CAFÉ PARADISE

Patricia Comb

2QT Limited (Publishing)

First Edition published 2013
2QT Limited (Publishing)
Lancashire LA2 8RE
www.2qt.co.uk

Cover design Hilary Pitt
Cover images supplied by shutterstock.com and istockphoto.com

Author website www.patriciacomb.com

Printed in Great Britain by Lightning Source UK Ltd

A CIP catalogue record for this book is available
from the British Library

ISBN 978-1-908098-93-1

To my husband Peter, with love.

Acknowledgements

To Karen Holmes for being a dear friend and mentor throughout the writing process and to Terence Flannagan for his guidance on legal matters in the book. To 2QT Publishing for the production and to Hilary Pitt for her design on both this and the eBook covers.

To Connie Scanlon for all her patient proof-reading and forebearance with my early tangled plots and most of all to my wonderful husband, Peter, who lived with a variety of characters bouncing around the house for many long months.

PROLOGUE

Even before she opened her eyes, Jackie knew that something was wrong. She lay still in bed trying to work it out. What was it? Her semi-conscious mind was registering that something was different. What? Jackie opened her eyes and shut them again immediately. Full daylight filtered through her closed eyelids making patterns dance before her eyes.

Daylight! Jackie opened her eyes again and sat up, staring at the window. It was only January; it should be pitch dark out there. What time was it? She turned to look at the clock on her bedside table. Hells bells! 9:00 a.m. She peered at the settings and realised she hadn't set the alarm the night before.

Jackie jumped quickly out of bed and began to throw on the clothes she had carelessly strewn on the chair the night before. She grumbled away to herself as she wrestled, bleary-eyed, with bra straps, tights and the too-tight zip on her trousers.

'I don't know, Mother. If you're not the most awkward, cantankerous woman in the whole of North Yorkshire, I don't know who is. You knew I had to be up early today so why couldn't you have given me a nudge? I know damned fine you'll be downstairs feeding yourself and that mangy moggy of yours and I'll have to go out hungry.'

Jackie hurriedly dragged a comb through her short fair hair, avoiding looking at herself in the mirror. She knew she would look a sight in crumpled clothes, with her wavy hair sticking out at all angles.

Picking up her handbag and car keys she ran downstairs. She raced through the lounge and on into the dining room where her mother sat at the table.

To Jackie's disgust, Samson, Marilyn's adored cat, was sitting on the table contentedly lapping at a plate of porridge clearly meant for Marilyn. Barely checking her stride, Jackie swept the cat off the table. He somersaulted elegantly and landed on all fours, spitting and growling at her.

'Oh Mother!' she exclaimed, 'do you have to share your breakfast with the cat. From what I can see he spends most of his time licking his backside, but if that's who you like to share with…'

Jackie headed into the kitchen and began rummaging around for something to put in a sandwich. She opened the fridge door and peered in. A packet of sliced ham caught her eye. That would do, quick and easy. She could sneak into the Ladies and scoff it once she'd shown her face at the supermarket. Quickly she buttered some bread and slapped the ham inside.

As she was doing this Samson sauntered into the kitchen. He sat down and curled his long black tail around him, staring up at her, mee-owing plaintively.

'Bugger off you ugly, over-fed, smelly mog,' Jackie snapped. She called out to her mother, 'He might have had your breakfast but he's not having mine.'

Marilyn made no answer. She of the acid tongue and mistress of the put-down was silent. This was so unusual it made Jackie pause. She glanced back into the dining room. Marilyn sat very still and silent at the head of the table.

Uneasiness stirred. Why didn't Marilyn snap back at her as usual? She turned and walked back to her mother. Marilyn sat very still, staring straight ahead. Bending down, Jackie looked more closely at her. Marilyn did not move.

Jackie peered into her face. She saw all the colour had drained from Marilyn's usually pink cheeks and no warm breath came from her lips. Her skin had taken on a waxy tinge; her eyes were unseeing.

Jackie gasped and jumped back. No, she couldn't be …, not Marilyn, her feisty, domineering mother. She was invincible; always had been. She was the one who dealt with any trouble: had seen off Jackie's more dubious boyfriends in her younger days; dealt with the teenage crises and, generally kept the show on the road. She was only sixty-four, she couldn't possibly be…

'Come on now.' Jackie shook Marilyn by the arm. Her mother fell forward, her head landing straight into the bowl of porridge. It splattered over Jackie and she backed away, tripping over Samson in her rush for the door. He dug his claws hard into her leg and dragged them slowly down, ripping the skin beneath her trousers. Jackie felt pain flare through her leg as she stood dumbly in the doorway, staring in horror at her mother lying lifeless across the table, plastered with lumps of cold, grey porridge.

Icy sweat beaded her forehead and trickled into her eyes, mingling with the tears that began to roll down her cheeks. Somewhere inside her head a voice was telling Jackie that her mother had just died and she should pull her out of that plate of porridge. She had never touched a dead body before. She shuddered, Mother would be cold. Jackie backed towards the kitchen.

In the same instant a thought occurred to her. Who would run the café today? With Mother… Jackie shied away from the word. She would have to go herself and see to things. Café Paradise wouldn't run itself and Mother had never missed a day.

She turned and ran, slamming the door behind her and racing down the path to her car she wrenched the door open and flung herself into the driver's seat and drove away at speed from No. 2 Mayfield Grove.

Inside all remained quiet. Pleased with his revenge on Jackie, Samson jumped back on the table and delicately licked at the porridge splattered on the cloth.

CHAPTER 1

The rain lashed relentlessly down on Walter Breckenridge as he leaned his bike against the window of the café.

'Come on, Walter lad, find the bloody key. You're not dressed for this weather.' Muttering to himself, Walter fished a large bunch of keys from his sodden pocket and raised them to his face, peering at them short-sightedly, trying to find the one that would open the café door.

'No, well you're not dressed for this weather because that stupid woman on the weather said it was set fair,' he continued. '"Brisk winds pushing the showers away," my arse. If she'd told the truth I'd be wearing my waterproofs instead of standing here soaked through to my vest.'

He fumbled through the keys. It wasn't only wet, it was pitch black too. Marilyn used to leave some of the lights on through the night after they'd closed, but had recently stopped.

'I'm not wasting electricity and contributing to global warming,' she'd said po-faced when he'd complained he couldn't see to open up in the mornings. Then she'd suggested he bring a torch. Bring a torch! As if it was his responsibility. He needed to check; there must be some health and safety regulations that she was breaching by making him struggle to open the bloody door.

Global warming! She's no more interested in global warming than I am; just too tight to pay the electricity bill.

He found the key he needed and fitted it into the lock. Even as it turned smoothly he cursed himself for a fool because the burglar alarm immediately started its monotonous beeping. He could hear it and see the small red light on the console flashing through the plate-glass door. He had one minute before the siren started to wail and the light above the door flashed. Then the police would arrive and the neighbours in the nearby flats who would be woken by the din would nail his nadgers to the nearest tree for waking them up again at six in the morning.

'Alarm code, Walter,' he said to himself. 'What's the bloody code?' 70 96 14, was that it? Or was it 70 14 96? Or 76 40 98? 'How the hell am I supposed to remember?' he wailed. 'If I had a head for figures I'd be an accountant not a cook. And I'd be making a lot more bloody money for a lot less effort.' The beeping seemed to increase in volume and the red light flash brighter.

He feverishly searched his pockets for the piece of paper on which he'd written the code after the last time the alarm had gone off. He wasn't supposed to write it anywhere, but needs must – and if it was a choice between Marilyn finding out that he'd committed her precious code to paper and the police hauling him in for questioning as a suspected burglar, he'd take his chance with Marilyn.

The scrap of paper was in the bottom of his jacket, soggy from the rain; the numbers smudged almost to the point of illegibility. He leaned back to try and catch the light from the nearest street lamp. There were only seconds left before the siren went off.

70 14 96. He punched the numbers into the keypad beside the door. The alarm tone rose by a note, seemed to become even more frantic.

'Shit, that can't be right.' Was the 70 really a 76 or the 96 a 70? It was hard to tell from the sodden paper. Sweat broke out across Walter's forehead, mingling with the raindrops. The alarm was starting to scream, preparing for lift off. He took a deep breath and tried again. Frantically he pushed the buttons, trying a different combination. For a heart-stopping moment he waited, then… Nothing. No wailing sirens, no flashing lights. Just silence, blessed silence.

The trouble was, Walter couldn't remember what the sequence of numbers was that he had just used. And if he asked Marilyn, she would ask why he wanted to know…

Walter slammed the door closed behind him and turned the lock. Welcome to the start of another day at the Café Paradise.

By seven the rain had stopped which meant that the woman from the Met Office had been right after all, provided that you accepted seven as early. For some people, Walter thought, it's the middle of the bloody morning. Some of us have been up for hours.

Walter watched the last drops trickle down the window at the front of the café as he stared out into the January darkness. He was looking at the café's name backwards but, even from that position, he could see that it needed a bit of tarting up. The tail of the R had disintegrated so that it read Papadise which sounded like a Greek kebab house. And the window itself was mucky again. The window cleaner only came round once a fortnight and it wasn't enough, but Marilyn was too tight to shell out for more frequent cleaning.

The central heating didn't come on until eight, so the place was bitterly cold. Strange how odd a café seemed when it was empty of people and life. The smell of fat was a lot stronger for a start, and everything looked shabbier. When the punters were spreading their papers over the chipped Formica tables you didn't notice the dents and scratches. Now they looked what they were, ancient and probably a health hazard. And another of the chairs had a rip in the seat. Marilyn wouldn't be too pleased about that.

Moira Stewart was reading the news, all deep measured tones as she told him how the world was going to hell in a handcart. He liked Moira Stewart; she had a bit of class. Which was more than you could say for Chris Evans with his manic jabbering. Whose brilliant idea was it that the world needed a wake-up call instead of being gently eased into the day? After all this time, Walter was still unhappy with the shouting and laughter and loudness of the music. Walter had been a Terry Wogan fan, one of the TOGs, Terry's Old Geezers. Terry knew what people needed when they reached a certain age, knew that a gentle awakening was less likely to trigger a heart attack, knew that not everyone was searching for their lost youth. This Evans chap – Walter felt sorry for his producer. It must be like trying to put a lid on a cartload of monkeys, keeping control of that young man and his fast-flowing ideas.

'You're getting old,' Walter murmured to himself. But sixty-four – well, sixty-five next week – wasn't really old. Not old enough for Radio 3 or Classic FM. No, he'd have to stick with Chris for a while longer. And anyway, if he tried to change the station Penny and Kate would lynch him. He sighed and went back into the cramped kitchen. There was a pile of spuds waiting for him and they wouldn't scrape themselves.

The front door swung open and Penny walked in. Walter looked at her appreciatively. She was a fine figure of a woman, considering her age. Not that she admitted to her real age, of course. To the rest of the world she was forty-seven but Walter had taken a quick look through her employment file one morning when nobody was around and the thought of tackling the day's chores didn't appeal. Forty-seven; going on fifty-two. Not that she looked it. Walter liked a woman to take pride in her appearance and Penny never disappointed. Her thick, black hair was cut within an inch of its life every week by Mr Antoine. There was scarcely a wrinkle on her face. Walter wondered if it was the Botox that he'd heard her discussing with Kate one lunchtime in the staffroom, or just clean living. He rather hoped it was the Botox because a woman like Penny shouldn't be reduced to clean living, not with a shape like that.

'Good morning, beautiful,' he shouted, as she walked quickly past the kitchen.

Penny scowled at him. 'What's good about it?' she snapped and pulled open the cloakroom door. Her feet skidded slightly on a smear of grease as she moved forward. 'And get this greasy floor cleaned up before we all break our necks on it,' she shouted. The door slammed behind her and Walter stared at it thoughtfully.

Whose husband forgot their wedding anniversary again then? He shook his head sadly. Some men just didn't know their luck. If he had a wife like Penny he'd cherish her, treat every day like an anniversary, bring her flowers and leeks, freshly dug from his smallholding, make sure that there were new laid eggs for her breakfast every morning…

He shook himself out of his reverie and went to fetch his mop.

The front door opened again and Kate walked in, her coat and umbrella still wet from the rain. Another bonny lass, Walter thought, though not really his type. For a start she was still in her twenties and Walter knew that he wasn't sugar daddy material. And she was a bit … intense. She'd done too much with her life, that was the problem. All that travelling, flitting from one place to another, all that university education, it put her well out of his league. And he had to say, all that experience didn't seem to have made her very happy.

Even so, with that red-gold hair and green eyes, she was a picture. If he were twenty, well maybe thirty years younger …

'Good morning Kate,' he said pleasantly.

Kate glared at him. 'You… You…' She struggled for words.

'Me, Walter: you, Kate?' Walter supplied helpfully.

'You,' she shouted. 'You MAN.' She pushed her way angrily past him and joined Penny in the cloakroom. 'And if you're mopping the bloody floor, get it done now before we all break our necks,' she threw over her shoulder.

Walter stared at her retreating back. 'The new boyfriend hasn't come up to scratch then,' he murmured. He sprayed some cleaner on the floor and ran the mop over the offending patch of grease. No point in winding either of them up still further.

Women! Never at their best first thing…

The door opened again and Jackie came in.

'Morning, Jackie, nice to see you,' Walter said unctuously. 'How's your mum? Is she alright? Is she coming in today?'

'She's never been better,' Jackie snapped. She sidestepped the wet patch on the floor. 'Can you get this dried off before we all break our necks on it? We can do without being sued for every penny we haven't got.' She walked past him to the little cubbyhole beside the cloakroom that Marilyn had designated an office and closed the door firmly.

'Good morning, Walter,' Walter said, imitating her tones. 'And how are you on this beautiful morning? Well, I trust?'

'Very well thank you, Miss Dalrymple-Jones,' he replied in his own voice.

'Splendid, splendid,' he continued in a falsetto. 'Must get on, customers to keep happy, money to make.' He bowed towards Marilyn's office door.

So what was up with her? She was never the easiest person to negotiate. Thankfully, she didn't often make her presence felt because her job at the supermarket kept her out of the way. When she did come in, it usually meant trouble.

* * * * * *

Jackie slammed the door behind her and leaned against

it, closing her eyes. Bloody Walter! Honestly, he didn't get any better. The state of that floor! And him! Café Paradise might only be a greasy spoon café but surely there were limits. Marilyn had let him get away with murder.

Funny that really: he wasn't much of a cook. He could do all-day breakfasts and after that he struggled. Yet Marilyn had kept him on all these years. Well that was going to change for a start. There was more dirt on his hands than there was on the mound of potatoes he had to peel every day. God knows what he brought in on his hands from that smallholding of his. He might give the spuds a nasty disease. And that apron he was wearing. It would keep an environmental health officer in work for years.

Jackie opened her eyes and looked round the dismal little office. Apart from a few dated health and safety posters and some old postcards, the yellowing walls were bare. The carpet was worn and greasy, testimony to the hundreds of times bloody Walter and his bloody work boots had tramped in the grease from the kitchen.

There were two battered filing cabinets and a bookshelf with a row of cookery books. Not that any of them had been opened. Who needed cooking tips when the Café Paradise punters survived on a diet of fry-ups and builders' tea?

Throwing a pile of newly-washed overalls onto the floor, Jackie slumped into the nearest chair: a scuffed old desk chair, upholstered in black fabric that was now worn to a faded grey. Marilyn's chair.

Well now, she thought. I've sat in it, just like that. I've never done that before. When I'm in here with Mother I sit in the visitor's chair, or perch on the edge of the desk.

Jackie looked around nervously, as if Marilyn might materialise at any moment and snap at her as she often did, 'Get a move on, our Jackie, no good sitting there all day.' But nothing happened and Jackie sat quietly, staring at Marilyn's desk.

It was piled with neatly-stacked papers, beside which was a pen tray full of biros, pencils, paper clips and elastic bands. Jackie picked up the bright yellow tray and moved it from right to left and then placed it at the back of the desk. She moved some papers in front of it and placed a paperweight on top of them.

Marilyn's desk …and Marilyn's chair…

The paperweight was a glass globe. As she moved it, a snowstorm started up inside and caught her attention. She picked it up and shook it gently. Desultory white flakes floated about the two little skaters frozen forever in the snow. She shook the ornament vigorously. The snow swirled about the boy and girl, clinging to their faces and clothes. Still they smiled at each other. Jackie shook the glass again, harder this time then suddenly, threw it with all her strength at the wall. The paperweight shattered, spraying shards of glass all around the office and into Jackie's hair and clothing. Tears coursed down her face as she sat immobile in her mother's chair.

There was a knock at the door. Jackie wanted to scream, 'Go away, leave me alone,' but the words would not come. The tears rolled down her cheeks and dropped off her chin, falling unheeded on to the papers on the desk.

On the other side of the door, Kate stood holding a tray of tea and biscuits. 'Jackie?' She knocked again. 'Can I come in? I've brought you some tea.'

Tea? Typical! Tea at a time like this?

'I'll bring it in, Jackie, I don't want it to go cold and upset Walter.'

Kate opened the door and swung in with the tray, ready to set it down on the desk. She stopped short, seeing Jackie with her head in her hands, glass fragments glinting in her hair.

'Are you OK, Jackie?'

Jackie looked up, as if she were surprised to see Kate

standing there with a tea tray in her hands. When she spoke, her voice sounded – to her own ears – surprisingly normal.

'Aren't you going to put it down?'

'Well,' Kate hesitated, 'there's a lot of glass. Has something happened?'

Jackie considered this. Nothing had happened. That was the problem. *Nothing* had happened. She'd overslept and rushed down for breakfast and it wasn't there. Her mother was sitting at the table, just sitting there.

'I spoke to her,' she said aloud, 'told her off for letting the cat share her breakfast.' Jackie looked up at Kate. 'She likes me to have a good breakfast before I go to work so I don't snack on any of the rubbish at the supermarket. That's how she sees it. Anything not cooked from scratch is the devil's fodder. I do eat at work, I just don't tell her. There's no point is there? She'd only nag at me. She never needs an excuse to do that. And I'm not getting into a slanging match because I choose to have a doughnut for my elevenses. Why poke the crocodile, that's what I say.'

Kate looked at her, confused. Jackie could be unpredictable but this was odd behaviour even by her standards. Tired of holding the tray, she placed it carefully on the edge of the desk. 'Jackie, you're thirty-five. I know your mother's a bit of a dragon, but you're allowed to get your own breakfast. She's not going to breathe fire and incinerate you for doing that.'

Jackie eyed Kate up and down and felt a stab of envy: young, beautiful, with her straw-coloured hair and green eyes, lithe, slim and free. She didn't have a domineering mother at her back, always harrying her. Nothing Jackie could do was right and yet Marilyn would take to her bed if Jackie ever talked of independence, of setting up in her own flat. No, Kate was free from all those sorts of pressures.

'You don't understand. I thought she'd fallen asleep at the table, so I went close up to her to have a better look and she looked funny. Odd. All white and waxy. Then I touched her and she keeled over right on to the table, into a plate of porridge. She was dead, Kate. Dead. Just sitting there, dead.'

Kate stood absolutely still for a moment, totally at a loss. Many things had happened to her in her short life, many adventures and dramas. But dealing with someone whose mother was lying dead in a plate of cold porridge was a first.

Uncertainly she said, 'Well look at it this way, Jackie, it might be a matter for congratulations.'

Jackie looked at her, shocked. Bloody hell, that took the biscuit. 'That's not very nice!'

'Nor was your mother. You detested her, from what I could see.'

Jackie drew her breath in sharply. She may well have detested her mother but had her feelings been so obvious?

'I bet she's giving Satan the run around right now,' said Kate.

Jackie sighed. It was pointless trying to defend the domineering old witch. 'You're probably right,' she agreed. 'Marilyn will soon sort Satan out.'

Feeling that she had struck the right note, Kate warmed to her theme. 'Well, it's not going to be God, is it? Not with her track record.'

Jackie thought of all the shady deals Marilyn had engaged in in the past: the goods stacked up in the office allegedly damaged and claimed for against different companies and still used; the cash deals done and taxes not paid; the waitresses underpaid, even their tips lifted from the bowl sometimes. Kate was right. Marilyn wouldn't be meeting God any time soon.

'Are you sure she's dead?' Kate asked.

Jackie shrugged impatiently. 'I've already told you that she'd keeled over. Of course she's dead, out cold, stiff. I wasn't going to give her the kiss of life, I might have caught something.'

Kate was looking perplexed. Jackie wasn't sure why. It was *her* mother that was dead. Why should Kate be bothered?

'But you've come here, Jackie,' said Kate. 'To work. I mean, shouldn't you be…' Her voice tailed off because she wasn't actually sure what Jackie should be doing. It seemed pointless to call an ambulance if the old bat was already dead and she doubted that a team of top detectives and forensic staff would be called in to investigate a deceased woman in a plate of porridge. So she changed the subject.

'And what have you smashed? There's glass everywhere.'

Suddenly Jackie started to cry. 'I released them, the two little skaters in the paperweight. They were trapped just like me, but not anymore. They're free … and so am I.' She looked wonderingly up at Kate as this knowledge started to sink in. 'I'm free, Kate, and I've come here. Mother's dead. Someone's got to run the caff, so it will have to be me. I haven't had any breakfast though. Do you think Walter could rustle up a bacon sarnie?' Jackie hunted in her handbag for a handkerchief to dry her face.

The door closed behind Kate. Jackie hoped she would remember to tell Walter about her sandwich.

* * * * * *

As Kate passed on Jackie's order for a bacon sandwich to Walter, she avoided his eyes. She wasn't going to be the one to tell him about the morning's drama. That was up to Jackie, though judging by Jackie's present state it could be some time before she got around to telling anyone. No, best keep it brief.

'Can you do a bacon bap for Jackie?' she said. 'She's not … er … had time for breakfast. I'm just going to make her another cup of tea.'

Before Walter could ask the inevitable questions — why

hadn't Jackie had breakfast? Where was Marilyn? Was the rain ever going to stop? What was the current level of the FTSE? – Kate slid away into the storeroom, past the piled-up boxes in the dingy back room. Judging by the layers of dust and cobwebs on some of the boxes they must have been there for years.

The smell of old fat, fried onions and stale cigarette smoke that pervaded the café had seeped through to the dark, dank little room. At the back, a small corner was used as a rest area for the staff. A few plastic chairs around an old wooden table with years of grease and dirt ground into the scratched and peeling varnish served as their staff canteen.

Wrinkling her nose in distaste at the awful smell, Kate wondered for the hundredth time how she could have been so stupid as to run from a broken romance in Cyprus and throw away sun, sand, sex and cheap wine for this. Alright, her heart was broken but even so – the surroundings were more palatable and the chances of finding a new bit of excitement and passion more likely.

She leaned against the dusty boxes waiting for the kettle to boil. She could hardly believe she was here, aged twenty-nine, working in this run down greasy spoon café down a side alley in York; dishing out endless plates of fatty bacon and eggs swimming in ancient lard that was speckled with odd bits of God knows what. Why were the great British public so attached to their morning fry-ups? All that cholesterol gathered together on one plate. Kate was a bowl of muesli and soya milk girl, even if Walter did call it hamster food.

As she waited for the kettle to boil, she wondered what she was going to do next. *What Katy did next.* Kate smiled wryly to herself. What Katy in the novel did was get off her backside and get herself a life. I suppose I should do the same, she thought. Make use of that history degree. Train to be a teacher. Kate considered the prospect as the kettle billowed steam unheeded. In theory, yes she could teach, but could she really see herself staying calm and benevolent in front of a class of stroppy fifteen- year-olds? Decidedly not. Kate knew herself well enough to realise it would only take one child to get uppity and she would tell it exactly where it got off. Or worse. There were penalties these days for clouting adolescents. Besides, teaching the same stuff year in year out could only get boring. No, she wanted more variety in her life.

The hot steam roused her from her reverie and she turned off the kettle. This was ridiculous, too. Here she was working in a café with oceans of tea and coffee for the customers, and the staff had to bring their own. Kate knew she shouldn't think ill of the dead, but really, Marilyn was a tight-fisted old bag. Hopefully she was being put to good used now, providing fuel to roast some good coffee beans.

As she stirred the teabag in the cup, the dim light of the room was cut off altogether as a pair of hands locked over her eyes.

'Tell me the password to release you,' said a deep male voice.

Oh God, not Stan again. Stan, Stan, the suntanned man. Did he never give up? God's gift to Café Paradise and every bakery in the area. So he thought.

'Let go, Stan, and bugger off.'

'That's not today's password but I'll overlook it seeing as it's you.' He released Kate and she swung round to face him. She had to admit he was good looking, if you liked that sort of thing; six foot four, rangy and muscular with a shock of black hair above lively blue eyes.

Yeah, and a girl in every store so I've heard, she reminded herself.

'And how is my most beautiful, most adored girl in the world today? I've brought you baps, cakes, gateaux and loaves, only three though. Whitby got the rest, all the chip butties they do.'

'What are you telling me for? I'm only a waitress.'

'Walter's not in the kitchen and Marilyn's not about. Someone's got to sign for all this stuff or my boss will think I've sold it off the back of the wagon and pocketed the cash. So come on, Kate, fair dos.'

God, he did go on. 'Stan, you've worked for that firm since leaving school, they're not going to think you've suddenly turned into the great bakery robber, à la Ronnie Biggs.'

'But I must have a signature. I suppose I could forge Marilyn's. I've seen her sign often enough.'

'Not today, you can't,' Kate said quickly. 'Now keep your voice down, we've had a bereavement.'

'Has that mousetrap finally worked?' Stan rubbed his hands gleefully. 'Shall I dispose of the corpse for you?'

Kate winced. If only it had been some poor inoffensive little mouse and not the messy situation they found themselves in. 'It's Jackie.'

Stan's face registered his shock. 'Hell's bells, she's only the same age that I am…'

Kate stopped him. 'No, not her. Not Jackie. It's her mother. She died in the night.'

Stan stared at her for a moment and then smiled. 'The old bat's finally kicked the bucket, has she? I thought she'd never go. She was my teacher at school, you know, before she bought this caff. The things she could do with a two-foot cane. She should have been a stripper in a nightclub: canes and whips and all that stuff.' Stan looked wistful.

Kate gazed at him wonderingly. Maybe she'd been a bit unfeeling when she spoke to Jackie about Marilyn's demise but she certainly wasn't in Stan's league.

'That's typical of you. Only you could bring a conversation about bereavement down to strippers and sex. And as for your nightclubs…'

Stan grasped Kate around the waist and tried to dance around the greasy table with her.

'Come live with me and be my love, And we shall some new pleasures prove.' He looked down at her. 'We could dance the night away at that new club in York.'

Kate looked up into Stan's smiling eyes and was tempted to say yes, but Penny's warning 'he's got a girl in every store' rang in her head. She detached herself.

'Oh go away. It's just not – appropriate right now. Fetch the cakes in before the cream melts on them and you'd better find some more loaves from somewhere. We'll be through those by lunchtime.'

'I'm not Jesus, but for you, Kate, I am as Achilles. I'll fly like the wind to the Pickering depot and get some. For you, mind. Not for the bereaved Jackie, although she should be hanging the flags out. Only for you, my Helen, my Cleopatra. I am your slave.'

'Yeah and so is every other pretty waitress, from what I hear.'

'Lies, all lies. Don't listen to idle gossip, Kate. You have my heart. See you at lunchtime. I'll come like a Greek God bearing gifts.'

'Eight loaves will do.' Kate picked up the tray and walked to the door. 'Now get out of my way. Jackie needs another cup of tea and Penny will be wanting her coffee. She's up to her armpits in bacon butties.'

Stan blew her a kiss as he left with the bread trays. Fancy him quoting from John Donne. Well he'd put himself about a lot too, hadn't he? The poet and the baker... Kate shook herself mentally. She would keep Stan at arm's length.

CHAPTER 2

After the plummeting temperatures over Christmas and New Year, large potholes and cracks had appeared in the roads. The little Fiat Panda rattled over them, bouncing Walter off his seat and banging his head on the roof of the tinny car.

Walter glanced across at Jackie as she hunched over the wheel, watching the road ahead intently. Her hands gripped the wheel so tightly that the blood had drained from her hands and her knuckles showed starkly white against the black plastic. Walter shivered, pulled his jacket more closely round him and huddled down in his seat. The Fiat did not run to an effective heater. Jackie had to keep a window open to stop the windscreen fogging up.

He wondered how to broach the subject. Shock did funny things to people. Well, Jackie was a good example, just leaving poor Marilyn like that and coming to the café this morning. Still, he'd best get on with it. Something would have to be done with her. They couldn't leave her where she was.

'Your mother was a very orderly person, Jackie,' he ventured.

'Yeah, she made the Olympic organisers look like a bunch of headless chickens. So what?'

Well that's a great start. Try again, Walter. 'Did she ever make her wishes known, you know, as to what...?' He stopped.

Jackie frowned and looked at him. 'What?'

Don't bloody make it easy, will you, lass? 'Well you know, after she died, what she wanted.'

'Well what do you want when you're dead, Walter? A tub of marmite flavoured ice-cream, seat at the Test Match, box at the opera? I don't think so, you don't want anything. It's too late then. Too late,' she echoed herself drearily.

Oh, Marilyn! Walter felt the familiar exasperation rise in him. I had forty years of you driving me up the bloody wall and now your daughter's starting. She'll have me in the funny farm soon, if she isn't in there first. He waited a moment, trying to control his irritation and choose his words.

'Did she ever express a preference for the disposal of her remains?'

'Her remains?'

Good God, had Jackie's brain died along with her mother? 'Burial or cremation?' There. How clear did you have to be?'

They hit another pothole and careered across the road. Jackie fought for control and managed to bring them back to their own side of the road, a whisker away from the bumper of an oncoming car. The sound of the driver's horn blaring on and on rang in Walter's ears.

'Hell, Walter, how do I know? She was only sixty-four. I thought she had years in her yet. If I'd have known she was going to up and die on me I'd have had it sorted, wouldn't I? Not left it to the last minute like this. She wouldn't like it, having nothing sorted.' Jackie's face screwed up and reddened and huge salty tears splashed down her cheeks.

Oh, that's all I need, Walter thought, a wailing woman. Make my day, God. And she's bloody driving too. 'Pull over Jackie,' he said, 'you can't drive in this state. I'll drive the rest of the way.'

'You don't drive, Walter, or had you forgotten?' she

hiccupped through her sobs.

'I've got a licence. I know I haven't driven for years but it's like riding a bike. You never forget. I'm still legal on the roads.'

'Thanks, but no thanks, Walter. You stick to your bike. I don't want to join Marilyn just yet.' Jackie dried her eyes.

'What about your fa ... your Dad? What happened to him?'

'He died.'

'I know he died!' Walter tried to keep a rein on his frustration and took a deep breath. 'Was he buried or cremated?'

'He was buried, in St. Martin's Cemetery.'

Now they were getting somewhere. If he was already in situ ... maybe they'd made some long-term arrangements. Marilyn had always been one to broker a good deal. Had she gone for two for the price of one? Careful, Walter, he said to himself, you might get your head bitten off again here. This was a delicate matter. The trouble was, he didn't do delicate.

'When Marilyn buried your fa ... your Dad, was it just a single or a double?'

'Sounds like she was getting on a bus,' said Jackie.

Was she doing it on purpose to wind him up? How old was she when her Dad died? Twenty-five at least, so surely she must know something about it.

'Was it a very deep grave, you know...?'

'No, I don't know.'

Sighing, Walter decided to go for the jugular. 'Deep enough to get two of them in, one on top of the other, united in death.'

Jackie jammed on the brakes and the Panda screeched to a halt in a cloud of smoking tyres. The acrid smell of burning rubber seeped in through the open window. They had stopped outside Jackie's home. 'God, Walter, do you have to be so visual? She's only just died. It was bad enough seeing her head down in a plate of porridge without thinking about…'

'I'm sorry, lass, but we'll have to make arrangements. Come on now, let's go in and make a start.' He got out of the car and walked round to help Jackie out. She sat immobile in her seat, white faced, a pulse throbbing in her cheek as her teeth clenched tight.

'Come on, Jackie,' Walter repeated. 'Let's get it over with.'

'No,' Jackie whispered, not looking at Walter. 'I can't. I can't … I just can't. I don't want to see her again … like that.'

Women, Walter thought. Why, oh why, God, did you ever create women? You just made a whole load of trouble for poor unsuspecting men. Now what am I going to do? I can't drag her in by the hair, the neighbours might be looking. And I don't doubt she'd do me for assault.

'Supposing she's not dead?' Jackie said suddenly.

'Oh yeah, like Monty Python's parrot "just restin". I don't think so.'

'But if she isn't,' Jackie persisted, 'she'd be so mad I left her like that. I'd get a right earful.'

If Jackie was to be believed, she'd left the woman out cold and stiff as a board. How dead did she have to be to convince Jackie? Mind you, Marilyn being Marilyn, she was quite capable of coming back from the grave.

Walter sighed heavily. 'Right, stop there if you want to. Give me your key and I'll go in.'

The door opened smoothly and silently. There was no smell other than that of polish. Walter wasn't sure what he'd been expecting – did death have an aroma so soon after it happened? The only strong smell that he was conscious of was that of cooking from his clothes and a faint whiff of the farmyard from his boots. Before he stepped over the threshold, he kicked them off. On the few occasions he'd visited Marilyn at home, she'd never let him inside without him removing his boots.

Walter stood in the over-furnished dining room and stared down at Marilyn Dalrymple-Jones. Jackie had not been mistaken; she was as dead as a doornail and had been for some time.

Walter had no fear of death; he'd had livestock die on his smallholding over the years and was used to handling dead bodies. This was a bit bigger than his chickens, though. He tried to sit Marilyn up in her chair but she was already stiffening up and he couldn't move her. Yes, she was definitely dead.

A wave of sadness swept over him. Poor Marilyn. Sixty-four wasn't old these days. She'd gone too soon. All that wheeling and dealing, grubbing about just to make an extra bob or two, and for what? To work so hard and get so stressed that you drop dead at sixty-four?

Walter looked around the room. Marilyn had always had good taste and the room was furnished in the most expensive style that money could buy. The oak table and chairs must have cost a fortune and as for the carpet, best quality Axminster no doubt. Marilyn never stinted on herself, Walter thought wryly, only on everyone else.

She hadn't always been like that. He looked affectionately down at her dyed blonde head firmly wedged in a large bowl of cold porridge. Walter remembered her as she was when they were young, her long glossy brown hair and melting brown eyes dancing with merriment, always up for a lark, leading him on, bewitching him.

Oh, how she'd bewitched him. He'd fallen in love with her, silly fool that he was. He believed she loved him too, at the time. They had been so right for each other. And then suddenly she'd upped and married Barry Dalrymple-Jones, rich civil engineer, and Jackie was born not long after.

Walter sighed. If only she could have settled for him and

life on a smallholding. No, being poor would never have made Marilyn happy. But that Barry hadn't either. She bought the café with his money and put her heart into that. And silly bugger that I am, I've followed her ever since. He patted her gently. Too late now, love. We could have had a lovely life, you and me.

CHAPTER 3

Even with the extractor fan going full tilt in the café kitchen; it was filled with smoke billowing up from the large pans of frying bacon. No healthy grilling of meats went on here. The fat swirled around the thick red slabs of bacon in the pan.

'If I'd have known I was going to be stuck in this greasy kitchen all day, I wouldn't have put my nice frock on,' Penny said to Kate. 'After all, I signed up to be a waitress not a cook. I can do this at home. But I suppose Walter was the best one to take Jackie home.' She shuddered suddenly. 'I wouldn't fancy seeing Marilyn just now. It was bad enough when she was here alive and telling us what to do as if we didn't know already. I suppose we all have to rally round in a crisis but really, how many all-day breakfasts and bacon butties can one city eat?'

Penny pushed a stray curl back under her hat and cracked two eggs to sizzle alongside the bacon. She spooned the fat over the eggs and their bright yellow yolks turned milky opaque as it rolled over them.

Kate waited, her tray ready with bread and butter laid out on a thick china plate. 'Anyway,' resumed Penny, 'like I was saying earlier, it's not as if he's the size to carry it off. He's built like a barn door and has all the equipment to go with it.'

'Lucky you,' said Kate.

'No, I don't mean that, even though he has, is – oh, you

know what I mean. He's very masculine. There's nothing feminine about him. He looks ridiculous in frills.'

'Frills, what? Like frilly shirts those naff dancers wear on *Strictly Come Dancing*, or gigolos on cruise ships?'

What was wrong with Kate today? She wasn't usually this dense. 'No, no, he can't dance at all. I'm not talking shirts, I'm talking blouses. My blouses. George has been wearing mine. Remember that one I wore to last year's Christmas party?'

'The pink one?'

'It's not as if it's even his colour.' Penny shook her head, irritably. 'And now he's burst the seams and ruined it. It's pure silk. You can't just mend silk and the repair not show.' She scooped the bacon and eggs out of the pan and slid them on to the waiting plate. Kate turned to take the tray to the waiting customer.

'I'll be straight back. This sounds fascinating. You start table three's breakfast. It's for Barney.'

Penny slapped four rashers in the pan. Young Barney needed building up. Those lovely blue eyes of his seemed sunk right back into his head. Where were those really large eggs? He could have two of those as well. Only the best for Barney. Now he was a real man. Penny wasn't so sure that hers was.

Kate re-entered the kitchen carrying a tray set for Barney's breakfast. 'Go on, what's all this about your old man?'

Penny wasn't sure where to begin. Since yesterday afternoon her mind had been in turmoil. How can you be married to someone for thirty years and never suspect they had a whole different side to them? But then you read about it in the papers every day.

'I went home early yesterday, if you remember. I wasn't feeling so grand. I think those Mrs Ebworthy's pork pies weren't all they're cracked up to be. I knew the minute I bit into it, so why I carried on with it I don't know.'

'George, Penny,' Kate persisted. 'What about George?'

What was up with Kate today? She wouldn't let Penny get the words out. What was the hurry? Walter was going back home with Jackie. The cats were all away, the mice could play.

'I got home early, didn't I? *Unexpected*, as you might say. Certainly not expected by George, as became obvious.'

Penny stopped, re-running the scene in her head. She'd been feeling queasy and looked forward to taking some Alka Seltzer and lying down quietly on her bed for a while. No-one would be at home. The two eldest boys were working away now and Alexander, the youngest, was in his second term at university. 'I got such a shock, Kate. I mean, George's car wasn't on the drive so I wasn't expecting to see him.'

'He does live there,' Kate pointed out, 'and he's there every day, so where's the shock value in that?'

If she'd just stop interrupting and wait a moment she would find out.

'You didn't see what I saw.'

'Oh, are we going all Topsy now, seen something nasty in the woodshed? Wasn't his secretary, was it? Was she young and pretty?'

Maybe that would have been easier to cope with, Penny thought as she rescued the bacon from the pan. It was a bit well done but Barney wouldn't mind.

'How does he like his eggs?'

'Runny yolks.'

Penny cracked the eggs into the pan and added some tomatoes and mushrooms. Barney was a lovely young man, so polite. He deserved special treatment.

'I went upstairs and there he was.'

'All naked and gorgeous and ready to rock and roll?'

Penny looked at her severely. 'You're not taking this seriously.'

'Well get on and tell me then. What catastrophe has

occurred to get you in this state?'

'He was ready to rock and roll as you put it, fully dressed in *my* clothes, admiring himself in the mirror, in full make-up and a wig.'

With a flourish Penny emptied the pan on to the plate and handed it to Kate. 'Is that catastrophic enough for you?'

CHAPTER 4

Opening the café door early the next morning, Jackie sniffed the air. Yesterday's fry-ups still lay heavy. Bacon, sausage, fried bread with a top note of heavily spiced black pudding. The stale, slightly rancid smell added to her sense of gloom. How had Marilyn stood this for forty years? No wonder she had always been crabby.

Jackie didn't want to end up like her mother. Things must change. She had to start somewhere and today she would take the first step. Walter was not going to be an easy nut to crack. He'd been working in the kitchen for thirty years, in the same clothes by the look of him. It wasn't going to be easy to get him to change his ways or his clothes.

Taking a deep breath, she pushed back her shoulders and forcefully pushed open the kitchen door. Walter was already there like a – like a troll in its grotto, she thought, malevolently.

'What're these?' he asked, eyeing the package she held out.

Impatiently Jackie ripped open the bag and shook out the contents. Then she unfolded the new chef's whites to show off the crisp white jacket and trousers. 'Any more clues needed?'

'I can't wear those.'

'Why not?'

'They'll show the dirt.'

'Exactly. They show the dirt so you have to keep them clean. Then the customers know that we keep a pristine kitchen.' He stared at her blankly. 'The idea is, Walter,' she went on impatiently, 'that you take them off and wash them and put a clean pair on before they get grubby. In fact, you change them every day.' She watched Walter's mouth move silently, echoing the phrase 'every day', his bushy eyebrows meeting his hairline.

'But, Jackie, that would mean…' He stopped incredulously. 'Six jackets and six trousers to wash every week. I don't know if my old washing machine is up to it, let alone my wallet. Think of the cost of all the water and soap.'

'I very much doubt if your old washing machine is up to anything at all, looking at your clothes right now, Walter. It would probably blow a gasket or expire altogether. Take that look off your face. I'll see to the laundry. And the girls need new uniforms too, so you're not being singled out. Now go on, put them on. Your bacon will taste better when you wear them.'

Jackie thrust the clothes into Walter's hands and shooed him off to the Gents. He muttered all the way. 'Bloody women, bloody Jackie, bloody Marilyn,' was heard at intervals. Jackie pictured Walter shedding his dirty farm jeans and struggling into the stiff new chef's trousers. When she got to his spindly legs she stopped. The thought was too horrible to bear. 'Ooh no, enough.'

* * * * * *

Barney Anderson pushed open the door of the Café Paradise and was enveloped in the familiar fug of warm, steamy air laden with the smells of coffee and frying bacon. He made his way to his usual table in the corner and sat down, calling across to Kate as she cleared a table near the coffee counter.

'Hi Kate, how are you today?'

'Missing the Cyprus sunshine, Barney. What am I doing here?'

'Ah, the eternal question, Kate. I can't answer that one

for you. But as for me, I'm here for an all-day breakfast. One of Walter's finest. There's no rush, just as and when. And maybe a large mug of coffee to be going on with.'

Kate moved to the coffee counter where Jackie was unloading a tray of mugs and cups still warm from the dishwasher. Leaning against the counter, she faced Barney.

'How's life in the squat?' she asked.

'Pretty good just now, thanks. I've made space for a young couple. The parents threw them out when they found out she was expecting. They don't like kids, not even their own daughter, so it seems.'

'Oh, poor things.'

'Yeah. The squat will be OK for now but we'll have to get them fixed up with a flat soon. It's not the warmest of places.'

Kate shook her head and turned back to Jackie. 'A mug of white coffee for Barney, please.'

'Who the hell is he?' hissed Jackie. 'Is he the local dosser? He certainly looks like it. I thought Walter had cornered the market in shabby but this … Barney, you call him? What's he all about?'

'I think he lives in the squat down in the Market Gate area,' Kate replied quietly. 'He's a lovely man, he helps loads of people. Anyone in trouble can go to Barney and he can usually sort them out. And isn't he just divine? Tall, fair, blue eyes and has a beautiful speaking voice. I could squat with him anytime.'

Jackie stared across at Barney who was engrossed in *The Times*. She had to admit he was very good looking. 'Never mind his looks, look at the state of his clothes. There's not a thread on his back that wasn't made before the Ark set sail.' She sniffed disapprovingly. 'What you're telling me is that he's a freeloader living in a squat. He's probably claiming all the state handouts he can get those soft, well-kept hands on and stuffing his pretty face in here every day at mine and every other hard-working taxpayer's expense.'

Kate looked horrified. 'Ssh, keep your voice down. He's not like that, Jackie. Look, if you just get to know him a bit you'll see. He's well educated, went to public school by the sound of him. He's not a scrounger. I don't really know what he does for a living, but I know he's always got a lot of irons in the fire, helping people in different ways. So don't be so judgemental. Barney's a good bloke.'

Jackie looked unconvinced. 'I'm not having any layabout scroungers in here. He needs to get a proper job. What's he up to, anyway?'

Kate turned round. Barney was spreading documents out on the table. 'He'll be filling in forms for someone, I expect,' she said. 'A lot of people he comes across aren't very good at reading and writing, and forms just baffle them. Barney does it for them – acts as their advocate.'

'Doesn't matter what fancy title you give. He's probably encouraging other shiftless idlers in the same way.' Jackie slapped the mug of coffee on the counter and glared across at Barney. 'He's not the sort of customer we should be encouraging.' Feeling her gaze upon him he looked up from his papers and smiled. Jackie scowled discouragingly.

Kate took the coffee over to him. 'Do I take it that our esteemed new owner does not approve of me?' he asked.

'Well,' Kate hesitated, 'maybe you're not going to be her favourite customer.'

'She's not even spoken to me,' Barney said indignantly, 'so how can she form any kind of opinion?'

'She thinks you're just another layabout scrounger. Well, you're not exactly a suit and tie man, are you?'

'So? Never judge a book by its cover, young Kate. I've been stung by suit and tie men in the past, and I don't trust them now. I go my own way. If that is what impresses Miss Snooty Pants over there, she'll have a long wait to be impressed by me. I don't do suits any more. Well, just occasionally, if I'm up in court.'

Kate looked down at him, slightly alarmed. Up in court? That little titbit of information she would keep to herself. It wouldn't do anything to improve Jackie's opinion of Barney.

Barney looked across the café at Jackie. He raised his coffee mug, smiled and saluted her. She turned away. Picking up the empty dishwasher tray, she headed for the kitchen. He might have a smile of particular sweetness, he might have charm in spades, but *she* wasn't going to fall for all that, like Kate and Penny had.

Walter was tossing tomatoes and mushroom in the frying pan. Jackie stopped dead, scarcely able to believe her eyes. Walter had his pristine new chef's whites on and his old greasy apron on top. He grinned at Jackie. 'See how clean I'm keeping them.'

Jackie swallowed hard and clenched her fists. 'Give me strength not to strangle him, Lord,' she muttered beneath her breath.

CHAPTER 5

Penny put her tea on the table and flopped down in a chair in the storeroom. Jackie was already there eating a late lunch, one of Walter's doorstep bacon and egg sandwiches. As she took a bite, melting butter and bacon fat oozed out of it and ran down her chin. She dabbed it up delicately with a paper napkin.

'I've been eating Walter's fry-ups for the last four days. I think that when things settle down a bit I'm going to have to get myself organised with a packed lunch like Mother used to do or I'm going to end up like a house side. How does he stay so thin when he eats them all the time?'

'Works it off on that smallholding of his. Always chasing after sheep or hens or some wildlife or other. And he has a big vegetable and fruit garden. I suppose he does a lot of digging.'

Thinking of digging reminded Penny of Marilyn's funeral. She was going to be buried alongside her husband according to what Walter had been telling Kate earlier.

'Will we be shutting the caff on that day, then?' she asked Jackie.

'What day?'

'When we bury your mum.'

'We're not burying her. We'll be attending, although God knows I don't want to.'

Not wanting to go to your own mother's funeral? Penny was shocked.

'Why ever not? I know you two didn't always get on but surely things weren't that bad.'

Jackie screwed up the napkin and threw it forcefully into the waste bin. Things weren't that bad? Oh weren't they? That showed how much Penny knew. If Marilyn hadn't upped and died when she did, Jackie might have run her through with the carving knife. All her carping and nagging. The endless criticism about Jackie's appearance, speech, manners – God! Her mother had even said she breathed too loudly. Then there was the guilt about having all these feelings and sometimes wishing her mother was tormenting the devil instead of herself … and then to come downstairs and find her stiff in the chair. Jackie couldn't get her last sight of Marilyn out of her mind.

'It's not that I don't want to go, Penny, it's just … I keep seeing her sitting there at the table, all dead and cold. I can't get past it. That's not how I want to remember her. I must have some good memories – surely there must be *something* she did that I can remember fondly! But all I can see is her with her face in bowl of porridge and her second-best slippers on. I hated those slippers. They were worn right through at the toes and they made her look like an old bag woman but she wouldn't get rid of them. And now she's died with them on her feet.' Jackie's voice rose steadily towards hysteria.

'You need to go and see her,' Penny said firmly.

Her words stopped Jackie in her tracks. 'Pardon?'

'You need to visit her.' Penny nodded her head, looking wise.

'I'm only thirty-five and I don't want to go where I think she's gone yet, thank you, Penny.'

'At the undertakers, Jackie,' Penny went on patiently. 'You need to see her now. They'll have … tidied her up and she'll look at peace. It'll give you a nicer lasting memory than seeing her in the chair at home – with the porridge.'

Jackie put her bacon sandwich down carefully. Penny had some crack-brained ideas sometimes. No wonder her husband didn't know whether he was George or Georgina.

'I don't think visiting a corpse is the answer, Penny.'

'You don't know till you try. And you need to go soon, before they screw the lid down.'

'And why would they do that?' Jackie asked, shocked. 'She's not going to climb out?'

'No, she's definitely dead,' Penny said reassuringly. 'Although some people ask to be buried with their mobile phones these days, just in case they aren't. But supposing they couldn't get a signal? It might depend upon your network. I don't suppose anyone's actually tried it, have they? I mean, who'd want to be buried six feet under to test out a theory? Anyway, Marilyn doesn't need her mobile in with her, but I think it might help you to go and see her. I went to see my Uncle Fred you know.'

'And did it help?'

'No, not really. They'd padded his cheeks out and he had someone else's teeth in because they had lost his, and they didn't fit. He looked a bit like Bugs Bunny with rouge on.'

As always in her dealings with Penny, Jackie felt she was swimming through treacle. 'But you're recommending this to me?'

'Well, it would be different. Marilyn didn't have false teeth and they won't have done funny things to her.'

Jackie picked up her sandwich. 'I'll think about it.'

* * * * * *

That afternoon, standing nervously outside the undertakers' premises, Jackie wondered how on earth she had let Penny talk her into this. She wanted to turn tail and flee, but somehow … no, she would have to face Walter tomorrow. She couldn't bear the look of disappointment in his eyes if she told him she'd ducked out of it. He'd been so full of admiration when she had walked into his kitchen and announced: 'I'm going to see my mother. Penny thinks it will help me, give me a good last memory of her. Heaven knows I need one.'

Walter had looked steadily at her and nodded agreement. 'Aye, lass, it's time you looked at her properly and stopped being a big girl's blouse. There's nothing to be frightened of. She's at peace now.'

'That's what Penny said.'

'Well for once she's talking sense.'

Jackie had laughed uncertainly. No-one had ever heard Penny talk sense. How come she was now?

'Go on, Jackie,' Walter had urged her. 'Be your mother's daughter. Square up to things. Marilyn always did. You never know, you might come out smiling.'

So here she was, clutching Penny's arm and feeling a bit sick. From a long way off Penny was calling her. 'Come on, Jackie, you're worse than my lads. They used to drag their feet like this when I took them to the dentist.'

Fillings, root canal treatment, even extractions, suddenly seemed attractive to Jackie.

Penny pulled her up the steps and they entered the offices of Messrs Baldwin and Fitch 'Undertakers to the Quality since 1807'. Jackie wasn't sure Marilyn ranked as Quality having only been the proprietor of a side street café in York, but Walter obviously was, as he had chosen the undertakers.

Mr Baldwin, or was it Mr Fitch, came bustling out of his office to greet them. In his early forties, he had mousy slicked-back hair above pale blue eyes set in a long lantern-jawed face. He was tall and very thin, and resembled a drain-pipe in his shiny funeral blacks. He proffered a bony white hand to Penny, a professional look of sympathy on his face. 'Miss Dalrymple-Jones.'

Penny ignored his hand, smiled and pointed to Jackie. He

transferred his sympathy to Jackie.

'I'm Mr Fitch. You've come to see your mother, the late departed,' he finished in a conspiratorial whisper.

Jackie was very tempted to say: 'Yes I know she has,' but resisted.

'Well,' he smiled, showing sharp incisors and rubbing his hands. 'Mother's all ready for us, if you'd like to come this way.' He said it very grandly, as if inviting them-to take tea with the Queen.

Jackie really didn't like it but Penny wasn't going to let her back out now. They moved off in Mr Fitch's wake, walking down a corridor with walls painted in pale green and highly polished floors. It reminded her of a hospital.

They turned right and entered a dimly-lit room where piped music was playing a funereal march. Not Marilyn's style at all. She was more a *Sound of Music* woman, except when she was in a temper and her tastes turned to heavy metal. Jackie remembered that their last row had been followed by a solid hour of Def Leppard. There was no denying her mother had been an unpredictable woman.

The coffin was in the centre of the room, flanked by two tall, gilded candlesticks with plastic candles topped by battery operated flames.

Mr Fitch ushered them in and made a queer little obeisance towards the coffin. He drew two chairs up to it and stood behind them, indicating that Jackie and Penny should sit down.

Penny drew Jackie forward and nudged her down into the chair. Mr Fitch made as if to withdraw and Penny started to follow. Jackie turned in her seat to protest but Penny said gently, 'Just sit with her for a while and then, when you're ready, have a look at her. Say your goodbyes properly.'

Jackie pointed to the coffin. 'You first, just to be sure.'

'Of what?' Penny said impatiently.

'That she's, you know … alright.'

'She's as alright as she's ever going to be. OK. Let's have a look.' Penny peered into the coffin. 'Hello, Marilyn, love,' she said, 'it's me, Penny.'

'I hope she can't hear you,' Jackie muttered.

'No, she can't, but it doesn't hurt to be polite. And if you want to know, she looks fine, just like she always did. Now isn't that lovely? They've done her hair and nails just as she liked them. She would be pleased.'

Visions of Mr Fitch or Mr Baldwin tending Marilyn's golden tresses revolted Jackie. She jumped up. 'Let's get on with it.'

She peered into the coffin at Marilyn lying in state.

Penny put her arm around her. 'What do you think? Not a bit like what happened to my Uncle Fred.'

Penny was right. Marilyn looked just as she always had done: formidable. 'I thought folk were supposed to look peaceful when they died. Trust Marilyn to buck the trend.'

They were silent for a few moments gazing down on the dead woman.

Then it struck Jackie. 'You know, Penny, this is the first time I've been in the same room as my mother and been able to get a word in edgeways.' Slowly she began to smile. 'I could get used to this.'

CHAPTER 6

Barney Anderson pushed his plate away with a happy sigh. Thursday lunchtime all-day breakfasts were the best. Walter reckoned Thursday was very nearly Friday and therefore the start of the weekend, so he always added an extra sausage in celebration of the fact. If Walter were a woman he would marry him tomorrow, just for his cooking alone. Maybe that was too sexist a thought these days. Whatever; if he ever met a woman who could cook as well as Walter, he would marry her anyway.

As if conjured up by magic Walter was suddenly at his side, wiping his hands on his new white apron.

'Have you got a minute, Barney? I need a word.'

'Yeah, sure, Walter.' Barney gestured to the empty chair opposite. 'After a breakfast like that I was just thinking I might have to marry you.'

Walter looked alarmed and Barney laughed. 'Not for real, Walter, don't worry. But you have a great way with a fried egg.'

Looking over his shoulder to check if Jackie was about, Walter slid into the chair across from Barney.

'What can I do for you?' asked Barney.

'You know I live on a bit of a smallholding just outside the city, Claygate way? Well, my few fields march alongside my neighbour's, Albert Patterson. He farms in quite a big way, owns a lot of land round about there. The other day, when I got home from work, there's one of his men putting up a fence on my land, four foot inside my boundary. Patterson's claiming that's where his land starts, but that's always been my patch.'

Barney was interested. Big men trying to crush little men didn't go down well with him.

'So what did you do?' he asked

'I tore the bloody fence down and told the bloke to get lost, only I used a bit stronger language than that, I can tell you. Told the bloke to go back to his boss and tell him straight that it's my land and to keep his fat hands off.'

'And did he go quietly?'

'Yes, he did. I was a bloody sight bigger than him so he saw sense. But that boss of his, Patterson, he's had the cheek to send me a solicitor's letter.'

Walter reached below his chef's apron into his trouser pocket and fished out a crumpled letter dotted with brown marks. Barney raised his eyebrows quizzically.

'Sarah, my oldest hen, got on the table and had a go at it,' Walter said apologetically.

Barney quickly scanned the letter. 'Sabre rattling, Walter,' he said.

'Come again?'

'It's bullying. They know they haven't got a solid case but think that this letter might scare you into giving up some land.'

Walter sat up straight in his chair, red faced with anger.

'I don't scare easily and I'm not giving up one inch of my land to Patterson.'

'No, of course you're not, Walter. Now, first things first. I would need to take a look at the Deeds to your property to ascertain the exact curtilage of your boundaries.'

Walter stared at him. 'Now you're talking like that letter.'

Barney chuckled. Good for Walter. He had got carried away for a moment and fallen back into the old ways. That would never do.

'We need to look at the Title Deeds of your holding, Walter. They will show exactly where your land meets Patterson's. Do you have them at home, or are they lodged with your bank or solicitor?' I can get a lot of information from the Land Registry online, but they won't show who owns which boundary wall. I need to see your Deeds for that.'

Barney's heart sank as he watched Walter thinking it over. How many times had this scenario played itself out before him over the years? The most important document that proves your right to the roof over your head and people just completely lose track of it down the years, stuffing it down the back of a drawer or in an old shoebox in the wardrobe. Once, after many days' searching, Barney had finally found some Title Deeds under a dog's bed. He was so thankful to find them, he didn't get around to questioning the old lady on the logic behind her hiding place.

Barney waited patiently. Eventually Walter said, 'They're at home, I know that much.'

Wait for it…

'Trouble is, I'm not sure where. Long time since I've seen them. I mean, I've lived at Claygate for forty years and they're not something you need every day, are they? Once the place was mine I couldn't wait to get digging and planting and building my hen house and sheds for my ducks, all that stuff.'

'Tell me you haven't wallpapered a duck house with them, Walter,' Barney said, holding his head in his hands in mock sorrow.

'Don't be daft, Barney,' Walter said scornfully. 'You don't wallpaper duck and hen houses – the birds would strip the stuff off straight away, bad for them. No, they'll be in the house, I just can't think where to lay my hands on them immediately.'

Barney was serious now. 'When you go home from here

today, Walter, you'd better have a good hunt for them. Without the Deeds, Patterson can lay claim to anything and you can't disprove it. I'll have a look at them tomorrow and we can reply to the letter then. Don't worry, Walter. We'll hang on to what is yours and send old man Patterson packing.'

* * * * * *

'And you've looked everywhere?' asked Stan.

'Everywhere. I spent the whole evening and half the night searching every nook and cranny of that house and I can't turn them up. I'm cross-eyed with looking for them. I don't know what I'm going to do.'

Stan hated to see his old friend looking so tired and upset. He knew Walter's smallholding was very precious to him and how hard he'd worked over the years to make a success of it.

'What if I come and help you tonight? Two heads are better than one. I can come to it fresh and likely think of places you might have missed.'

Kate came into the kitchen with a tray piled with dirty dishes and headed for the dishwasher.

Stan leapt across the kitchen to her. 'Kate, Kate, my lovely Kate. You can't resist this wonderful opportunity to spend time with me tonight. Just think – our first date and at the same time helping a friend: a work of charity.'

He felt he had to seize the moment, the perfect opportunity to spend time with Kate outside the café. She might even get to like him.

Kate considered. 'A, it's not a wonderful opportunity, B, I don't want a first date and C, who's the friend?'

'The friend is Walter here. He's lost his Title Deeds, somewhere in his house, and he can't find them. He needs help sharpish or his neighbour is going to swipe some of his land.'

Kate was impressed with Stan's brief summation. She knew he was good friends with Walter. 'So what's the deal then?' she asked warily.

'We go to Walter's tonight and ransack his house until we find these Deeds and I buy you supper afterwards.'

'Mmm.' Kate looked a bit doubtful. She might be dirty and dusty after all that searching; she'd been to Walter's before.

'Or,' Stan improvised, 'if it's too late for supper we'll make it another night, wherever you would like to go. Name your place. We'll wine and dine in style.'

She had to hand it to Stan, he made the most of every opportunity. She was keen to help Walter, but with Stan in tow would she be getting into something she hadn't bargained for? Walter needed help, though, so she agreed to go with them after work.

'I have this picture in my head,' said Walter, 'of putting them somewhere safe, like in a biscuit tin, some thought of protecting them from fire perhaps. Don't know what biscuit tin it was though, or if it was a tin at all….' He tailed off wearily.

Stan clapped him on the back. 'We'll find it, Walter. Leave it to Kate and me. What a team! you'll never get better.'

He grinned from ear to ear, his deep blue eyes sparkling with delight at the prospect of seeing Kate away from the café.

'What have I let myself in for?' Kate wondered as she stacked the dirty plates into the dishwasher.

CHAPTER 7

By some miracle all three of her flatmates were going out on Friday evening leaving Melissa Gatenby free to take her pick of their clothes and possessions for her own night out with Barney Anderson. After lots of heavy hinting he was finally taking her to a very posh restaurant tonight and she wanted to look her best. Unfortunately, modelling jobs had been in short supply lately and funds were low. She would have to borrow a frock from one of the girls for the evening even though she had been expressly forbidden to do this ever again after the last time. But hey, memories were short and she knew they wouldn't mind really, especially if she netted Barney on the strength of it.

She sat demurely on the sofa feigning absorption in a high-brow documentary on global warming presented by some bearded intellectual droning on about greenhouse gasses and emissions. Her flatmates, drifting through the lounge at intervals between the bathroom and their bedrooms, raised their well-shaped eyebrows in amazement at the sight of Melissa so unusually occupied, actually concentrating on something for once.

'Don't forget to clean the microwave, Melissa,' Rachel said before she left. 'I don't know what you put in it yesterday, but it exploded and there's burnt stuff spattered everywhere.'

'Never mind watching TV,' Imogen snapped as she passed through the lounge. 'For God's sake clean that bloody oven, Melissa. No-one can use it as it is.'

Beatrice, in slinky black trousers and crop top which showed her tanned flat stomach, was almost out of the flat door before she too remembered the oven. 'It still stinks out there, Melissa. What did you do, cremate an old skunk or something? Just for once, clean up your own mess.'

Well, now they had all gone and who the hell cared about some mouldy old microwave. If they thought for one moment she was going to spoil her carefully polished nails doing cleaning… She leapt off the sofa and headed off to Rachel's room. Rachel had a good job in a merchant bank and earned shedloads of dosh, consequently she had the best wardrobe of clothes to choose from. Luckily they were the same size and Melissa was spoilt for choice as she happily riffled through the dresses in the wardrobe. Mmm, she should go for the sexy low-cut little red number or the chic long black one? She decided on the red dress and bore it off to her own cluttered untidy room.

There was no hot water left for a bath so she made do with a grubby flannel around her face and neck and climbed into the red dress. She looked at herself in the mirror: very nice. Now, make-up. Imogen had the best collection.

Melissa trotted into Imogen's room. It reflected Imogen's personality, clean and orderly. Her trays of make-up were neatly arranged on top of an old wooden chest covered by an embroidered white linen cloth. Melissa trawled amongst the pots and powders and found a dusky violet eye shadow she liked. She applied it to her eyelids, the excess powder dropping on to the linen cloth. Melissa dusted it off; it only left a few smudges behind, you could hardly tell. Imogen had a new mascara that made lashes look twice their length. Melissa applied it lovingly thinking of how she would lower her eyelashes sexily at Barney. She sprinkled sparkly gold dust over her cleavage and over the dressing table. It fell over Imogen's pots and snowy cloth. Melissa half-heartedly swiped it away and went into Beatrice's bedroom.

This was a night for the Chanel N° 5. It would be the clincher. Barney would only need one whiff of that and he would be hers for the taking. She could be wined and dined in style whenever she wanted. She liberally doused herself from Beatrice's bottle. The room smelt a touch strongly of it now, but no matter. By the time Beatrice came home the smell would have faded. Hopefully.

* * * * * *

As he dressed for his Friday evening date with Melissa, Barney Anderson asked himself for the twentieth time, why, oh why, oh why did I ever agree to this? How, the hell, did I ever get into this mess? It's not as if I even like her. She's a little gold digger. She talks rubbish and hardly has a brain to speak of.

Barney was a man who knew himself well, whose honesty and integrity had been tested to its utmost and yet, here he was about to go on a date with a bimbo.

He sighed deeply. OK, so she had been balm to his spirit when he gave her a lift home. All that obvious and over the top admiration of him and everything he did. She had extravagantly praised his smooth gear changes and laid a hand caressingly on his leg. Not good for a bloke when he was negotiating busy city traffic.

He had been downing a few whiskies in the pub, brooding on Jackie and her barbed remarks about him being a dosser and a no-good. Alright, so she thought about him as someone she might side-step if he was on the pavement with a begging bowl. He could disabuse her of that idea in two sentences, couldn't he? Tell her the truth, what he really did, and his true circumstances. But for some reason he rebelled at this idea. Jackie should like him for who he was and not what she wanted him to be. He wasn't sure why he was brooding on this; what people thought had never mattered before.

The whisky fumes warmed his head. Jackie's soft fair hair and deep violet eyes filled his thoughts. Then he heard her words again in his head: 'It's a pity I pay so much council tax, double in fact, here and at home to keep the likes of you in luxury, squatting in homes you don't own and giving you an income you don't earn. Good job we're not all like you, Barney Anderson, you'd bring the country to its knees.' He drank the last of his whisky down and turned to leave, cannoning into a young lady standing behind him at the bar and spilling her drink down her dress.

His profuse apologies followed. He renewed her drink and one for himself at her insistence. She had been with a large crowd of people but now remained by his side.

'Admit it, you fool, she is good for your ego,' he told himself. 'What man of forty wouldn't like a beautiful twenty-five-year-old blonde on his arm? You are a vain fool, but after tonight at the Fox and Pheasant it's time to stop the show. She's no substitute for a certain sharp-tongued café proprietor that you feel attracted to, so be honest and let her go.'

* * * * * *

The Fox and Pheasant prided itself on its small but perfect menu and its beautifully cooked and presented local food.

Melissa and Barney were shown to a table for two in an alcove. A plum-coloured velvet curtain shielded them from any draughts and created a cosy intimate space.

The waiter held Melissa's seat for her. She practised batting her eyelashes seductively at him as she lowered herself into the chair. Unmoved, the waiter handed her a menu and asked Barney if he would like to see the wine list. Before Barney could say Cabernet Sauvignon, Melissa cried, 'Champagne. This is a special occasion after all.'

Barney looked nonplussed, but nodded agreement to the waiter who promptly departed.

'A special occasion?' he asked.

Melissa fluttered her eyelashes again and pouted at him. 'Our very first date. I think that's something to celebrate, don't you?'

She leaned forward, the low neck of Rachel's red dress exposing white breasts glittering with gold dust in the lamplight. She held the pose for a moment, giving Barney ample opportunity to study her assets. He made no comment and, a little disappointed, she leaned back again in her chair.

The waiter brought the champagne and poured a little into Barney's glass. He took a sip and wrinkled his nose. 'They all taste the same to me, too sweet and bubbly,' he said.

'It's Dom Perignon, sir.' The waiter sounded hurt. 'We only serve the best at the Fox and Pheasant. Shall I pour for the lady, sir?'

Melissa held up her glass enthusiastically and toasted Barney. 'Happy first date,' she cooed. 'Let's hope there'll be many more to come.'

Barney took a swig of his champagne and spluttered as the bubbles went up his nose. 'Told you so, all bloody bubbles.' He motioned to the waiter. 'Bring me a decent red, for God's sake. I can't stand this girly stuff.'

Melissa ordered the home-made pâté for starters and munched her way through the generous portion whilst watching in fascination as Barney deftly dealt with his moules marinières.

'You don't get much at the end of it all,' she observed. 'You have to prise open the shell and there's only a little moule inside after all that effort, not even a mouthful.' She gestured to her hearty chunk of pâté balanced on a thick slice of toast and butter. 'I like a good mouthful, darling.' She lowered her lashes at him seductively and wiggled her breasts, giggling.

Barney rinsed his fingers and thought of Jackie. They could have shared a bowl. He could have fed her moule marinières all night and enjoyed wiping the cream from her seductive mouth….

'Why is it called Beef Wellington?' Melissa's voice interrupted his fantasy.

Barney slewed his mind back to the present. Beef Wellington, what was she talking about? Oh yes, she'd ordered it for her main course. Bit heavy after the pate, he thought, but it was her choice. She would go out on a high note anyway.

'Well, it's said it might be named in honour of the Duke of Wellington, although it seems the dish was only recently invented, 1960s, I think. Or it might have been named after it was introduced at a civic reception in Wellington, New Zealand. No one source can agree, but I like to think if it as honouring the Duke of Wellington.'

'Yeah,' Melissa said admiringly. 'You know so much, Barney. You're so clever. What did you order for mains?'

'Sole Verde, it's a sole stuffed with cream and herbs in a white wine sauce, not too heavy. I don't sleep well if I eat a lot late in the evening.'

'Who said anything about sleeping?' Melissa blew kisses at him and somehow managed to rub his thighs with her bare toes under the table.

Did she have legs on elastic? he wondered uneasily. He didn't know what she had in mind after the Fox and Pheasant but he intended going home alone. He would have to find a way of letting her down lightly before they reached her flat.

He nibbled absently at his meal whilst Melissa chomped her way through a large Beef Wellington along with vegetables and crushed potatoes, followed by a cold chocolate pudding with whipped cream. He wondered how she stayed so stick thin and fell to imagining her in middle age. Would she still be a bag of bones, all narrow shoulders and pointy breasts? His mind wandered back to Jackie. Now there was a proper woman, deep bosomed and curvaceous. He imagined her in a red dress opposite him with gold stardust on her breasts. Mmm….

'You've got chocolate sauce dribbling down your chin,' Melissa pointed out.

'Oh, God.' Hastily Barney dabbed at his face and decided the evening had to end. It wasn't fair on Melissa and his mind was on … well, other things.

Driving back into York Melissa suggested a visit to Boothams Nightclub. 'I think my flatmates might end up there, I could show you off.'

Trophy man, he mused to himself. Led by the nose around the dance floor as her prize exhibit. I don't think so.

He swung the car in the direction of her flat. 'Not tonight, Melissa,' he said aloud. Not any night, if he had any say in the matter. 'I've got work to do at home and have an early start with appointments tomorrow.'

Melissa pouted her disappointment. 'Don't be such a spoilsport, Barney.' She placed her hand on his thigh. 'We could have such fun.'

Barney removed her hand. 'No. In fact, Melissa…' He took a deep breath to prepare for ending things between them.

Back came her stroking hand. 'Well, I tell you what,' she cooed invitingly. 'The girls are all out. Why don't you come up to the flat for a nightcap, a little drink and … who knows…?' She caressed him again.

Barney was only human. He removed Melissa's hand again before his resolve could weaken. Drawing up outside her flat, he firmly declined her offer. 'Look, Melissa…' he began again.

She was clearly insulted by his failure to succumb to her charms. 'No, you look. What does it take to get you into bed,

Barney Anderson?' she snapped. 'Aren't I beautiful enough for you? Sexy enough? Don't you want to take me in your arms and have mad passionate sex with me?'

She was tearful and angry and didn't wait for an answer to her questions. Wrenching open the car door she jumped out. 'Go cuddle up to your mouldy old papers,' she shouted at him. 'See how warm they'll keep you.' She slammed the door and made to walk off. The hem of her dress had caught in the door and Barney heard a loud ripping noise.

'Hell.' Melissa pulled open the car door and rescued the rest of the dress from the car. Slamming it once more, she ran off and disappeared up the steps and into her block of flats.

'Hell,' Barney echoed and punched the steering wheel. 'You handled that really well didn't you, Barney boy. Now she probably thinks you're gay and you haven't even ended things properly.'

* * * * * *

Up in her flat Melissa dropped her bag and examined the torn hem of Rachel's dress. It wasn't too bad, she would be able to repair it and put it back tomorrow. Dejectedly, she dried her tears and drifted aimlessly about the room. It wasn't the end to the romantic evening she had envisaged. A nightcap and slow seduction on the sofa…. Thinking of nightcaps, Melissa wandered into the kitchen and opened the fridge. What luck! Imogen's almost full bottle of white wine was still there. She could have a glass and it wouldn't be noticed.

She found a glass and went back into the living room. She enjoyed the wine, sitting in front of the TV watching old celebrities suffering in the jungle. Melissa was soon absorbed in the programme and absently poured herself more wine. She could top the bottle up with water and put it back later.

Much later the bottle was finished and Melissa slept soundly on the sofa, her make-up smudged and black mascara streaked down her cheeks. The torn and crumpled red dress, now spotted with wine stains, was wrapped around her sleeping body.

She slept through her flatmates' arrival home and their disbelieving stares as they surveyed the dress and the empty bottle and glass cast aside on the floor.

Before Rachel could shriek her anger Imogen motioned her to silence and pointed their way into the kitchen. Quietly the three of them huddled together.

'Leave her to sleep it off.'

'First thing in the morning.'

'Bags packed for her and ready to go.'

'Where will she go?'

'Who cares. She's not staying here one more night. She's a lazy, thieving slut. We should never have taken her on in the first place. No wonder the Carrington crowd threw her out.'

'We'll write her a cheque, refund this month's rent. She can find somewhere else with that.'

In full agreement, the girls crept back through the living room, past the sleeping Melissa.

Any lingering sympathy for Melissa soon vanished when Imogen found her spoiled make-up table and Beatrice recoiled at the strong smell of her Chanel N° 5 when she opened her bedroom door.

Realising the extent to which she had raided all their possessions, they quietly set to work with a will. As they packed up Melissa's bags, they found several of their own lost things amongst hers. She was a magpie, taking the brightest and best.

CHAPTER 8

At 6:00 p.m., a blue Kia people carrier was standing outside the café. Stan was waiting patiently at the passenger side, but as soon as Kate came out he leapt to open the car door for her. He bowed low and said, 'My lady.'

Despite herself, Kate was impressed. Sir Walter Raleigh couldn't have done better by Queen Elizabeth, she thought. She was touched by his gesture, in spite of all her resolutions to resist him.

Stan was a careful driver. Years of travelling around the cities and winding country roads of North Yorkshire had honed his skills. Kate relaxed, tired after a busy day's labour.

'We could be all night at Walter's,' Stan said with relish. 'He's a bit of a hoarder, you know. One of the "it might come in useful one day" brigade and knowing Walter it probably does. He could have invented the re-use and recycle movement. To be fair to him, he's probably not in the house long enough to have much of a clear out. After a day at the caff he likes to be outside with his birds and tending his land.' He paused, then continued, 'If we don't find these Deeds tonight, Kate, we'll have to come back again tomorrow.' A wide grin broke across his face and his blue eyes danced gleefully.

'I'm sure we'll find them tonight, Stan,' Kate said firmly. 'Walter is sure they're in the house somewhere, and with three of us turning the place upside down we're bound to find them. Then Walter can get this land thing sorted out.'

'But we're still on for going out, aren't we?'

Stan looked so anxious Kate knew she couldn't disappoint him. Besides, Walter would have her guts for garters if she didn't give Stan his chance.

'Saturday night, Stan.' She glanced across at him and couldn't help responding to the smile in his eyes. 'We'll dine and dance the night away. We haven't got an early start on Sunday.'

Stan was speechless with delight. He gripped the steering wheel tightly and looked out happily at the darkening city streets.

Walter was already home when they bumped up the rough track that led to his house. The lights were on, beaming out a welcome into the dark night. As they turned into the last bend, the house came into view. Nestling beneath the hillside, it was a large building built of stone taken centuries before from the nearby monastery that had been sacked and looted by Henry VIII's henchmen. Two storeys high, the house was divided into two halves – one side for living accommodation and the other for sheltering farm animals. Walter's home still had the roof on but the old byres attached to it were now open to the skies. The pantiles were long gone and only the wooden roof spars remained, giving the house a sad, neglected air.

Stan's people carrier bounced to a halt as the track petered out into a gravelled parking area. Kate wondered idly why he needed such a large car. She hoped he didn't have ideas of back-seat seduction later on. If he did, he would soon feel the benefit of her self-defence training classes. But maybe she was being alarmed at nothing. Dismissing her thoughts, she got out of the car and stared at the house and shadowy fields beyond. Then she turned to Stan.

'It's a lovely place, but Walter must like his own company to bury himself out here, far away from everyone.'

'I don't think it's his own company he likes, Kate. I think

it's more a case of he can't stand other people most of the time. He likes to work away in his kitchen at the caff, have a few good spats with Marilyn and enjoy the peace and quiet out here.'

'*Had* a few good spats,' Kate reminded him, emphasising the past tense. 'They were like an old married couple in some ways and now she's gone Walter seems so lost.'

'Well they worked together for forty years. Walter saw more of her than her husband did. I think they grew up together and grew old together and now...' Stan stopped, looking pensive. '...she's left him behind, out here.' He looked about. 'With nothing more than his bloody hens and ducks and purple sprouting broccoli for company.' Kate shivered and started walking towards the back door. Walter opened it and a stream of bright light flooded the dark stony path.

As she stepped into the kitchen, the scene was like something out of a bad dream. At the Café Paradise, Walter ran an organised and tidy operation. Years of drilling by Marilyn, always a stickler for order, had made him neat and economical in all his actions. He cleared up as he went and his kitchen remained orderly and clean however heavy the day's trade might be.

Walter's home was an entirely different matter. Here he was king and could do as he liked. Chaos ruled. Kate's eyes were dazzled by the profusion of objects and clutter littering every surface. Tins, jars, dishes, cups, seed packets, even freshly dug vegetables lay on the draining board, their dark muddy roots soiling the yellowing stone sink. On the kitchen table, amongst the stack of clean plates and cups, a pure white hen with a red comb snuggled down on a large square sod of turf. She cackled protectively at Kate's and Stan's entrance.

'Don't mind Sarah,' said Walter apologetically. 'She got broody but she's always in here with me so I made her a nest on the table there. She wouldn't want to be in the byre on her own. She'd get lonely.' He stroked the little bird affectionately. 'She'll soon get used to you. Now, would you like a cup of tea before you start?'

Kate eyed the cups stacked all around the hen and passed on Walter's offer.

'Maybe later,' Stan said, seeing the panic in Kate's face. 'We'll make a start, Walter.'

'Perhaps you could get going in here,' Walter suggested. 'If you don't mind Sarah, that is. She won't be any trouble. She's been out for a feed and a walk around, so she should settle now.'

Walter looked around his large kitchen helplessly. 'I did have a look about in here but it's got a bit, you know … I'm that busy outside I never seem to get time to sort out in here.

'Never,' seemed about right to Kate. Forty years of outside busyness and never a thought for the inside. Everything was piled up and had clearly gone way beyond Walter's control. Old papers and bills were stacked up in heaps on the floor. How did he ever find anything?

'Come on, lass,' Stan said encouragingly. 'Let's set about this dresser here.'

He turned to Walter. 'Why don't you try your bedroom, Walter? Maybe you could check out your wardrobe or on top of it, or under your bed. I bet you've got hiding places everywhere that you could look in.'

Not wanting to play gooseberry, Walter left them to it and went to start his search upstairs.

Sarah, the broody hen, watched quietly from her warm nest as Stan and Kate worked slowly through the mass of items on Walter's dresser. Every now and again she clucked softly to herself, rose majestically, ruffled her feathers and then settled herself comfortably once more on her clutch of eggs. Kate and Stan worked in companionable silence. Occasionally one or the other would open an envelope, tin or box to find it contained something evil smelling and indescribable and exclaim at the contents.

Why would Walter keep a box full of old grass, or a wartime tin of dried egg? Kate tried to prise the lid off a large battered and ancient looking tin, thinking it looked old and grand enough to contain the Title Deeds to nearby Castle Howard, never mind Walter's Claygate home. Stan saw her struggling and came to help. He took a sturdy knife from his pocket and eased the lid off.

A foul smell rose from the tin. Kate and Stan stepped back. Sarah clucked her disapproval from the table. Covering her mouth and nose Kate motioned to Stan to replace the lid. He looked inside and grinned at her. 'I know what this is.'

'I don't care what it is,' Kate shouted, then put her hand over her mouth to stop herself throwing up. She ran to throw open the back door. 'Just put the lid back on.'

'It's horse glue,' Stan said happily.

'Horse glue?' Kate gasped as she gulped in fresh air. 'Stan, I know you think that most women are pretty but dim and gullible, but I assure you I'm not one of them. You don't glue horses. They are living creatures.'

Stan laughed loudly. Kate felt miffed. He needn't take her for a complete fool.

'Horse glue, my lovely Kate, is not for gluing horses, as you rightly point out. It is *made* from horses, boiled bones and all that. It has many uses, particularly for gluing furniture. It's excellent for stage scenery, good strong stuff.'

Kate was still standing by the open back door. 'What's Walter doing with it? Does he make his own furniture?'

'Yeah, I think he did make some of it. You can pick up any amount of good quality wood for free if you keep your eyes open. People are always getting rid of it.'

Sarah clucked loudly and shivered on her nest as the cold night air filled the kitchen. Kate closed the door and returned to searching the dresser and its contents. Sometime later she said casually, 'Stage scenery, eh?'

'You what?'

'You said it was particularly good for gluing stage scenery. Is that what you do in your spare time, amateur dramatics?'

'Me!' Stan exclaimed. 'No, oh no. I have … er … friends that do that kind of stuff, that's all. I help them out from time to time.'

To Kate's amazement, a deep flush suffused Stan's cheeks and he looked guilty and embarrassed at the same time. Her curiosity was aroused, but this subject would have to keep for another time; they had a job to do.

Nothing quite as smelly as the horse glue troubled them for the next hour, although they came across over-ripe bags of old hen food and some mouldering dog biscuits in a dark and dusty corner. Kate learned quickly to delve carefully amongst all the items crammed into the drawers. She didn't know what she might put her hands on.

Stan approached the task with his usual cheery gusto, pulling out drawers and rifling through them, checking everything quickly as he went. Suddenly he whistled long and low and stood up, holding a paper in his hand. Sarah took exception to the noise and cackled back at him.

'Have you found it, Stan?'

'No, sweetheart, I haven't, but come and take a look at this.'

He held out a paper and Kate reached out to take it. 'Oh no, come here and see it with me.'

Kate sighed and rolled her eyes. This had better be good. She stood next to Stan and looked at the paper in his hand. It was an old photograph taken when Walter was a young man, with his arms around a beautiful young woman. He was gazing adoringly into her eyes and she looked back at him smiling, her dark eyes shining with love. It was a young Marilyn.

'Well, he's a dark horse,' said Stan wonderingly. 'In all the years I've known him, he's never mentioned any relationship with Marilyn. I wonder what happened.'

'It's none of our business, Stan,' said Kate. 'It's private, between the two of them. If they've never said a word about it then they don't want anyone to know, so we'd better put the photo back and pretend we've never seen it.'

Stan turned the photo over and studied the back of it. 'Listen to this, Kate,' he said excitedly. '"To my darling Walter. A memory of the best day of my life, February 1975".'

'Put it back, Stan,' Kate urged. 'We're not here to pry into Walter's private life. I don't like it.'

'We're not prying,' insisted Stan. 'He asked us to search and that's what we're doing. I can't help what I find.' He looked at the photograph again. 'By heck, she was good looking.'

Kate took the photo from him and replaced it in the drawer. 'Title Deeds,' she said firmly. 'Keep looking.'

'You're a hard taskmaster, Miss Johnson.' Stan sighed and moved on to the next drawer.

Another half hour passed. Kate slowly became aware of Stan standing very still and staring into space. She looked at him. He was staring at his feet as if he'd never seen them before.

'You've got a left and a right one, Stan, size eleven by the look of them, had them for, ooh, forty years maybe.'

Stan looked at her. 'What?'

'Your feet, you're staring at them.'

'No I'm not, I'm thinking.'

'That's what the noise is.'

'Listen to this, Kate. Jackie's birthday is November, right?'

'I don't know.'

'Well it is. Do the maths, Kate.' He shook her arm, 'Walter and Marilyn were clearly a very close couple in February 1975. Jackie is born in November 1975. What does that say?'

'That Marilyn was married to Mr Dalrymple-Jones in 1975 and after that Jackie was born. Don't go making stories where there aren't any.'

'I bet there are,' 'Stan said slowly. 'A lot of stories.'

Kate resumed her searching, feeling uneasy. She didn't know Stan well enough to be sure that he would keep this information to himself.

'I doubt Jackie even knows that they were ever involved,' she said cautiously.

'Probably not.'

'So let's keep this information to ourselves,' she went on quietly. 'We don't want to open a Pandora's Box.'

It was Walter himself who finally found the Title Deeds. They were carefully taped up in polythene and hidden in an old hat box belonging to his mother and then stuffed in a dark corner in the spare bedroom.

It was 10:30 p.m. and Kate was drooping with tiredness. After congratulating Walter, Stan took hold of her hand and steered her towards the door.

'Come on,' he said, 'we'll just catch the chippie before he closes and then I'll get you home. What about you, Walter?'

'No thanks, lad,' Walter said. 'I see enough chips at the caff. I might just have a nice egg sandwich and keep old Sarah here company.' He stroked the hen and she crooned softly to him.

Kate paused on the threshold to wish Walter goodnight, thinking again of the photo of young Walter with his Marilyn. Was that why he had never married? She tried to picture Marilyn in this setting. No, never in a million years!

She felt sad as Stan shepherded her out of the house, looking back to wave once more at the lone figure in the doorway, holding his old white hen in his arms.

* * * * * *

It was late Saturday morning before Melissa awoke. Her tongue felt too large for her dry mouth and her throat was sore. She sat up on the sofa, setting off a hammering inside her head. Looking down, she realised that she was still wearing Rachel's dress. With rising panic, she realised if Rachel had come home last night she would have it. Hell's bells! she'd really be for it now.

Feeling like death, she tip-toed into her bedroom. It was her bedroom, wasn't it? She paused uncertainly in the doorway and looked about her. She knew she was hungover, but surely not all her wits had gone astray. Her three suitcases were packed and stacked neatly on a stripped bed. How had this come about? Had something happened last night and she'd forgotten about it?

'You're awake at last.' Rachel's voice made her jump.

'Wha … wha … who…?' Melissa gestured to the bare room in front of her.

Rachel eyed her up and down frostily. 'My best Jennifer Morgan dress and you had to go and ruin it.' She took a step back and called down the corridor. 'Our little magpie is awake and functioning. Call the taxi, girls.'

Melissa turned to face Rachel. 'I'm sorry about the dress, Rachel, really I am. I didn't mean to…'

'No, of course you didn't,' Rachel said sweetly.

'I don't suppose you meant to use my make-up and spill it all over my grandmother's linen cloth,' said Imogen, appearing at Rachel's side.

'Or use my best Chanel Nº 5 and leave my room smelling like a bordello,' added Beatrice, materialising from nowhere.

There was a constant throbbing pain inside Melissa's head. She fished about in her brain for the words to come out, but could only stand there, wordlessly gaping at them.

'Time to go, Melissa,' Beatrice said. 'Last night's shenanigans was one borrow too many.' She handed Melissa a folded cheque. 'There's a refund of a month's rent. At least you'll have money for a down payment on your next place.'

'The further from here the better,' added Imogen.

'Your bags are packed and the taxi is booked.' Rachel pushed past Melissa and passed the suitcases out to Imogen and Beatrice. Carrying one herself, she made for the flat door and opened it.

'Goodbye, Melissa. You can always go home to Mummy darling. At least she will put up with your thieving ways.'

Beatrice prodded a shocked Melissa in the back and guided her to the front door. 'Bye, Melissa. Buy your own perfume next time.'

Imogen closed the door, leaving Melissa and her baggage standing on the other side. A taxi drew up at the kerb. 'Where to, love?' the driver called out.

Where to indeed? Where on earth was she going to go?

* * * * * *

That Saturday evening Barney parked his car in the residents' car park at the rear of his block of flats. He slumped back in his seat and rubbed his tired eyes. It had been a long day. He had seen a succession of clients, all bringing complex personal or financial problems to his office. In the normal run of things Barney would have relished the challenge of each one of them, but somehow the unfinished business with Melissa last night lingered on in his mind and ran like a troubled undercurrent throughout his day. He resolved to see her that evening and end things properly.

He let himself into his flat and stopped abruptly in the hallway. The television was on in the living room and a girl's voice was joining in loudly with the band singing on the screen. He strode into the room. 'Melissa!' he exclaimed. 'How the hell did you get in here?'

Melissa turned away from the TV screen. 'The key

was under the mat, Barney darling. I thought it would be, everyone leaves one there, don't they?'

Barney cursed himself silently. The key was meant only for his street friends when they needed to talk or had decided on a change of direction. 'It doesn't mean that you can just let yourself in and help yourself to my home, we hardly know each other.' His voice was sharpened by the anxiety of not knowing what she was up to.

Melissa tripped lightly over to him. 'Don't be cross, Barney. Awful Rachel made me leave the flat and we only had the *tiniest* of arguments. But she's *soooo* short-tempered and you've no idea how nasty she can be, so really I was quite happy to leave. But with Mummy and Daddy being away in Australia at the moment the house is shut up, and I had nowhere to go, no-one to turn to except for my faithful, devoted Barney.' She slipped her arms about his neck and kissed him softly on the lips.

With a sinking heart Barney knew he was trapped for now. 'This is just short-term, Melissa,' he said, removing himself from her embrace. 'You can't stay here for long. You'll have to start looking for a new place in the morning and …' A thought occurred to him. 'Where have you put your things?'

'I found your spare room.' Melissa pouted sexily at him. 'A girl doesn't presume, you know. She likes to be invited into a man's bed.' She waggled a finger playfully at him. 'You can't hold out forever, Barney, you'll see. Now if you don't mind, I'll just go and use that divine shower of yours and maybe then we could think about dinner. I'm starving. Can you cook, Barney?'

She sashayed out of the room in her high heels, swinging her hips and twinkling over her shoulder at him.

Barney watched her go, transfixed with horror at the prospect of Melissa becoming enmeshed in his life, the very last thing he wanted.

* * * * * *

It was an overcast Saturday at Café Paradise and Walter was preparing himself a late lunch. He slipped two doorstep-sized chunks of bread into the pan sizzling with hot bacon fat. He licked his lips with anticipation. He was ravenous; his breakfast had been hours ago and cooking meals for everyone else all day had sharpened his appetite as usual. The bread slowly absorbed the fat and he turned it over, waiting patiently until it was golden and crisped to perfection. He opened the oven and took out a plate on which lay two perfectly fried eggs and rashers of bacon. He added the fried bread to the plate and made his way out of the kitchen to the dingy staff coffee area at the back of the café.

As he sat eating his solitary meal, Stan rushed in from the delivery door. Walter nearly choked on his fried bread as Stan danced in with shining eyes and grabbed him in a big bear hug.

'Here, steady on,' he coughed.

'Walter, Walter, Walter, you'll never guess what?' Stan beamed.

'You've bought some new boots and you're climbing Everest tomorrow.'

Stan flung himself down in the chair opposite. 'Don't be daft. It's better than that anyhow. I've got a date; a real date with the beautiful, delectable, delightful Kate. What do you think to that?'

Walter grunted and took a slurp of his tea. 'Hmph. Going to be fish and chips again?'

'That might be your idea of showing a girl a good time but it's not mine. I'll take her wherever she wants and we can go dancing afterwards.'

'You must have been flogging a lot of bread rolls lately. It sounds expensive to me.'

'When God made tight-arses, Walter, you were his model. I bet there's a whole colony of moths in your wallet.'

'I'm just careful, that's all. I can't help it, I'm a Yorkshireman. Actually, I'm amazed Kate has agreed to go out with you at all. Your reputation goes before you. She'll have been warned.'

Stan's face fell and he was silent for a few moments. 'My trouble is, Walter, I love women as a species. You know, like you can be a cat lover or a dog lover and be drawn to them. Well I'm drawn to women. They're all gorgeous. I don't pretend to understand them but I love them all. Notwithstanding that,' he went on earnestly, 'I've really fallen big-time for Kate. This is the real thing.'

Walter raised his eyebrows sceptically and chewed on his fried bread.

'No, honestly, she's completely taken me over, every waking moment, every sleeping moment, I dream about her. She's the *one*, Walter, I know it.'

'You'll have a hell of a job convincing her of that,' Walter said, dunking his bread in a runny egg yolk.

Stan sighed. 'I know, but I have to. It may take a while but I will,' he said with quiet determination.

Walter wiped his plate with the last of the fried bread. Now he was full he could give Stan his full attention. 'Kate is a lovely lass, Stan. As you say she's beautiful, she's clever and she could probably have the pick of any men she chose to. What makes you think she would settle for you?'

'Well I know I'm not beautiful like her,' Stan said humbly, 'but I'm intelligent, knowledgeable. Look at all the work I do with the Historical Trust. I bet she would be fascinated by that. I can't wait to take her along to a day.'

'Hold your horses, lad.' Walter held out his hand as if to slow Stan down. 'Don't hit her with all that boy soldier stuff just yet. You might frighten her off.'

'It isn't boy soldier stuff,' Stan said indignantly. 'It's

re-enacting history and educating the public. They can see exactly how life was lived under the Romans in York. We provide living history, not playing soldiers. And in any case, I'm not a soldier, I organise it all. When we can find a suitable expert in the field, we would like to build a full villa showing the heating and drainage systems; we might build a Roman bath house…'

'You see, you're off already. Don't go chewing Kate's ears off with all that stuff.'

'But it's a huge chunk of my life, Walter. History is what I know. What else can I talk about?'

Walter was exasperated. 'No wonder you can never keep a woman. Politics, current affairs, the theatre. What's on at the Theatre Royal this week? Or exhibitions at the art galleries. Women like that kind of stuff.'

'Oh, like you would know, bachelor boy.' Stan groaned and rubbed his eyes.

'I could woo them if I wanted to,' said Walter. 'I had my moments.

Stan remembered the dedication on Marilyn's photograph and said soberly, 'Yes, I know you have, Walter. I'll try to think of a few things before tonight.'

CHAPTER 9

That same evening on the other side of York, Penny Montague chewed reflectively on her chicken tikka masala and gazed across the table at her husband, George. He was a big man, six foot four inches tall, and after years of hefting about double-glazed windows and conservatories he had developed bulging biceps and a six-pack that a twenty-something youth would be proud of. The shadow of a day's growth of dark beard darkened his cheeks and glinted in the lamplight as he shovelled his food into his mouth hungrily. In his large hands the cutlery looked like it was made for a doll.

This evening George wore an emerald green satin dress with a full skirt decorated with small seed pearls. Penny eyed it enviously. It would look so much better on her.

'Unlucky colour, green,' she said. 'My Granny wouldn't have it in the house.'

'Never?' asked George, looking up briefly from his curry.

'If you came in with anything green on you had to go outside, turn around three times, spit, and come in again.'

'Mmph,' grunted George. 'She must have had a mucky doorstep. Green's a very popular colour.'

Mentally cutting the dress down to fit herself, Penny asked, 'Where did you get it anyway?'

'Harrogate. We were there on a job and I went into one of them posh dress shops and asked if they had anything in green satin. I love satin, it always looks sexy and I wanted to try it out.'

'You never tried it on!' Penny was scandalised.

'Course I didn't, you muppet. I told them my wife was a big woman, my kind of size, and she showed me this.'

'I bet she wasn't deceived for one moment, George. A six-foot-four wife with a 42-inch chest? She'll have known it was for you. They've seen it all, those women in dress shops. You won't be the first man that's gone in looking for a frock for himself.'

George thought she was probably right and as she had brought the subject up he decided to pursue it. Upstairs, in one of the boy's rooms, he had cleared out the wardrobe and hung up his new, treasured dresses. Until Penny had caught him in one of his dressing-up sessions, she had never seen them. She still didn't know the extent of his collection and now he wanted to show them to her, show off a little to someone, and maybe get some advice on widening his choices.

'You mean Philip's wardrobe is full of them?' Penny was glad that she was sitting down. It was a lot to take in. She'd thought the other day was just a freak notion. 'How long have you been doing this?'

'Months!' George said proudly. 'I've got some cracking good gear.'

He had finished his meal. Now he jumped up, eager to display this newly discovered side of himself.

Penny pushed aside her half-eaten curry. It had lost its appeal. As George hurried her out of the dining room, she was grateful it was winter and the curtains were drawn. At least she was saved from a passing neighbour catching sight of George in full rig and kitten heels.

George had commandeered their eldest son's bedroom for his study when Philip had moved into his own flat four years earlier. He had re-decorated the room in a neutral colour, painting over the youthful experiments of black and purple. He had put up extra bookshelves to house his ever-expanding book collection and the new shelves were overflowing with books of all sizes and subjects.

Philip had taken his bed with him and in its place George had installed a new desk with his computer and printer placed neatly on it. A black leather easy chair completed the ensemble. Only the old fitted wardrobes looked familiar to Penny. It was now very definitely a man's den. Yet bizarrely, when George flung open the wardrobe doors with a flourish, Penny beheld a rail full of beautiful dresses in bright colours and patterns that lit up the room.

George handled them lovingly: a sheer, floaty, pink dress; a shiny, silky, long, red skirt; a bright orange, ruffled blouse. Penny had to hand it to him, he had terrible taste.

'Aren't they just beautiful?' George crooned, hugging a satin polka-dot dress to his chest.

'As individual garments, George, maybe,' Penny agreed dubiously. 'But what are you going to do with them all?'

'I want to wear them. Go out with you, both of us dressed up to the nines, all our make-up on. Then, we could go dancing. What do you say?'

She wanted to say that she would sooner dance naked on top of the Empire State Building with Skippy. 'I think you've lost the plot altogether, George. That's what I say.'

His face fell. 'I knew you wouldn't understand. Well, I'm not giving it up. This is only the beginning. I'll find someone else if you won't go with me.'

He wore the same mutinous expression as his son Philip at the age of fourteen, when he was going through a difficult adolescent phase. Penny sighed.

'It's a bit like asking me to climb a mountain when I haven't even walked down the road yet,' she said.

'I don't want to climb mountains,' George said moodily.

'I never said you did.'

'You just did, you said…'

Philip aged fourteen all over again. 'Forget mountains. All I'm saying is, let's take one step at a time. What do you know of being a woman out and about?'

George gaped at her.

'Quite right. Nothing. You've no idea about what it's like being a woman. How *could* you know? Why don't we just try one short outing in the daytime, dressed in ordinary clothes?' She pointed to the dresses in the wardrobe. 'Not anything fancy. We'll see how you get on. See if you like it.'

George smiled happily. 'I knew I married the right woman. Let's do it soon.'

Penny tried to smile back at George, her cheeks aching with the effort. 'But did I marry the right man?' she asked herself. She had never imagined George in Audrey Hepburn green satin. Well you wouldn't, would you? And did she want a girly husband? What if he didn't want to be a man again, where did that leave her?

CHAPTER 10

Monday morning dawned clear and crisp. A light frost lay over the fields. Bright sunshine flooded into Walter's farmhouse, bringing a hint of spring warmth to the January day.

Walter leaned out of his open bedroom window and sniffed the air appreciatively. The smell of damp earth was strong as the dazzling diamonds of frost melted slowly away.

He was grateful for the fine weather. It was going to be hard enough saying good bye to Marilyn for the final time without it being a grey rainy day. She had always hated those.

He drew his head in, shivering a little now. 'It's still only April, lad,' he told himself. 'Get your overcoat on.'

He shut the window, went to his wardrobe and looked at his reflection in the long mirror. His dark suit hung loosely from his thin frame. Even with his braces holding them up, the trouser waistband gaped. He would have to keep his jacket buttoned up to hide this and the wide red braces. Why did the shop only have red braces? Bloody bright red: not suitable for a funeral. He thought they went out of fashion with Mrs Thatcher's stockbrokers: but not in Yorkshire. Sighing, Walter fastened his jacket buttons and reached into the wardrobe for his best winter coat. He would need that for the cemetery.

Slowly he went down the stairs. Sarah was sleeping on her nest on the kitchen table, her head tucked beneath her white feathers. Walter moved quietly about the kitchen, gathering the teapot and mug for a hot drink before he faced this most painful day.

By the time he poured his tea Sarah had woken up and was looking about her in her quiet stately way, content to brood over the new lives developing beneath her warm body. Walter sat down at the table and stroked her.

'You'll have to be a good lass on your own today,' he told her. 'You see today' he stopped as his chest tightened and the tears welled up in his eyes 'we have to let Marilyn go, lass. Forty years, and now she's gone. I can't bear it. They're going to put her in the ground today with that daft bugger she was married to. Dalrymple-Jones,' he said scornfully. 'She only married him for his money. Didn't love him like she loved me. Yes,' he looked Sarah in the eyes, 'she did. She loved me, Sarah, and I loved her. We were made for each other but she couldn't see it. She could only see that I had nowt. Wouldn't come here and live with me like this. I wish I could have let her go. But I couldn't. I had to be near her. And then there was Jackie. She's mine. I don't care how much Marilyn denied it. We're so alike, we strike sparks off each other.'

The memories overwhelmed him and he gave way to them, burying his head in his hands. Heavy sobs shook his thin body. Sarah pecked gently at his sleeve.

When it was over Walter wiped his face and got up. 'Time to go, lass, Jackie will be waiting. It's her we have to think about now.' He patted Sarah's head one more time. 'Be a good lass and look after your eggs. We need new blood round here.'

* * * * * *

Jackie brushed her black suit fiercely. Marilyn's bloody cat: it always seemed to be moulting. Didn't it ever stop? And why did it rub itself against her all the time? She hated the thing. Hadn't she read somewhere about cats sensing those who disliked them and making a deliberate bee-line for them? That would make sense. Perverse; just like Marilyn. Well, that animal might be making a tin of cat-meat sooner than it thought, if it didn't look out.

The animal in question yowled loudly from behind the kitchen door.

'You're not coming out, Samson,' she shouted. 'I'm going to my mother's funeral, *and* cat hair free. You'd probably jump in the funeral car for a ride, given half a chance. Well no chance today, pussy boy. You can stay put.'

She slipped the suit jacket on and checked herself in the full-length hall mirror. Mm, still beefy. Her mother's sharp voice echoed in her head. 'I see my death hasn't stopped you eating well. You're putting on weight again, Jackie. You'll never get a man like that. They don't want elephants. They want svelte sexy girls, more like me. I don't know what you're eating down at that supermarket, because you don't get any rubbish at home.'

Jackie poked her tongue out; at her mother's image dancing before her in the mirror. 'Well there won't be the supermarket any more, Ma,' she told her. 'I'll be down the café and it won't be Walter's chips I'll be stuffing my face with.'

She turned away from the mirror and put her coat on. Mercifully the cat had not been near it. She sat down in a chair and waited for Walter to arrive. For the first time since her mother died, Jackie had silence and time to think.

Life had been a constant whirl of activity: making the funeral arrangements; contacting her mother's friends, relatives and business acquaintances; taking over running the café where Marilyn left off; ordering supplies; keeping the books; seeing the solicitor, the accountant...

With her increasing knowledge of her mother's world,

Jackie was slowly getting some kind of order into her life and her confidence was growing. She was free of Marilyn's constant nagging and jibes about her appearance. People listened to her, looked to her for leadership. It was a very new and very satisfying sensation.

Jackie suddenly felt light-hearted and happy. Then she was immediately beset by a rush of guilt. 'For heaven's sake, you're burying your mother today,' she told herself. 'It's a really sad occasion, laying her to rest alongside Dad.'

So why did she feel like kicking her heels up, liberating the cat from the kitchen and going out and getting drunk?

Jackie had to admit that Walter had been right. If it had all been left to her, she would have driven to the church in her own car. Mr Fitch of Hamilton and Fitch Undertakers by Royal Appointment since 18-something-or-other had looked shocked at the very idea of not having a car filled with mourners following the dearly beloved.

'Your mother was a well-respected businesswoman in the city, Miss, if you don't mind my saying so, and I feel she should be attended to the church in the style that befitted her life.'

When she re-told this scene at the café, imitating starchy Mr Fitch, Walter had reproved her strongly.

'Aye, and it's not funny neither, Jackie. It's your mother we're talking about. He's quite right, she deserves respect and a decent Christian send-off.'

'But she never darkened the church door, Walter,' said Jackie.

'That's nowt to do with it. She were married there and you were christened there. She'll get properly buried there too, and that's an end to it. So ring Mr Fitch about that car and I'll be in it alongside you. I'm her oldest friend and I want to do right by her.'

There was a defiant note in Walter's voice. There was to be no arguing over this one.

Now here they were sitting in the back of the large black Daimler following slowly behind the hearse carrying Marilyn's coffin.

Jackie wondered if the Queen felt like this. People gawped as they moved up the street. She resisted the temptation to try out a wave, a slow regal dip of the hand as Her Majesty did.

She sneaked a look at Walter. He stared straight ahead, his jaw clenched and his hands clasped tightly together in his lap.

Pity she's not alive to enjoy it, Jackie thought. She would have loved all this, the big cars, the flowers, all the attention.

The cars made their stately way up the drive to the church and swung round precisely at the church door. The vicar and pall-bearers were waiting for them.

Suddenly it was all very real to Jackie. This was it. Marilyn's journey was in the hands of others now. She gripped Walter's hand. 'Stay close, Walter,' she said. 'It's all a bit...' She didn't quite know what she meant but Walter seemed to understand.

'It's alright, lass. I'm here.'

With quiet dignity, the pall-bearers loaded the coffin onto their shoulders and slowly made their way into the church, the vicar intoning the opening prayers of the funeral service behind them.

Walter and Jackie followed on. As they entered the main body of the church Jackie gasped in amazement at the gathered crowd now standing up respectfully at their entrance.

Jackie had put a notice in the paper inviting friends and old colleagues to attend, but who were all these people? Jackie hoped they had come to the right funeral and people didn't start leaving when the name was announced. It had been known, she'd seen it on the TV. People turned up to the wrong weddings sometimes, too.

Walking down the aisle, she spotted Penny and George with Stan and Kate next to them. Penny smiled encouragingly at her. Jackie smiled back and thought how handsome George looked in his suit. She had heard about George's secret pastime from Kate. She was right. He would never make a good-looking woman. She wondered if Penny had ever discussed that aspect of George's new hobby with him, or perhaps he didn't care.

Walter ushered her into the pew and sat down beside her. The Bible and flowers were placed on the coffin and the vicar took his place at the altar steps.

He was an elderly man, almost a stereotype of a Church of England vicar. Tall, with a large bony frame, he was wearing a white cassock over clerical blacks that looked a size too small for him. Wisps of white hair were carefully combed over his head. He wore thick-lensed glasses behind which pale blue eyes beamed placidly out on a world which in the main he found to be full of virtuous people who were willing to do God's work and help each other as much as he was.

Walter had been relieved to find St Martin's was led by such a prelate. He couldn't stand trendy vicars, all beards, sandals, and guitars in the church. Walter liked his religion the old-fashioned way, stirring hymns accompanied by the organ and a sensible sermon you could understand delivered by a properly dressed vicar in a frock.

He knew Marilyn preferred tradition too, so he had made it his business to accompany Jackie when she went to the vicarage to arrange the details for the funeral. It was to be a simple but dignified service with three hymns, an address given by the vicar relating to events of Marilyn's life, prayers for the deceased and a final hymn as the coffin was taken out to the churchyard.

Walter had to be satisfied with that. For him, black-plumed horses drawing Marilyn's coffin mounted on a gun carriage and trumpeters announcing her arrival into the church wouldn't have been too much. But he knew Jackie wouldn't wear that, nor possibly would the Very Reverend Crispian St John Bellamy, vicar of St Martin's.

The Very Reverend Bellamy stepped forward to welcome everyone and the service began. The congregation rose to sing the first hymn, 'Abide With Me.' Jackie sang the words of the hymn lustily, inwardly glad her mother wouldn't be abiding with her anymore and looking guiltily across at the flower-covered coffin standing at the altar.

She became aware of Walter beside her. Feeling his body shaking, she looked up at him and saw the tears pouring down his face. She slid her arm into his and wished she could cry too. She would have to try or people would think she was really cold hearted.

'Think of the saddest thing you can, Jackie,' she told herself sternly. 'Surely burying your mother is the saddest thing, isn't it?' Then she thought: I suppose it's sad for Marilyn, it's obviously sad for Walter, but it's not my kind of sad.

She pondered whilst the verses of the hymn rolled on and then it came to her. Her beloved dog Rollo died when she was twelve years old. Rollo had been her constant companion until he died suddenly one morning. It was like losing part of herself and she felt her heart would break. The memory of darling Rollo did the trick and Jackie's tears flowed. Walter put his arm around her and they sat down to listen to the vicar's memorial address.

Reverend Bellamy waited a few moments for his flock to settle themselves. In the brief silence that ensued before he began, a mobile phone rang. The resonant tones of William Tell's Overture echoed about the church. The congregation looked about them, embarrassed and amused, ready to stare down the guilty party.

Many people immediately dived into their pockets and

pulled out their phones to check them, but the Overture played on. Reverend Bellamy looked on in distress.

'Really, this is hardly the time…' he began.

Phones were shoved back in pockets with relief as the music stopped. Then the taped message began. 'You have reached the phone of Marilyn Dalrymple-Jones. I'm sorry I can't take your call at the moment, but please leave your message after the tone and I'll get back to you.'

There was a collective gasp from the mourners as a woman's broad Yorkshire tones did as she was instructed.

'Hello, Marilyn love, it's me, Jessie. I'm just back from my world cruise. Can't wait to tell you about it, the handsome men and the dancing. You'll have to come with me on the next one. Give me a ring when you've got a mo and we'll meet up for lunch soon. Bye for now.' The message tape clicked off.

Hastily stifled laughter rippled about the church. Walter's face was thunderous. He would have the undertaker's head on a plate for this and dissect his brain with a meat cleaver. How dare they do this to her?

'Don't you worry, lass,' he whispered to Jackie. 'I'll deal with Mr flaming Fitch about this. Leave it to me. He'll be needing one of his own coffins before I'm done with him.'

The Reverend Bellamy was transfixed as if his shoes were nailed to the floor. His mouth opened and closed but no words would come. Never in fifty years of his priesthood had anything like this happened to him. Someone had put a phone in the coffin.

An embarrassed silence fell. Then a deep male voice whispered, 'Well, at least she hasn't answered it.'

It was too much; the mourners erupted into laughter. The happy sounds rolled around the church, much to the vicar's consternation and Jackie's joy. She jumped up to face the assembled congregation. Nodding to Reverend Bellamy she said, 'I'm sorry, Vicar, that happened at a most inopportune moment, but in a way I'm glad it did. I knew my mother had died, but still there was a part of me that wondered, you know… Sometimes doctors get it wrong and people regain consciousness. I didn't want it to be too late for my ma if she did, wherever she was, so I put her phone in her coffin when I visited her at the undertakers. I felt better then, felt she had every chance I could give her. Anyway, she never went anywhere without her phone, did she? So that's it really. Thanks to Jessie, we know she's really gone and that's set my mind at rest.'

She sat down suddenly, her legs giving way beneath her.

Spontaneously the congregation stood up and applauded her. Walter, looking bewildered, put his arms about her. The applause re-energised the vicar; he took control of the service again and Marilyn's funeral proceeded without further drama.

* * * * * *

As the organ played the resounding last notes of the seafarers' hymn 'For Those in Peril on the Sea', the pall-bearers moved into position and removed the Bible and flowers from Marilyn's coffin. Slowly they carried her out of the church and across the damp lawn surrounding it. Frost still lingered in the shady corners of the church walls, untouched by the unusual January sunshine.

Jackie and Walter followed the Reverend Bellamy and made their way to the open grave in the cemetery. It was lined with pieces of artificial grass which spread out over the banked up earth around the grave. Any sign of her father's coffin was carefully hidden from Jackie's view.

The mourners streamed out from the church and gathered around the graveside as Marilyn's coffin was carefully lowered into the ground. The vicar intoned prayers that had been used over the centuries. 'We now commit her body to the ground; earth to earth, ashes to ashes, dust to dust, in the sure and certain hope of the resurrection to eternal life.'

Jackie cried. It didn't need memories of Rollo this time. She had been fond of her father, even though they had never quite connected, and now here was Marilyn being laid to rest with him. She hadn't always been a sharp-tongued old bat; in fact she had been a good mother when Jackie was growing up. 'Hang on to those memories,' she told herself.

Standing at her side, Walter was weeping unrestrainedly. Jackie took his hand and he clung on fiercely. Stan came to his side, gently putting an arm around him as if he were a wounded child. He nodded to Kate. It was time to move away now that the service was over.

Kate led Jackie to the waiting funeral car and settled her in. 'What a fright I must look,' Jackie sniffed. 'All tears and runny mascara.'

'Don't worry about it,' Kate said. 'You can tidy yourself up when you get to the hotel ahead of all the crowd arriving for the bun-fight.'

She saw Stan approaching and straightened up. 'Where's Walter?'

'He just wanted a few moments to get himself together,' Stan said.

He waved to Jackie. 'I'll see you at the hotel.' Then he drew Kate away towards his Kia which was parked way down the drive. 'Actually, I think Walter wanted to have a last few moments on his own with her to say his goodbyes. He asked me to leave him.'

Back at the graveside Walter took a red rose from his inside his jacket and placed it tenderly on Marilyn's coffin.

'My forever girl,' he whispered. 'Goodbye for now, my love. You were always my love.'

He straightened up and turned away, blinded by his tears. He stumbled off to find his way back to Jackie waiting in the black Daimler.

* * * * * *

The Golden Lion Hotel was living up to its reputation for good food and wine. Jackie had ordered a hot and cold buffet for the occasion with wine or beer of the guests' choice. When she placed the notice in the local paper for the funeral arrangements, she thought it would attract a good response. No-one would pass up the opportunity of a slap-up lunch at the Golden Lion.

Jackie gazed about the crowded room and wondered how many of the guests had actually known her mother. People were standing in groups drinking and chatting quietly, others were seated, giving the buffet their serious attention.

Walter had collected his wits and made sure that she had a hot cup of tea and something to eat. Eventually he directed her attention towards a knot of people standing near the bar.

'Now, lass, it's time you circulated. There are a lot of people here who knew your mother for many years. You need to say hello to them. And I reckon some folk have come a long way to pay their respects today, so off you go. It's time to meet and greet, even though you don't feel like it.'

'I can't just swan up to people and say, "Hi, I'm Jackie, who are you?".'

'Don't be bloody daft. Didn't your mother teach you anything? Just go and introduce yourself and they'll do the rest.'

He gave her a light shove in the back as if she were a boat he was launching on the pond.

Nervously she approached the group at the bar. 'Hello, I'm Jackie, Marilyn's daughter. Thank you for coming today.'

Walter was right, as usual. The group immediately widened to include her and people introduced themselves.

It turned out that they, and many of the people present, had been Marilyn's colleagues at the city's Trades Council.

Jackie had been aware that Marilyn flitted off to some meetings or other but had never really taken much notice. According to the well-groomed woman speaking, Nina she thought her name was, Marilyn had been a leading light in promoting commerce in York and especially the catering establishments in the city.

'Your mother was a most interesting character,' a man called Tom said. He'd introduced himself as the President of the Trades Council. 'She knew she only ran a greasy spoon caff, so to speak, but she knew her trade from top to bottom. "Horses for courses," she always said. I think she could have run the catering operation at Buckingham Palace; she was so organised and enthusiastic. She used to run great training days for some of our members, introduce them to proper service, staff discipline and duties, book-keeping and all of that. Oh, your mother had such style.'

Jackie tried not to let her jaw drop with amazement. How had Marilyn managed to dish out all that advice when she ran the Café Paradise? She was still trying to take it in when Tom invited her to join the Trades Council.

'We always need young blood, Jackie. You'd be very welcome. I expect you'll have a lot to learn now you're taking over from your mother and I'm sure we could be of help to you. Don't forget that. Come along to our next meeting, they're always held on the first Monday of the month. Here, as a matter of fact.'

She was turning away when he asked, 'Just one thing, and I hope you don't mind my asking, but why the seafarers' hymn at the end of the service? Did Marilyn have a connection with the sea?'

'Oh no,' said Jackie brightly. 'She was terrified of water, so she always supported the Lifeboat Service in case she ever needed rescuing, even though she never set foot in a boat.'

'Right,' Tom said politely, looking bemused.

'Yeah, I never got it either,' she agreed.

It was the same story from every group she approached, all old Trades Council friends. Marilyn seemed to have known every business in the city intimately.

'How she ever got the time to run her own business I'll never know,' said one elderly restaurateur. 'She was quite selfless in helping others around the city.' Jackie knew very well how she managed: getting me to do all the cash and carry runs, write up the books and do the stock-taking while she swanned about being Lady Bountiful, she thought.

She shook herself. That was all in the past. She was her own boss now, in charge of her own operation. Hadn't they asked her to join their ranks? Well, she would then and get all the help she needed.

Penny watched Jackie doing the rounds. 'Who'd ever have thought of her doing that?' she mused.

'Now what?' asked George.

'What Jackie did, putting a phone inside the coffin. I wonder if they took it out before they buried her. Imagine it going off in the cemetery if someone was ringing her. You'd drop dead of fright if you were nearby.'

Walter, a rare pink tinge flushing his cheeks spoke up. 'I think it was a brave thing that she did. She's got guts, that lass, guts,' he repeated solemnly. He raised his glass in salute to Jackie across the room. 'Here's to Miss Jacqueline Dalrymple-Jones, a woman of courage and kindness and the … and the courage of her convictions.' He stumbled slightly over 'convictions' and drained his glass.

'Haven't you had enough now, Walter?' Stan suggested.

'No, never. This is a day that will never come again.' He poured himself a glass of wine from the bottle on the table. 'This is Marilyn's passing. Someone should make a speech. That's it, a speech.'

Before Stan could stop him, Walter jumped up and

thumped on the table. 'Speech, speech,' he cried.

The loud chatter died away. Walter climbed on to the coffee table and unbuttoned his jacket. The wide red braces holding up his trousers hove into view. Walter swayed slightly, clutching his wine glass in his hand.

'Friends, colleagues,' he began solemnly. 'Today is a sad day for all of us. We are saying goodbye to a much-loved and admired friend and for some of you,' he looked beadily around the room, 'a mentor. I knew Marilyn,' he went on, 'when she was just a slip of a girl. She was beautiful, ambitious and driven. Yes, you may well stare. Yes, she was driven, because in those days we didn't have a penny to bless ourselves with. But I tell you what we did have: ambition. Drive and ambition. We weren't going to work in some poxy factory twelve hours a day for ten bob a week. And you know what, ladies and gentlemen? We didn't. We did all sorts of jobs, the pair of us, worked all hours God sent and saved every penny.

'I wanted my own little farm one day, wanted her to share it with me. But it wasn't to be. Marilyn was too good to be running after pigs and ducks and the like. She wanted her own life and she went out and got it. And made a success of it, too. Look at everyone here today. I bet there isn't one person who hasn't learned something from Marilyn and been a better person for knowing her. So raise your glasses please to Marilyn, a woman in a million.'

Everyone raised their glasses. 'To Marilyn' echoed around the room. Walter drank deeply and swayed. Quickly Stan stood up and went to him, catching him just as he fell down in a stupor and they landed in a heap on the floor.

In the ensuing silence Penny remarked, 'He doesn't look like a man who would wear red braces, but there, you never know.'

CHAPTER 11

Two days later Barney popped in to see Walter at the café. 'There you are, Walter, I sent that letter off to your Mr Patterson yesterday. That'll keep his sticky hands off your land in future. Here's your copy. Keep it somewhere safe.' Barney Anderson passed the letter over to Walter. He'd just finished a late lunch and in the afternoon lull they were enjoying a cup of tea together.

Walter read the letter carefully and looked at the attached plan of his property. 'Aye, that's it, lad. You've nailed it good and proper. That's all my land you've outlined and you've made it right clear to him in that letter too.' He peered again at Barney's letter. 'You've letters after your name. What's LLB, then?'

Barney leaned forward and whispered to Walter, 'It's my law degree, Walter. Shows I'm a proper solicitor and licensed to practice.'

Walter's mouth fell open. 'A solicitor!' he exclaimed.

Barney laughed. Walter made it sound on a par with thieving or street-walking. 'Ssh, keep your voice down.'

'What for?'

'Well, Miss Snooty at the counter there thinks I'm a dosser and a no mark. She passed judgement and sentence on me before I even opened my mouth, so why tell her different if she's made up her mind?'

'I thought you just helped folk, writing letters to the Social and that.'

'Well, I do that; and other stuff as well.' Barney grinned. 'Keep it under your hat, Walter, there's a good chap. We'll keep our own counsel for now.'

'This LLB thing, Barney … you say it makes you a real solicitor?'

Barney smiled, "Fraid so, Walter.'

'I thought they all had big offices full of files tied up with pink ribbons, like you see on the telly.' Walter eyed him suspiciously. 'You don't have any of them.'

Why did everyone have to think in stereotypes? Barney wondered. He gazed around the café and looked at the people going about their business. The waitresses: all so different. Who would guess Kate was a qualified historian or that Penny had problems with a transvestite husband? Barney wouldn't have, until Penny had unburdened herself to him recently. Look at Jackie talking so animatedly to Penny: who would know she had just buried her mother? What about Gus, finishing his meal on Table 4. He'd elected to be a solitary road sweeper because it gave him time to compose his poetry as he worked. He'd had two collections published. Stereotypes! No such thing really.

'I choose not to wear a suit and tie, Walter, but I work for the Citizens Advice Bureau. I have an office there and it's full of files tied up with pink ribbon. Will that do for you? Does that make it official enough?'

Walter took a long drink of his tea and eyed up Barney. 'I've been thinking for a while about making a Will. If I come to your office, is it in your line of things? Could you do one for me?'

Barney was pleased that Walter was beginning to think of other things besides his friend's death. 'Yes of course,' he said gently. 'Just make an appointment with Maria at Reception and we can soon sort it out for you.'

Walter looked happy at this.

'Well now,' he said, looking directly at Barney. 'That's my

affairs being sorted out. Let's catch up on the news. How are things with you? Found yourself a decent girl yet?'

Barney grimaced. 'If only! You have no idea of the mess I've managed to get myself into Walter and right now, I don't see any easy way out of it.'

'Sounds serious lad, what've you been up to?' Walter asked in concern.

Barney related the whole sorry tale of meeting Melissa and her unexpected move into his flat. 'I never wanted her there in the first place Walter,' he said despairingly. 'I was going to end it after the first date. I knew I never should have started it in the first place. I was really stupid and now I'm stuck with her. Her parents are away in Australia and she's no job or money. And she's hardly house-trained!'

Walter laughed at this. 'You make her sound like an old stray dog you fetched in off the street.'

'I'd sooner it was,' Barney said fervently. 'At least I'd have some chance of training a dog. Melissa takes no notice of anything I say.'

'Best find her a job quick and then she might move out,' Walter advised. 'Plenty more fish in the sea, lad. Must be a good 'un amongst them, just be a bit more choosy next time.'

He drained his mug and got up to leave. He looked over to Jackie at the coffee counter. 'I'd best not linger, Barney. She's worse than her mother. Doesn't like staff sitting about, only the customers. I'll be off but I'll see you soon.'

'LLB,' he mused as he made his way back to the kitchen. 'Who'd have thought it?'

Barney still had work to do and he also got up to leave.

'Time for our afternoon nap, is it?' Jackie said as she gave him his change.

'Something like that,' Barney replied pleasantly. He hitched his rucksack up on his back. 'Can't be all work and no play, can it now, Jackie?'

He heard her snort derisively as he went to the door. 'Any work from you would be a miracle. I'll keep praying for one.'

Barney chuckled as he stepped out into the busy, darkening street. Her insults were great; he wouldn't miss them for the world.

Inside the café, Walter was not as amused as Barney at Jackie's sharp remarks. When she came into his kitchen he rebuked her. 'You've no call to be rude to Barney like that Jackie. He's a good lad and he's got more than his share of problems at the moment to put up with.'

'Oh yeah.' Jackie was unconvinced. 'Like whether to get up at ten or ten thirty before a stroll down here for his breakfast.'

'Nothing of the sort,' Walter retorted. 'You've got him all wrong. He's got girlfriend trouble. Lass called Melissa. Bit of a handful by all accounts.'

Jackie snorted derisively. 'Well, if that's all he has to do with his time… '

'No, he's a busy lad,' Walter protested. 'He's full on at the ...' He stopped short, remembering his promise to Barney to keep quiet about his work.

'Don't tell me, busy at the coal-face. Cutting edge of things,' Jackie said sarcastically and went back to her coffee counter.

Absently she served the waiting customers with coffee and cakes, a feeling of disappointment settling over her. Of course Barney would have a girlfriend. He might be scruffy but there was no denying he was good looking and had a certain charm about him. Not that she fell for that. She could see through it. That's probably how he made his way in life, charming his way around people. Well, he didn't charm her, Jackie told herself.

Nevertheless, in the quiet moments when the queue for coffee-to-go had thinned to a slow trickle, Jackie gazed about the busy café, watching her customers eating and laughing together. After a few moments of this she turned away, busying herself in an effort to stave off the unfamiliar sense of loneliness that filled her.

* * * * * *

The Citizens Advice Bureau was housed in a large, red-brick building that was part of a long, three-storeyed terrace block just out of the centre of York. Walter had managed to prise the time off out of a reluctant Jackie.

'It's only an hour,' he'd protested. 'I'll work through until 4 o'clock and then go.'

'I'm not running a slave camp, Walter,' she'd said drily. 'You'll need a break. But don't make a habit of it. We're not like the old speaking clock, you know: at the first stroke it will be 4:00 p.m. precisely and so everyone stops eating. Someone's going to have to cover the kitchen. You might have to work your charm on Penny, if you've got any.'

Penny had been fine about it and now here he was, on Thursday afternoon, sitting nervously in Reception waiting for Barney. After about ten minutes he appeared.

'Sorry, Walter, someone telephoned just as I was about to come down for you. I had to take the call.'

Barney started to lead the way up a flight of steep stairs.

'Bloody hell, Barney, I didn't know I was going mountaineering,' Walter grumbled. 'I'm getting a bit old for the north face of the Eiger. I'm sixty-five.'

Barney laughed. 'Keep taking the Omega 3 capsules, Walter. Sixty-five is the new forty-five these days. You're in your prime now.'

He led the way into a small cramped office and waved Walter into the spare chair. Walter sat down and looked about him. 'So this is where you do your LLB stuff is it? Aye, this is more like it,' he said with satisfaction, eyeing the files piled on every surface and spilling over on to the floor.

Barney laughed. 'Do I look like a real solicitor now?'

'Not really. I mean jeans and a jumper, don't look legal to my way of thinking, but I know I can trust you, so you'll do for me, Barney lad. Since Marilyn died it's made me re-think a bit.'

Barney drew a pad towards him and took a pen out of his drawer. After he'd noted down the usual preliminary information, they came to the details of the Will.

'I take it you know how you want to dispose of your estate in this Will,' Barney said.

'I do,' Walter agreed. He hesitated and shuffled about on the chair. 'The thing is … it's not just straightforward.'

Barney sat back in his chair and waited. 'Take your time, Walter,' he said. 'I'm sure we can sort things out as you want them to be.'

Walter's eyes ranged all over the pink beribboned files. Would his sad little story be reduced to one of these soon? He reached into his coat pocket and pulled out a large brown envelope, placed it on the desk between them and instructed Barney to open it.

Barney picked up the envelope and pulled out the contents. He held it up to look at it properly. It was a photograph of a young woman aged about 35 dressed in a severe suit of 1930s vintage. Barney looked questioningly across at Walter. Walter remained silent. Barney looked more closely at the photograph and his blonde eyebrows disappeared almost into his fair head.

Carefully putting the photograph down between them, Barney said, 'Who is this lady, Walter?'

'My grandmother, Rebecca Matthews, a farmer's daughter from Haxby way. She married a local farmer, Walter Cartwright. They had a daughter Mary and a son John. Mary was my mother.'

'Why have you bought this photograph along today?' Barney asked quietly.

'You can see it, can't you?' Surely he wasn't imagining things. It was plain to see: she was just like her great-grandmother.

'Walter, if I am to be your solicitor I have to deal in facts. I can't just go seeing things that might not be there. You tell me what you see and we'll take it from there.'

'I see Jackie Dalrymple-Jones as the spitting image of my grandmother, Rebecca Matthews, there in that photograph.'

'Perhaps you do, Walter, but is that in any way relevant to the business we're discussing today?'

Walter was beginning to feel angry and frustrated at Barney's cool reaction. He jumped up from his seat and walked about the little office. He'd screwed up his courage to finally get all this off his chest today, get something official written down and here was his friend Barney asking him if it was relevant.

Barney rose and went over to Walter. 'Come on, let's have a drink. I can see there's a story here that needs airing. You sit down a minute and I'll go and rustle us up some tea.'

Barney went out and Walter sat down in his chair. He picked up Rebecca's photograph and stared at it. It was Jackie to the life, surely Barney could see that.

In a few minutes Barney was back with a tray of tea and biscuits. He settled them both down and made Walter drink before he allowed him to embark on his story.

'My grandfather was killed in an accident on the farm and so that put an end to the farming life for my mother and her brother. They were only tenant farmers and they had to find somewhere else to live and find work. My grandmother went back into service and her children went to relatives for a few years until they were old enough to go out to work. Grandma used to visit them on her days off. That's how come she's all dressed up in the photograph.'

'So that's where you get your love of farming from,' he suggested.

'I think so. My father worked in a factory all his life. He wasn't interested in the land at all. I suppose it skipped a generation and came out in me. Like Rebecca Matthews … she's skipped a generation and come out in Jackie.'

Barney smiled gently at him. 'Just take your time and tell me the rest, Walter.'

'I grew up in a poor area of York. Marilyn Langley, as she was then, lived in the same street as me. In a way I was lucky, I had my mum and my dad. Marilyn didn't have much at all, not even a dad. He'd beggared off and left Marilyn's mum early on. Sometimes I was jealous of that. Can you believe it? My dad had what I suppose they would now call post-traumatic stress disorder left over from the war and he could get into terrible rages over nothing. I tell you Barney, you dived for cover then.

'But not having a dad really affected Marilyn. I'm no psychiatrist but when I look back now I can see it. She always felt insecure. Her world had collapsed on her once and she never wanted it to happen again. It made her want to be in charge of her life, in charge of everything connected to it, really be in control.'

Barney nodded, 'Yes, you could see that in her at the café.'

Walter leaned forward eagerly, his face alight with memories. 'We worked hard in those days, the pair of us, determined to have more than our parents ever had and be in charge of our own lives. We did all sorts of jobs and saved and I thought Marilyn was going to be mine forever.'

Walter stopped, his brown eyes darkening a little with remembered pain. Barney waited.

'I saved and planned and plotted. I had my eye on that Claygate holding. I wanted it for us, somewhere no-one could take away from us. I loved her, she loved me and I would have looked after her.'

'So what happened?' asked Barney.

Walter fixed his gaze on the bookshelf behind Barney's head. 'I bought Claygate. I thought that was what she wanted. Turned out she didn't.' His voice was bleak now. 'She didn't want a life buried away on a farm, no matter how much I loved her. She wanted to make her own way, whatever that meant. We were lovers, I thought she was going to be my wife but she took fright and ran off. I never clapped eyes on her for another three years. She just upped and left without a word. Next I see her she's married to that Dalrymple-Jones fella and running the Paradise with a little girl of two and a half called Jackie.

'I could see my grandmother in her straight away and I did the sums. I knew Jackie was mine but Marilyn would never admit it. Maybe that's why she ran away. She didn't want to be trapped into a situation she wasn't in control of. Turns out she married this Dalrymple-Jones soon after. He was well-off and she could do as she liked.

'I didn't really care. Once I'd found her again I could never leave her. She was the other half of me and I stayed with her to the end.'

It was Barney's turn to lean forward. 'I don't want to upset you, Walter, but you say Marilyn never acknowledged you as the father of her child, so apart from a resemblance to your grandmother you have no proof.'

'Proof!' Walter shook his head in disgust. 'I know. We were lovers right up to when she left in February 1975. I have a photo of us that she wrote the date on. Jackie was born in the November. That's clear enough for me. She found out she was pregnant and all she could see was Claygate farm with me. Now I'm older I can understand it. She could never have stood that life. She wanted more, she wanted to be secure, and Dalrymple-Jones gave her that. She must have run off and married him and told him Jackie was early. But I know she's mine.'

Barney sighed and ran his hands through his hair. 'So

short of telling her and asking her to take a DNA test, what are your plans?'

Walter sat back in his chair and steepled his fingers. 'I'm not telling her, it's not the right time. She's just lost her mother. She doesn't need any more shocks just now. I may never tell her, but that doesn't mean to say she should never know in the future. You could tell her.'

'And what if I'm run down by a number 9 bus the day after you've died?'

'Mmm, hadn't thought of that one.'

'I can think of a way around all this,' Barney said and drew his legal pad towards him. 'We can draw up your Will leaving everything unconditionally to Jackie, no mention of kinship, etc. This is all for public consumption and if any nosey-parker wishes to read the terms of the Will, which they're perfectly entitled to do, that's all anyone will know. So far so good?'

Walter nodded.

'Now, regarding the speculative kinship or otherwise.' Barney held his hand up to silence Walter's protests. 'You could write a private and personal letter to Jackie containing whatever information and speculation you care to make in it and then you could take an official DNA test witnessed and attested by me and leave the results on your file. I, or my successor to my practice, would give the letter to Jackie to take the matter forward if she so wishes.'

Barney looked up from making his notes and waited for Walter's response.

'You can't half put it together when you get into your legalese stuff, Barney,' Walter said after a few moments. 'I can understand you better when you don't talk like a solicitor, but I think I get your drift. Aye, I like your ideas, excepting for the fact that I have to write that letter. I'm not much good with words.'

Barney smiled across the desk at Walter. 'You can do

it,' he said confidently. 'Tell it in your own words, just like you've told me.'

'Why is nowt ever as straightforward as you want it to be?' Walter asked gloomily as he got up to take his leave.

'It's called life, Walter,' Barney chuckled.

'And now I've got to descend that bloody mountain again.' Walter surveyed the steep stairs and turned to Barney. 'Tell 'em they need to get a lift installed. Never mind sixty-five being the new forty-five, my knees are knackered.'

CHAPTER 12

That same day, Jackie was again up to her ears in steam from the erratic coffee machine when the old black telephone on the counter rang out shrilly.

'Oh hell. Why now? Can't you see I'm busy?' She motioned to Penny to answer it whilst she served a take-out customer.

'Mr Who?' Penny queried, leaning closer into the phone and covering one ear against the noise of the café. 'Mr Young? Oh yes, the Trades Council. Just hang on a minute I'll get her for you.' She put her hand over the mouthpiece. 'It's that Mr Young, President of the Trades Council; he'd like a word with you.'

For a moment Jackie looked puzzled and then her brow cleared. 'Oh yes, he was at mother's funeral. He suggested I might like to join them in her place. I'll go into the office, Penny. You take over here.'

Jackie flung herself down in Marilyn's old chair and picked up the phone. 'Hello, Mr Young. Nice to hear from you.'

'Hello, Miss Dalrymple-Jones. You remember me then?'

How could she possibly not. Six foot two and impossibly handsome. 'Oh yes indeed,' she gushed.

'Good,' he said smoothly. 'We're having a little soirée in a few weeks time; drinks and a buffet and a general meet and greet, you know the sort of thing.'

'Of course,' she said, never having been to one before.

'Excellent. Well I was wondering if you would like to come along. It will be on a Saturday evening to the Golden Lion Hotel, seven thirtyish if you can manage it.'

'I'd be delighted.'

'Excellent,' he repeated. 'We'll get your membership sorted out and then you can get to know some of the brethren during the evening.'

Jackie came off the phone all aglow. She would be one of the brethren, whatever that meant. She wasn't sure what the Trades Council did, but it couldn't be a sect of any kind as Marilyn would never have been a member. She had been far too irascible and independent for any of that nonsense.

'The Trades Council?' Walter repeated in dismay when Penny relayed the news to him. 'That oily insurance broker, Tom Young? Marilyn could handle him but he'll gobble up Jackie for breakfast and then be looking for afters.'

Penny was intrigued 'What do you mean?'

'He's a wolf in sheep's clothing, that's what he is. He'll convince Jackie she must have all sorts of insurance that she doesn't need at all. Put the wind up her, this might happen or that might happen, and she'll end up paying him a small fortune when she could get a much better deal from honest brokers who belong to the Chamber of Trade and Commerce. They wouldn't have the likes of him anywhere near them. They're all the same that Trades Council lot. She should have nowt to do with them.'

'Marilyn did,' Penny pointed out.

'I never liked that either, but at least she was fly enough to deal with them. Jackie isn't. All she's ever known is that daft supermarket she worked in. No, them Trades Council lot are a bunch of vultures.'

'Are you going to tell her, then?' Penny would like to be a fly on that wall. Walter trying to tell Jackie anything always got the fur and feathers flying.

'Aye I will, and right now before she goes and does

something daft.' He stripped off his white apron and marched out of the kitchen and into the café. Jackie was back at her coffee counter.

'We need to have a word,' he said.

'What about?' Jackie carried on cutting a wedge of chocolate cake for a skinny spotty youth who looked like he needed more than coffee and cake to keep him upright.

'This Trades Council lark.'

What bee had got into his bonnet now, Jackie wondered. 'What about it?' A cloud of steam covered her as she espresso'd the coffee.

'You're not to join it.'

Jackie gave the spotty youth his change. Penny must have been gossiping in the kitchen. She gave her attention to Walter. 'What *are* you on about now, Walter?'

'That set of rogues at the Trades Council; you're not to go and join them. Join the Chamber of Trade and Commerce instead. They're much more reputable and respectable.'

'And from your vast experience of running an international conglomerate, otherwise known as Claygate Smallholding, you would know, wouldn't you?' Jackie glared at him. 'I'm not going to discuss it with you, Walter. It's none of your business.'

'It is my business. You're my business. I've known you since you were a little girl and I'm not going to stand by and watch you throw yourself to the mercy of wolves.'

He'd be telling her he changed her nappies next. She laughed. 'It's the centre of York, Walter. I don't see too many wolves roaming the plains here.'

Walter was obstinate. 'That's the trouble, you don't see the wolves and they're gathering ready to gobble you up, lass.'

Jackie wondered if Walter had been at the wacky baccy again if he was seeing wolves. She sighed and motioned to her office door. 'Let's go in there and you can get if off your chest, whatever it is.'

They glared at each other across Marilyn's desk. Walter said nothing at first but let his gaze roam about the room whilst he tried to put the words together in his head that might persuade Jackie against this new venture.

His glance came to rest on an old postcard from Cumbria that he'd sent to Marilyn years ago. The colours had faded and the view had taken on the sepia tones of a bygone era. But Marilyn had kept it there all these years, so he must have meant something. Walter took heart from that. Marilyn had known her way about the world and the Trades Council suited her perfectly, but it wasn't the place for her daughter.

His faraway look irritated Jackie. Did she have to sit here all morning whilst he got his act together?

'They're all sharks; they'll fleece you soon as look at you,' he began.

Wolves, sharks and sheep. What was going on in Walter's head? Jackie waited.

'Years back,' Walter continued, 'there was some funny business at the Chamber of Trade and a bunch of them got chucked out. They're the ones that went on to form this Trades Council outfit. Now what kind of a foundation for an organisation is that?'

'Well, what kind of funny business was involved?' asked Jackie.

'I don't rightly know. Nobody would talk about it at the time, it all got hushed up. But if you want anybody to part you from your money quickly it's that lot at the Trades Council.'

The now-familiar sensation of exasperation in her dealings with Walter came over Jackie. 'You've just said you've no idea what went on in the past, so you're going on hearsay and gossip. That's not enough for me, Walter. I haven't seen anyone queuing at my door from the Chamber of Trade with an invitation, but Tom Young and a few others came to Marilyn's funeral and he rang me today to ask me along to their next social evening at the end of March. Now I don't know what you call it, but I call it kindness.'

'A sprat to catch a mackerel,' Walter said darkly, 'you mark my words.'

* * * * * *

Later that day Walter tried to enlist Barney's help.

'She won't take a blind bit of notice of what I say,' Barney said. 'She thinks I'm just the local dosser, so what do I know?'

'Well tell her different, lad,' Walter said patiently. 'I don't know why you keep up the pretence of being a layabout. Anyone with half a brain can see you're not.'

'She must only have half a brain, then.' Barney wasn't sure why, but he wanted Jackie to accept him just as he was, without having to have chapter and verse on his background and employment. 'One day she might be civil enough to have a proper conversation with me, but until she does I'm just the local dosser. So I wouldn't know anything about the Trades Council let alone be in a position to recommend the Chamber of Trade to her.'

'Barney, please,' Walter pleaded. 'You're my last hope. She won't listen to a word I say. She's hell bent on throwing in her lot with them and you know they're a bunch of no-goods. Just one other person backing up my view might change her mind.'

'It might give her pause for thought if I said how wonderful they all were.'

'You wouldn't!' Walter said indignantly. 'Barney, I thought you were a friend.'

'Reverse psychology, Walter. If I say how good the Trades Council is she might well go and do the opposite for the hell of it. After all, if people like me were in it, we might get her to the Chamber of Trade that way.'

Walter stroked his stubbly chin thoughtfully. 'I take your point, Barney.' He ran his finger over a deep groove in the chipped pine table and fished out some long-buried grease. 'No, too risky,' he said at last. 'She's so dead set on it even you praising it might not put her off. No, you must warn her off; make her see it for what it is.'

Kate approached their table. 'Sorry, Walter, but Mrs Martin and her grandson want two large brunches, pronto. They're in a bit of a hurry, but she doesn't fancy cooking tea tonight.'

Walter rose and stared intently at Barney. 'It's all down to you now, lad,' and was gone, back to his kitchen and frying pans.

'Nothing like giving a bloke enough rope …' Barney mused.

Kate brought him his lunch and a pot of tea. Barney ate without noticing, reading and re-reading the papers in front of him. This afternoon's appointments at the Citizens Advice were all about personal debt and house repossessions. The recession had wrecked so many people's lives. Barney was determined to do his best to help. He was absorbed in his papers when a shadow fell across the table.

'Here you are, Barney darling! Jake said you'd be in here but I really didn't believe him,' Melissa cooed as she looked about her. 'I mean, you … in a greasy spoon! Not your style, surely!'

Melissa, dressed from head to toe by Harvey Nicholls, with full make-up and WAG-blonde curls, attracted interested stares from the regular café customers. Inwardly wishing her to hell and back, Barney jumped up and pulled out a chair, sending all his papers sliding on to the floor. As he scrambled to collect them and re-assemble them into some kind of order, Melissa gently chided him.

'I don't know why you bring your work in here, Barney.' She fanned herself. 'It's hot and noisy and,' she wrinkled her nose, 'a bit smelly.' She eyed his empty plate. Ooh! You've been having a fry-up. Look at that greasy plate! Oh, and is that your cup? Gosh, I bet even the road navvies don't have such thick ones. And it's chipped!

Melissa didn't trouble to keep her voice down. An angry flush spread over Barney's face. He pulled Melissa down on to the chair.

'For God's sake, Melissa,' he snapped.

'What, Barney darling?' she asked innocently.

'You shouldn't come here, to my favourite café as it happens, and start criticising it from the minute you walk through the door.'

Melissa looked at him earnestly from beneath her heavily-mascaraed eyelashes. 'But I wasn't, Barney darling. I was just making an … what do you call it? That's it, making an observation.' She sat back in her seat, proud of having produced such a statement.

Out of the corner of his eye Barney could see Kate and Jackie staring grimly at Melissa from behind the coffee counter. Penny was making her way into the kitchen with an order. She walked in crab-fashion, hardly able to take her eyes off Melissa. Barney groaned. She'd be filling Walter in any minute now.

'What's the matter, Barney?' asked Melissa.

'Oh, nothing.' No point in explaining. Melissa wouldn't understand in a million years. 'What do you want anyway, Melissa?' he asked.

She eyed his empty plate and pouted. 'Well, it's too late anyway. I was going to take you away from your stuffy old work and out for a lovely lunch, but as you've already eaten, I shall just have to go on my own.' She rose to go.

Barney was intrigued. Allegedly, Melissa had no money, so how had she intended to pay for lunch, he wondered.

'And where would we be going for this surprise lunch?' he asked.

110

Melissa sat down again. 'There's this really cool new place near Coppergate,' she enthused. 'Le Maison Blanc, it's called. Everyone's talking about it. I thought we could try it out.'

Barney had heard about Le Maison Blanc. Nouvelle cuisine and the bill in inverse ratio to the portion size. When Melissa said *she* was taking *him* out to lunch, he had no illusions as to who would be footing the bill. God bless Walter's sausage and chips, he'd had a lucky escape.

'Not today, Melissa,' he said firmly. 'In fact, not any day. It's all talk and no food in that place. I'm very happy here at Café Paradise, thank you.' He said this last statement loud enough for the scowling Jackie to hear. She tossed her head and vigorously steamed a jug of milk. Barney noticed Walter standing at his kitchen door, staring at Melissa and shaking his head. 'I've just had a wonderful lunch,' he said desperately.

'Bully for you. Well, I'll just have to lunch on my own then,' Melissa said crossly, recognising defeat. 'Only…'

Barney waited. He had an idea of what was coming.

'Could you lend me twenty pounds, Barney?' Melissa asked.

Silently Barney reached into his wallet and pulled out a twenty pound note. 'We need to get you a job, Melissa, and back to independence.'

'Oh, you and your work, Barney. Sometimes you can be very boring. I'll see you later.' Melissa snatched the note from his hand and was out of the door in an instant.

Barney tidied his papers back into his rucksack. Glad to be rid of Melissa, he lingered over another cup of tea. He turned his attention again to the problem of Jackie and the Trades Council and wondered what on earth he could say to put her off. Should he try the light touch? 'Great idea Jackie, go for it, they're some of my best friends.' Or the heavy-handed approach? 'Please, please don't touch them with a barge pole; they're a bunch of conniving thieves and will take you for every penny you've got and a lot more besides.' Then he remembered Marilyn had been a member so he couldn't very well say that.

What about the polite softly, softly approach? 'I hear you're thinking about joining the Trades Council. I have heard several reputable traders prefer the Chamber of Trade. Perhaps I could get some of their literature for you so you could make an informed judgement.'

Yes, that was polite, non-confrontational, even if it did have undertones of 'please don't jump into this with your eyes shut.' He wasn't actually saying that, so she might agree.

He made his way to Jackie's coffee counter and till point. He smiled politely as he handed her his bill. 'How are you today, Jackie?' he began pleasantly.

'Working *hard*,' she said with heavy emphasis.

'As I see,' he agreed. 'You're a great credit to your late mother.'

Jackie looked up at him. Was that a hint of amusement in his tone? Just because he was tall, blonde and handsome didn't give him the right to take the mickey.

'More than your mother could say about you, I expect, or that girlfriend of yours.'

Barney had an almost irresistible urge to reach over the counter and take hold of Jackie and shake her hard. 'You blind, opinionated little fool,' he wanted to shout. 'What do you know about me and mine?' OK, so she might be right about Melissa but his lovely mother? She was a beautiful and kind-hearted woman, always ready to help anyone in need. How proud she had been of her son when he had chosen not to pursue a barrister's career like his father.

'I believe my mother agrees with my present career path,' he made himself say mildly.

Jackie rolled her eyes. 'I suppose it takes all sorts.'

'I believe so,' Barney replied blandly. Why did she always

have to be so obnoxious and so alluring at the same time? He couldn't afford to respond to her rudeness today. He needed to keep as much sweetness and light between them as he could and that wouldn't be much when she pursed her lips as if she'd been sucking on lemons all day.

He gave her his prepared speech about the Chamber of Trade and offered to bring her some information leaflets about it. He was as polite and persuasive as he knew how.

'You've got a cheek, Barney Anderson,' she replied scornfully. 'Coming in here and telling me what I should do. It's laughable. What you know about business I could probably write on this till receipt. You come in here and sit on your backside for half the day, your girlfriend slags my café off and then you have the brass neck to claim to know all about the Chamber of Trade. I can make my own decisions, thank you, without any help from you.' She slapped his change down on the counter and moved away. 'Yes, sir,' she greeted a new customer

Barney made his way out into the street. A cold wind whistled down the alley. He turned his collar up and headed for the office.

To hell with Melissa and Tom Young. I knew I should have recommended the Trades Council, he thought ruefully. If she thought I was a member, she'd have gone hell for leather for the Chamber of Trade. Grey skies and cold raindrops falling on his face chimed with his sombre mood. . She disliked me enough before today and now Melissa's visit really put the tin hat on it and made things even worse. Damn and blast the girl. However am I going to have a reasonable conversation with Jackie, if ever? he asked himself. He looked up at the grey sky and pulled his collar up as cold raindrops began to fall on his face. He walked up the street in sombre mood, a heavy shower of rain sweeping over him.

CHAPTER 13

It was Friday morning. Jackie had been in charge of Café Paradise for nearly three months. She stood behind the counter, wrestling with the coffee machine. A cloud of steam belched out and billowed up, falling like warm rain all over the mugs, and spread out on the counter.

'This bloody temperamental machine.' She flicked the lever left, right, left and still steam churned out and engulfed her.

Kate rushed over and clicked a knob at the side of the machine. The steam subsided. 'I think it's seen better days, Jackie,' she said. 'If it starts that lark again, switch it off for a minute or two and then it will be ready to go again.'

Seen better days, Jackie thought to herself. Completely clapped out, that's what it is. Marilyn's let everything go to pot. The kitchen's a wreck, the plates and mugs are chipped, the tables are wonky. How the customers don't get their dinners in their laps, I'll never know.

Aloud she said, 'I know a wreck when I see one, Kate, you don't have to be polite.'

'Your mother understood its funny little ways,' said Kate.

'She would, she had plenty of them herself.'

Kate shrugged non-committally and went back to her tables.

Jackie had not enjoyed the monotony of her work in the supermarket but now she was beginning to appreciate how well run it had been. If a piece of equipment broke down, a highly skilled team moved in immediately and repaired or replaced it and the life of the supermarket continued apace.

Café Paradise had none of these merits. To Jackie's critical eye everything here seemed on the verge of collapse. Surely the next visit from Environmental Health would close them down. Had Walter ever been on a food handling and hygiene course? Getting him to change his chef's whites was a daily battle.

Depression settled over her and she slumped over the counter.

Barney Anderson had just finished his breakfast and came across to pay his bill.

'What's up, Jackie? You look like you've lost a shilling and found sixpence.'

Jackie straightened up and scowled at him. 'I don't remember that far back, Mr. Anderson. Your era was it? You'll have to give me a history lesson on it sometime.'

'Mee-ow! Who's been sleeping in the knife drawer? Come on, what's up?'

Jackie sighed. 'Oh I don't know. Well I do. I've just been looking around here and seeing how clapped out it all is. Dingy, old fashioned, everything needs replacing ... it's horrible.' She tailed off.

'Well change it then,' he said.

Jackie was startled.

'It's your café, isn't it? You can do what you like. If you don't like it, do something about it. I changed my life completely and I'm much happier.'

'Oh, so moving squats really worked for you, did it? I think it will take a bit more than that to transform things here, but thank you anyway. I'll bear it in mind and when I really need advice you'll be the first man I come to.' Jackie smiled up at him, the biting sarcasm in her voice making Barney flinch.

Barney slapped a five-pound note down on the counter.

'That covers it, doesn't it,' he said and headed for the door. 'Got to dash, need to see a man about a dog. Now *he* really does need my advice.' Why did he let her get to him?

The door banged and Jackie stared after him, his words whirling around in her head. Change it. Could she? Would she dare? She imagined Marilyn's horrified face and caustic tongue lashing her as she forcefully expressed her opinion at her daughter's daring to meddle with her precious café.

All the more reason to do it then, she thought. She looked about her with fresh eyes. Unconsciously she echoed Barney, It's mine now and I can do what I like. I'm not under the old bat's thumb anymore.

For the first time in years, Jackie felt the beginnings of a new emotion stir in her; excitement. The café was in a good position in the city centre even though it was down a side street. She could turn that to her advantage. If it had a rather exclusive tag, went upmarket, people would seek it out.

Yes. She would do it and she would go along to the Trade Council meetings, get help and advice. They owed her after all the work she'd done for her mother over the years.

'Two eggs, chips and beans and two sausage baps please, Walter,' Kate called out as she neared the kitchen.

Eggs and chips, sausage baps. Not for much longer.

'Cassoulet with crusty French baguettes, best French cheeses and pâté, served with outstanding French wines, or, or…'

Penny stopped clearing tables and stared at her.

'Paella with Spanish wine. Yes, that's it. We could celebrate Europe, have themed weeks. Be Spanish one week, paella, tapas, special oils and breads, stuffed olives, that kind of thing. And entertainment …'

'Dancing with castanets and Walter dressed up as a matador. I'd like to see you run that by him.' Penny rested her dishes on the counter. 'What are you on about, anyway?'

'Change, Penny,' Jackie announced. 'It's time for change. Marilyn might have loved her caff but I don't. I want a café, not a greasy spoon: a proper café that visitors and residents of this city will be drawn to; a microcosm of Europe here in the centre of York. Keep some staples on the menu of course, but feature a different country regularly, get a website up and running to advertise.'

Jackie was enthralled with her new ideas. Penny looked around the café. 'You might need to get some new tablecloths, perhaps,' she said uncertainly.

'Never mind new cloths,' Jackie said grandly. 'New everything. We're going to have a complete overhaul, make the Café Paradise the hottest spot in town.'

'No more egg and chips then?' asked Penny

'Out with the egg and chips, in with paella, spaghetti, linguini, cassoulet, croissants, sauerkraut, rye bread, German sausage, pumpernickel, Irish barmbrack and Guinness and all things European.' Jackie paused for breath. 'Imagine ...'

Penny imagined herself in a little French maid's outfit or Walter in Lederhosen for Austrian week. She shook her head. Could this ever happen?

Jackie hummed happily to herself as Penny drifted off to the kitchen to update Walter on the latest news.

'She wants to do what?'

'Dress you up in lederhosen or a matador's outfit.'

'Has she gone kinky, or what?'

'She's gone European. We're going to be a European café, all baguettes and crostinis, pumpernickel and sauerkraut,' she said.

'Not ruddy likely.' He stomped out of his kitchen and glared at Jackie over the counter. 'Over my dead body,' he said.

'That can be arranged,' Jackie said tranquilly, stacking the chipped mugs next to the coffee machine.

'Bloody Europe. Why do we want to be European?

What's wrong with being Yorkshire?'

'We can be Yorkshire as well, Walter. We can serve fat rascals and curd tarts and Yorkshire puddings, but regularly feature other countries. I'm going to get a drinks' licence and serve wines and beers and all different foods.'

'Like what?' Walter spat out.

'Well, for Greece for example, we could do moussaka, feta cheese dishes, taramasalata, houmus, kalamari or for Italy; pasta, lasagne, bolognaise, panini.'

'Pan what?'

'Ni ni; ni ni.'

'Panininini.'

'Oh, don't be daft, Walter, you can say it.'

'What is it anyway?'

'Italian bread.'

'Well there you are then. It's all Berlusconi and dancing girls and bunga bunga. We're not having any of that in the Paradise caff. What's wrong with good white sliced bread and a bacon buttie, that's what I want to know?'

'Walter, you're a dinosaur. Left to you we'd still be living in caves and thinking about inventing the wheel. Change happens, Walter, and we have to change with it.'

'We're alright as we are,' Walter said stubbornly.

Jackie was losing patience. 'How old are you, Walter?'

'Sixty-five.'

'Exactly. You've spent forty years in that kitchen frying sausages for Marilyn, it's time you had a change too. You're near retirement. You can go off and enjoy life on your smallholding instead of slaving away in that hot kitchen.'

'Who says I want to?' Walter asked defiantly. 'You can't sack me when I get to sixty-five you know. The law has changed. I can work on if I want to.'

'Yes you can,' Jackie conceded, 'but maybe in a different role. I would need a different style of chef, but you could still do the preparation work and assist him and probably learn a whole lot of new tricks even if you are an old dog.'

'Bah.' Walter gave up. She was just like her mother. She'd got the bit between her teeth and was bolting off. As usual, he would be running behind trying to keep up with her and watching events unfold.

'Hang on to your hat, Walter, old lad,' he told himself as he went back to the kitchen. 'This is going to be a bumpy ride.'

CHAPTER 14

It was early Saturday evening in early April. Kate was wavering between a full-length blue coat and a shorter suede jacket. Stan was collecting her in his car, so presumably they would only have a short walk to a restaurant. A coat might be an encumbrance. It was a cold night but clear and dry. She decided to risk the jacket.

She gazed at herself in the mirror without vanity. She was very striking with her red-gold hair, green eyes and porcelain complexion. She wore her beauty lightly, more interested in other people than in herself.

She had worked at Café Paradise for some months now and it was time to move on with her life. Sunny Cyprus and Dave seemed a long way away. Until recently she had missed the place desperately but now she knew what a fool she had been. Thinking about it, she realised with relief that she was over him. With an effort she tried to conjure up his face but his features remained blurred in her mind. Strangely, his voice had taken on the timbre of the retired boxer Frank Bruno. She smiled at herself in the mirror. 'Know what I mean, Harry?' she growled his catchphrase at her reflection.

For too long she had hidden away in her little flat nursing her emotional wounds and the memories of finding Dave with a gorgeous brunette one night when he had told her that he would be working. She had fled home to York and changed her mobile phone and email address so as not to receive his urgent and contrite calls. She had worked long hours at the café, as many as Marilyn could give her, and gone to bed exhausted to sleep a dreamless sleep not haunted by Dave's handsome face.

Now the year had turned and Kate was missing Cyprus less. Spring was in the air and stirrings of interest in life were beginning anew. After weeks of indecision, she was finally going out with Stan tonight, in spite of Jackie and Penny's dire warnings.

'You've agreed to it?'

'A proper date?'

'You must be mad.'

'Thought you had more sense.'

'Better taste.'

'They call him octopus arms you know.'

'I've heard that Kia of his is called The Passion Wagon.'

'He knows every dark lay-by in the town.'

'He'll have the clothes off you before you can say knife.'

'Out to dinner, hah!'

'His idea of haute cuisine is like Walter's. Ketchup and chips and it doesn't matter which way round.'

'He's taking you dancing? It'll be chasing you round the nearest gooseberry bush more like.'

'It will be "oh if it's Saturday it must be Kate's turn".'

'You want to see your doctor, you're obviously overworking.'

Kate found Stan kind and funny and she thought she would enjoy his company. 'But just remember, my girl,' she told herself, 'Jackie said he has a girl in every store, so keep tight hold of your heart.'

At that moment her doorbell rang. Stan was waiting on the doorstep for her. In spite of her good resolutions, her heart lifted at the sight of him. He had obviously taken trouble with his appearance and wore a gleaming white shirt and smart trousers. He'd scrubbed up remarkably well.

Stan was feeling nervous, excited and panicky all at the

same time. He had tried for so long to get the girl of his dreams to go out with him. Now that he'd succeeded, he was terrified in case he messed it up and she would never see him again.

* * * * * *

Stan held the car door open for Kate and gently helped her in as if she were a piece of precious porcelain. He handed her the seat belt and made sure she was securely strapped in and comfortable before going to his side of the car and climbing in. He looked across at her and grinned, 'And where would mademoiselle care to dine tonight?'

Kate considered for a few moments and then said, 'How about an Indian? There's a lovely one in Bank Street. The waiters all dress in Indian costume and the food is fantastic. Have you been there?'

Stan's heart sank. Indian. He'd only eaten Indian food once, a long time ago. He was going out with a petite redhead at the time. She had multiple body piercings and studs all over her body, on her face and even in her mouth. It wasn't the best feeling to be grazed by one of those in the middle of a passionate clinch. He didn't remember too much about the food, only playing footsie under the table. He dragged his mind back to Kate.

'OK, my lady, if that's where you would like to go, Bank Street it shall be. I am yours to command.'

Silently Kate admired his patter.

He started up the engine. 'Bank Street here we come.'

Stan was a good driver. Kate felt quite safe as they went through the dark streets of York. She watched his large capable hands on the wheel and noticed how well kept they were in spite of him heaving bread and cake trays about all day.

She studied his profile outlined sharply by the street

lights. His black hair was neatly cut and she glimpsed his clean shaven neck rising out of his crisp white shirt. His smooth square jaw was set in a firm line as he concentrated on finding his way.

Into the silence Stan said lightly, 'Well, will I do? You've been looking for long enough.'

In the darkness, Kate blushed. 'Sorry, Stan, I didn't mean to stare. It's just that I don't get time at the café. We're all whizzing about so much.'

'So what's the verdict, now you've made your survey?'

'Providing I see you in profile all evening, you'll do. I reserve judgement on the full face.'

He chuckled. 'You'll have to put up with looking at it in the restaurant. I'm not plug ugly, so I've been told.'

'Oh! By one of your many conquests, I presume,' Kate said drily.

'I don't have many conquests, as you so delicately put it.' Stan turned to her in exasperation. 'Kate, I've so looked forward to going out with you tonight. I'm not interested in anyone else.'

'Sorry, Stan, your reputation goes before you. Jackie and Penny warned me about you.'

Stan ground his teeth. 'Wait till I catch up with those two sourpusses. Kate, I swear I only ever went out with two girls from different stores and that was a long time ago. The jungle drums started beating and my reputation was cast in stone,' Stan finished bitterly. He turned to look intently at Kate. 'I'm a one-woman man and that woman is you.'

Kate directed his attention to the road ahead. Sez you, she thought silently to herself, we'll see Mr Pretty Peterson. We'll see.

* * * * * *

Seated inside the restaurant, Stan looked about

appreciatively. Murals were painted on the walls and the tables, set with sparkling white cloths, were not too close to each other. The lighting was low and intimate, and Indian sitar music played softly in the background.

He started studying the menu. A shish kebab? A shami kebab? What was the difference? Oh God, there was such a long list of curries. What was Tarka Daal? Indian fried otter? Nimbo Chicken? Indian limbo chicken? How the hell was he supposed to know what he wanted? Why did she have to choose Indian, the one nation he knew nothing about. He could end up looking a right idiot. Now if it had been Italian, or the foods the ancient Romans used to eat, he could have told her all about that, the garum sauce made of fish waste and salt that was left to fester in a barrel for several weeks, delicious by all accounts. No Stan, lad, he chided himself, don't start going down that route. Remember what Walter said.

He looked up to see Kate smiling at him. 'You're looking very serious. Are you confused by the choice of starters? I am. I don't know what to have.'

Stan hedged his bets. 'Take your time, there's no hurry, plenty of time to choose.' He had better have whatever she had. He didn't want to end up with a piece of dog or horse, even donkey. Did the Indians eat dogs like the Chinese? That could be those kebab things. He tried smiling at her confidently.

'Have you decided?' she asked.

'Like you, I'm just not sure,' he said breezily.

'Right pair we are,' laughed Kate. 'I'll make a decision, for me at least. I'll play safe and stick with an onion bahjee. Do you like those? They're not too heavy before the main course.'

'Onion bahjee,' Stan repeated slowly. What the hell was that? A small Indian that works on the canals fried up and served with rice. 'Yeah, good choice, we don't want to fill ourselves up with those shit kebabs do we?'

'Shish kebabs?'

Stan consulted the menu again. 'Yeah sorry, shish kebabs. And what about a main course?'

'What are you going to have?' asked Kate.

Stan pretended to consult the menu again. What was Nawabi Karahi Chicken, Chicken Nentara, Planet Special Bhoona? How was he supposed to make sense of any of this lot? When he couldn't pretend to consult the menu any longer he said, 'We're just spoilt for choice, Kate, I'll have whatever you're having.'

'Well…' Kate hesitated. Slowly, she started to smile.

'Go on,' said Stan, 'what's it to be?'

'I usually have a Chicken Bangalore Phall and a Naan Bread, it's my favourite but…'

'Just the job,' Stan agreed. 'We'll make that two and have some wine, or beer if you prefer.'

'But…'

'No buts,' Stan interposed. 'We'll have whatever you like, make it a night to remember.'

Stan snapped his menu shut, relieved the major hurdle of the night had been jumped so easily. Kate was gorgeous and beautiful and a pushover. He'd carried it off with style and panache.

The young waiter, dressed in jewelled blue satin trousers and tunic with matching turban on his head, approached their table.

'You are ready to order, sir?' he asked politely. He raised his eyebrows when Stan got to the Bangalore Phall. 'It's a hot dish, sir,' he commented, his pencil poised over the order pad.

'Yes, it is,' Kate agreed. She looked across at Stan. 'I don't know if you like hot food…?'

'Hotter the better,' Stan said recklessly. 'Bring it on. Man food, I call it, can't be doing with all this namby-pamby stuff.' What was he saying? Well, what *could* he say? She was having it. He couldn't let her think he was a complete wimp.

The waiter bowed and took their drinks order. They decided on beer and when it arrived Stan proposed a toast: 'To Kate, the most beautiful girl in the whole of York. I'm a lucky man tonight.'

Don't get any ideas about your luck, buddy, she thought. But she felt a bit uncomfortable about letting him order the Bangalore Phall. He obviously had no idea about Indian food, but the little devil in her head said serve him right. He should have been man enough to admit it. And he'd been covertly ogling the beautiful Indian maiden reclining by a limpid pool in the mural on the wall. Right under her nose, too. The man was incorrigible.

She acknowledged his toast and put her glass down carefully. Both fell silent. Kate fiddled with her cutlery. Now that they were here, she realised she didn't know much about Stan at all. Then she remembered the scene at Walter's house a few nights ago when he had blushed and looked guilty when she'd asked him about amateur dramatics. Yes, there was a mystery there. Now was as good a time as any to unravel it.

'We were talking the other night about amateur dramatics, Stan,' she began.

He looked startled and sat bolt upright in his chair. 'Were we?'

There it was again, that guilty look. What did he get up to?

'Yes,' she persisted, 'at Walter's house. You said you'd used horse glue in making scenery, helping your friends out at the amateur dramatics?'

'Oh that? Yes, well from time to time I lend a hand.'

It must be easier getting information from an Atlantic Clam, Kate thought. What had he got to hide? A thought crossed her mind. Perhaps he liked dressing up like

Penny's George; maybe he had a penchant for playing the pantomime dame every year. Now he wouldn't want that information put about, would he?

Stan had gone fiery red and was blustering now. 'Kate, that's all I do. I ... I just glue scenery for them once in a while. I don't get involved. I told you, there's nothing to tell,' he ended crossly.

'OK, keep your wool on. I was only asking.' I bet he does make the pantomime dame every year, she thought.

Silence fell between them again. Kate stole a look at Stan. His glance had strayed to the lovely Indian girl by the pool again. Fancy being upstaged by a painting, even if she was beautiful.

The evening had started off so well, but what had happened to chatty Stan? Perhaps she should widen the conversation.

'So what are your interests outside work, Stan?' she asked.

He withdrew his gaze from the little Indian lady and focused on Kate. 'Erm, erm…'

'Well you must do something besides watching girls. Hunting, shooting, fishing, metal detecting, ballroom dancing…?'

Stan looked at her thoughtfully. Was that a brain cell she heard clanking away? Kate let the silence roll on.

Eventually he said, 'I like history.'

Thank God, something to go at. 'Any particular period?' Again, 'erm, erm…'

What was it with this man? Didn't he know what he liked? 'Second World War.'

Kate pounced. 'Now that is a fascinating period to study. My Uncle was at El Alamein with Monty's troops. He was in the 46th Royal Tank Regiment. He told me a lot of stories about the battle.'

'Oh yeah?' Stan's gaze wandered back to the Indian maiden lying by the pool. 'El Alamein, Monty, the battle,' he said uneasily.

'Yeah, you know, the big one against Rommel.' It was a decisive battle, he must know about it. 'Bletchley Park had got hold of and deciphered Rommel's battle plan in advance and so knew…'

'Yeah, Bletchley Park, great place I believe.' Stan hadn't lifted his eyes from Miss India.

Kate wanted to slap him. 'I like the Romans and Vikings myself,' she said with a tinge of defiance. 'Now there's history for you. York is full of it in every street.'

Stan looked across at her and the old Stan re-appeared. 'Well, as a matter of fact…'

He was cut off by the approach of the young waiter with their onion bahjees. Stan watched Kate squeeze her lemon over the bahjee and take some raita from the side dish on to her salad. He followed her example and tried the food.

'Very nice,' he said in a slightly surprised voice.

'You sound like you didn't expect it to be good,' said Kate.

'Oh yes, of course I did,' Stan said. 'I just wanted it to be perfect for you.'

Me and the Indian maiden and every other pretty girl in York too, reflected Kate.

They concentrated on their food. Stan showed no inclination to expand on his history hobby and Kate was wondering what to try next. Suddenly Stan blurted out, 'Politics, we could talk about politics, that's a good subject.'

'Which Party?' asked Kate.

'Conservative.'

'Labour,' said Kate.

There was another silence. The food was finished and they sat back. Kate was wondering whether to try the history tack again when Stan jumped in.

'What about football? You've got to like football. York City are really coming on these days. We could go to a game if you like.'

Kate couldn't think of anything worse. 'Sorry, Stan, I hate football. They score a goal and then go jumping on each other and kissing. All a bit weird to me. I like rugby, that's a proper game, the likes of Martin Johnson and Lawrence Dallaglio.'

'Holidays,' Stan rushed in. 'It will soon be time for them. Going abroad, all day sunshine and sea, golden sands. I bet you can't wait.'

What was wrong with this man? Had he forgotten that she'd left all that sunshine behind for a reason? 'I've just come back from two years in Cyprus, Stan, a broken romance, remember? I've had all the sun and sea I want for now, thank you. I'll holiday at home this year.'

Kate felt very confused. Where was the merry, twinkling-eyed Stan from the caff? She seemed to be out tonight with a doppelganger with Tourettes Syndrome.

The waiter took their plates away and their conversation lapsed as he set the table for their main course. Silently he brought the two Bangalore Phalls, some rice and naan breads. He set them on the metal hot plate in the centre of the table. When he'd arranged the dishes to his own satisfaction, bowed and said in a low voice, 'Sir, Madam, I hope you enjoy your meal,' in a tone that clearly indicated he had no hope of this at all, and he withdrew.

Stan indicated to Kate to go first. She helped herself to some rice and then spooned the Phall on to the plate beside it. She tore off a hunk of the naan bread, ready to dip into the fragrant sauce. Stan watched her take a mouthful. Kate closed her eyes in ecstasy as the hot sauce rolled around in her mouth, the chilli oils making her eyes and ears tingle.

Stan followed suit and spooned some rice and a small portion of the Phall on to his plate. Kate waited as he ate a spoonful of the sauce.

It was like lighting the touch papers on a thousand fireworks all at once. He felt as if his mouth and head were exploding. He erupted from his seat as if propelled by sticks of dynamite. His face was bright red and even his ears glowed as he danced up and down wild-eyed holding his quivering mouth.

'Are you trying to bloody kill me?' he spluttered. He was an ugly sight as slivers of sauce dripped off his paralysed tongue. He leaned over the table and grabbed his pint glass of beer, guzzling it down in one. Then he reached for Kate's beer and poured it over his head.

* * * * * *

'You said you liked hot food,' Kate insisted stubbornly as they made their way to the car. 'Man food, you called it. Bring it on, you said.'

'There's man food and mad food,' Stan replied. 'How or where did you ever get to try something like that in the first place?'

'Four years at Leeds University, poor student and the best cheap curry houses in Britain. I made friends with the owners of one of them and waited tables in exchange for my dinners. I ate like Indian royalty.'

'Whatever happened to kids living off beans on toast and spam fritters?' Stan said mournfully.

'Passé, you old dinosaur.'

They had nearly reached the Kia. 'Speaking of royalty let's live a little and get fish and chips and then we can try out that new club down Albermarle Street,' Stan suggested.

Kate sighed, regretting their quick exit from the restaurant. She would have asked for a doggie bag but after Stan had knocked over two chairs and the neighbouring table she didn't think Mr Khan would have been too receptive to that idea.

Now they were out of the restaurant, Stan seemed to have regained some of his usual ebullience. 'Watch this, Kate,' he called out. He was framed in the light of an old fashioned wrought-iron lamp-post. 'Great trick with keys this,' he said. 'Watch closely now. The Great Suprendo will make them disappear before your very eyes.' He threw the keys up in the air and twirled around. As the keys came down he reached out for them and missed. Just out of his reach, they fell to earth and down into the street drain.

For some moments they stood still and silently contemplated the drain. 'I catch them, hold my hand out and they disappear and that's the magic,' Stan said uncertainly.

Kate felt beyond calm now. The whole night was taking on a surreal quality. 'They've certainly disappeared, Stan, and I don't think any amount of magic is going to bring them back. What are we going to do?'

'I'll have to go home and get my spare set. It's miles away. It'll take me the rest of the night to get there and back.'

Kate shivered in the cold night air. Large drops of rain splashed on her head and shoulders. 'Bloody Met Office wrong again,' she thought. Very quickly the rain became heavy and Kate's thin jacket was soaked.

'Come on,' Stan said miserably, 'let's find you a taxi. At least you might get home half dry tonight.'

Stan had been right: it was a night to remember alright.

CHAPTER 15

Across the city that same evening, Jackie hummed happily to herself as she stepped out of the bath. She reached for the thick fluffy towel from the heated towel rail and wrapped it around herself. Moving across to the full-length mirror, she wiped a circle clear of steam and examined her face. Hmm, not bad. Her spots were finally beginning to clear. Keeping off Walter's fry-ups and taking up healthy eating was beginning to pay dividends.

It was strange when she thought about it. Marilyn had constantly been shoving healthy fat-free food and all manner of fresh fruit at her in an effort to get her weight down. In defiance, Jackie had pigged out on junk food at the supermarket where she worked, her frugal Marilyn-packed lunch fed to the ducks on the river. The ducks were obviously omnivorous and greedily gobbled up everything Jackie threw at them; carrot batons, celery sticks with fat-free dip, crispbread spread with the vile, truly disgusting fish paste.

But now that Jackie wasn't being forcibly backed into a dietary corner she felt more relaxed around food. After Marilyn's death she had enjoyed Walter's big breakfasts but lately even those had lost their appeal and she found herself shopping for fruit and vegetables and, unheard of for her, making salads at home.

She finished drying herself and hung the towel neatly on the rail to dry. Padding into her bedroom, she fished out clean underwear and tights from her drawer. OK, so no-one was going to see her lacy bra and panties; well, not unless these Trades Council dos got racier than she'd heard about. But if she felt nice and smelled fragrant it would give her confidence to face this new social world she was stepping into.

An expensive new dress hung on the wardrobe door. Jackie had splashed out on a figure hugging little black number for the occasion. She remembered how Marilyn had always been dolled up to the nines, hair, make-up and nails always immaculate. Jackie didn't aspire to be in Marilyn's league. 'No,' she told herself determinedly. 'I am my own person. I am not like Marilyn and, with a bit of luck, I never will be.'

The cat flap in the kitchen rattled. Samson, Marilyn's cat, stalked into the bedroom and jumped on to a chair. He fixed his green eyes unblinkingly on Jackie and then slowly and delicately began to wash his black paws.

Jackie was not pleased to see him. He was truly the cat from hell. Marilyn had had him from being a tiny kitten and he'd been very much in tune with her. Like her, he was independent and went his own way. He could be wayward and bad tempered, spitting and scratching for no apparent reason. Jackie detested him and had hoped he would find a new home after Marilyn had gone. She felt obliged to feed him if he was around but took no notice of him otherwise. Often he rubbed himself around her legs or jumped on her lap when she was watching TV, only to dig his claws in and scratch her for no reason. In spite of being thrown out of the door several times he still came back, demanding food in his malevolent and surly way.

Jackie sighed and gritted her teeth at the sight of him. She would have to do battle with Samson before she went out tonight. No way was she leaving him in the house without her. She would have to catch him and put him out, locking the cat flap shut behind him, until she came home.

She turned to reach for her new dress hanging on the wardrobe. She stopped in her tracks and gasped in horror. Deep claw marks had gouged tram-line strips out of the dress from top to bottom. Samson had used it as a scratching post, swinging on it and tearing the hem. A cold fury took hold of Jackie. This was really the end of the line between them. He'd ruined her lovely new dress, almost as if he knew how much it, and this evening, had meant to her.

Slowly she turned. Already the cat was up on its feet, back arched, stretched ready for flight. 'Samson!' she hissed venomously, 'you evil, spiteful, mangy, hell-cat. Come here so I can kill you.'

She raced and pounced on him but was too late. He slipped from her grasp. Samson knew when his ninth life was at stake and fled the scene. Like greased lightning he streaked out of the room and through the cat flap before Jackie was even at her bedroom door.

She flung open the kitchen door and looked out into the night. Samson mocked her from the safety of a nearby sycamore tree.

'Don't bloody mee-ow me, Samson!' Jackie shouted and shook her fist at him. 'You ever come back in here and I'll have your guts for violin strings, make no mistake about it. And I'll feed the rest of you to the ducks on the river; they're not fussy what they eat. You've been warned!' She slammed the door so hard that the mugs rattled on the worktop. Reaching down she locked the cat flap shut. 'There, that will fix you tonight, you little fiend.'

But what was she to do now? She couldn't possibly wear the dress, it was completely ruined. And finding a replacement outfit was not going to be easy.

She ran back into her bedroom and flung open the wardrobe door. A quick survey revealed she had very few suitable outfits. Hurriedly she flung a few dresses on the bed and started trying them on. The first one, a red flouncy number was too tight and a bit tarty. 'Must have been my defiant stage,' she thought. Her mother had had exquisite taste in clothes and always dressed elegantly. The second dress was even worse. Orange did nothing for her dull fair hair. Orange! Why? Her friend Aurelia had said it suited her. Fancy believing her, when Aurelia was away with the fairies most of the time. The dark purple number was the last resort. Jackie breathed in and struggled to do up the zip. It only just closed. If she stood up really straight all night and didn't breathe out too heavily she might just get away with it.

Time was getting on. She threw a black pashmina around her shoulders. 'That should cover a multitude of sins,' she thought, and slipped on the new spiky black shoes she had bought for the occasion. At least Samson hadn't attacked those.

She was glad it was a buffet tonight and not a sit-down meal. She decided to select only things she really disliked and then she wouldn't wolf them down as she usually did. She could nurse a plate all night. This dress didn't have room for mini vol-au-vents, mini dim sum or mini anything, come to that.

She was feeling nervous about meeting a whole new bunch of people so to distract herself she tried to conjure up all the finger foods she most disliked; blinis piled with caviar, smoked salmon and horseradish sauce, mini fish and chips with those awful mushy peas ...

The hotel car park was almost full but she managed to squeeze her Fiat Panda in between a hulking Shogun and a Discovery. 'Size isn't everything,' she told herself as she made her way into the hotel. I am small but beautifully made and pack a powerful punch. I am just as good as Mr Shogun or Mr Discovery... Yeah, and you'll be running for Prime Minister next week too, she thought. Get real. You're the new kid on the block and know nothing. Watch and learn, watch and learn.

Jackie didn't have to ask directions to the Trades Council soirée. The loud chatter and laughter of a ballroom full of people spilled out into the big hall of the Golden Lion. The door was open and guarding it like a well-dressed bouncer was the President, Tom Young.

He saw her hesitating in the hall and came towards her, his hands outstretched in greeting.

'Miss Dalrymple-Jones.' He smiled engagingly down at her and took her hand in a warm handshake, enveloping her small cold hand in his tanned, well-manicured ones.

'Please call me Jackie, such a mouthful the Dalrymple-Jones bit.' He was absolutely drop-dead gorgeous. Move over George Clooney. What was Tom Young doing here running a Trades Council? He could be in Hollywood making millions and have women dropping like flies in his path. Perhaps they did already. He was so perfect. Tall and lean with a Kirk Douglas jaw, perfect teeth and the most melting brown eyes she had ever seen.

Jackie pulled her pashmina around her and straightened up. She could do attractive with the best of them, as long as she didn't breathe too much.

'Jackie,' Tom purred.

Shivers of excitement ran up and down her back. No-one had ever made her name sound sexy before.

'I'm so glad you've come. There are lots of people you must meet. They know all about you from Marilyn and they're really looking forward to meeting you.'

'What's the old bat been saying behind my back?' Jackie asked, assuming a brightness she did not feel.

'Only good things I assure you,' Tom laughed. With his hand under Jackie's arm, he steered her through the crowds. As they passed a waiter holding a tray of drinks he took two glasses and handed one to Jackie. He raised his own glass in a toast. 'To Jackie: our newest and prettiest member of the

136

Trades Council, welcome.'

Jackie blushed and took a sip of her wine. 'I had no idea my mother was so involved with events here,' she said. 'She never really spoke about it at home.'

'She was a very busy lady,' Tom said. 'She probably never had the time, always dashing about from her café to her courses. She spoke about you sometimes, she was very confident you would rise to the challenge of Café Paradise when the time came.'

'It's a pity she never shared that belief with me,' Jackie said drily. 'However, time has moved on and so have I. I've decided to completely re-vamp the cafe. We have thousands of visitors to York every year from all over the world and especially from Europe. I'm going to give the café a European Union flavour. As well as offering a traditional British menu, we'll have themed weeks, taking a different EU country's foods and traditions each time. I shall re-fit, re-decorate and re-launch the Café Paradise,' she ended a little breathlessly, trying to talk and not burst the seams of her dress at the same time.

Tom toasted her again delightedly. 'My brave Jackie: to launch a new venture in these difficult times. I applaud you.'

'Or have me locked up for insanity maybe,' she grinned.

'No, no,' he said smoothly. 'Now, there are people here you will have to meet. You've come to the right place. We have the best designers and trades people that York can offer here tonight. I'll introduce you to them. As fellow Council members, they would do you a good deal. You'll be getting the best of the best.'

Jackie was impressed and slightly overwhelmed. As the tasty Tom trawled her about the room she could see why he was the Council President. He had charm in shovelfuls as he made introductions and schmoozed and flattered electricians, decorators and shopfitters. Business cards and email addresses were swapped and promises to come and quote were made. Finally they came to Nina, the elegant and beautiful interior designer who had spoken so warmly at Marilyn's funeral.

Tom put his arm around Nina and hugged her gently He introduced Jackie and briefly explained Jackie's ideas for the café. 'You might be able to help her with some ideas for the re-vamp,' Tom suggested.

'I'd be delighted,' Nina said. 'Would you like to book a consultation now?' She reached into her bag and pulled out her diary. 'Now, what about next month? That's the earliest I'm free.'

Jackie hadn't thought about employing an interior designer. Did she need one? How much designing did a café need? Tables and chairs and a good coffee and cake counter and the business end of things, the kitchen, serving and washing-up areas hidden away at the back. She could choose equipment and colour schemes herself, couldn't she? Couldn't she? The whole enterprise suddenly seemed more complicated than she had envisaged. Maybe she could use a little advice.

'OK,' she agreed and got out her new Blackberry. She still wasn't quite sure of all of its operations but thought she could manage the diary. In the event, she was wrong and a stream of gobbledegook galloped across the screen. Not wanting to look a complete idiot in front of this elegant woman Jackie agreed to the 11th of May and pretended to punch the information into the machine. She rammed the Blackberry back into her bag before Nina could catch sight of the screen and smiled brightly at her.

'There, the 11th it is. I shall look forward to it.'

'Excellent,' Nina cooed. 'I'm sure my team can come up with some great design ideas. Europe is such an exciting project. I can't wait to get them started.'

Alarm bells began ringing in Jackie's head. A team! That's not what she wanted at all. Just one lady casting her eye over the place and making a few suggestions was all she'd had in mind. How was she going to get out of this one? It sounded expensive.

Nina held out her hand. 'I'm sorry, I must dash off now. I only popped in for an hour. I have to meet another client at nine. He's a busy industrialist and this is his only slot in the day.' She shook Jackie's limp hand. 'I'll see you on Friday, Jackie.'

'But …' Jackie began. Too late: Nina was gone, swallowed up in the throng now crowding around the buffet.

An electrician she had met earlier beckoned her over. 'Come on, Jackie, time to tuck in. They're a right bunch of vultures here. You need to get in quick or they'll strip it clean before you can blink.'

He handed her a plate. 'Here have a blini. There's all sorts here: caviar, fish, chips and mushy peas, pastrami and beans, lovely stuff.' He wafted the plate under her nose and Jackie stepped back revolted by the strong smell.

Thank you, God, all my least favourites. She selected a caviar blini and then a smoked salmon and horseradish one and smiled at Ed. 'What a lovely buffet, thank you.'

The electrician stayed by her side for the rest of the evening. Jackie wasn't convinced it was her irresistible charm and good looks that kept him there. He was just coming to the end of a big contract, he told her, and the café would slot in nicely before a certain large council project had to be started. He couldn't say any more, but a certain councillor had tipped him the wink… By the end of the evening he was saying it like it was a done deal between them and he would definitely be re-wiring and installing new power points for Café Paradise.

Jackie wasn't sure just where along the line she had agreed to anything but Ed was talking so confidently she felt that she must have.

At the end of the evening she sought out Tom Young

and said her goodbyes. He gently kissed her goodnight on the cheek as if he had been doing it for years and suggested they have lunch soon. 'We have much to discuss, Jackie,' he said. 'We must make sure the café is well insured whilst all this work is going on. I'll check your policy and make sure your level of public liability insurance is up to scratch and give you a ring.'

Wearily she retrieved her Fiat Panda from between the Shogun and the Discovery. It was dark and raining heavily. She backed out of the space carefully; pranging either car would be an expensive mistake.

Her head ached and her ears were ringing from the noisy chatter. She was too tired to make sense of all she had heard and seen. It would have to keep for tomorrow. One thing she did know, she would have to invest in some new magic pants and only look at a lettuce leaf for the next month if she wanted to look her best for lunch with Tom.

Back home, she put the car away in the garage and locked the door. The rain splashed down heavily on the path, spattering up her shoes and legs as she made a dash for the back door. She opened the door and put the light on. Turning to close the door for the night she looked out briefly.

A faint mewing noise came from the sycamore tree in the garden. She halted, holding on to the door. It was slightly pitiful. Samson, drenched and bedraggled, was sitting on a low branch waiting for an invitation to come inside.

'Samson,' she exclaimed, 'you have got to be kidding. You're trading on borrowed time already. Remember the little black dress, the very, very expensive little black dress?'

'Mee-ow,' yowled Samson bleakly.

'Up yours, Samson,' Jackie gestured skywards with one finger. 'Go curl up under a leaf for the night. Oh dear, it's only just spring and there aren't any yet. Just have to get wet, won't you?'

She banged the door and leaned against it. A loud yowl sounded behind the door.

'Bugger off!' she shouted.

Samson wailed.

She sighed, slowly opened the door a crack and looked out at the unremitting heavy rain pouring down from the dark sky.

'Oh, get in then,' she snapped. 'But don't come anywhere near my bedroom. Have you got that, you mangy lump?' she shouted after him as he fled to the safety of his basket.

Jackie made her way to bed. Samson licked at his wet coat and purred contentedly. There was always tomorrow. Another day: another battle.

CHAPTER 16

Saturday morning dawned dry and bright. George was up early riffling through the outfits in his wardrobe trying to decide what to wear.

Penny, still lying in bed, sipped her coffee and listened to him padding about as he pulled one dress after another out, only to discard it with a, 'oh that's not right either,' or, 'why did I buy that?' She would cheerfully welcome a hurricane or tornado, floods, fire, anything but to get up and go to Thirsk this morning. She looked at the clock. Nine o'clock already. She would have to get out of bed soon.

She sighed to herself. How could two people who had been married for thirty years and up to now shared everything, find themselves so far apart? George was obsessed with this transvestite carry-on. It's not as if he'd ever had leanings that way. He'd always been such a manly man, testosterone overload if anything, and it seemed a bit late for a mid-life crisis at fifty-four... Penny didn't know what to make of it.

George put his head around the door. 'You still in bed? Come on, it's a lovely morning, almost like summer. Come and see my outfit, see what you think.' He disappeared back into his den.

Reluctantly Penny dragged herself out of bed and pulled on a dressing gown. In the den George paraded before her in a blue mohair sweater teamed with a black swirly skirt and chunky black shoes. Penny would have killed for the sweater, it must have cost a fortune. She fingered the mohair enviously, 'You could have bought me one too,' she said.

'Couldn't run to it at the time,' George answered, stroking it lovingly. 'Next time perhaps.'

Crumbs from the rich man's table, Penny thought grumpily. She chose a plain brown suit for their outing. She wanted to look as inconspicuous as possible, if indeed that was going to be possible at all walking with George. She decided to walk a bit ahead of him on the street so as not to be associated with him, in case any of her acquaintances might be visiting Thirsk this morning. Mentally reviewing George's outfit a thought occurred to her.

She returned to the den and looked at him more closely. 'You've got bosoms,' she said. 'Where did you get them from?'

George pushed his chest out proudly. 'Got them off the internet. Found a website for clothes for the larger man, transvestites of course. Good aren't they? I'm in the outsize category, all that working-out I do. Not much call for this size they told me.'

'No, I don't suppose there is,' Penny said pensively.

George had opted for the black wig to tone with his ensemble. The whole outfit was very well put together, but there was no denying that George was a man.

'Can you walk in those shoes?' she asked.

'Yes, watch this.' George strode about the room confidently in his wedge heels. 'I've been practising.'

'Where?'

'Outside in the garden, done several laps when I'm home before you. I've got really good at this high heel lark. It's good fun.'

Penny shuddered. No doubt the neighbours would have had great entertainment, especially nosy Mrs Redmond from number thirty-four.

'Have you watched how women walk, George?'

'Well they just walk, don't they? One foot in front of the

other, like men do.'

'They don't stride, George. You're striding out with a man's stride, women don't do that.'

'Well what do they do?' George asked impatiently.

Penny couldn't believe she was doing this. She picked up George's handbag and sashayed up and down the den demonstrating shorter steps. 'Ladies don't gallop along like men.'

George watched closely and tried again. His next effort was slightly better; that was as much as Penny could hope for.

Penny drove them to Thirsk. Initially George had got behind the wheel but found his thick wedges got stuck under the pedals. He couldn't get his foot off the accelerator and shot off the drive and into the road before he could release it. Thankfully there was no other traffic coming along the road.

Penny hated driving George at the best of times, but this Saturday morning was particularly bad. George was excited and keyed up about the expedition. Penny was miserable and anxious about the whole ridiculous nonsense. Why am I going along with it?' she asked herself, turning up the demister to number four to clear the fogged-up car. After a minute George turned it off and Penny turned it on again. 'Don't interfere, George, I need to see where I'm going.'

'I'm frying in this jumper. I'll overheat and die.'

'Don't be so melodramatic. We'll be there soon and you'll be out in the freezing cold. That will soon sort you out.'

George muttered into his jumper and Penny ignored him. They drove on in silence. Thirsk on a Saturday morning was always busy and the cobbled town centre was already full of tightly parked cars. Penny slowly weaved her way amongst the lines of cars looking for a space.

'That one will do.' George pointed between two Discoveries.

Penny eyed it up. 'Far too narrow,' she decided. 'I'd scrape the car getting in.'

'Don't be daft. You could get a tank in there.'

'When we have a tank, you can try.' Penny circled around again.

'In there, quick,' George barked, waving at a very slim space at the end of a line of cars.

'It's not a space, George, and if it was we'd have to be half the width we are to get into it.' She turned to look at him. 'Do you need glasses, George? You couldn't get a sardine in there let alone this big thing.'

'Typical woman,' George jeered, 'unless the space is big enough to take a tractor you won't consider it. Can't park, won't park. Here, let me do it.'

George made to get out of the car but Penny accelerated sharply flinging him back in his seat. 'You sit tight and shut up. I'm in charge today, George.'

Slowly she made another circuit of the market square and found a space right on the edge that she felt confident of getting into. She would have completed the manoeuvre with confidence, but a keyed-up George couldn't help but interfere. Penny had no idea what 'left hand down a bit' meant, or 'over to me' or 'mind your offside.' If only George would shut up and leave her to it.

Stuck out half on the road and half in the space, Penny stopped the car. 'Get out, George,' she shouted.

'What?'

'You hear, get out. I'll park this car a lot better without your, "left hand down a bit", and "up a bit, down a bit." I won't move another foot until you're out.'

George wrenched open the car door and stood scowling on the pavement, still twirling his fingers around an imaginary steering wheel as Penny competently parked the car. She got out and slammed the door triumphantly. 'See, George. Perfect parking.'

'Your nose is too far out on the road.'

Penny looked back at the car. 'No it isn't. That's just sour grapes. Come on, now I'm here I might as well get my shopping.' She walked off towards the butcher's on the main street.

'Wait for me,' George called and followed her, teetering over the cobbled stones in his wedge heels. He caught her up as she was placing her order with the butcher and she motioned him to stand behind her. The butcher stared hard at George and raised his eyebrows but made no comment as he assembled Penny's meat order.

'Do you want the oxtail chopping, Mrs Montague?' he asked.

'Yes please.'

'Oxtail?' George queried in a whisper. 'Since when did we eat ox?'

'It's not ox you chump, it's a cow's tail.'

'Cow's tail, yuk, sounds disgusting, do we have to?'

'You've been eating it in stew for thirty years, George, and never complained.'

'Oh, is that what that brown lumpy stuff is. I don't really like it anyway.'

'It's only taken you thirty years to say so.'

The butcher stood waiting patiently holding up the oxtail. 'Well, do I or don't I?' he asked.

'No,' said George 'Let's have some fillet steak instead.'

'Yes, sir, I mean, madam.' He went away to his cold store.

'Do you know the price of fillet steak, George?' Penny asked crossly.

'Well I'm not eating oxtail,' he said mutinously, 'nor tripe, trotters or tongue or any other bits.'

The butcher returned with the fillet steak. 'That will be thirteen pounds, madam,' he said.

'How much?' George exclaimed in his booming male voice.

'Thirteen pounds, sir,' the butcher said.

'You and your fillet steak. You'd better enjoy every bite, George, because it will be a long time before you see any again.'

Other customers had come in during this exchange and were watching them curiously. Flustered, Penny paid for their goods and, avoiding looking at anyone, hurried outside as discreet whispering broke out.

She thrust the bag at George and hurried off up the street. 'I'm going for some bread,' she said. George, hampered by his wedge heels, followed on more slowly. By the time he caught up with her she was inside being served.

Penny had a very determined tilt to her jaw and so George decided to wait outside. He looked at the array of cakes and pastries in the window. Some particularly fine looking meringues filled with whipped cream caught his eye. Now they definitely had his name on them. He decided to risk going inside.

Penny was receiving her change and avoided eye contact with him as he entered the shop. Undeterred, he took the shopping bag from her.

'Meringues,' he whispered.

'Well spotted, it's a bakery,' she said.

'Two beauties in the window. Let's take them home for afternoon tea.'

'No chance.'

'Why not?'

Penny hustled him out of the shop. Out on the pavement George pointed to the meringues. 'Aren't they beauties?' he drooled. 'Go on, Penny, let's treat ourselves.'

'If I said yes to every time you said that we'd both be like house sides. No, George.' She tapped his chest, 'Cholesterol. We have to watch it now you're at a funny age. Come on, let's go and get a coffee before the rush starts. I might treat you to a scone instead.'

Giving one more loving glance back at the meringues, George followed Penny into the Cosy Teapot Café. She chose a table at the rear of the café and ordered coffee and scones for them both.

'Butter or Flora?' asked the waitress.

'Bu...,' George began.

'Flora,' Penny said firmly.

'Cream?'

'Yes.'

'No,' said Penny, 'and no jam either, thank you.'

Eyeing George curiously, the waitress moved away.

George sat back in his chair and stroked his mohair jumper appreciatively. 'This is my favourite,' he said, 'it's so soft and sexy. It makes me feel ... fantastic.'

'Keep your voice down, George,' Penny hissed at him and glanced about her fearfully. 'I don't think everyone wants to know what turns you on.'

'You worry too much, Penny.' George smoothed his skirt down. 'People are far too involved in their own affairs to be listening to us. I tell you what though, much as I love wearing a skirt, it's a bit draughty in this weather. I'm glad I've got warm tights on, but what a job I had getting into them.' He laughed loudly. 'I'm only practised in getting them off women, not putting them on.'

George's voice was attracting attention. The level of chatter had died down as the other customers tuned into their conversation. Penny was purple with embarrassment. Her nose almost touched the table as she hid her face from view.

'Shut up, George.' She handed him a scone with a smear of Flora on it. 'Eat that whilst it's still warm.'

George eyed the small scone askance. No butter, no cream, no jam: terrific. 'All one bite of it,' he said and wolfed it down.

'You'll thank me for it when you live to a ripe old age,'

Penny hissed.

'I'll be too old and gaga by then to enjoy it.' George drank his coffee and looked sadly down at his empty plate.

The lady at the next table stifled a snort of laughter. Penny had had enough. She threw her napkin down on the table and got up. 'There's just no pleasing you, George, is there? You're never satisfied. I've had enough. I'm going to the supermarket on my own and I'll see you back at the car in twenty minutes.' She gathered up her bag and ran out of the café.

George looked after her in disbelief. She was at a funny age, he'd best make allowances. He sat back in his chair and considered the situation. Well now, if she didn't want him at the supermarket and he had twenty minutes to kill … maybe the baker's hadn't sold those meringues yet…

He finished his coffee and made his way through the café to the pay desk. He was conscious of people staring up at him as he passed their tables. 'Bet they love the jumper,' he thought.

The waitress at the till giggled as she gave him his change.

Coming out into the street, George pushed his handbag up his arm and holding on to the shopping bags made his way up the street to the baker's. He saw with satisfaction that the meringues were still nestling in their frilly wrappers. In a moment he was in the shop and buying them.

Out in the street again he wasted no time. He bit into the crispy meringue and the smooth cream squidged down his chin and on to his jumper. George took no notice. He closed his eyes in delight as the meringue melted in his mouth. In no time both were gone. George licked his sticky fingers and dabbed the cream from his chin. Feeling full and happy, he made his way through the Saturday crowds to find the car in the market square.

The shoes were beginning to pinch and a blister was forming on his heel. The cold wind whistled up his skirt and whipped around his midriff, now exposed under his thin skirt as his tights had slipped down his hips and were in danger of coming down altogether. Fairly satisfied with his morning, George decided it was time to go home.

He reached the car just as Penny staggered across the square with her supermarket shopping. Tottering around to the back, George opened the boot and lifted in the bags. Penny glanced up to thank him and gasped, 'George, how could you?'

'Now what have I done? Don't you like the way I've stacked the bags?'

'You went back for those meringues, didn't you?'

'No I didn't.'

'Yes you did, they're all over you, stuck in your five o'clock shadow and there's cream on your lovely jumper. Oh, George, how could you?'

'Well, what if I did.' He grinned at her. 'They were lovely. I ate yours as well.'

Penny burst into tears. 'All I try to do for you and this is how you repay me. I gave up my precious Saturday to come out in the freezing cold to support you in your cross-dressing fetish when I could have been tucked up warm at home. And all you can do is stuff your face with cakes and cream...'

'I didn't eat cake,' George protested.

Penny ignored him. 'And you'll be dead soon. You'll just go off pop 'cos your arteries will all be clogged up with cream and cholesterol and serve you right. I'll be a merry widow and collect on all your insurances and, and ... I'll get myself a toy boy. Oh you needn't look like that, George, I'm still young enough.' Penny blew vigorously into her handkerchief

A small crowd was gathering in the square and looking on with interest as George and Penny went at it hammer and tongs in a blazing row. The ripple went around the crowd, 'Was that the fella from the pantomime?'

'The sky isn't going to fall just because I had one little meringue.'

'Two.'

'Well, two then. It's more than I ever get at home. All I get is a chunk of bony oxtail in brown goo.'

'Are you saying I can't cook?' Penny demanded. 'Thirty years we've been married, George, and you've never complained before.'

'That's because you've never asked me before, and since you're asking, I think you're cooking can be crap sometimes.'

'That's never stopped you eating it,' Penny threw back at him.

'Don't be daft, the dog gets most of it under the table. Why do you think he's so fat? He doesn't taste it, just gobbles it down.'

'Well, if my cooking's crap, your attempts at Mr He-man DIY are rubbish. Look at that garden path you tried to lay last year. It's all kinks and bumps. I can hardly walk on it without falling over.'

'There's nothing wrong with my path, it's as straight as a die. It's you; you want to take more water with it.'

'Are you suggesting I drink?'

'I think there's more gin than tonic goes in your glass.'

Penny and George raked up old scores and flung them at each other, oblivious to the crowd gathered about them.

'You are so untidy, leaving your clothes in a trail behind you.'

'*I'm* untidy! Look at the state you leave the kitchen in after you've cooked up one of your so-called specials and I have to clean up.'

'And what cleaning up do you have to do? Stack the dishwasher? Oh life is so tough on you, George.'

'Believe me, it can be tough living with you, Penny,' said George.

'Ooh, that's nasty,' said a little old lady.

'Best to get it out,' said a man.

The crowd began arguing heatedly amongst themselves. 'Well, he's right, he says she drinks, probably gives him a dog's life.'

'You can talk, Joe Brierly. Not known for your sobriety, are you?'

'Don't start on me, Madge Parsons. It doesn't take half an hour for the postman to deliver letters to you, does it?'

'And what does that mean…?'

The noise level grew, attracting the attention of more onlookers and particularly a beat bobby who crossed the road to see what all the noise was about. He pushed his way through the jostling crowd and saw Penny and George, now without his wig, at the centre of the disturbance.

'Now, sir, madam, what's all the bother about? Do you realise you're disturbing the peace and,' he gestured to the arguing crowd, 'possibly causing an affray? I'll have to arrest you if you don't move on.'

'Don't go blaming her,' a woman shouted from the crowd. 'He's a nasty piece of work. You want to arrest him and take him down to the station, leave the lassie alone.'

As the policeman separated Penny and George, both red-faced and panting hard, the flash of a camera caught their attention. They looked around suddenly aware of the crowd.

'*Thirsk Trumpeter*,' the photographer said. 'Thanks a lot.' He went off down the road beaming. Copy was always short on a February Saturday. His boss would be delighted. He could see the by-line already. "Pantomime Frolics in Thirsk. Scintillating Sisters Fall Out In The Market Square."

Penny drove home in silence and dumped the car on the drive. She stormed tearfully into the house and slammed the door. So much for an anonymous visit to Thirsk! If word of this got out they would be the laughing stock of the village.

CHAPTER 17

'I don't know why I let you hatch these chicks, Sarah,' Walter said, exasperated. For the third time that afternoon he rescued a stray chick and placed it back in the box on the floor.

'I thought you were going to be a good mother. After all, you've had a good example from me. I've brought you up properly. Maybe I've spoiled you.'

Walter sat down in his chair and drank his coffee. It had gone cold whilst he chased the birds around his kitchen. He sighed. Sunday afternoon stretched aimlessly before him. Every day seemed long now that Marilyn was gone from his life. Even working on his smallholding didn't bring the same pleasure it used to.

There was a knock at the door and Stan appeared carrying a bottle wrapped in tissue paper. 'Ah, you're in, Walter, that's good. Have you got time for a chat and a brew? I've brought something to put in it.'

'Come in, lad, come in.' Walter got up and cleared a chair for Stan to sit on. 'It's good to see you. I could do with some company. I can't seem to get going today.'

He got up and put the kettle on, taking clean mugs from the dresser whilst Stan sat down, unwrapped his bottle and put it on the table.

'Whisky, eh?' commented Walter. 'Are we celebrating?'

'No,' said Stan gloomily. 'Commiserating. Last night was not my finest hour.'

Walter sighed to himself. He could see he wasn't going to be cheered up today.

'Are we talking about Kate, lad? Ooh, mind out, there's a chick right by your foot there.'

'What the…' Stan scooped up the yellow ball and stood holding it in his hands.

'Behind you, there's a box full of them. They hatched out two days ago and they're very adventurous already; keep getting out of that box somehow. I shall have to find something else to put them in. Mind you, Sarah's not putting herself out too much to look after them. I've just been telling her she's spoiled. Put it back in the box for now, I'll find summat later.'

Stan slumped back into the chair and Walter set the mugs of tea on the table. He sat down opposite Stan and offered him a biscuit. 'All butter shortcake, lad. My neighbour, Mrs Longbottom, made 'em. She's a bit sweet on me, keeps trying to seduce me with her fruit cakes and homemade biscuits, but I don't fancy a set to with Mr Longbottom if he found out. He's six foot five and built like a barn door.'

'At least you've got someone who wants to be seduced,' Stan said glumly. 'I doubt I'll get a second chance with Kate after last night. After months of trying, I finally get her to agree to go out with me and then I make a complete hash of it.' He opened the whisky bottle and poured generous measures into both mugs.

Walter's eyes widened. He wondered what had gone so wrong for Stan to drown his sorrows in this way. 'What happened then?' he asked.

'I made the mistake of giving her the choice of what to eat.'

'It wasn't Outer Mongolian Yak or Russian vodka-marinated moose?'

'Worse. Indian.'

'Indian, as in Tikka Masala, recently voted Britain's

favourite. 'Nowt wrong with that, is there? How could you fall out over that?'

'If only it had been Tikka whatever it was you said. Thing is, Walter, I know nowt about Indian food. I've only had it once and that was years back. I was more interested in the bird I was with at the time than the food. Anyway, when Kate chose Indian what could I say? She knew this really good place down Bank Street in the city centre, really impressive it was. The staff were all dressed up in silks and turbans and there were these beautiful murals painted on the walls, thick white tablecloths and napkins…'

'Hang on a minute, lad.' Walter jumped up and rescued a couple of chicks as they ran across the floor cheeping excitedly. Sarah cackled from her box on the floor. Walter caught the birds and dumped them back with their mother. 'Sit on them for a bit, Sarah,' he said. 'Show them who's boss.'

Stan finished his tea and poured some more whisky. 'I thought I would be safe if I just ordered the same as her. How wrong can you be?'

'She didn't order a vindaloo, did she?'

'I don't know what one of those is, Walter. She asked for something with chicken. A Bangalore Phall, that was it.'

Walter looked at Stan in wonderment and said with a tinge of awe in his voice, 'A Bangalore Phall? I've heard of those but I didn't believe anyone actually ordered it. I was having a weekend away once in Scarborough with a mate of mine and we went for an Indian. This bloke wanted to order one of them Phalls. He'd had a bit to drink and his mates were egging him on. It was on the menu right enough: Vindaloo (Hot); then Tindaloo (Very Hot); and then, this Phall (Explosive Hot). The waiter wouldn't let him order it, said it would be irresponsible of him. It was only on the menu for show really. And she ordered one of them…?'

Stan collected three chicks that were inspecting his shoes

and carried them back to Sarah. 'They'll be taken into care soon, Sarah, if you don't show some mothering skills. Yeah, we had these bahjees to start with and they were fine, very nice really, and then they brought out this bloody Phall.'

'You must have put on a convincing act that you knew what you were doing,' Walter observed. 'But that's typical you, you're always full of blether, Stan, you know that.'

'Thanks, Walter, yes I do know that. I just didn't want to look like an idiot in front of her. I wanted to impress her, take her out and give her a lovely evening, then she might consider me in a whole new light. She'll do that now alright.'

'So what happened?' Walter said patiently. 'Did you eat this Phall?'

'I only had a mouthful. I thought my head was going to explode. I asked her if she was trying to kill me.'

'Mm. Mebbe not the best thing to say on a first date.'

'No. And I knocked the chair over and that sent the food flying. Then I banged into the bloke sitting at the table behind me and his food went west. I was covered in beer and so was the table. The bloke wanted to put one on me…' Stan stopped, looking miserable at the memory.

Walter shook his head. 'By, lad, you don't do things by halves.'

'That's not the worst. We were asked to leave.'

'So instead of impressing her, you embarrassed her.'

'Oh there's more, Walter. Pass that whisky. I can't bear the memory of it.'

The bottle was getting well down now. Stan's eyes narrowed as he focused on getting the whisky safely into their mugs. 'Cheers,' he said bitterly as he raised his mug in a toast to Walter. 'Here's to women.'

'Yes, here's to women, God bless them,' Walter said quietly.

There was a silence as the whisky fumes warmed and relaxed them. Walter reached down and scooped an errant chick up and gave it back to Sarah. He was a little unsteady on his feet and nearly missed the box. Sarah cackled disapprovingly. 'Well, stick them under your wings then,' he said, 'or the cat will get them.' Sarah nudged the chick under her wing, chattering quietly to it.

Walter collapsed back into his seat. He couldn't get past the Bangalore Phall. Kate was some woman. 'Before this food from hell, did you manage to keep her entertained with a flow of small talk?' he asked.

'No,' said Stan flatly. 'I was so nervous about putting a foot wrong I mostly talked rubbish. You told me to keep off the history stuff and the re-enactment society and then she goes and says she likes history. Vikings and Romans. I should have followed it up then, instead of making an idiot of myself.'

'Well why didn't you?'

'You'd frightened me off it, I didn't dare.'

'Quite right on a first outing. There are other things you can be talking about besides re-enactments. Did you even try?'

'I made a complete mess of it all and now she'll never give me another chance.' Stan downed his whisky miserably.

'Don't be such a wimp, lad,' Walter said bracingly. 'She never will if you go about with that attitude. Apologise and ask her again. Exert that famous charm on her. It works on all the other ladies.'

'Kate sees right through it,' Stan said. 'You haven't heard it all yet.'

Suddenly the chicks made a mass break out and the kitchen was filled with squeaking birds. Unsteadily both men dived about the floor trying to capture them.

'How many should there be? 'Stan asked, red-faced from the whisky and throwing himself about the dusty floor.

'Noh shure,' panted Walter. 'She had ten eggs but only eight hashed, I think.'

'I've only got five,' said Stan, catching another and stuffing it down his shirt with the others.

'Thash the lot then,' said Walter. 'I've got three. Lesh shove 'em back in here and put a cloth over 'em for a while. They'll think ish night and go to shleep.'

Stan looked out of the window at the darkening February afternoon. 'Shoon will be, Walter.' He shrugged. 'Who cares, lesh have another drink.'

They sat down at the table again. 'I did that magic shrick with the car key,' he said. 'Wanted to make her laugh.'

'Making them dishappear up your sleeve?' Walter said. 'Clever that.'

'Only I mished and they went shtray down a drain.'

'Dish you try and fish 'em out?'

'It was raining shtair-rods by then and Kate was getting so … so … soaked. I had to shee her into a taxi home. Then I got filthy lying on the ground in the muck and groping for the keys. Cap it all, Walter, I got a parking ticket on my windshcreen, out … out … over my time.'

'Good night was had by all then,' Walter commented.

'Terrific.' Stan downed his whisky and poured them some more.

Walter drank and eyed Stan beadily. 'Nothing venshured, nothing gained,' he enunciated carefully. 'Fight for her, give it everything you've got. I didn't and I've regrt, rregrr, regretted it ever shince. I stood back and ashepted things. Don't you do it, lad. Look at me now and learn.' Walter sighed and shuffled up to light a lamp.

'You mish her a lot, don't you, Walter?'

'Aye, I do,' Walter said gruffly, staring out into the darkness. 'She was always my ness breath and now ….' He shrugged and turned to face Stan. 'There's thish empty space, nothing to look forward to every day.' He sat down again.

'Jackie …?' Stan asked tentatively.

'Aye. Need to keep an eye on her, but I 'spect she'll find her feet soon and take up with someone from thash Trades Council of hers. Won't need me then.'

Pouring the last of the whisky, Stan raised his mug to Walter. 'I'm your frien, Walter, and I'm telling it like a frien should. Marilyn's gone and you've got to fashe up to it. Move on … thash what you've got to do.' He swung his mug to and fro to echo his thoughts. 'Start living again. Get yourself a life … different life. You're shtill young enough.' Whisky sloshed on to the table. Stan mopped it up with his sleeve.

Stan wagged his finger at Walter. 'Come to a re-en … renact…' Stan drew himself up and took a deep breath and very slowly said, 're-enactment day with me. Always a lot to organise. I could use another pair of handsh. Meet new people. Would be something 'pletely different.'

Somewhere in Walter's fuddled brain this seemed a good idea but his mouth was paralysed and couldn't frame the words to express his thoughts. He nodded solemnly at Stan and slowly slid down in his chair, his head coming to rest on the table, one hand still clutching his drink

Stan, happy they had come to some conclusion, briefly rested his head on his arms. In a moment he too was out cold.

Sarah cackled disapprovingly as her little yellow chicks bravely climbed all over the two sleeping men and hoovered up the shortbread biscuits on the table.

* * * * * *

Things weren't going well for Barney on Sunday afternoon. Melissa had been occupying his spare bedroom for several weeks now and had gradually spread her clothes and possessions around the flat. Walking in the door, his arms full of supermarket shopping, Barney found himself tip-toeing around bags, shoes, discarded newspapers, clothes and dirty cups and dishes. His lips tightened.

Enough was enough. He dumped the shopping on the table and went in search of Melissa. On his way to the living room he noticed his bedroom door standing open. He paused. Since Melissa's arrival he made sure he always shut his door firmly, as a polite hint to her to keep out. He walked towards his door and peeped in. To his intense relief she was not waiting for him inside. But… Barney stepped into his room. Who's been sleeping in my bed, he wondered, as he surveyed his rumpled bedclothes. Not Goldilocks that was for sure. Melissa? Surely not. Where was she now?

Barney tried the living room. The TV was blaring away as usual when Melissa was at home, but for once she was not stretched out semi-comatose in front of it. That meant she must be holed up in the spare bedroom. Mentally he braced himself and knocked on her door.

'Melissa, are you in there?' he called.

'Hi, is that you, Barney darling. You can't come in. I'm in the middle of my Sunday beauty routine.'

Barney ground his teeth. Since when did Melissa confine herself to Sundays to spend hours tarting herself up? 'Sorry, Melissa,' he called loudly. 'This can't wait. We need to talk. No, not just talk, we need action around here.'

As he said this Barney opened the door and walked in to Melissa's room. He stopped short. Melissa sat up on her bed, her face encased in a mud pack. She had just painted her toe nails, each toe carefully separated from its neighbour by cotton wool and now she was carefully painting her finger nails.

'Barney! I said you can't come in. Now look what you've done! I'm not supposed to talk with this face pack on and now it will be cracked and ruined. It cost me a fortune too.'

Barney was unmoved by Melissa's plight. He sat at the foot of her bed and eyed her sternly. 'What,' he asked her in a cold voice 'were you doing in my room this afternoon?'

Through her mud pack Melissa tried to look coy. 'Oh, Barney darling, I was just trying it out. You know … just in case you changed your mind, or…' She brightened at her next idea, 'I managed to change it for you.' She leaned towards him, sensually puckering her lips, but the effect was spoiled by bits of mud flaking off and falling on to the bed.

Barney was in no mood for her wiles. 'Keep out of my room, Melissa,' he said. 'It's the only part of this flat that's not cluttered up with your stuff, which is why I've come in here anyway.'

Melissa's head drooped. 'I thought you wanted to come in and see me, Barney darling, not tell me off in that horrid old way.'

'I do want to see you,' Barney began. 'Not in that way,' he said hastily, seeing the renewed gleam in Melissa's eyes. 'I wanted to see you to ask you, no, to tell you to clear up your mess. It's one long trail of stuff from the front door, through the living room and into here. And I can hardly get into the bathroom for your essences and oils, at least ten different types of shampoo and bottles of fake tan, not to mention the pile of used bath towels festering away in the laundry basket. I assume you know how to use a washing machine?'

'Course I do!' Melissa exclaimed in hurt tones. As she replaced the top on her nail varnish bottle she studied it meditatively and added, 'Well, actually, now I come to think about it, no I don't.'

Barney felt he was fast losing his grip on the situation. Dealing with Melissa reminded him of trying to eat his first Chinese meal with chopsticks and losing most of it in the process.

'Well, at least you'll know how to wash up,' he said firmly. 'There's a stack of it in the kitchen, so you could make a start on it right now.'

'No, Barney darling, I couldn't possibly!' Melissa looked

horrified at the idea. 'I've just done my nails and washing up would ruin them. Besides,' she went on, an accusatory note creeping into her voice, 'I don't know why you haven't got a dishwasher. Mummy has and we *never* wash up. I'm not used to it, Barney, you shouldn't ask me.'

Barney stood up and made for the door. 'I've a large stock of Marigolds, Melissa, so you'd better make a start.' He didn't wait to hear her retort. He headed back to the kitchen, picking up sundry items of Melissa's discarded clothing along the way and piling them up on the sofa.

After a few minutes, Melissa made her way through to the kitchen where Barney was putting the shopping away. She had wiped the mud pack from her face, though traces still lurked in the faint crows-feet around her eyes. Sulkily she pulled on a pair of rubber gloves and ran some water into the sink. As the steam rose around her, she crashed the dishes into the sink and sloshed the water around them. After a few moments she lifted the whole lot out and banged them down on the draining board.

Barney winced and stole a glance at the steaming plates. The top one was still swimming in the watery remains of Melissa's latest take-away. Before he could ask her to have another go at them, Melissa crashed another set of plates and screeched as they hit the white ceramic sink and shattered.

She backed away from the sink, stripping off the rubber gloves. 'I'm not doing any more, Barney. You're treating me like a slave and what's more it's too dangerous! You shouldn't make me do this. It's so dark ages. You'll have to get a dishwasher like everyone else.'

Barney looked at his dinner plates lying in pieces in the greasy water. Maybe it had been a mistake to let Melissa loose on them. But he wasn't giving up easily. 'Don't be so dramatic, Melissa. I only asked you to wash a few dishes. But if you're not capable of that, surely you can tidy away your own clothes and clear up the mess you've left in the bathroom? Or did you have a maid to do that for you at home too?'

Melissa flung down the gloves. 'You're too horrid, Barney. I don't know why you ever invited me to stay with you. I wouldn't have come if I'd known you were going to make this much fuss over every little thing. A few frocks here and there and a bottle of shampoo in the bathroom. If I'd known you were going to be such a fussy old woman…' Melissa stalked out of the kitchen and banged the door behind her

Barney stared at the door. *I* … invited *her* to stay! How did she work that one out?

Half an hour later after Barney had finished in the kitchen, he made his way back into the living room. He was pleased to see that Melissa had made efforts to tidy up and had removed her trail of clothes and shoes. Only now the carpet was revealed, her evening snacks of chocolate and crisps could be seen scattered over the carpet. There was no sign of Melissa. Barney wondered if she had resumed her Sunday beauty routine. Well if she had, he was jolly well going to interrupt it again. The flat still looked untidy and dirty and if she was going to stay any longer, she needed to shape up a bit.

He strode to her door and knocked loudly. 'Come on out, Melissa,' he called. 'We haven't finished yet. The flat needs hoovering and dusting and I'm not clearing up any more of your mess for you.'

Melissa's head appeared round the door. 'Oh, Barney, this is too much! First, you invite me stay, then you try and turn me into your maid of all work, like you're some kind of white slave trader.'

'I never invited…'

'Well it won't work with me, Barney. I'm up to all the tricks. My mother warned me about men like you. I've done your horrid old washing up, I've tidied your flat for you and cleaned your bathroom, though goodness knows I don't know why. It's not my mess in there. You should try and be more tidy, Barney, then I wouldn't have to clean up after you. And I'm not going to start on your hoovering or anything else now. I've done quite enough for one day. I'm quite exhausted. I'm going to put another face pack on, so don't bother me again tonight.' She slammed the door.

Barney slowly made his way back through the living room and to the hall cupboard. He pulled out the hoover and began to clean the hallway, baffled as to how Melissa had twisted her way out of everything.

CHAPTER 18

The icy rain hurled itself at Walter and trickled down his neck as he rode his bicycle through the dark streets of York. 'How much more miserable could life get?' Walter wondered. 'A cold April morning, slinging it down with rain and a Monday. Oh bloody joy. Jackie wants us to be all things European at the caff and I'll get to work under Moosewer Gaston, or some such geezer, pretending to be wonderchef. Forty years of bacon butties and I come down to this. Thank you, God, you're a real pal.'

Walter parked his bike outside the caff and pulled up his waterproof cape to search for the shop keys in his jacket. He tried each pocket in turn, the breast pocket and then the inside pocket, but there was no tell-tale jingling.

He sighed and struggled to unbutton his jacket beneath the cape. The rain beat down on his head and dripped into his eyes. He blinked the drops away. His fingers were cold and stiff. He delved into his trouser pockets but the keys weren't there.

Seriously alarmed, Walter patted his legs and rear pockets in an effort to locate the keys. He felt them near his knee. Bugger, they'd gone down into the long truncheon pocket. A retired policeman friend of Walter's had passed his old uniform trousers on to him and now the keys were stuck. Walter twisted and gyrated like some crazed pole dancer lucked out on ecstasy in an effort to fit his big fist into the narrow tube formed to take the truncheon, but to no avail.

He jumped up and down trying to dislodge them, but only succeeded in kicking up puddles of rainwater and soaking his trousers whilst the keys stayed firmly put.

'Bloody Jackie, bloody caff, bloody life, why do you do this to me?' he shouted at the dark cloudy sky. 'Isn't it enough you took Marilyn from me without making my life impossibly difficult now?'

Wet through, hot and panting, he kicked his shoes off and, ignoring the icy cold water seeping through his socks, whipped his trousers off, held them upside down and shook them hard. The keys dropped out into a large puddle.

Walter fished about for them, muttering about all the things he would like to do to a capricious God if he ever came face to face with him.

Quick footsteps sounded behind him. Mrs Walker, from the specialist cake shop on the main street, hurried past. She smirked at his bare backside mooning to the skies. 'Nice day for it, Walter,' she called out and hurried on.

Walter straightened up and grabbed his dripping trousers to cover himself. Cursing at Mrs Walker's retreating back he retrieved the keys and punched the code into the alarm system. Thankfully, he managed the right numbers in the right order and let himself into the caff.

* * * * * *

An hour later, in his clean chef's whites and with a hot cup of tea and bacon buttie inside him, Walter viewed the world in a slightly better light. He wondered if he should pop round to Mrs Walker at the cake shop and explain his earlier actions. She'll never believe me, he decided sadly. Spect she thinks I often do things like that. She's seen too much already, that's her trouble.

He was busy peeling potatoes when he heard the front door bang. Looking out of his kitchen he saw Penny stomping through the caff.

'Good morning, Penny,' he called out.

She marched up to him and glared into his face. 'Good!' she exclaimed. 'Good! Good, it is not. Never say good to me again, Walter.' She wheeled about and went off to the staff room.

Walter's heart sank. It was going to be one of those mornings. He wondered if Kate had got over her Saturday night out with Stan yet. He didn't have to wonder for long. Kate stalked through the café and up to Walter. 'Remind me, Walter, never to listen to you again. "He's such a nice lad",' she mimicked Walter, '"just give him a chance; you won't regret it; he's a gentleman; you'll have a lovely time".' Kate ticked off all Walter's phrases on her fingers, scowling at him. 'Wrong, on every count.' The staff room door banged behind her.

Mm, Stan didn't exaggerate then, it wasn't exactly a success, Walter thought. It just needed Jackie to arrive in a foul mood and that would make a full house. The door opened. In for a penny, Walter, he thought, live dangerously, lad.

'Good morning, Jackie,' he called out heartily.

Jackie wasted no time. She grabbed the lapels on Walter's chef's whites and nearly lifted him off his feet. 'Don't, Walter,' she growled through clenched teeth. 'Just don't, OK, if you want to see sixty-six.' She let him go and marched off into her office slamming the door behind her.

Walter raised his eyes heavenwards. 'Thank you, God' he said. 'You, me and three hormonal women on a wet April Monday. What could be nicer?'

* * * * * *

In the dingy staff room at the back of the café, Kate made coffee for Penny, herself and Jackie. The room was very quiet except for Penny sniffing miserably into her handkerchief.

'The shame of it, Kate,' she wailed. 'Imagine, George and I on the front page of *The Thirsk Trumpeter*, arguing, and him all dressed to kill. What if my neighbours see it? Everyone will know and I'll never live it down. We'll be a laughing stock, have to move, emigrate maybe.'

Kate turned away to make the coffee. She couldn't help but smile at this notion: George as Georgina in *The Trumpeter*. Someone would be bound to put it on Facebook and that wouldn't be so funny for them.

Jackie tried to comfort Penny. 'It's not all bad, Penny, perhaps this will put an end to his nonsense now and he'll go back to being a man.'

Penny sniffed loudly into her handkerchief. 'No, he didn't mind a bit,' she croaked out between sobs. 'He said it's his life and he can do what he wants with it. He likes dressing up and there's no law against it and he's going to carry on. But I don't know if I can stand it.'

A sudden idea came to her and she dropped the hankie from her face. 'Supposing the boys find out now it's in the paper? Whatever will they make of it? Their father a …a…' She couldn't bring herself to say it.

'He's still their father,' Jackie said practically and passed Penny a mug of coffee. 'Here Penny, have a hot drink and calm yourself down. We've a day's work to do and you can't go out front in that state, you'll frighten the customers.'

If Jackie hoped the gentle joke would raise a smile from Penny she was disappointed. Penny disappeared into her handkerchief and Jackie gave up.

Kate brought her coffee to the table and sat down. 'Well at least she got to go out which is more than I did,' she said flatly.

'I thought you were seeing the bachelor baker boy on Saturday night,' Jackie said

'I did and what a disaster that turned out to be.' Kate

sipped her coffee and reflected bitterly. 'I should have listened to you two.'

Curiosity got the better of Penny and she raised her swollen eyes from her hankie. 'We told you it was called the Passion Wagon. Did he live up to it?' Penny asked.

'Did he try that lay-by over the bridge down by the river?' Jackie asked

'None of the above,' Kate said dolefully. 'No octopus arms, no ripping my clothes off with breathless passion, no dinner, no dancing.'

Jackie and Penny were all ears now. They looked at each other questioningly. Who was going to grill her first? Penny dived in. Years of trying to extract information from a houseful of unco-operative males had honed her skills to perfection and she soon had the sorry tale of Kate's Saturday evening with Stan laid out for their dissection.

'He sounds a bit schizo to me,' Jackie said, 'all Mr. Schmooze one minute and a raving looney the next.'

'You'd never think it the way he handles those bread trays,' Penny mused. 'Those lovely blue eyes like limpid pools, you could drown in them. And he's got lovely hands.'

'Oh, Penny.' Kate wanted to hurl her cup of coffee at her. 'Lovely eyes and lovely hands, my foot. Where did that get me? Soaked through, my new suede jacket ruined and a cheese toastie *on my own* at Chez Kate. What a wonderful weekend.'

A short silence followed Kate's outburst.

'Tried to warn you,' Penny ventured.

'Said it was risky,' Jackie agreed.

'Yeah, I know. Sorry girls. It's Walter's fault really, he talked me into it.'

'There's a lesson in there somewhere, Kate,' Jackie said briskly. 'Take it from me, never ever listen to Walter and if you do, do the opposite.'

'Speaking of "dos",' Penny said. 'How did you get on on

Saturday night at that Trades Council thingy you went to? Was it alright?'

'Yes and no,' Jackie said thoughtfully. 'First of all I had to wear a dress that was a bit too tight for me 'cos Marilyn's bloody cat had ruined the little black number I had bought to go in. I'm not sure purple's my colour and I could hardly breathe in it, so it wasn't a great start.

'There was a buffet laid on, with all my least favourite foods, so I took a small plate of everything I didn't like as the only way not to burst out of my dress.'

'So your night out wasn't much better than mine,' Kate said gloomily.

'Well some of it was OK. Tom Young, the President, is drop-dead gorgeous and he's asked me to have lunch with him soon.'

'Get the magic pants out,' Penny offered.

'I'm ahead of you,' Jackie said. 'It was going great and I made a lot of useful contacts to help with the doing up of this place, but…'

'And there's always a "but".'

'Right at the end Tom introduced me to this Nina woman. Mountford-Blayne it says on her card. She came to Marilyn's funeral. I met her there briefly and vaguely remembered her on Saturday so I felt well disposed to her to start with. Turns out she's an interior designer.' Jackie paused looking pensive. 'She's going to re-design the caff. She's got a whole team ready to pounce on us.'

'So…' Light was dawning on Penny and Kate.

'I hear expensive bells ringing,' Kate said.

'Why does she need a team, can't she think on her own?' Penny asked.

'It's her and her team that worry me,' Jackie said slowly. 'I don't know how she did it. I didn't invite her to help on this project, it just happened. One minute we said hello and the next it was "see you on the 11th of May". What am I going to do with her?'

'Ring her up and put her off,' Kate suggested.

'But Tom introduced me especially. He made me so welcome that night; I don't want to throw his kindness back in his face. He might change his mind about lunch with me.'

'And your magic pants.'

'Exactly. They take a stone off me at least; make me look twenty-five instead of thirty-five.'

'Zumba dancing, that's what we need,' Kate said from nowhere.

Penny and Jackie looked at Kate enquiringly. Jackie checked Kate's pulse.

'Mm, normal.'

'What's a zumba got to do with magic pants?' Penny asked.

'You won't need them after a few sessions zumbering. Energetic dancing, South-American style,' she answered Penny's unspoken question. She warmed to her idea. 'That's exactly what we need, all three of us. Forget our troubles and dance the blues out of ourselves and into a size twelve.' She nodded at Jackie. 'You'll drop a few dress sizes in no time. How about it?'

'I don't think…' Penny started to say.

'Not sure if it's for me,' Jackie said.

'Great, I'll take that as a yes then and book the classes. Saw a notice of a beginner's class starting next week in the Hall on the Harrogate Road. Keep Wednesdays free, girls, get ready to zumba.'

* * * * * *

Kate was having a break in the bleak little staff room at the back of the café. It had been two weeks since the disastrous date with Stan. He'd tried several times to ask her out again, but she was having none of it. He could cajole and persuade all he liked; why put herself through all that again? By the time she had got home she was soaked and hungry and, to cap it all off, probably wouldn't dare show her face in her favourite restaurant again. 'No, no, Mr. Peterson, I'm proof against all your charms.'

Kate sipped her coffee reflectively and pondered the world of men. Would she ever find one who would share her interests, and more importantly, stay faithful?

Walter came in and sat down opposite her. He placed a large mug of tea and a doorstep bacon buttie on the table.

'Late breakfast,' he said, indicating his food. 'I slept in this morning and didn't have anything at home. My neighbour had trouble with a ewe lambing. She was a late one and she needed a bit of help. I don't know why the daft bugger keeps sheep. He goes to pieces in a crisis and comes running to me. So there I was, two o'clock in the morning with my hand up a ewe's insides trying to get a load of legs sorted out. She had triplets see. It's a bit like mud wrestling in the dark with an octopus, legs everywhere and you've no idea who they belong to. Got 'em sorted out in the end though, and they all came out alive.' Walter took a bite of his sandwich with relish. 'I'm ready for this, lass.'

Kate smiled and sipped her coffee. 'But at least you've done something worthwhile. That's more than I can say.'

Walter put his sandwich down looking concerned. He leaned across the table. 'Sounds a bit serious, lass. What's up?'

'Oh I don't know, Walter. I think I've got a fit of the blues. I enjoy working here. The staff and customers are lovely, but…' She tailed off.

'Itchy feet?' Walter asked. 'Well that's not surprising is it? Girl like you. You've got brains, good qualifications, time you were using them, lass.' He took another bite of his sandwich and took in Kate's slumped shoulders and listless expression.

'Get the paper. Check over the jobs. Get down the Job Centre. There'll be something for a girl with your titles, Kate. How long have you been here now, nearly a year? Aye, I remember when you first came, full of fury at all men you were. You used to crash pots and slam cutlery down and scowl at any bloke that so much as asked for an extra slice of toast. I don't know how Marilyn put up with you. That chap of yours in Cyprus has a lot to answer for, but it's behind you now, lass, time to move on.'

Kate looked around the dark little staff room and silently agreed. She enjoyed waitressing, she wasn't knocking it, and the new Café Paradise sounded a great place to be if Jackie put all her plans into action. But Walter was right, it was time to move on and she had known it for a while.

'He's not worth it you know,' Walter said.

'Who?'

'That Dave fella in Cyprus. You deserve better. An honest, straightforward Yorkshireman. A man like Stan, for instance.'

Kate rolled her eyes. Walter just had to be kidding. 'No thanks,' she said. 'We tried it remember. Not the most memorable date of my life and I've no wish to repeat it.'

'Women,' Walter reflected as he drank his tea, 'all the bloody same. Never give a man a fighting chance.' Remembering Stan's despair at never being given another chance with Kate, Walter pressed on.

'Alright, so he messed up a bit.' Understatement if there ever was one, Walter thought to himself, but he'd said he'd try. He leaned forward across the table and took Kate's small fair hands in his leathery ones. 'Stan's a good lad, Kate. He's as honest as the day is long. He's kind, he'd never do anyone a bad turn. In fact, he's helped me out loads of times on my holding, would never take a penny for it either. He's always cheerful, he makes you laugh and best of all he thinks the world of you. Give him another chance, lass.' As he waited for Kate's response, Walter thought, Now if that didn't melt a girl's heart then it must be made of ruddy marble.

'Stan the man with a girl in every store,' Kate quoted Penny, 'I don't want that, Walter – "if it's Saturday it must be Kate" routine I want something a bit more meaningful, real, maybe even lasting. Is that too much to ask?'

'He stopped all that nonsense long ago,' Walter said. 'It's just Penny and Jackie have bloody elephant memories. Yeah it went to his head for a few years, girls used to nearly throw themselves at him. How was he supposed to resist? Young, single and good looking. You'd have to be a plaster saint not to. But that was then and this is now. He's grown out of all that, grown up if you like, bit late on maybe but at least he's got there. He's like you, ready for a serious lasting relationship.' Another thought went through Walter's mind, And if that doesn't even the slate up between us, Stanley boy, nothing will.

'Did he put you up to this?' Kate asked suspiciously.

'No of course not,' lied Walter at his wide-eyed and innocent best. 'Stan's too much of a man to get someone else to do his work for him. He knows nowt about it.' If she said yes Stan owed him big-time. His duck-house roof needed renewing and was a two-man job. 'Say yes,' he urged, 'he thinks the world of you, Kate. Just say yes. You've nowt to lose have you, lass?'

Kate weakened. Oh, maybe Walter was right, perhaps she should give Stan another chance. After all, nothing else beckoned on her particular horizon. 'Oh alright, I'll go out with him again. As long as he doesn't pull any stunts like last time.'

Ree-sult. Short of going on the date with him, Walter could do no more. 'You won't regret this, Kate, I promise you,' he said. 'You'll have a great time with Stan. He knows how to treat a lady.'

Memories of spilt beer, crashing tables and running for a

taxi in the pouring rain came back to Kate.

Walter wiped the last of the bacon fat from his plate and popped the bread into his mouth. 'You'll not regret it, lass, I promise you. In fact,' he stood up and brushed away the crumbs, 'you'll be thanking me.'

Walter returned to his kitchen. Left alone once more, Kate contemplated her empty coffee cup. What would Stan have in mind this time? Maybe she enjoyed being put through embarrassing moments, had a masochistic streak in her, like banging her head against a wall. It might be better to do that than risk a second time with Stan. But too late now, she had agreed to it.

CHAPTER 19

The morning had not gone well and tempers were starting to fray in the café. Walter's wet clothes, smelling of the farmyard, were gently steaming dry in the staff room. A strong whiff of eau-de-cowpat intermittently filtered through to the café whenever the door was opened.

Jackie ground her teeth. How many more ways could Walter find to drive her up the wall. Added to that, she had a long queue of customers waiting for their mid-morning coffee and as usual the coffee machine, now almost on its last legs, was playing up. Clouds of steam erupted from it every time she went near it, adding more moisture to the already soggy atmosphere in the café. Customers were standing steaming in sodden clothing and pools of water collected into puddles as coats dripped off the backs of chairs.

Penny was helping Walter in the kitchen as the old range cooker was misbehaving and only Penny had the patience and knack to deal with it. Walter would have taken a hammer to it. Kate was left on her own to fly around delivering breakfasts and mid-morning snacks at high speed to try and keep up with the demand.

Into the mayhem stepped the elegant and sultry Nina Mountford-Blayne. She paused in the doorway for everyone to take in her turquoise coat with its deep sweeping collar and contrasting silk scarf threaded underneath. Her pose showed off her long slender legs encased in cream leather boots. Raven black curls set off her tanned olive skin and brown eyes to perfection.

For a few seconds the loud buzz of conversation in the café was muted. As the moment passed, Nina moved into the body of the café, hand outstretched to greet Jackie. Flustered, Jackie wiped her hands on her apron and returned Nina's handshake, 'You're a bit early, Nina.' She gestured to the queue of people at the counter. 'I'll have to serve my customers before I can give you any time. Would you like to take a look round and then have a seat? Is *he* with you?' she gestured to the willowy youth standing a little apart.

'Oh yes,' Nina said a little surprised, as if she'd forgotten she had brought him. 'Aubrey, my Assistant.'

'Chief Assistant,' Aubrey added firmly. 'PA, really. I'm in charge of everything, next to Nina that is.' He gazed at her adoringly.

'Yes, well, give me ten minutes and we can have a chat. Look, that couple's leaving now. You go and sit at that table and I'll be over as soon as I can. I'll get Kate to bring you some coffee.'

Nina eyed up the heavy pot mugs and declined the offer. 'I'm a lapsang souchong girl … don't suppose you…? No, never mind then.'

She and Aubrey drifted over to the table at the back of the café. Aubrey opened his briefcase and pulled out a laptop which he set up on the table. Diving into the bag again he produced a laser tape measure.

'I'll leave you to measure up and get it all logged in, darling,' Nina said to him. 'I'll have a little walk round and get to know the old place. I need to bond with it before I can bring it to life again; get to know its ways, its feelings and the vibrations that pulse through its very walls.' She hugged a supporting pillar as she said this and stroked her hands slowly down its length.

'I feel purple,' she said.

'Purple,' Aubrey tapped into the laptop.

'Mustard.'

"Mustard,' repeated Aubrey.

'With tartan swathes as a nod to our cousins over the border.'

Nina wandered off towards the kitchen and Aubrey got on with the task of measuring up the café. He tapped everything into his laptop and in no time at all had a three-dimensional model of the room up on his screen. Very soon Nina was back. She sat down opposite him.

'There's a philistine in the kitchen,' she announced. 'He's never heard of Martins of Mayfair. Says we can do equally as well at B&Q or Wickes.' She shuddered. 'Mass produced units that every Tom, Dick and Harry has at home. That's not for us. This is a Mountford-Blayne creation. I see cupboards handcrafted from seasoned oak or maple, Farrow & Ball pastels, Liberty fabrics, *objets d'art* in every corner for famished customers to feast their eyes on.'

'Delicious darling,' Aubrey breathed. 'You're a genius.'

In the kitchen Walter stabbed his knife into a potato and twisted it forcefully to remove the embedded dirt. 'Nina Mountford-Blayne, of all the people.' He stabbed another potato and jerked out a growth. 'What does she know about equipping a kitchen? She only lives on a lettuce leaf, you can tell that. Is Jackie out of her mind employing her? She'll fleece her.'

'It's that Trades Council.' Penny deftly flipped the sausages in the pan. 'Nina sort of wished herself on Jackie before she knew where she was. She doesn't want her at all, but doesn't want to give offence and send her packing. That President, Tom Young, recommended her and she fancies him.'

'Who does?'

'Jackie.'

'That girl hasn't the sense she was born with. He's another one like that Nina, take the eyes out of your head and come

178

back for the sockets. Shall I get rid of the lass?'

'No, leave it to Jackie,' Penny advised. 'She's got to find her feet. This might be the way to do it.'

'Bloody expensive way by the sound of it.' Walter decapitated a frost-bitten potato. The blackened head rolled along the table and he hurled it into the bin. 'Bloody Mountford-Blayne,' he muttered.

Nina might have picked up the colour vibrations emanating from the café, but thankfully Walter's venomous thoughts did not make their way out to her as she was now seated at the back of the café. Aubrey was still tapping instructions into his laptop.

She looked about her. The man and woman at the next table were tucking into a fine looking fried breakfast with extra toast and marmalade lined up to follow. Nina raised her eyebrows. Glancing behind her a woman with two young children approached with a tray laden with milkshakes and chocolate-covered cream cakes.

'You know, unsweetened juice and a handful of nuts and raisins would be much more nutritious,' she said to the mother.

'Pardon, love? Wait a minute, Emily, the lady's talking.'

'Or a banana with fat-free yoghurt mixed in. You should be more responsible in your children's food choices, set them a good example.'

The mother on hearing this became red-faced and furious. 'You mind your own business, madam. I didn't ask for your advice and I certainly wouldn't want to be a stick like you.' She banged the tray down on the table and the milk-shake spilled out. The children started to cry. 'Now see what you've done.'

Nina shrugged her shoulders and turned her attention to the couple quietly eating their breakfast. They had looked round to see what the commotion was about.

'You can't help some people can you?' Nina smiled

sweetly at them.

'What was all that about?' asked the man.

'I was simply pointing out the dangers of all the food that mother was loading up her children with. It could lead to their early deaths.'

The man looked alarmed. 'Could it?'

Nina leaned forward earnestly and pointed to his plate. 'Look at all that,' she commanded. 'A heart attack waiting to happen. Madam,' she nodded to his wife, 'get your husband some muesli or porridge for his breakfast, not this greasy stuff. It's disgusting.'

'Now look here,' the woman rose angrily, 'don't you go telling me how to look after my husband. A perfect stranger coming in here and flinging your weight about, not that there's much of that. I bet your old man cuddles up to a bag of bones of a night-time. You push off and mind your own business.'

'She says you're killing me,' the husband chimed in. 'Are you trying to get rid of me? She says this is all fat.'

From behind the coffee counter Jackie could see that Nina was causing some disturbance. She left her queue of customers and hurried to the back of the café.

'Is something the matter?' she asked the couple.

'We only came in for a late breakfast and you set the thought police on us,' said the wife angrily.

Jackie was icy. 'Miss Mountford-Blayne is a designer and has no business to comment on my customers' choices. If you would like to step into my office, Miss Blayne, I will be with you shortly.'

She pointed to her office door. Nina shrugged her shoulders and moved off. Aubrey sat open mouthed. 'Shall I…?'

'You sit tight, young man,' Jackie barked. 'Your employer will not be long.'

Jackie marching towards her office door caught a frazzled

Kate. 'Look after the counter for five minutes, please. I'll be as quick as I can.'

'And shove a broom up my ar…'

'And sweep the floor as you go. Yes, if you like.' Jackie continued on into her office. She closed the door firmly behind her and turned to face Nina who was leaning back in Marilyn's old chair studying Jackie's latest invoices.

'How dare you!' Jackie snatched the sheaf of invoices from Nina's grasp. 'Your mother obviously never told you to respect other people's privacy. Thanks to you, I've probably lost good customers this morning. What were you thinking of, telling them how to live their lives?'

Nina's brown eyes darkened and she tossed her glossy black curls back defiantly. 'That's where you're wrong, Miss Dalrymple-Jones. All people need to be told how to live their lives. Mostly they are not clever, they are too simple to know how to live properly. They need directing. I am someone who can do this.'

'What?' Jackie was incredulous.

'Yes, you may look, but it's true. Look at those people out there. They eat and drink all that's bad for them and then they get sick and can't work and are a drain on our state. They become useless.' She banged her fist on Jackie's desk. 'They have to be told clearly and firmly what to eat, where to live and always to work hard. I do that. I tell the people wherever I go. All the world should be like that. I am going to stand for the Council, then be an MP, and when I get into power everything will be different. So. There we are. I'm sorry you've lost some customers today, but I might have saved their lives. They will thank me.'

Jackie put her hand over her mouth to stop her jaw from falling open. 'As you see, we're very busy this morning, Miss Blayne. You've had the opportunity to look around and I see your assistant has made a model of our premises on his laptop, so perhaps you'd like to return to your own offices now and come up with some ideas for us.'

'Very well, Miss Dalrymple-Jones,' Nina rose and offered her be-ringed hand to Jackie. 'I'll consult with the top members of my design team. Don't worry I'll return with some great designs. You'll adore them.'

Waving them off, Jackie had a hunch that was the last thing she would feel about Nina Mountford-Blayne's designs.

Walter stood in his kitchen doorway and watched them go. 'So what did you make of her?' he asked Jackie.

'Completely barking,' Jackie said tranquilly. 'About two minutes away from a straightjacket, I would say.'

'Aye,' Walter assented. 'Told me me and my kind would be expendable soon. Folk will only eat fruit, seeds and nuts according to her. She reckons we only need a juicer and a smoothie machine in the new kitchen and maybe a coffee machine, but only because she likes George Clooney.'

'Did she call you expendable?'

'Yeah. I would have preferred redundant. Did she get it wrong?'

'No, I think she meant it. I told you; she's more than a few slates off, the whole roof's obviously gone.'

* * * * * *

'She said it was the devil's food.' Penny briskly buttered a toasted teacake and put it on the tray along with dishes of butter and jam.

'Man's humble banger,' Kate exclaimed.

'Yes, along with the bacon, eggs and mushrooms on the plate too. Said if she had her way I and all the others like me would be re-programmed into healthy eating. She must think she can flick a few of our switches and we'll instantly change, like Aubrey's pictures on his laptop.'

'She says she's going to run for the Council and then for

parliament.'

'She'd make York City a fat-free zone as her first action,' Penny mused. 'Do you remember when places used to be called nuclear-free zones, I never could work that one out either.'

'It'll never happen. Jackie says she's completely barking and could get carted off any day.'

'Anyway,' Penny paused in her buttering, her knife held mid-air, 'I expect the devil loves bangers. He wouldn't get any better than Walter's finest when he's on form and the stove's not playing up. So really there's nothing wrong with devil's food is there. Do you think she was paying us a compliment?' Penny added doubtfully.

Kate gave up. There was nothing to be done with Penny in this mood. She changed the subject. 'How's George getting on these days? Has he got over Thirsk yet?'

Penny shuddered. 'Never mention that place again, Kate. It is forbidden territory in our house. Thankfully, my boys never got to hear about it.'

'Only because you drove around buying up every copy of *The Thirsk Trumpeter* you could lay your hands on.'

'Cost me a fortune,' Penny said. 'Well not me. I made sure George paid up. It was his fault after all, making an exhibition of himself in the middle of the market square.'

Kate loaded up the tray with the pot of tea and waited for Penny to finish the teacakes.

'He still dresses up at home, but he's gone off going out in his frocks. He didn't like being stared at, but what did he expect? Six foot four, was he ever going to look like a woman, I ask you?'

'Well at least you'll be spared that again.' Kate was sympathetic.

Penny looked up from her work. 'There … are … clubs...' she whispered.

'Clubs?' Kate repeated.

'For, you know, people like him, who like to, you know…'

'Oh yeah, that kind of club. Wow, is he going to try one?'

'So he says,' Penny sighed.

'Is he going all dressed up?'

'I suppose so. I don't know. Suppose they got stopped by a policeman or had an accident and got taken to hospital, imagine that. Perhaps they get dressed up when they get there.'

'Sounds serious stuff,' Kate commented. 'Does he want to take it further?'

'I don't know,' Penny said, 'I don't think he knows, maybe that's why he's going. I *think* he just wants somewhere he can be himself along with others of the same kind. I think I can live with that if I have to, but supposing he wanted to … you know … really be a woman. What then? Where would that leave us?'

Penny piled the teacakes on to a clean plate and dropped it on to Kate's tray. 'Would it be Mrs and Miss Montague then?'

'Hey,' Kate put the tray down and gave Penny a hug. 'Let's not get that far ahead. He's still George. He's a man, he goes to work, he loves his wife.' Kate paused. 'Is he still interested in…?'

'Sex?' Penny finished for her. 'No. I think we're at that age where he just doesn't really see me any more. If I danced naked in front of him, except for a strategic rose or two, he wouldn't notice. Probably ask for a second helping of pudding.'

* * * * * *

Stan came in the back door of the café and into the kitchen laden with trays of bread, rolls and teacakes. He began to unpack them on to the shelves. After years of delivering to Café Paradise, he knew where everything was kept.

Walter came in for some eggs. 'Now, lad, I've got some good news for you.'

'I could do with some, Walter. Kate's been giving me the cold shoulder, my boss has gone into deep depression because we didn't reach the target of a million loaves last week and he's snapping at our heels every minute of the day to sell, sell, sell. Doesn't he know there's a recession on? Then my mother fell on the ice and broke her leg so I'm round her house every morning and night and then I have to walk that daft French poodle of hers last thing. So as long as you're not cancelling your order or wanting your dog walking, anything's good news.'

Stan emptied the last of his trays and turned to face Walter. The broad smile on Walter's face brought him up short. 'You haven't…? She hasn't…? Has she?'

Walter nodded. 'I used all my tact and finesse, lad, and eventually triumphed.'

Stan danced Walter about the kitchen. 'Didn't know you had any, Walter, but thank you, thank you, thank you. I owe you big-time.'

'Well you'd best make hay while the sun shines, lad.' Walter extricated himself from Stan's arms. 'She's waiting on in the caff just now. Nip in and surprise her. Go in with a definite plan. You know like, Friday, Peter's Jazz Club, supper at Dino's.' Walter shuffled off to the back kitchen. 'And talking about owing big-time, I've a new duck-house roof to put on. I could do with a hand.'

'I'll be there Saturday, Walter, just put that vicious old drake of yours out of the way before I get there. He nearly had my leg off last time.'

'Monty?' Walter was surprised. 'Never. He's as gentle as they come.'

'About as gentle as a piranha fish after meat. I've the scars to prove it. Lock him up, Walter, please.'

'Wimp,' Walter muttered as he went back to his work.

'Monty's a vegetarian, doesn't go for meat.'

Left behind in the kitchen, Stan took a few moments to ponder the situation. He needed to woo his Kate afresh. This time he wasn't going to let her slip through his fingers like his keys did last time.

He strode into the café. Kate was stacking crockery at the old dresser. Stan spun her around to look at him.

'It is my lady; O it is my love! O that she knew she were!'

'Appropriate. Romeo Act 2, Scene 2.'

Stan held firmly on to her. 'Saturday, The Fair on the Green, then supper at Dino's. I'll pick you up at eight o'clock. I can't make it earlier as I've to see to my mother and the dog, she's broken her leg.'

'The dog?'

'No, my mother. She's laid up so I walk her dog. Poncy French poodle. I feel a right idiot, but don't want it peeing in the house, so needs must. Never mind about that, just say yes, please. We can have some fun. Think of it, Kate, the waltzers, the flying horses, ferris wheel, and I'll win you a teddy at the shooting gallery. What do you say?'

'Yes, I'd love to, Stan, but maybe not the ferris wheel,' Kate said. 'I suffer a bit from vertigo.'

'Oh, you'd be fine on it,' Stan grinned happily. 'It goes really slowly, nothing to be frightened of and the views from the top are fantastic. I'll look after you.'

'Read my lips,' Kate enunciated slowly, 'ver ... ti ... go, as in don't like heights.'

'It's not really high and you're secure in this glassed-in box, so you're quite safe. You'll love it, Kate, I promise. I took my mum up before she broke her leg. She didn't break it up there by the way, she fell on the ice and she loved it, not breaking her leg, the ferris wheel and she doesn't like heights either so there you go.'

'Yeah. Mm, we'll see.' Kate was still dubious.

'Great, see you on Saturday. "Sleep dwell upon thine

eyes, peace in your breast. Farewell".' He kissed Kate gently on her cheek and let her go.

Feeling elated, he made his way back out of the café and encountered Jackie checking the supplies.

'Those Yorkshire Fat Rascals and Curd Tarts are going well,' Jackie commented.

'It just so happens I've got extra on the van today,' Stan said rubbing his hands. 'I'll let you have first crack at them.'

'Is your boss having a sales drive again? Got new targets?'

'You're getting as bad as your great-aunt Madeleine, Jackie,' Stan said mournfully.

'I'll take that as a compliment.'

'It isn't.'

'And you know what you can do with your Fat Rascals.'

'Supply you with two dozen extra,' he said hopefully.

'No.' Jackie ticked the last items off her list and turned back to the café. 'And if you're taking Kate out again, make a better fist of it this time. She deserves it. We'll be watching.'

'Well, thank you, Miss Dalrymple-Jones,' Stan said to her retreating back. 'And Fat Rascals to you too.'

Back at her coffee machine Jackie looked at Kate and felt a pang of envy. How lucky she was to have Stan chasing after her. She felt very much alone at that moment and then tried to console herself with the thought of the promised lunch date with Tom Young. She waited for the familiar wave of excitement to flow over her, but instead Barney Anderson's handsome face and blue eyes took his place. Shocked, Jackie stood still.

'Two coffees and bacon sarnies please, love,' went unheeded as Jackie tried to dismiss the dosser boy from her thoughts.

CHAPTER 20

Barney Anderson lugged the shopping out of his car boot and up the stairs to his flat. He hoped that by now Melissa would have managed to tear herself away from the TV and have tidied the place up a bit. His mother had instilled tidiness and consideration for others into him in preparation for life at boarding school. Barney knew that for people to live and work together harmoniously, these two virtues were a must.

Unfortunately, Melissa's family had not found these virtues important or instilled any kind of moral behaviour into her. Now that they had lived cheek by jowl for several weeks, Barney had discovered her to be an almost feral animal, living for herself, in the moment, with no thought or consideration for others.

Matters had reached a head last night when Barney came home late, tired from a long day at the Citizens Advice Bureau and visits to the local police station. He found the flat once again like a bomb site with Melissa's now familiar trail of wet bath towels, clothes and make-up everywhere and a now ruined coffee table stained and burned with her nail polish remover.

Melissa, oblivious to all the mess around her, was beautiful, bright-eyed and dressed up to the nines, waiting to be taken out to dinner. Barney hit the roof. What had Melissa been doing all day other than sleeping, eating and beautifying?

'But that's my job, Barney darling,' Melissa protested

tearfully. 'We models have to take care of ourselves. My face and body are my shop window. I have to spend time on myself.'

'Have you been in touch with your agency about a job?'

'Yes of course I have, Barney darling, but there isn't much around for me at the moment. I am trying, honestly.' Her baby-blue eyes were at their widest.

'Well, if there isn't modelling work about, Melissa, it's time you looked for something else and learned to support yourself and stand on your own two feet.'

Melissa started to cry, but Barney stood his ground. A few months of having Melissa and her slapdash, lazy ways in his flat had hardened his heart.

'You've been here for over two months already, Melissa. I took you in on the understanding it was to be a temporary arrangement and I don't think you've done a day's work since you've been here.'

He gestured to the bag of shopping. 'You could have done this, maybe prepared a meal even, or at the very least cleaned up this unholy mess. Tomorrow, Melissa, things are going to change big time.'

He took a deep breath and made himself say what he had wanted to say for weeks now, in fact ever since the night Melissa had moved in.

'I am not your boyfriend, Melissa, I never have been. I think I'm just a meal ticket.'

'Barney,' Melissa exclaimed and flew to throw her arms about him.

He held her off. 'It's OK, I'm too old for you, you're too young for me, let's just leave it at that. But I mean what I say. Tomorrow we find you a job and then hopefully a place of your own.'

Regardless of all he had said, Melissa attempted to snuggle into his chest. 'Can't we go out to eat, just tonight,' she coaxed. 'I promise I'll be good tomorrow and do all those things you said.'

Barney pointed to the shopping. 'I've bought some fresh mackerel and pasta for supper, you'll love it. Oily fish, great for your heart and circulation. It will keep you young and beautiful.'

'Mackerel! Yuk! Pleb food.' Melissa pouted. 'Can't we go out to Dino's? They do a lovely steak tartare.'

'Too much red meat is bad for you.' Barney grinned. He had recovered his good humour. The thought of finally getting Melissa out to work and out of his life lifted his spirits. 'Mackerel, or starve, my girl.'

'Well I'll starve then, you old meanie.' Melissa turned and ran off to her room.

Barney's grin widened. He would give her half an hour. She had the appetite of a hard working navvy. There was no way she would do without her supper.

As he stuffed the fish with fresh herbs and made a light sauce he imagined Jackie sitting down to eat with him. They would drink chilled white wine and fork up tiny portions of the flaky fish for each other.

'Yeah, and in a parallel universe I'm James Bond.'

* * * * * *

'I've made the appointment for this afternoon. Mornings are no good to Melissa; she doesn't open her eyes until noon. At least the Job Centre's a starting point. She's a complete nightmare, Jake. It's like inviting a wild animal into your house that you've no hope of ever house training. Only, I didn't invite her, she just landed on me.'

Barney and his friend Jake were having coffee at the Citizens Advice Bureau.

'But enough is enough, I've got to get her a job and then out of my flat. I can't stand her much longer.'

Jake whistled. 'She's so fantastic, Barney, I'd take her on

anytime if she'd look at me, which she wouldn't. I'm too poor and plain.'

'And there you have it, my friend. Our Melissa is after rich and handsome, which I'm not,' he added modestly. 'But it's time she was out of my hair.'

'Rich and handsome eh?' Jake's craggy face looked thoughtful. 'Barney my boy, I have the answer to your prayers.' He jumped up and bustled out to the general office.

'Susie!' he shouted.

A young woman working at a desk looked up. 'Steady on, I'm not deaf.'

Jake ignored this. 'Did I dream it or did I hear you talking about Tom Young at the Trades Council looking for a new receptionist?'

'No dream, honey,' replied Susie. 'His last is moving to London, got taken on by a modelling agency, so he's looking for new eye candy.'

'Terrific.' Jake grinned widely at a puzzled Susie and departed. He stopped in Barney's doorway and bowed. 'Rich and handsome Tom Young, President of the Trades Council, seeks blonde bimbo, nominally as receptionist cum secretary, whereas in fact solid Mrs Carson actually does all the work. Blonde bimbo' Jake continued, 'a.k.a. Melissa Gatenby seeks rich and handsome escort. Voilà, if that isn't a marriage made in heaven I'll eat hay with all the donkeys in Yorkshire.'

Barney could hardly contain his delight. 'Jake. Man, I could kiss you. No, I promise I won't,' he added hurriedly as Jake backed off in alarm. 'Young is the answer to a maiden's prayer and most certainly mine. How do you know about this?'

Jake sat down and picked up his coffee again. 'Heard Susie telling Marsha this morning. They were doing that woman thing – you know – He isn't? He is? Is he??? lark, and then – He never! Then, He never!!, then, He DID!!!

Did he???? So I gave up and did the man thing and made the coffee.'

Barney paced up and down his office looking thoughtful. 'This could be our chance, Jake,' he said sitting down again. 'We've wanted to nail Tom Young for long enough. If I can keep Melissa on side we might learn a lot more about the goings on in his office.'

'You might have to put up with her at home for a bit longer,' Jake commented.

'It might be worth it just for that. Yes, let's do it,' Barney said decisively and swallowed the last of his coffee.

* * * * * *

Barney pushed open the door of the Café Paradise and the familiar aromas of coffee, chips and bacon hit him. He was very hungry but tried to ignore the rumblings of his stomach. He was on an urgent mission. Jackie was in her usual place at the coffee counter. He had to contain his impatience whilst she served the two customers in front of him.

'We...ell,' Jackie drawled looking him up and down. In his haste Barney had forgotten it was a court day for him. He was dressed in a suit and tie. Jackie slowly poured his usual cappuccino.

Life's so bloody unfair. Dosser Boy in a suit and he looks drop-dead gorgeous.

'What's the occasion?' she nodded at his clothes.

Barney looked down at himself. 'These. Oh, I'm in court today. I like to impress the magistrate, you know. Show I've taken a bit of trouble.'

He stood there hoping desperately she would ask the right questions and he could tell her what he did. Stubbornly, he didn't want to just come out with it.

'What you up for?' She shook the powdered chocolate

over his coffee.

'Non-payment of council tax. Final demand and all other channels have been exhausted, so this is the end of the line.'

'Humph.' Jackie tried to take in what Barney was saying but just the sight of him standing before her, clean-shaven, his blonde hair nicely cut and brushed made her slightly weak at the knees.

Why did God give the good looks to all the wrong people and, no, you don't fancy Barney Anderson, Jackie, do you hear me? Jackie thought. Never mind his beautiful face, lovely voice and spadesful of charm, sexy bum or anything else. He's a dosser boy OK. He's just had the brass neck to stand in front of you and admit it. He'd sooner go to court than pay his way.

Why does it have to be this way? Why can't that be a business suit he's wearing? Why can't he be on my side of the fence and why am I so conventional?

'Why can't she see beyond the clothes, really look at me, talk to me, try to get to know me?' Barney asked himself. 'Why do I like her so much, find her sooo attractive? Her lovely peachy skin and deep bosoms. Oh God, Jackie Dalrymple-Jones, if you only knew what you did to a man.'

The cappuccino stood cooling on the counter between them and they stood motionless staring at it.

Penny passed by with a tray of buttered crumpets. 'Ooh Barney, you look gorgeous enough to eat. George is working tonight. Can I take you home as my toy boy?'

The spell was broken and Barney found himself breathing again.

'I need to ask you a favour,' he said.

'Go on,' Jackie wiped her cloth over the sparkling counter and did not look at him.

'Melissa Gatenby, who is staying with me at the moment,' he began.

'Your glamorous girlfriend,' Jackie said morosely.

'She's not my girlfriend,' Barney said.

'Not what I heard.'

'Then you heard wrong,' Barney said firmly.

'Why's she living with you then? Another dosser?'

'I'm not a dosser. She's not a dosser. She's a model but work is slack just now and she's looking for a job. I hear your friend Tom Young's looking for a new receptionist and wondered if you might put a good word in for her.'

'Why?'

'Why not?'

'Why would I put a good word in for her? I hardly know her. Only seen her in here a few times. She looks more ornamental than useful.'

And I am just so jealous, thought Jackie.

'I'm sure Tom would find her extremely efficient,' he lied. 'Please, Jackie.' He hunkered down to make her look at him. 'If Melissa gets a job she can get her own accommodation, move on and stop driving me round the bend. Please.'

Violet eyes locked on to blue.

'Alright. I'll give Tom a ring. Tell her to get herself round there this afternoon.'

Elated, Barney leaned over and kissed her cheek. 'Thanks, Jackie, thanks a lot. You won't regret this, I promise. What goes around comes around.'

He dashed out leaving the cappuccino on the counter.

Oh yeah, and what's coming round for me, I wonder, Jackie thought sourly.

* * * * * *

Several fruitless phone calls later and Barney eventually roused a sleepy Melissa from her bed.

'A job,' she squeaked, 'this afternoon? Oh Barney, it's only eleven o'clock. I haven't even started my beauty routine. You can't seriously expect me to be in town by one o'clock.'

'I seriously do, Melissa, or your bags will be packed and you'll be out on the street again.'

'Oh alright, you old bully you. I'll be there.' A very cross Melissa put the phone down.

'I'll suffer for this when I get home,' Barney grinned across the office at Jake. 'Melissa's mess will meet me at the door and she'll tell me it's all my fault because I made her rush. But I don't care, if it gets her a job and out of my life. Cross everything you've got that our Melissa is just what Tom Young wants in a receptionist.'

* * * * * *

At one o'clock Samantha Rawling admitted Melissa into the Trades Council offices. The two highly polished young women eyed each other up and down like a pair of feral cats preparing to fight.

'Mr Anderson says you're a model,' Samantha began doubtfully, reading the information Barney had supplied and looking at Melissa.

Melissa tossed her glossy blonde curls. 'Yes of course. Only I have been so busy with assignments lately that I felt I needed a change, something completely different, sweetie.' Melissa sat down, crossed her long, elegant legs and looked at Samantha defiantly.

'Of course, darling,' Samantha purred. 'That's exactly what I said when no-one wanted me. But times change and maybe they will for you too, darling. I'm off to London tomorrow, the toppest of top agencies has signed me, so you can have darling Tom with my blessing.'

Tom's buzzer sounded and Samantha conducted a defeated Melissa into the inner sanctum.

Tom Young came forward from behind his desk, smiling appreciatively at Melissa. Working from her blonde hair downward, he took in her lithe slim body. She would do

195

nicely. A young sexy blonde to grace his reception and, who knows, maybe even his bed if he played his cards right.

He dismissed Samantha with a nod. She was yesterday's news. 'Well, hello, Melissah,' he crooned. 'How lovely to meet you. Come and sit down.' He indicated an expensive looking sofa and slid into the seat beside her. 'Tell me all about yourself. In fact, I've got a better idea. Why don't we discuss this little matter over a long and very expensive lunch? Trades Council expenses, of course. Interviewing has to be thorough and *rrrigorous.*'

He rolled his tongue over the words. Oh yes, I'd like to be rigorous with Miss Gatenby here, he thought.

'Oh, Mr Young, how lovely.' Melissa batted her eyelashes at him and produced a dazzling smile.

'Tom,' he purred, entranced already. 'Call me Tom.'

Two hours later, sated and a little tipsy, they emerged into the watery March sunshine. Melissa kissed Tom on the cheek. 'Such fun, Tom, thank you. I'll see you on Monday. It's going to be lovely, I just know it.'

'As lovely as you are, O beautiful Melissa.' He hailed a passing taxi and put her in, standing in the street to wave her off.

Later that evening, when Barney finally arrived home from his office, Melissa was tucked up watching the latest soap opera, and drinking his finest Merlot.

'Celebrating, darling,' she called out to him without taking her eyes from the screen. 'I'm a working girl.'

'Who hasn't actually done any yet,' Barney remarked drily. 'Don't suppose you thought about supper.'

'I had the most divine lunch with the divine Tom, I don't need supper now.'

'No,' said Barney flatly. 'So I suppose I don't either. That's OK, Barney,' he said to the air, 'you just quietly starve in the corner here. Don't make a fuss. No-one will notice.'

'Sshh, you're spoiling *Eastenders*,' Melissa called, sipping her wine.

'Oh pardon me.' Right now Barney didn't care. Melissa had got a job, freedom beckoned. He skipped happily out to his kitchen.

CHAPTER 21

Stan parked his car and rushed into his house. That wretched dog of his mother's would pick tonight of all nights to be sick all over her best rug. It had taken him ages to clean it all up, especially with his mother watching him from her chair and pointing out all the bits he had missed. If he'd gone on much longer, he'd have shampooed the entire room.

Heading up the stairs, Stan shed his clothes as he went. He grabbed his razor and shaving gel and got into the shower. He didn't want to be late to collect Kate so he'd just have to risk the shower/shave combo.

If only his mother hadn't broken her leg and been laid up for so long. If only she'd never gone and bought that wretched poodle and spoilt it rotten. No wonder it kept being sick. A diet of best steak and chocolate wasn't ideal for a small dog. But the silly woman had a complete blind-spot where the mutt was concerned and wouldn't listen to himself or the vet.

Soaping himself vigorously Stan imagined re-incarnation as a golden Labrador and being fed rump steak and dark chocolate. It would be OK, especially if Kate was doing the feeding.

He cleaned the steam from the small mirror perched on the shower tray. Swiftly he stropped the razor over his face to remove the days growth of beard.

'Oh hell,' he exclaimed and 'hell' again as one, then the

other, side of his face spurted blood. Obviously it was time for a new blade.

He stepped out of the shower dabbing at the blood running down his face and rummaged in the bathroom cabinet for some cotton wool. He stuck a piece on either cheek and tried to dry himself without any further mishap.

In the bedroom he took his best shirt off its hanger and slipped it on. Buttoning it he moved to the mirror to check his face. To his dismay he saw he had managed to transfer blood from his hands on to his shirt.

Stan ripped the shirt off and ran back to the bathroom to rinse his hands and check out his cut face. Thankfully the cotton wool was doing its job and mopping up the blood.

He ran back to his wardrobe, searching for another shirt. In despair he rejected them. They were mostly the old shirts he kept for his re-enactment days. With a sinking heart he realised his other good shirts were still awaiting ironing.

He kept his ironing board set up in the spare bedroom and ironed his shirts when he needed them. Cursing his own laziness Stan grabbed another white shirt from a loaded basket and flung it across the board.

Whilst the iron heated up, he hurried into his trousers and shoes and brushed his hair. Gently he dabbed some aftershave on his cheeks, wincing as the spirit dried on his sore face. He could almost hear his mother's favourite expression, 'more haste, less speed, Stan, how many times do I have to tell you?' He grimaced at himself in the mirror. For once she was right. He looked like he'd just gone a couple of rounds in the ring.

Well he couldn't help that now. He went back to iron his shirt. Quickly pressing out the creases his mind went anxiously back to yesterday when he and Walter were putting the new roof on the duck house.

'Just be yourself, lad.' Walter had urged him. 'She knows you already as the happy go lucky Stan, like she sees at the café every day. That's the lad she likes. You don't have to impress her with all your history stuff. Don't expect she's ready for all that. Just take it steady. Aim to go and enjoy yourselves. You can't go wrong at the fair, can you?'

Stan paused a moment, cheered by this thought. It was Easter Saturday, holiday time. They would just go out and have some fun, have a bag of chips and a hot dog. That wouldn't cause them any trouble tonight.

As these reflections ended, so did the life of Stan's shirt. An acrid smell of burnt linen rose up from the ironing board. Stan looked down and yelped in disbelief. His second best shirt now had a deep brown scorch mark right in the centre. Why couldn't it have been on the tail or sleeve where it wouldn't show under his jacket?

Frantically, he rummaged in the basket and found a floral-patterned shirt. That would have to do. No other good ones were clean. Silently, he sent up a plea-bargain, 'God, I promise I'll be a model of all things housewifely after tonight, if you'll just let me get dressed and get to Kate on time.'

Stan must have been in favour as nothing else happened to delay him and he made it across the city to Kate's flat in record time. It was a fine April evening and she was waiting outside for him. Stan got out and went round to open the car door for her.

She eyed his floral shirt and the cotton wool balls stuck on his face. 'Did I miss something?' she asked.

'Eh?'

'It's not the first of the month is it?'

'Course not, you know it isn't. It's the twelfth.'

She grinned up at him. 'Thought you'd been playing white-rabbits at home. You know, where you go down the stairs backwards being a white rabbit, to bring good luck for the month ahead.' She touched his cheek. 'All that cotton wool…'

In his haste Stan had forgotten to remove it. He snatched it off his cheeks and stuffed it in his pocket. 'I was late home and shaved in a hurry, made a bit of a mess.'

His words tailed off as he looked at Kate. She took his breath away she was so gorgeous. She wore slim-fitting jeans and a warm woolly jumper. Stan could hardly take his eyes off her. He stood staring down at her, just smiling.

Kate smiled back. 'Come on then, let's not stand here all night like a pair of numpties.' She jumped into the car and made herself comfortable.

'Were you late home from your round today?' Kate asked as they made their way to the fairground just outside the city centre.

'No, it wasn't work that was the problem. It was my mother's broken leg and the dog again. It hasn't mended as fast as it should as she's older; my mother, not the dog. So I'm still walking the mutt, a pampered poodle. And it's as unco-operative as she is. I took it all around her roads; poop scoop and bag at the ready, and it did nothing. The minute it got home, it cocked its leg on her armchair, poohed on the carpet and, just to really finish things off, was sick all over her best Chinese rug. Needless to say, poodles are not my favourite species just now. Nor is my mother. She overfeeds it and then wonders why it gets poorly. Rump steak and doggie chocs all day. I ask you, Kate, wouldn't you be poorly on that lot'

'I might, but I'd really enjoy it. Only make it proper chocolate and then I'll be in heaven.'

The evening seemed set fair. Stan relaxed, pleased to be in Kate's company. For once all was going well.

The field next to the fairground had been set aside for car parking and it seemed as if all York had turned out as hundreds of cars were already parked up. Stan managed to find a space and squeezed the Kia in. Soon they were strolling arm in arm towards the fair. It was in full swing.

Loud music and the screams of the terrified revellers filled the air. The waltzers were whizzing round, lights flashing and music blaring, whilst the twister rose and fell in the distance. Kate and Stan walked around, watching excited children drive their parents around in the dodgem cars, squealing with delight as they crashed and banged their way around the course.

Interspersed, were the gentler rides for children. Kate smiled as she watched wide-eyed toddlers sitting very still in the giant cups and saucers as the merry-go-round slowly revolved.

The fish and chip and burger vans were doing brisk trade. People strolled by eating chips, candy floss, striped sticks of rock and hot dogs.

'Did you want something to eat now, Kate, candy floss maybe, or a bag of chips and then eat at Dino's later?' Stan asked.

'You really know how to treat a girl, Stan,' Kate smiled at him. 'Maybe a candy floss when we've been around the fair.'

Stan was relieved. He didn't want to part company with a bag of chips half-way round the waltzers.

They spent a happy couple of hours trying most of the rides. Kate enjoyed the waltzers and the carousel. They were fast but mostly ground-based. Stan's eyes shone at the sight of the twister and Kate didn't have the heart to disappoint him, so she endured the ride, mostly with her eyes shut and teeth clenched tightly. After that she declined the offer of a ride on the flying horses. They looked so innocent; magnificently painted steeds that at first sight seemed too gentle and decorous for a fairground, but Kate knew that once the ride was underway they went too high and too fast for her.

They opted instead to wander around the side-stalls. Kate won a little rag doll from the hoop-a stall. She tied it on to her bag. 'All that netball and hockey at school,' she laughed, 'sharpens your eyes and your aim.'

Stan felt fairly confident at the shooting gallery. He'd spent many hours at Walter's smallholding clay pigeon shooting and was sure he could shoot all the targets down. Kate was eager to have a go but only managed two out of the six targets. Taking a deep breath, Stan stepped forward and picked up the air rifle. Taking careful aim he swiftly potted all six targets.

The stallholder scowled at him. 'Professional are yer?' he asked.

'No, not at all,' Stan said. 'Just the odd bit of clay pigeon.'

'Might ha known,' said the man. 'Here.' He reached for an enormous white teddy bear and handed it to Stan. 'You've won the top prize. I don't know what yer'll do with it, but it's yours. Might keep you warm at night.'

Stan took the bear to enthusiastic applause from Kate. He bowed solemnly and handed it to her. 'For madam. The spoils.'

Kate's eyes widened as she took the bear. He was almost as big as her. 'He is lovely,' she said and reached up to kiss Stan's cheek. 'Thank you.'

For a moment they stood there shyly in the darkness, flashing lights and squeals of terror going on around them.

Stan bent down and kissed Kate lingeringly on the lips, the bear between them.

'Yeah, yer could regret winning that,' grinned the stallholder to Stan. 'He could be a right passion killer; started already.'

Ignoring him, Stan put his arm round Kate and they moved off.

'What are you going to call him?' asked Stan.

'Bertie, I think, after Bertie Wooster. Bertie Bear. He's got that slightly anxious, vacant look Bertie often has.'

'Come on then.' Stan took Bertie from Kate and carried him along. 'Let's take Bertie for a ride on the ferris wheel, show him the sights of York.'

'Oh no you don't, Stan. I told you before, I don't like heights. I'm not going on that.'

'It's OK Kate, honestly. I took my great-aunt Madeleine on it and she's like you.'

'Thanks a lot,' Kate said tartly.

She doesn't like heights,' Stan said drily. 'But she was fine. She loved it. You're in a very secure cage and the wheel goes really slowly. Don't look down, just look straight ahead and you get the most magnificent views of York: the Minster, the river, Cliffords Tower. It's beautiful. Come on, surely you're not chicken, Kate.'

Chicken! Kate drew herself up and took the bear from Stan. 'Come on, Bertie, he'll only call us chicken once.'

The pods on the ferris wheel were surprisingly large and comfortable. Stan made sure Kate and Bertie were properly strapped in before he sat down beside them and secured himself.

Why am I doing this? Kate asked herself, as the ferris wheel began to move. Does it matter if Stan thinks I'm chicken? Unaccountably, Kate felt it did. Stan faced things head on and she didn't want to trail in his wake, afraid to try new experiences. Even so, Kate kept her eyes tightly shut as they made their slow ascent above York city.

Stan put his arm gently round her. 'Open your eyes, Kate, and look straight ahead; it's beautiful.'

Kate willed herself to keep calm as she opened her eyes. The movement of the wheel had been so slow and smooth, she had not realised how high they had ascended. She drew in a sharp breath. She saw the spire of York Minster towering above the streets and shops with the River Ouse winding its way through the city and on to the outskirts, where the landscape changed to a patchwork of fields, some green with spring crops, others newly-ploughed brown earth.

'It is beautiful, Stan,' she agreed. 'We're lucky to live in such a great city, full of history and lovely ancient buildings, all the snickleways and The Shambles area. I'd love to look down at them, but I daren't.'

'Has it been worth the trip?' Stan asked.

'Yes and no,' she said. 'I'm not chicken and it is amazing up here, but I'll be glad to get back down to earth.'

Stan hugged her. 'Just like Aunt Madeleine,' he said. 'No, not to look at, believe me. She's sixty-five and could do with a shave, but she's a game girl, just like you.'

They were right at the top of the wheel now. Kate closed her eyes again, wishing now that it would speed up and set them back down again.

'Funny,' said Stan uneasily, 'I'm sure we haven't moved anywhere for the last five minutes.' He looked out of the window and down at the ground below. 'Yeah, we're not moving. Oh…' He paused. 'What's going on down there? No, don't look, Kate, won't do you any good. Concentrate on Bertie and I'll keep looking out.'

Kate obediently stared at Bertie, willing herself to concentrate on him, how his soft white fur went in different directions and how one eye was slightly higher than the other. Anything but think of all her nightmares come true. She couldn't possibly be stuck right at the top of a ferris wheel in a small metal pod, could she?

As this information sunk in and the evening breeze rocked the pod, a wave of vertigo and nausea swept over Kate. She held tightly on to Stan, fighting down the bile that rose in her throat. That would be the final indignity, to throw up all over him.

Stan held her close and stroked her hair. 'It's alright, Kate, nothing to worry about. The engineers are fixing it now. We'll soon be down.'

Soon couldn't come soon enough for Kate. The evening air was growing chilly. Kate shivered as the cool wind whipped about them. She clung on to Stan, in no mood to appreciate the very expensive after shave he had invested in for the evening.

She wanted to scream like a small child, 'Get me down, GET ME DOWN. Why ever did I listen to you, or your nutty friend, Walter? Next time anyone suggests I need a visit to the fair, please remind me I need my head testing first, just in case I decide to say yes.'

The jumble of thoughts went on, as Stan held her and stroked her. From the depths of his jacket she heard him say, 'I'm so sorry, Kate, this was never meant to happen. It was just going to be a short ride to see the sights, just like with Aunt Madeleine.'

Bloody Aunt Madeleine, sixty-five and bearded. She had a lot to answer for by enjoying this damn ferris wheel. If Kate was ever unfortunate enough to meet her, she … well, she didn't know what she would do, but she'd do something.

After an hour, that seemed to stretch to eternity, the pod jolted suddenly and dropped six feet. Kate screamed, thinking they were falling to earth. But the pod stopped and rocked crazily like a swing boat.

'Stan Peterson, if I ever get out of here alive,' panted Kate clinging on to him, 'I'll, I'll…'

'You'll kiss me with fervour, grateful for our deliverance,' he said cheerily, now that they were nearly down.

'I'll shred you and feed you to that poodle of yours.'

'He's a fussy eater. I don't think he's keen on men.'

They came into the unloading platform with a bump. Kate tottered off clutching Bertie tightly, leaving Stan to receive apologies from the operators.

She waited a little apart, swaying slightly as the vertigo subsided. Stan caught her up and took firm hold of her. He looked at her anxiously. 'You're very white, Kate, well a bit green, really. It matches your eyes. Do you want to sit down for a while?'

Kate declined. She wanted a stiff drink in a warm pub. 'Let's go and find the car and get into Dino's,' she suggested.

Stan grinned at her and took hold of Bertie. 'And you're too young for Dino's,' he told him. 'You can stay in the car, young fella, whilst I escort this beautiful young woman to the nearest hostelry.'

Which he would have done: if only they could have found the car. Neither of them had paid the slightest attention to where Stan had parked the car on their arrival. In a field full of cars in the dark, with no particular landmarks to go by, their search seemed impossible.

They walked up and down the rows searching for the Kia, the shouts and screams from the fairground ringing in their ears. Drizzly rain began to fall and soon they were squelching along puddled grass that was quickly turning to mud. Kate's jeans were spattered up to her knees and her thin sneakers ruined as she stumbled over the muddy field. A long time later too weary to take another step, she stopped and rested against the bonnet of the nearest car.

'I've got to hand it to you, Stan, you sure know how to show a gal a good time,' she drawled, in her best Mae West accent. 'I ain't seen mud like this since I was   at   Peter Jackson's health spa … aaawl wrapped up head to toe in it I was.' She smiled wanly at Stan, shivering now, her clothes soaked through.

Stan stopped, some way in front of her. He couldn't believe this was happening; the girl of his dreams getting a soaking. Once, yes, maybe, but again, and on date number two! In the darkness Stan cast his eyes skywards. 'Thank you, God,' he whispered through clenched teeth. 'Remind me to do the same for you sometime, soon.' He turned to Kate.

'Look, Kate,' he said, 'I don't suppose it's any good my saying how sorry I am about this. But really I am. This has never happened to me before. We've either missed the car in the dark or it's been stolen. Either way, I think you've had enough for one evening and you've got work tomorrow at the café. Let's go and get you a taxi home and I'll have another go on my own.'

Kate protested, but Stan was having none of it. Dejectedly, they walked to the line of taxis waiting at the edge of the fairground. After the ordeal of the ferris wheel and searching for the Kia Kate felt exhausted and was glad to be going home, but she hated leaving Stan to search alone for his car. What if it had been stolen?

'Then I'll get a taxi too. Don't worry, Kate.'

He kissed her gently on the cheek and saw her into the taxi. He smiled ruefully. 'Another wonderful night out, Kate. We must do it again. Imagine what could happen to us next time?'

As Stan waved her off, Kate gently banged her head against the cab window. 'Never, never, never again,' she told herself. 'Yes, he is a lovely man but he is also a walking disaster and I don't think I'm the cavalry.'

CHAPTER 22

The Kia bumped up the track to Walter's smallholding. On either side of the lane large banks of bluebells nodded in the early morning breeze. Stan was grateful for the fine clear day. It was a sunny Sunday morning and they were expecting large crowds for their battle re-enactment day at Southmere House.

He tried to banish thoughts of Kate from his mind. He still couldn't believe that an evening that had begun so well could have ended yet again in disaster. At least he would be too busy keeping the day at Southmere House running smoothly, to dwell much on his troubles.

As Stan drew up to the house Walter came out and locked his door. Stan mentally shook himself. Come on now, he told himself. You've managed to lure Walter out to something at long last, Make it a really good day for him. Slap on a smile and get on with it.

'Morning, Walter,' Stan said brightly as Walter got into the passenger seat.

'Good morning, Stan.' Walter smiled at him. 'You've got a grand day for your Romans today. I'm looking forward to it, something different. Make a change from running after sheep and ducks. Lambing's finished, so they can all get on with it for the day.'

Stan set off back down the lane. He was pleased to hear Walter sounding so positive. In the three months since Marilyn's death Walter had been very low, but with the coming of spring he was cautiously beginning to emerge from his grief.

Walter rubbed his hands together enthusiastically. 'Well, lad,' he began. 'Don't keep me in suspense. How did you get on with the lovely Kate last night? I bet she's eating out of your hand now, isn't she?'

Oh, if only, Stan thought. Every other woman he'd taken out had been a pushover, but the one he really wanted, had fallen head over heels in love with... Well, he just made a fool of himself every time, probably driving her further away with each stupid incident.

'Well?' Walter enquired again.

'Not well, Walter.' Stan said, trying to keep his voice light. 'It didn't quite go according to plan.'

Walter looked across at him questioningly. 'Oh?'

'It wasn't all a disaster,' Stan said. He needed to put a positive spin on this, not wanting anything to cloud Walter's day. 'Yeah, we had a fantastic time on all the rides, went on loads of them. She's lethal on the dodgems, never seen anything like it, carved everyone up. I wouldn't like to be a passenger in her car I can tell you.'

'And then?' Walter wasn't going to be side tracked.

'We did the side stalls. She won a rag doll and I won a teddy, life size, the star prize, Walter, on the shooting gallery. Thanks to you and the clay pigeons I got a bulls-eye on every target. I gave the bear to Kate. She's calling him Bertie. Great name, eh? And she kissed me. Progress, Walter.' Stan kept the smile on his face.

Walter looked puzzled. 'So what happened that made it not go so well?'

'Ah well.' Stan stared through the windscreen, oblivious to the passing countryside. How could he put it to Walter without it sounding like the finish of things. 'I took her on the ferris wheel,' he began.

'You did what?' Walter cut across him in an astounded

voice. 'What did you do that for? You know she doesn't like heights.'

'I know, but you get such a good view from the top. I thought she would enjoy it. And she did, just like my Aunt Madeleine did and she doesn't like heights either. That's what I told Kate. Everything would have been fine, we would just have come slowly down and Kate none the worse, only the machinery got jammed and we were stuck right at the top for an hour.'

'An hour,' Walter exclaimed. 'Poor lass, how ever did she cope?'

'She hid her face in my jacket and held tight on to me,' Stan grinned. 'That bit was lovely. I kept my arms around her and stroked her hair. I could have stayed there for hours.'

Walter made a noise in his throat like a strangled duck. 'I don't know why I wasted my breath on you, Stan, getting you this second date. How could you go wrong at a fair?'

'We didn't do too badly at the fair, Walter,' Stan said. 'We got on great. She's a lovely lass and she likes me too. She kissed me. Only...' he hesitated, wondering whether to tell Walter the rest. But he might as well know; he would only hear the next bit from Kate if he didn't hear it now.

'We decided to go for a drink and to Dino's after we finally got off the ferris wheel. So you see it was still OK with her. Only, when we got back to the field where we'd left the car, we couldn't find it.'

There was silence whilst Walter digested this. 'You didn't take note of where you left it,' he said flatly.

'No, I was so thrilled to be with Kate I just lost the plot. All I could think about was her and making sure she had a nice time.'

By now they were pulling into the grounds of Southmere House. 'What happened then?' Walter asked.

'The rain came on and the field where we were parked soon became boggy. Kate was getting soaked and caked in mud. She was tired, cold and hungry so I put her and Bertie in a taxi home and trailed around for another hour trying to find the car. Believe me, in a dark, unlit field, it's not easy. Then the police stopped me as a suspected car thief and I had to produce my documents, which, of course, were in my car, so they helped me to look for it. They had torches and we soon found it and I went home alone, again.'

Walter shook his head in disbelief. 'She might forgive you once, but twice?… I don't know.'

'Yeah well,' Stan said brightly. 'Let's not worry about that now. I want you to enjoy the day, Walter, not worry about my love life.

'I might manage to do both,' Walter said lugubriously and got out of the car.

They had parked at the back of the house. As they walked around to the front, Walter could see the manicured parkland of Southmere House set out before him. Cattle and sheep grazed in the home farm fields and beyond ploughed fields showed the faint greening of new spring shoots.

For today, one of the home farm fields had been set aside for parking and already teenaged stewards in fluorescent waistcoats were receiving their instructions.

In the parkland below the house, Stan's Roman *legionarii* were beginning to lay out their armour and weaponry for the day whilst further away the native English tribe was also laying out their costumes for the day.

Stalls were being set up around the sides of the park with very un-Roman looking bunting around them.

Stan and Walter sat on the grass watching the scene. 'We only get a small amount of funding from the Historical Society and the legionaires' chain mail, armour and swords are quite expensive to make. That's before the authentically correct boots, soft tunics and all the other stuff. So we set up our stalls at every event for fund raising.'

'What sort of stuff do you sell?' asked Walter.

'Everything under the sun. Some of our members make copies of Roman jewellery and clothing, cloaks, belts, tunics, that kind of stuff and others bring what they can. We have bookstalls, bric-a-brac, plants, home-made jams, soft toys and we always run a raffle. Everything helps and people seem to enjoy getting involved.'

Stan started to get up. 'I'll have to go and see how everything is going Walter. It tends to be a bit chaotic first thing and I don't like to leave anything to chance. I need to make sure we've got everything and there are no last minute panics. You have a wander round the stalls down in the next field and we can have a cup of coffee when the refreshment tent is up and running.'

Stan headed off towards the crowds of soldiers milling about the field. Already two distinct encampments could be seen; the Roman soldiers with their mock-up fort to his right and the English tribe to his left. They seemed to be erecting a large hut with mud walls and a straw roof. From his vantage point above the parkland, Walter watched the unfolding scene with interest.

Some distance from them a woman was struggling to erect a large frame tent. It didn't look a difficult task but the frame was quite high and the lady was small. After watching her for a few minutes, Walter strolled down to the field to offer his assistance.

'Can I help you, lass? You look like you could do with a hand.'

The woman paused in her struggle with a recalcitrant rod. 'Oh, would you? That would be so kind. It's a fairly straightforward job, but I could do to be a bit taller to get the frame up. My name's Ellie Ward, by the way.' She held her hand out and smiled at Walter.

Ellie was small, just making five foot one. She was sixty-two, slim, with curly brown hair streaked with grey and had the merriest brown eyes Walter had ever seen. He felt a stirring of interest as he took her outstretched hand and introduced himself. 'Walter Breckenridge. I'm a friend of Stan Peterson.'

Ellie's lovely smile widened. 'Oh Stan. He's marvellous, isn't he? None of this would happen without him. Somehow he manages to keep us all together and put on a great show.'

Walter wondered how Stan could successfully bring all this together and yet in the simple matter of taking his best girl out without mishap, he failed miserably every time.

He took the tent frame from Ellie and together they put it up. In no time they had the old tent canvas draped over the frame and began securing the guy ropes. Ellie was graceful in her movements and Walter enjoyed watching her as they worked. He felt as if he had known her for years, so intuitive were they with each other as they made fine adjustments to the ropes and pegs.

When they had finished they stood back to admire their handiwork.

'What's it for anyway?' Walter asked.

'It's my sewing room for the day, well part of the day,' said Ellie. 'The Roman soldiers have long tunics under their chain mail, the Brigantes tribe have thick tunics, and they all have cloaks and hoods, and that's where I come in. Fighting men are prone to tear their clothes. The old Romans might have had their camp followers to do their running repairs and I'm the twenty-first century equivalent. I set up my sewing machine and needles and threads in here and I'm ready for all comers. But first of all I need a coffee. I see the refreshment tent is open for business now.'

Ellie smiled up at Walter. She had the sweetest smile he had ever seen. He stood transfixed looking down at her, aware that he should say something, but nothing would come.

'Well?' said Ellie, 'are you joining me for one?'

Was he joining her for one? He was joining her for lots,

hundreds. Only, there was Stan... 'Of course I want to join you,' he said eagerly, 'but what about Stan? He said he'd be back to join me for a coffee.'

'Oh don't worry about Stan,' Ellie said. 'He likes his coffee and he'll find us in the refreshment tent.'

Walter didn't need to know more. He went off happily with Ellie. Over coffee she told him about her career in nursing and how she had retired two years ago. Her husband had died in a car accident when they had only been married for three years.

Walter sympathised, but Ellie was brisk. 'It's so long ago, Walter, sometimes it seems like it happened to someone else. I've spent most of my adult life on my own; I got used to it.'

'And you never met anyone else?' he ventured.

'No-one I wanted to spend my life with. I'm an old fashioned girl, Walter. I wanted Mr Right and he never appeared.'

Walter knew it was early days, but there was something about Ellie that drew him to her. He told her about his smallholding at Claygate, his sheep and new lambs, his ducks and hens and of course, spoilt Sarah the hen. She laughed at his story of himself and Stan chasing Sarah's chicks all around the kitchen and the times he'd rescued the ducklings when they'd strayed away from their mother.

'Daft little birds,' he said, 'and their mothers aren't much better. They never seem to know how many babies they've got and if one gets left behind they don't seem to notice.'

They were laughing together when Stan entered the tent. He spotted them immediately. They had not seen him and he paused to watch them. He'd never seen Walter so animated before. He seemed lit from within.

'Well, the old dog,' he thought. 'Good for him. Look at them, they're best pals already.'

Walter looked up and saw Stan and he grinned happily at him. Stan made a decision. He went across to them. 'I can't stop, Walter,' he said. 'I'll grab a cup and get on my way, too much to do.' He looked at Ellie. 'Could you look after my guest Ellie? It's bedlam out there, worse than usual. I'm sorry about this, Walter.'

Ellie smiled in delight. 'If Walter doesn't mind putting up with me…' she began.

'Nonsense,' Walter interrupted robustly. 'The pleasure will be mine.'

They smiled across the table at each other. Stan felt distinctly in the way.

'Right, see you later.' He moved off to collect his coffee. Why ever hadn't he thought of Ellie for Walter before now, he wondered? She might have taken his mind off old Marilyn years ago. Stan made his way out of the tent. At least Walter was having some success with women. He would have to study his technique.

The sun shone on Southmere House and gardens all day. After their coffee Walter helped Ellie set up her sewing machine and tables and sat with her as Roman soldiers and English tribesmen came in with torn garments and went out repaired, looking as good as new.

Walter marvelled at her deftness with her needle and thread; the most awkward rips and tears were invisibly mended. It turned out Ellie's father had been a tailor and had passed on his skills to his daughter.

When it was time for the battle, Walter and Ellie sat outside the tent. Walter watched Ellie. He couldn't study her enough. She intrigued him. He watched how she held herself; how she rubbed her nose when presented with a new problem; how, when she smiled and laughed, her lovely brown eyes lit up.

Ellie watched the battle intently. The clang of iron swords clashing rang out as the soldiers roared terrifyingly and fought with each other. Eventually the Roman *legionarii* overcame the English Brigantes and declared York or

Eboracum for Rome and the Emperor. Walter saw and heard the spectacle as if from afar. When it was over the crowd cheered and applauded loudly. Both sides bowed their thanks to the crowds and drifted off, some to sit on the grass together amongst discarded chainmail and helmets, sharing food and drink as if the battle had never been.

Ellie turned to Walter. 'Wasn't that fantastic? Every time I see it, it's like the first time. There's always something different. It's amazing.'

'You're amazing,' Walter wanted to say, but managed just to nod his head in agreement and beam at her.

The crowd drifted away down the parkland and wandered happily around in the sunshine, prowling the stalls for treasures. Walter and Ellie began dismantling the sewing tables and tent. Walter was keenly aware that the day was drawing to a close. He couldn't let Ellie go without arranging to see her again. He hoped tonight. He hadn't asked a woman out in years; how was he to put it? Whilst he was still trying to frame his thoughts, Ellie broke across them.

'It's been a lovely day, Walter, thank you so much. I've really enjoyed meeting you; you made it really special.'

She was holding her hand out. Walter couldn't let this be goodbye. If she was being truthful and she had enjoyed it, surely she would see him again. 'Come on, Walter lad,' he thought, his old bravado re-asserting itself, 'ask her fair and square and don't take no for an answer.' He took Ellie's outstretched hand.

'Ellie lass, we've had a grand day and we're grown-ups now. We don't have to go home just 'cos it's tea-time. Our mums aren't waiting for us anymore. How about we take your stuff home and then go out for a bite of supper? I'd be honoured to take you out.' There. Walter held his breath. 'Pleeease God, you've saddled me with enough cantankerous women all my life, just let me have this one perfect one now,

217

he pleaded inwardly.

Ellie smiled and said yes, she would love to do that, and Walter breathed again. 'Thank you, God,' he prayed silently. 'I promise I'll treasure her forever.'

CHAPTER 23

During the following Monday afternoon lull, Jackie was checking over invoices in her office when Penny put her head around the door. 'Her ladyship and all her retinue are here,' she said.

Jackie looked up in alarm. '*All?*'

'A lot of gorgeous looking men and weedy Aubrey. You'd better come, she doesn't deal with minions.'

Oh God, Jackie thought, it's crunch time. I wonder what mad ideas she wants to waste my money on when I haven't got it to waste anyway. I wish I'd asked her hourly rate; I bet it's astronomical.

As they came into the café a procession of young men were coming towards them. Without exception, they were young and lithe, clad in black from head to toe. Penny was right, they made quite an entourage. Every young man carried a piece of equipment and an odd-shaped bag. Bringing up the rear, Nina Mountford-Blayne chivvied them on.

'We'll use the space at the back, darlings. That is where it will be built when all those awful fittings and furnishings are gone.'

Mmm, well it was never going to happen was it? Nina *tactful* Mountford-Blayne, Jackie thought wryly as she watched the men gather around Nina, their faces fatuous with adoration.

She must pay them well to do that. She might be clarted with make-up and fancy clothes but she's old enough to be their mother. Toy boys, I suppose. I wonder if she takes one home with her every night and devours him.

Jackie joined Kate and Penny standing by the dresser.

'She is so rude,' whispered Kate. 'Don't you want to punch her lights out?'

Jackie smiled. 'I told you, she's a basket case. I don't think the sensitivity and consideration microchips were ever slotted into her DNA.'

Nina approached the three ladies at the dresser. Ignoring Penny and Kate, she greeted Jackie. 'Miss Dalrymple-Jones, as you see, I arrive.'

Jackie's lips twitched in amusement. 'So you do, Nina, and we can't wait to see what you've brought.' Jackie was learning to lie with the best of them. She could wait all year if necessary, but Nina was here now and there was no place to hide.

'We?' queried Nina, a puzzled look in her chocolate dark eyes.

'Yes. Kate here and Penny, and I'll have to call Walter in for a dekko too. We're really looking forward to seeing your designs.' Your nose is going to grow sooo long Jackie…

'But these are for you only, Miss Dalrymple-Jones.' Nina drew herself up to her full five foot eleven. I design for you, not for these ... these…'

'Ladies,' Jackie said sweetly, 'and Walter of course.' She called him from his kitchen. 'This gentleman, too. We are a team, Nina, and I value their opinions. So,' Jackie pointed to the young men assembling their equipment, 'if you would like to show us what you have brought today.'

Walter came out from his kitchen wiping his hands on an old towel. Nina eyed it with distaste. 'You cook with that?'

'Course not, you daft bat. I've just washed my hands. What else am I supposed to dry them on?'

Why did he do this to her? Jackie thought. All the health and safety measures they had been through, food handling and hygiene until they were both blue in the face and he does this. Should she just kill him now?

Jackie took the towel from him. 'Could you have found an older or tattier one to bring out here, Walter? What's happened to the new ones I put in there?'

'Still in the packet,' he said proudly.

'Ooohh.' For once words failed Jackie. Killing would be too good for him; a slow skewering to the wall would be much more satisfying. She pointed to an empty table and chairs. 'Sit there, watch and say nothing. Miss Mountford-Blayne is going to show us her designs for Café Paradise.

'We're in for a treat then.'

'Don't start,' Jackie warned.

Walter beamed at her and zipped his lips. He sat back in the chair and folded his arms with the air of a man happily waiting to be entertained.

Two of the young men theatrically flung wide the café doors, making way for four men to wheel a huge polished steel disc through the café and park it outside Walter's kitchen. After they had locked it into place and slotted a second semi-circular disc across the centre of it, the thing completely blocked off the kitchen and serving area to the café. The men stood back, looking expectantly at Nina.

She flung her manicured hands out before her. 'A masterpiece,' she announced solemnly.

The young men applauded and smiled adoringly at her. Jackie, Penny and Kate stood silently at the dresser.

'Who's going to ask?' Penny whispered.

'Who fancies looking stupid this morning?' fielded Jackie. As the silence grew Jackie gave in. 'It might be a masterpiece to you and your team, Nina, but what exactly is it?'

'You are telling me you cannot see it?' Nina stalked up and down in agitation, her eyes raking contemptuously over Jackie. 'My art is wasted on you; all the creativity I have poured into your poor little project and you cannot see it.'

'No,' said Jackie flatly.

'It is a stage,' announced Nina proudly.

'You did tell her it was for a café, Jackie,' whispered Kate. 'She's not got us mixed up with the Theatre Royal, has she?'

'A masterpiece,' Nina said loudly, 'because it is a revolving stage, the backdrop for your café. I am a woman of amazing talents and ideas, but even I astound myself with this.'

'We're certainly astounded,' echoed Jackie. She gazed at the steel disc and semi-circular divider with a look of wonder. Holy moly! This woman shouldn't be let loose on society ever again, she thought, and maybe I shouldn't be for employing her. She tried to keep her voice neutral. 'I wonder, Nina, would you care to elaborate on your ideas for us.'

'Is it not obvious?' Nina was incredulous. She strode up to the disc and flicked it with her fingers. Slowly it rotated. 'This is just a rough model. Imagine a properly dressed one, set where you are now; it will hide all that so-hideous kitchen and stores behind and when you are being a Spanish café one week, you can be preparing Austria and the ski scene the next. Boys,' she clapped her hands, 'show these ... ladies and … gentleman our sets in more detail.'

Nina stood back and the young men, all sinuously dressed in tight black rollneck jumpers and trousers, sprang up to do her bidding. As if they had been choreographed for this moment, they glided to and fro unpacking their bags and sacks and, with some whispered consultations, set up both sides of the stages. Nina padded back and forth between the two like a prowling cat patrolling its territory.

Some new customers came into the café and Kate and Jackie went to serve them with coffee and cakes. Penny went to join Walter at his table and together they watched the proceedings.

The assistants dressed the steel disc stage as a mini beach with a backdrop of palm trees. Coconut matting parasols dotted the beach with sun beds placed beneath them. Large palm trees were placed about the café and a mini-bar set up complete with tequila cocktails, shaker and ice-bucket on it. Flamenco music echoed through the café and a young man began to dance.

'Didn't you go to Spain on holiday last year?' Walter asked Penny.

'Yes. Lumpy beds, endless paella, sunburn and topless girls who should know better.'

'Did you get your kit off then?'

'Course not. You need a little mystery in a marriage, not flaunting it all at once.'

'You've got mystery in your marriage alright,' agreed Walter. 'Is George still…'

'Yes,' Penny answered repressively.

'Ladies and gentleman,' Nina clapped her hands to command their wandering attention. 'I give you Spain.' She stepped back to reveal the mini-beach, the Spanish bartender mixing drinks and the flamenco dancer.

Applause rippled round the café as the customers showed their appreciation of the floorshow.

'Now, Miss Dalrymple-Jones,' Nina challenged Jackie. 'Do you see how you can be in Spain now and tomorrow,' she spun the stage set around and a dark cave setting was revealed on the other side, 'this.'

'I know some countries in the EU are not as advanced as others,' Jackie commented, 'but a cave….?' Did Nina think they were all Neanderthals in York?

'Miss Dalrymple-Jones, you are such a philistine. It is a backdrop only; a frame, for a picture. You can put in it whatever you like.' She snapped her fingers imperiously and her young men immediately jumped up and went forward to dress the cave.

It became a ski resort in the background with an Austrian tavern in the front with wine and beers set on the counter.

Accordian music began to play as the young men strung fairy lights and scattered dustings of snow around the café.

'You see how easily the tone of your chosen country can be set,' Nina said proudly.

Jackie could just imagine it: sand everywhere one week and snow the next, and Walter doing his nut when he had to clean it all up. I don't think so, Miss Nina Mountford-Blayne, thought Jackie. Much as she had the urge to strangle Walter most of the time she thought he might hang her guts out to dry if she took on this mad idea.

Jackie was still trying to frame some kind of reply to acknowledge Nina's display when a young man stepped forward with swatches of material. Nina took them from him and wafted them in Jackie's direction. 'I've chosen these for an overall backdrop for your café. I've studied the psychology of colour and can tell you that these will bring Mediterranean warmth and ambience to your rooms and at the same time can also be a study in the peace and tranquillity of the Alps. I'll leave this set of materials with you to bond with and let your staff become accustomed to them.'

Nina dropped swathes of material in deep purple and mustard on the table. 'You'll grow to love them and see how wise I've been in my choices. And now we have to go. Boys,' she commanded, 'new horizons await, new challenges to be conquered, we must be gone.'

Without waiting for Jackie's comments on her presentation, Nina walked towards the door. As she neared it Aubrey gave her a long white envelope. 'Oh, yes,' she said and wheeled about, heading for Jackie. 'For my installation and services,' she announced, putting the envelope into Jackie's hands and was gone.

'Can I speak now?' asked Walter rising from his chair.

'If you must,' said Jackie, opening Nina's envelope with shaking hands.

'Well, for my money that's the daftest collection of ideas I've seen in a long time. A bloody great big stage taking up half the caff and folks bumping into palm trees or icebergs at every turn.'

'And puke-coloured furnishings thrown in,' said Kate.

'It's taking money under the false pretences of being a designer, that's what it is,' added Penny.

'And if you think I'm clearing leprechauns, lizards, sand, snow, elephants, alligators or anything else in this caff at six o'clock in the morning then you *will* have another think coming. If mad Mountford-Blayne has her way I'll never get time to get to bed, let alone…'

'Yeek!' shouted Jackie sliding off her chair. 'Is she mad? She can't be serious. She wants seven thousand pounds just for this lot.' She waved the invoice at the set and materials. 'What would she charge for the full sized version?'

'No wonder she legged it quick,' observed Walter.

* * * * * *

Barney watched Jackie as she made his cappuccino. He thought she looked tired and worried. 'Don't suppose you'll tell me what's up, but I'll ask anyway,' he said.

'And give you the opportunity for a good laugh at my expense like the rest of the café already had today.' She shook chocolate powder over his coffee.

'Promise I won't,' Barney said gently. 'What's up?'

'Nina Mountford-Blayne and her so-called designs for the new café. I know.' Jackie held her hands up. 'You told me not to have anything to do with her and, bloody-mindedly, I did.'

Barney suppressed a grin. Bloody-minded just about hit the nail on the head but at least this was progress, she had been listening to him. But alarm bells were ringing. What had Nina Mountford-Blayne been up to now? 'So?' he asked taking his coffee from her.

'She designed a so-called masterpiece for us, i.e. that thing over there.' Jackie pointed to the stage sets at the top of the café. 'Her idea is that she builds us a full-size revolving stage that screens off the kitchens and stores from the caff and whilst the caff might be set one week for say, Spain, we can be tarting up the set on the other side ready for the next week.' Jackie gestured to the palm trees and fairy lights speckled with snow around the café. 'We've had Spain and the Austrian ski slopes this morning.'

'Right,' Barney said slowly taking it all in. 'The woman's mad of course, but you know that.'

'The whole idea is ridiculous. There would be no room left for any customers by the time she had installed her precious stage, and God knows how much it would all cost if I went ahead with it.'

Jackie pointed to the small set and the props. 'The worst thing, the totally worst thing is, for *that* and the most hideous colour scheme on God's earth, she has had the cheek to bill me for seven grand.'

Barney gaped. 'How much?' he asked in awed tones. Even in his wildest dreams, and boy he had had plenty of them where Jackie was concerned, he wouldn't have come up with that figure.

'Seven thousand smackeroos,' Jackie said glumly. 'How can she justify that kind of money?'

Barney started turning over possibilities in his mind. He thought he saw a knight in shining armour moment hoving into view.

'All those toy boys to keep,' he grinned. 'How many did she bring with her this time?'

'Six, plus awful Aubrey.'

'Mmm. She's got at least another six under wraps back at her offices. She usually has a round dozen in her stable at any one time.'

'I must be keeping them all,' Jackie said miserably. 'It's going to make a big dent in my renovations budget. No fool like an old fool, so they say.'

'Hey,' Barney protested, 'less of the old. You're a beautiful woman, worth a hundred Nina Mountford-Blaynes any day. Now listen to me, Jackie.'

Barney leaned back against the counter and contemplated Nina's designs.

'I know a thing or two about that woman she wouldn't want made public. Forget about that invoice. Miss Mountford-Blayne is going to send you a much revised account, or my name is not Barney Anderson.'

'And is it?'

'What?'

'Your real name?'

'Why wouldn't it be?' Where were they going with this? Why was Jackie knocking him down again?

'I don't know.' Jackie mentally kicked herself. Why did she say that?

'Do you think I would use a false name? What for? Oh, I get it. Dosser Boy making claims under different names. Is that it? You don't know how wrong you are.'

Barney was furious. He'd actually thought he was beginning to make some progress with this cantankerous, awkward, bigoted, narrow-minded woman but, as ever, she had proved him wrong.

He finished his coffee and put his cup back on the counter. 'I'll fix Nina for you and yes,' it was his turn to hold his hands up, 'it will be legit. Say hello to Walter for me, will you? Tell him I've got his bit of business sorted, he just needs to come and sign for it.'

He turned and was gone. Jackie gazed after him in dismay. A perfect end to a perfect day then. Was there anyone else she really liked that she could upset today? Probably, and she hadn't even been trying.

* * * * * *

Barney leaned back in his chair at the Citizens Advice Bureau and dialled Nina's number. As usual when dealing with Mountford-Blayne Design Services he had to run the gamut of her assistants and then Aubrey her personal assistant before finally getting put through to Nina in person.

'Mr. Anderson,' she said guardedly, 'do I know you? You've been very persistent and quite upset Aubrey.'

One up to me then, Barney thought. 'St. Ninian's Gardens project, Nina,' he said, 'August 2010.'

'I was inspired,' she said grandly. 'Only I could have designed such beautiful gates and artistic installations and now you have come back to me for more.'

'Mmm, that's not quite what I had in mind actually, Nina.'

Barney was beginning to enjoy himself. Should he keep her dangling or go in for the kill? He decided to be direct.

'You bill Jackie Dalrymple-Jones for five hundred quid and I will give you your invoice to a certain party for two thousand pounds for the making of the said garden gates that I happen to know you charged the City Fathers ten thousand pounds for.'

There was a long silence on the end of the line. Barney put his feet up on the desk. He could wait. He imagined the cold sweat breaking out on the smooth Mountford-Blayne brow and grinned.

'How do I know you have such a thing? You are making all this up.'

Barney grinned more widely to himself. She was definitely rattled. 'Take your chance, Nina. Five hundred pounds only to Jackie or you'll be all over the papers tomorrow. I am a man of my word and as soon as Jackie has a revised account and it's receipted by you, this invoice will be on your desk.'

'Deal,' she said, 'Aubrey will see to it now.' And the line went dead.

Barney punched the air. 'Yeesss. Nailed the old bat at last, and I bet she's a lot more careful in future.'

His heart thumping wildly, he dialled the number of the Café Paradise. Jackie had distrusted him, insulted him, she was rude and insolent by turns and yet just thinking about her made his heart turn over.

'You are the biggest fool walking this planet, you know that don't you,' he told himself.

Jackie answered the phone and Barney savoured her melodic voice for a moment without answering.

'Café Paradise. Hello?' she repeated.

'How does five hundred pounds sound, Jackie?' he gabbled.

'Depends. Are you giving it or taking it?' she answered.

'Neither. It's Barney. Nina Mountford-Blayne; write her a cheque for five hundred pounds and the job's done. Aubrey will be round with a new invoice shortly. Give him the cheque and *make sure* he gives you a proper receipt in full and final settlement for that amount. You'll hear no more from Miss M-B after that.'

'Barney!' Jackie exclaimed. 'How have you managed that?'

'All legit, as I said.' He felt a little smug. 'Let's just say I know our Nina's little ways of old.'

Mentally he polished up his suit of armour, mounted his white charger and rode off into the sunset with Jackie, perhaps to set her down on a sun-kissed beach of pure white sand, the white-tipped waves gently lapping around their feet as they sipped chilled wine.

Putting the phone down, Jackie realised how deeply indebted she was to Barney Anderson. What a mystery he was and how ever was she going to repay him? She didn't think free all-day breakfasts for life would suffice.

CHAPTER 24

Jackie closed her front door and slumped against it. What a day it had been. The outrageous Nina-Mountford-Blayne and her boys, another battle with Walter over using the new towels and finally, Barney Anderson.

At the thought of Barney, Jackie's mind veered off. She would think about some supper. With an effort she straightened up and kicked her shoes off. She padded through the hall, throwing Nina's bolts of cloth on to a chair. They landed with a thump, disturbing motes of dust that danced crazily in the hall lamplight. What on earth had she bought them home for? She couldn't see purple and mustard featuring in her colour scheme any time soon.

Jackie stood still and looked around the hall. It dawned on her that she hadn't properly looked at it in years, or the rest of the house come to that. She had just perched there. Slowly she inspected the walls, looking at the pictures hung on them: hideous chocolate-box images of golden-haired children and sweet little cats with bows on their heads.

She looked at the brasses on the hall window sill, dull now that Marilyn was not there to polish them; the heavy gilt-framed pictures of mist laden glens and heathery moorland. Jackie shivered just looking at them. They were not to her taste at all. She was a lounger by the pool and iced rum and coke girl.

Circling the hall slowly Jackie realised everything here was to Marilyn's taste; even the thick Axminster carpet underfoot. Jackie hated the pattern of it. Well… It was her house now

Tentatively she removed an old brass bell from the window sill. Better. She removed the other pieces: a candlestick, snuffer and another small bell. Cradling them in her arm she waited. No thunderbolt, no ceiling crashing about her ears. Nice. Less is more.

One by one she took down all the pictures and stacked them against the wall. She stepped back to inspect her handiwork. Yes, OK, the paper was marked where the pictures had hung but a lick of paint would fix that.

Jackie breathed more freely, liberated by the new sense of light and space in the hall. She listened to her breathing. It was the only sound to be heard. With a sharp pang Jackie noticed the contrast in coming home now to the days when her mother was alive.

Marilyn would have been bustling about getting a meal ready, chiding and chivvying Jackie on. 'What time do you call this? Hurry up, dinner's ready. Go and get changed and don't put those old grey trousers on. If I see them on you one more time…' On and on she would go. But never again…

It had been like background music, so constant that mostly Jackie had ceased to notice it. Now it was no longer there, she noticed the quiet of the house. She would get used to it; maybe even get to like it, and being on her own.

Jackie dragged herself upstairs to her bedroom and flung herself down on her bed. She was thirty-five and very much on her own now. How come she had never met Mr Right? A picture of Marilyn rose before her. Jackie tried to dismiss it. She couldn't blame her mother for everything.

Yeah, come on now Jackie, grow up and accept responsibility. You allowed Marilyn to keep you at home, do her books, go to the wholesalers and help out in the café. You never fought back and made a life of your own, so how were you ever going to meet anyone?

She closed her eyes and immediately Barney Anderson was there, his vivid blue eyes and sculpted mouth smiling mockingly at her. Dosser Boy! What was he doing in her head? Why did he have to be so impossibly handsome and do her a good turn out of nowhere; six and a half thousand pounds worth of good turn when she had only ever been incredibly rude to him?

She sat up. Nina Mountford-Blayne. She was beautiful and stylish if you liked exotic. Maybe Barney did. Were they lovers? That would explain Barney's influence over her. How else would Nina waive almost all of her bill out of the blue? But Nina and Barney? Mr Shabby? Mr Shabby Chic? Jackie didn't know what to think. Barney was always scrupulously clean and had a beautiful speaking voice. Sometimes it made her go weak at the knees, even when he was cross with her.

Oh stop it, Jackie, get a grip, she told herself. He would never look at you and would you want him to? Mr Help Everyone, man of the streets? A small voice somewhere deep inside was saying yes, yes, yes.

Jackie jumped up from her bed and went into the bathroom. She looked at herself in the full-length mirror.

'Still fat and plain, luv,' Marilyn's voice echoed in her ears.

'Well no, mother, actually, I'm not,' Jackie decided and looked steadily at herself again. 'I've lost weight. All that running around in the café. I only sat on my backside at the supermarket checkout. Now I'm on the go all day. And if I like these zumba dancing classes Kate's dragging us to, I might shed a few more pounds.

She peered at herself more closely. Her fair hair had grown down to her shoulders and framed her face. Her cheekbones were beginning to emerge and her skin and eyes looked clear and healthy.

'Dream on, Nina Mountford-Blayne, I'll give you a run

for your money soon. Not that I'm after your Barney. I'm not. Come to think of it he must put himself about a bit: he's still got dopey Melissa in tow. Maybe he has a girl for every night of the week.'

Depressed, Jackie wandered back downstairs and began preparations for her evening meal. The cat flap rattled and Samson walked into the kitchen. He sat down on the doormat and looked up at her, his green eyes glinting in the bright kitchen light. He jumped up on to the counter, spied the chicken breast Jackie had got out for her supper and meowed hopefully.

'Not a hope, you little beast.' Jackie batted him off the counter and on to the floor. 'Go catch your own supper, that's what cats do in case you didn't know. Marilyn might have stuffed you full of best chicken and smoked salmon but there's been a regime change, buddy, and I haven't forgotten what you did to my dress.'

Samson stared unblinkingly at her and waited patiently. After a while Jackie gave in and reached for the Kattibiks. 'The deal is, Samson,' she said pouring the dried biscuits into a bowl, 'you don't bring home any live or dead birds, mice or rats, in fact, anything living and furry and I will continue to provide you with as many Kattibiks as you can possibly stuff yourself with.'

She put the bowl down on the floor and Samson approached it. He sniffed it gingerly and gently lifted out a biscuit. He took a small bite and immediately spat it out, meowing angrily up at Jackie, his black tail swishing vigorously.

'I bought a bloody great big box of those, Samson. Are you telling me you won't eat them? Listen, friend, eat them or find a new home. I'm not bringing home the entire stock of Supashopper's cat food section so you can be Mr. Choosy Choosy.'

Samson stalked to the door, head held high, and ran off

through the house.

Jackie turned the radio on and the kitchen was filled with Pink Floyd's 'Brick in The Wall.' Good. Nice, loud music that would blot out her thoughts. She made herself concentrate on preparing supper, chopped up a red pepper and part of a leek; its fresh pungency made her eyes water. Carrot and mushroom followed and she tossed the whole lot into a frying pan with a teaspoon of oil. There, a small stir-fry alongside a skinless chicken breast was blameless enough.

She wondered if she would ever be able to teach Walter to cook like this or would he want to stick to his endless round of anything you could put in a buttie plus a portion of chips?

She put the chicken into the microwave and slammed the door on it. She had to change her life, here, now. She had made a start already hadn't she, removing Marilyn's pictures? Nina's designs were a disaster, but that didn't have to stop Jackie from taking the project forward.

Jackie ate her supper in the kitchen. Ever since Marilyn had died in the dining room, she hadn't been able to face eating a meal in there. She occupied herself with sketching out her ideas for the re-vamping of the café.

Time passed and eventually Jackie gave up the task. She was tired after a long day at the café. Her own ideas on colour schemes would have to wait until tomorrow. She stacked the dishes in the sink and decided to have a bath before bed.

It was a fine, dry night, Samson should go out. He hadn't touched the Kattibiks and if he was hungry he would only stalk about all night and yowl. Jackie went through the dining room and into the hall calling his name. He did not appear. The hall looked strange and bare, denuded of its pictures. Passing the carved hall chair, Jackie glanced down at Nina's bolts of cloth. She stopped and gasped.

Samson had had his revenge in style. Lesser cats might settle for Kattibiks, but not Samson. Torn pieces of cloth lay strewn across the floor and ribboned away up the stairs. Samson had had a field day, ripping, chewing and biting his way through every revolting length of the purple and mustard cloth.

Jackie stood transfixed. All that expensive fabric. Five hundred pounds' worth: ruined just like that. Wait 'til she got that cat. No wonder he wasn't coming when she called, the cunning little beast.

She began collecting the torn cloth, imagining how she would like to slowly dismember and fry a certain black feline. Following the trail upstairs, Jackie stopped in her tracks. For a few moments she stood motionless in the silence. What was she doing? She hated this stuff so why was she rescuing it?

Samson was right. For once in all of his misspent nine lives he had done something right. He had freed her completely from Nina's rubbish ideas and awful material. Where was he? He must be rewarded immediately.

She called to him more sweetly. 'Samson, come on out, come to Jackie. I promise I won't strangle you. You're the best cat ever, so good that we're going to break out the salmon for you. Come on, even you can't resist that.'

She skipped happily down to the kitchen and found a tin of salmon in the cupboard. She ditched the Kattibiks and put the whole tin into the bowl. Picking up a large pair of scissors and the bowl she went back into the hall and waved the dish about, knowing the aroma would tempt Samson out of his hidey hole.

Jackie put the dish down on the floor and set to work cutting and shredding the lumps of cloth. She was laughing so loudly that Samson was lured out from underneath Marilyn's bed. He slunk quietly to the top of the stairs and observed Jackie hacking away at the cloths. He smelt the salmon and his mouth watered.

Jackie looked up and spied him. 'Samson, you clever little cat you, destroying all this cloth. Come here and get your reward. See, a lovely tin of salmon.' Jackie got up and proffered the dish.

Samson backed off. His world was turning upside down. He'd destroyed all that stuff in the hall and she was offering him *best salmon*. She never offered him best salmon. No, that wasn't playing the game. She couldn't do this to him, he couldn't stand it. They had an agreement: she was the goody and he was the baddy, that's how it was. If she started being affectionate who knew where it would all end?

Samson hurtled down the stairs and shot past Jackie like a black streak. In seconds he was out of the cat flap and into the street. A nice mouse or passing vole would do him tonight.

Jackie shook her head. That cat would be contrary to the end. Well, if she was going to change her life and change the café she had better start somewhere. She fished her phone out of her pocket and looked up Stampwick Builders in her directory. She had met Mr. Stampwick at the Trades Council soirèe and he had been very keen to take on the re-development of the café. No-one was at home but the answerphone clicked in. Before she lost her nerve Jackie left a message asking him to call and discuss the proposed alterations. Smiling happily, she picked her way through the wreckage on the stairs and went to run her bath.

CHAPTER 25

The early evening drizzle had turned to heavy rain and bore all the signs of turning into a prolonged downpour. The wipers swished to and fro, trying to clear the windscreen.

'Just as well we're not going far tonight,' Penny commented. 'Knowing our luck, if this keeps up we could come out to a flood.'

'Have you been listening to the weather forecast again, Penny?' Kate asked. 'Big mistake, they're always wrong.'

'They haven't a clue have they?' Jackie agreed. 'I don't know why we fund the Met Office. I have this image of them sitting around all day, drinking tea and when it's time for them to do their TV and radio forecasts they stick pins in a load of words; sun, rain, sleet, wind, and use whatever comes up.'

'Well George said the forecast was for rain and it looks like he might be right.' Penny clung on stubbornly.

Jackie, in the front seat, turned to look at Penny. 'How is George? Is he still dressing up at home?'

'Unfortunately, yes,' Penny sighed. 'I really don't know what to make of it. He says he's getting in touch with his feminine side, he wants to be a more rounded human being.'

'I suppose the idea behind it is no bad thing,' Kate said thoughtfully.

'The idea maybe.' Penny was a bit tart. 'Last night he lit the bathroom with scented candles and soaked in a rose-scented bath. Said he wanted the experience. The house smelt like a botanical gardens. And if you could see him tonight…' Penny stopped for a moment to assemble her thoughts.

Kate and Jackie were agog. 'Go on,' they urged, 'don't stop there.'

'I left him dressed in pink satin, studying Delia Smith's recipe for cheese soufflé.'

'I didn't know George could cook.' Jackie was intrigued.

'He can't, well not up to now. He's never used a whisk before, only electric drills and screwdrivers. Not much call for balloon whisks when you're double glazing. He's costing me a fortune in fancy ingredients and then he leaves the kitchen like a bomb site.'

'It sounds like a mid-life thing; only pink satin and all that stuff … it's a bit more…'

'Crazy, that's what I call it, Jackie. I don't think I can stand much more of it. To be honest, I'm glad to get out tonight, leave him to it.'

'Well George was right about one thing.' Heavy rain swished across Kate's windscreen and she clicked the wipers on to fast speed.

'I hope it will be warm in this hall we're going to,' said Jackie.

'Maybe not too warm.' Kate turned the heater on to the screen to demist it. 'We'll be making our own warmth. After the initial warm-up, zumba is fast action dancing. We'll be hot and sweaty in no time.'

'We must be mad,' Penny said.

'No Penny.' Jackie turned round to her again. 'It will be good for us. We've all been a bit down lately; this might be just the thing to shake us up a bit. I've lost a stone since I took over running the café. I'm hoping the zumba dancing will do the rest and I'll look as gorgeous and svelte as you and Kate.'

'I can't argue with that.' Kate grinned at her.

The hall had a large car park and Kate soon found a space. They made their way through the wet car park and into the hall. Inside, it was brightly lit. People of all ages and sizes, dressed in loose comfortable clothing, were slowly moving and stretching their limbs preparing to zumba.

The three women looked about them with interest. A tall, dark-skinned man spotted them hovering uncertainly in the doorway and came over to them.

'Lay-dees,' he smiled warmly at them. 'You come to my zumba classes, yes?'

They nodded.

'Excellent, you make good choice with Enrique. That's me. Enrique Gonzalez, Madrid's finest export. I run the best zumba dancing classes in York, possibly the whole of your Great Britain.'

Enrique ran a professional eye over them. 'Three very beautiful laydees, just in need of a little…,' he wiggled his hips, 'like so. Put you in shape for the spring eh, when the young men come calling and *lurve* is in the air.' He rolled his eyes suggestively. 'Now, what are your names, laydees?'

Penny laughed nervously and introduced them. She didn't know what she had been expecting but certainly not a gorgeous Spaniard. Enrique was of medium height with black hair and melting brown eyes. He had a warm wide smile that showed his perfect white teeth. He wore a tight white T-shirt and frayed denim shorts that showed off his tanned and muscular legs.

Penny looked up at him and was smitten. She blushed. 'I don't know about *lurve*,' she said archly.

Enrique drew her to him. 'Oh Pennee, I'm sure you do. A beautiful laydee. Come I teach you zumba, we zumba together to the vibrant Latin music; salsa, merengue, samba. Oh Pennee, we gonna have fun,' He kept his arms folded in hers and drew her on to the dance floor.

Kate and Jackie looked at each other. 'Plonker,' they said in unison and laughed. Then they trooped after Penny and Enrique.

He began by putting everyone through their paces, bending and stretching and taking simple steps from side to side to get them warmed up. Soon the Latin fusion music was playing and the class was closely following Enrique's dance steps.

Enrique faced the class so that they could see the movements of his arms, legs and feet. It seemed to Jackie and Kate their limbs should be going in all different directions at once and their head in another, at the speed of an express train. Penny was faring no better. Whilst still shouting instructions Enrique danced in front of Penny and showed her how to place her arms and legs, sometimes dancing in a close hold with her.

Watching this out of the corner of her eye, Jackie nudged Kate. 'Look at Penny,' she hissed. 'I think she's got the hots for him. She's all starry eyed and steamy. George had better watch out.'

'Well if he stays in Georgina mode, he had. Penny might well be on the lookout.'

After the initial warm-up session the music got louder and Enrique pushed them at a fast and furious pace through the zumba steps. Everyone was sweating and panting hard as they threw themselves about to the music.

Enrique shouted, 'Come on folks, give it your heart, Latin is about giving your heart and soul.' He shimmied suggestively in front of Penny, his hips gyrating in time to the music. 'Heart, Pennee, give me your heart in your dance.'

'Oh Enrique,' Penny giggled and attempted to mirror his gyrations.

'Wonderful!' he shimmied back at her. 'I make you best zumba dancer.'

Crunching their way over the frozen snow to the car Kate

took Penny's arm and said in Enrique's deep voice, 'You come with me, Pennee, I make you best zumba dancer, we make beautiful music together, oh so beautiful Pennee.'

Jackie took her other hand. 'I so look forward to seeing you next week. It seems such a long time, my Pennee, mi querida. Adios.'

'He is fantastic, isn't he?' Penny said dreamily. 'I had the best time in years.' She turned to Kate. 'I'm sorry I rubbished it before. I'm glad you dragged me out. I never would have met Enrique otherwise. He's just so...' She floated over to the car wrapped in her own dreams.

'He's such a plonker,' repeated Kate indignantly. 'How can she fall for all that guff?'

'But when you're feeling neglected and unloved,' Jackie pointed out.

'Yeah, quite easily, I suppose.'

'I wonder if she'll tell George?'

CHAPTER 26

'Hasn't she gone yet?' Kate asked sympathetically.
'Unfortunately, no,' said Barney, 'but,' he grinned at Kate, 'there is light on the horizon. I've managed to get her a job and if she can keep it, which I think she will do as the boss is rich, good-looking and fancies her, I might get shot of her soon.'

'Poor Barney,' said Kate, 'Melissa really turned your life upside down, didn't she?'

'It's my own fault. Why did I ever ask her out in the first place? She was pretty and I was at a loose end… Anyway, enough of me! How are you and Penny getting on?'

Kate slid into the seat opposite Barney. It was Thursday afternoon. He had finished his meal and the café was quiet after the lunchtime rush. Jackie was in the office tackling paperwork. Just as well, she wouldn't like any of her staff wasting time with Barney, though why she so disliked him Kate couldn't understand. She settled down for a good gossip.

'Get this one, Barney. Penny has an admirer? A dark-skinned admirer from Madrid.'

Barney's eyebrows disappeared behind his floppy blonde hair. 'Is this her rebellion against George and his activities?'

Kate laughed, 'No I don't think so, not consciously anyway. We went to our first zumba dancing class, Jackie, Penny and I, and this Enrique is our teacher.'

'Enrique eh? Quite dramatic.'

'He is, believe me. Enrique Gonzalez, Five foot four of toned and tanned muscle. He's hilarious, Barney. You should hear him, totally over the top with his dramatic he-man carry on, but Penny loves it. Enrique adores Penny because she hangs on his every word and admires him so soppily.'

'And has George heard about this?'

'He must have. Penny goes on and on about him here, can't see her just switching off at home. She hasn't said what George makes of it. I think he's too deep into his cross-dressing just now to notice.'

'And what about yourself?' Barney asked.

Kate made a face. 'I'm a bit like you, Barney. I need my head examining. I went out with Stan again. We went to the fair on Saturday evening. Walter caught me in a weak moment and pleaded his case and, like a mutt, I said yes. Stan swore blind we'd have a lovely time, but I think I must have been bonkers to risk a second date.'

'Hey, Stan's a good bloke, Kate. Everyone's entitled to one mistake and poor Stan…'

The café door pinged open and they both looked up. A new customer approached the counter.

'Better run, Barney. I'll bring you a coffee, shall I?'

'Yes, please.' Barney was frowning. 'I know that face, just can't place him.'

Kate slipped behind the coffee counter and smiled brightly at the newcomer. 'What can I get you?' she asked.

'I've not come for coffee, lass,' said the man. 'I've come to see the owner, Miss Dalrymple-Jones. I'm Stampwick, the builder. She left a message on my phone about doing some renovation work here.' Mr. Stampwick looked about him. 'Aye, and not before time by the look of it. It's worse than I thought.'

'Is that your line in tactful, Mr Stampwick?' asked Kate.

'No point in beating about the bush, lass,' he said. 'Tell it like it is that's what I say. No sense in wrapping it up.'

'I'm sure Jackie will love you,' Kate said under her breath and went off to get her.

John Stampwick scratched his grizzled grey head as he stared about him. He took in the scratched and worn serving counter, the battered old dresser and frayed carpets. Never been touched since Marilyn took it over I bet, he thought. He took his pad from his pocket and rummaged for a pen. This could be a long list.

Jackie came out from her office smiling happily. 'Mr Stampwick, I'm so pleased to meet you. Tom Young from the Trades Council said you were the best. Come on into the office and we can discuss what needs doing.' Jackie shepherded Mr. Stampwick into her office and shut the door.

Kate returned to Barney. 'Well what did you make of him?' she asked.

'I know of him,' Barney said, 'and he's a good builder by all accounts, but I don't like that connection with the Trades Council. Never good news. Tom Young's up to something but I haven't found out what yet. I really should be back at my office now, but I think I'll hang around a bit and see what happens.'

'She'll only take it that you've got nothing better to do,' Kate pointed out.

'So I'll just confirm her prejudices then, won't I, by being here,' Barney said calmly.

Jackie took Mr Stampwick on a tour of the café, Walter's kitchen and storeroom, the staffroom and toilet facilities. At every new sight he pursed his lips and whistled soundlessly through his teeth. 'It is as it is,' he repeated enigmatically as he surveyed every new room.

Jackie wondered if this was good news or bad news. Mr Stampwick wrote extensively in his small notepad, his large fist travelling busily across the page. Jackie tried to read his notes but his writing was almost illegible.

Luckily Walter was on his break when Mr Stampwick checked out his kitchen. After the now familiar whistle and 'it is as it is,' he poked about the room. Jackie was starting to feel a little annoyed with him. Hell's bells, even she could see the whole lot needed ripping out and starting again, it didn't need all his whistling to tell him that.

Eventually the whistling ceased and Mr. Stampwick turned to Jackie. 'However have you been allowed to operate this long with a kitchen like this? It's a nightmare. Doesn't Environmental Health ever visit?' He poked his shoe into a hole in the lino on the floor. 'This should be a solid non-slip floor.' He stared about him in wonderment and the whistling started again.

'Look, Mr Stampwick, I know it's bad,' began Jackie.

'Bad? Yes, it's bad I'm afraid, lass. Sorry to say but I have to tell it like it is. I always do; tell it like it is. No sense in wrapping it up, that's my motto.'

Ooh, I think I'd like to wrap you up, thought Jackie, and tell it like it is to you. You're a right old woman. A blind man on a galloping horse can see it is bad. That's why we are gathered together brethren, so cut to the chase. Aloud she said, 'So what are we talking about and how much?' She might as well be as blunt as him.

'Re-wiring, new cupboards and counter tops, ovens, hotplates, sealed non-slip floors, extractor fans.' He poked at the old fan on the wall. It wobbled. 'I don't suppose anyone's had that to bits and cleaned it for years,' he commented and wrote lengthily on his pad.

He obviously didn't know Marilyn. I don't suppose she let anyone take it to bits, least of all Walter, he'd never get it back together again. Last time he took his bike to bits Stan had to sort it for him. Mother wasn't hot on repairs and renewals unless something was really dropping to bits; it would have eaten into her profits. 'How much then?' He must have some idea.

Mr Stampwick recommenced his whistling and strolled back out into the café. Walter was sitting having a coffee with Barney. Jackie frowned when she saw them together. Walter was enough trouble at the best of times; she didn't need Barney Anderson stirring him up in the background.

Mr Stampwick nodded towards Walter. 'Is that your chef?' he asked.

'Not chef really,' Jackie said, 'general cook really. He worked for my mother for years and has rather ossified like his menu, but that will change with the new menus for the café.'

'Ossified,' Walter leaned over to Barney, 'what's all that about?'

'Er, stuck in a rut, I think.'

'Cheeky little…,' Walter fumed. 'I might be in a rut but I have loyal customers that have come for years for my fry-ups. Half of York goes to work on my bacon butties and now she wants to change it all and me too.'

Mr Stampwick, unaware of the darts of dislike from Walter and Barney, snapped his pad shut. 'I'll be blunt, Miss Dalrymple-Jones,' he said, 'and I'm always blunt. I'm a Yorkshire man and I don't see any sense in beating about the bush. It is as it is and it's like this. It's going to cost you a packet, a top to toe re-fit and however you do it, it doesn't come cheap, so if you're determined to do it, brace yourself, lass.'

Jackie drew herself up. 'My mother left me sufficient funds to do the work, Mr Stampwick. The Café Paradise has to be dragged into the twenty-first century. The tourists and locals expect so much more these days and I want to be in there as one of the leading cafés in York. So how much?'

Mr Stampwick took to whistling through his teeth again and stared at the ceiling. 'Well, all things being as they are…' he began.

'And when there's an R in the month and the moon's on

the wane and the cat's been sick on the step – *how much?*'

Mr Stampwick's blunt manner seemed to have deserted him. He edged closer to the café door. 'It's not so easy just off the top of my head, Miss Dalrymple-Jones. I'll have to go away and study my notes and work on the project a bit before I can accurately tell you.'

Jackie got between Mr Stampwick and the door. 'How much, or I'll ram one of Walter's best bacon butties where you've never seen one before.'

'Forty thousand, maybe fifty,' squeaked Mr Stampwick and made a dash for the door. 'I'll be in touch.'

'He might be a good builder but, if he's any connection to Tom Young and that Trades Council of his, there'll be bad news in it somewhere for Jackie,' said Walter. 'Can't we talk her into getting other quotes, anyone away from that lot?'

'Are you going to try, Walter?' asked Barney.

'I thought you might,' Walter said hopefully.

'Look what happened the last time I mentioned the Trades Council to her. She immediately went and joined it, so I don't think I can stop her now.' Barney was gloomy.

'Well we've got to try,' Walter said determinedly. 'We can't stand by and see her get ripped off.'

Barney drained the dregs of his cappuccino. 'I know. But you try. She won't listen to me.'

Walter stood up and waylaid Jackie as she returned from seeing Mr Stampwick out. 'He's Trades Council, Jackie,' he said. 'Don't you think you should cast your nets a bit wider, lass, get quotes from other folk not connected with that lot?'

'There's nothing wrong with *that lot* as you like to call them, Walter. Mr Stampwick has been very helpful and I'm sure is quite honest and trustworthy. In fact, Mr Young recommended him.'

Barney couldn't help himself. He snorted with derision. 'Well if Tom Young recommended him, Walter, what can we say? Anyone who Tom recommends must be, well ... I'm not sure what really.' Barney stood up. 'Time to go.' He pushed his chair back and looked levelly at Jackie. 'Go to the Chamber of Trade, Jackie, get someone decent and reliable, not one of Tom Young's crowd, please.'

Walter held his breath, surely she would see sense.

Outwardly calm, Jackie returned Barney's level stare but, somewhere deep inside, a small voice said listen to him, don't be so pig-headed. But already it was too late, she had promised Mr Stampwick the work. She couldn't back out now and cancel. What would Tom Young say, especially after the Nina debacle.

'Save your breath, you two, he's already booked,' she said and swept off back to her office.

CHAPTER 27

Jackie took the new pair of elasticated pants out of their wrapper. Why it had to be a new pair for her lunch date with Tom Young, she wasn't sure. It wasn't as if he was going to get a look at them, not in broad daylight, in the middle of a posh restaurant. But, Jackie admitted, she might feel better about herself, more confident, knowing a gleaming, fresh pair of magic-pants were giving her the streamlined, nearly svelte figure she yearned for.

She really fancied Tom Young. He was attractive and sexy, *so* very unlike a certain customer at the café, who she most certainly did *not* fancy, did she? No she did not, Jackie told herself firmly. And in any case, Dosser Boy could never afford to take her to The Pear Tree Restaurant. Even the top-rate social security hand out wouldn't stretch to that. She would stick with Tom Young; at least he had asked her out to lunch, which is more than Dosser Boy ever did.

Jackie stood in front of the full-length bedroom mirror and held the magic-pants up against her. She shook her head doubtfully. They were supposed to be her size but they looked like they would only fit an anorexic elf. But they *were* stretch pants… She put one leg in and then the other and tried to pull them up. She made it to her knees and then started to struggle, squirming this way and that in a crazy dance, her face flushed and contorted with effort as she tried to pull them to her thighs.

Exhausted, and with the magic-pants only half way up,

she shuffled to her bed and flopped on to it. She lay panting and cross that her efforts had been wasted so far.

But Jackie wasn't Marilyn's daughter for nothing. Those magic-pants clearly stated her size on them, and having paid an exorbitant amount of money for them, she was jolly well going to wear them, come hell or high water.

Jackie reached down and grasped the pants firmly. With fresh determination she wriggled, heaved and tugged and wriggled some more until, eureka! with one last tug she forced them up and over her bottom and stomach.

Jackie lay back on her bed panting triumphantly. They didn't feel too bad either. In fact, she didn't mind having spent all that money now. These were the most comfortable pair she'd ever had.

Then she tried to stand up. The pants encased her so tightly she could hardly walk. She tottered to the mirror and looked at herself again. She smiled: they weren't called magic pants for nothing. Her stomach was flat and her bottom small. OK, so she could barely walk and they were incredibly uncomfortable, but if she looked like Gwyneth Paltrow for the day she didn't care.

Jackie had thrown Samson out of the door first thing, so that she would be able to shower and dress in peace, without either herself or her new dress being attacked by his sharp claws. She slipped the dress over her head and zipped it up. The pale blue suited her, the fine wool material clung to her curves and emphasised her new slim outline. For once Jackie was pleased with her appearance. She slipped on her high heels and picked up her bag. Bring it on, Tom, she thought happily. Be prepared to be charmed.

* * * * * *

The Pear Tree restaurant was a mellow red-brick building covered with ivy, tucked away behind one of York's many snickle-ways and had a proud tradition of serving fine food for over a century.

Although May was well advanced, the air was cool. Jackie had a warm coat over her dress. The waiter took the coat and showed her to the table Tom had reserved for them. Jackie eased herself gently down into the chair, glad that Tom was not there to watch the process. Now that she had sat down, the magic-pants jack-knifed her in two and kept her rigidly upright in the chair. She didn't know how she would ever get up again, let alone eat anything.

Now that she was settled, she looked about her, enjoying the few minutes alone, taking in the other diners and the discreet luxury and charm of the place. Even though it was early, the restaurant was filling up rapidly with business people in suits, older more casually dressed retired couples and tourists.

Jackie sighed happily. Café Paradise could be this popular after Mr Stampwick and his builders had worked their magic. Yes, she was on the up and life was getting better. She was lost in daydreams, her mind filled with pictures of long queues for the Café Paradise stretching down the street, when suddenly Tom was in front of her, leaning in and kissing her cheek.

'Sorry I'm a bit late,' he said, slipping into the chair opposite and smiling at her.

Her heart lurched violently. He was amazing and he was hers, even if it was just for lunch. Jackie tried hard not to show her excitement and delight and tried for a nonchalant, 'And how are you?'

'Oh, I'm fine,' Tom replied. 'Never better. But look at you, Jackie, you look lovely. Really blooming. You've lost weight since I last saw you. It suits you, if you don't mind my saying so.'

Jackie blushed guiltily. Yes, she had lost a few pounds running about the café, but the magic pants smoothed out all the lumps and bumps.

The waiter arrived with the menus and Tom consulted the wine list.

'Is red alright with you, Jackie, there's a cracking St. Emilion Grand Cru 1982 here. You must try it, it really is a stunner.'

St. Emilion. Well. Jackie knew from working in the supermarket that a bottle of that didn't come cheap, whatever year it was. She nodded agreement.

She opened the menu and her heart sank as she was presented with an almost endless list of dishes. The entrées and mains covered pages. She wondered how the kitchen ever managed to keep this lot in stock.

The waiter poured out the wine for Tom to try. He nodded approval and both glasses were filled. Tom raised his glass. 'I think a toast is called for. To you, Jackie, and to the success of the new Café Paradise.'

They clinked glasses and Jackie took a sip of her wine. It was soft and velvety. She took another sip. She could get used to this. The wine relaxed her and she looked more confidently at the menu.

'Have you seen anything you fancy?' Tom asked, smiling at her across the tale.

Only you so far, Jackie thought, and tried not to look as if she could eat him up. Everything on the menu looked delicious but, her pants were so constricting, she wasn't sure if she would be able to eat very much. She looked for the smallest and simplest dishes. Maybe not the soup: all that liquid, she might need the loo and however would she wrestle with the magic pants in a tiny cubicle? And even if she did get them off, she'd never get them on again. No, better play safe.

'Perhaps a small egg mayonnaise and the fish,' she said to Tom, her mouth watering as she read all the different meat dishes and styles and sizes of steak.

Tom looked at her quizzically. 'That's very restrained. You're not dieting today I hope, Jackie. You look beautiful just as you are.'

Jackie glowed at his compliment. 'Me, dieting? No, not at all. I don't believe in all that,' she lied. 'I was never going to be Twiggy, so I try to embrace my fuller figure. I mean, look at Adele, the singer. It hasn't done her any harm.'

Tom topped up her glass. 'As I said, my dear, a very beautiful figure it is,' he purred, licking his lips slowly.

This was almost too much for Jackie. 'I'll… I'll stick with the fish though, Tom,' she stammered and took a long swig of her wine.

Tom was a good lunch companion and kept up an amusing flow of anecdotes about the people he dealt with in the course of his work. No names were mentioned, but he was not particularly discreet and Jackie could make educated guesses to identify them all. He told his stories well as the food came and went and the wine flowed.

Conversation turned to Café Paradise. Tom was interested to hear all of Jackie's plans. After several glasses of St. Emilion, Jackie's guard was down and she told Tom in some detail of Mr Stampwick's visit and the proposed renovation of the café: taking out the old electrics and the pipe-work covering the walls and chasing in new electrics and fittings before re-plastering and fitting the new kitchen equipment.

Tom seemed very impressed with Jackie's plans and asked intelligent questions, encouraging her to explore and expand her ideas for the future.

By now the magic-pants were nearly cutting Jackie in two and she wriggled around on her seat to try and find a more comfortable position. Tom looked concerned. 'Are you alright, Jackie? Is your seat not comfortable?'

Jackie flushed. Fancy wriggling, like a silly girl, she thought.

'Sorry, Tom, no I'm fine. Where were we?'

Tom reached down to the briefcase he had placed at the side of the table when he first came in. He opened it and pulled out some papers. Clearing a space amongst their glasses, he got out his pen and consulted the forms in front of him.

'Sorry to bring this up now, Jackie, after such a lovely lunch with you, but from what you've told me we'll have to get your insurance for the café sorted out now.'

Jackie made a face. She was having such a lovely time. Why did Tom have to bring such boring old stuff up now?

'Because I'm your friend and I'm looking out for you.'

The St. Emilion had had its effect on Jackie. She threw caution to the winds. She reached across the table and stroked Tom's hand as it travelled across the page. 'We could be more than friends, Tom, we're both free…'

Tom looked up and smiled at her. 'I like the sound of that, Jackie, but first things first. Guns before butter as they say. I must get this proposal form completed for you and then I'll know you're covered for the café and the work you're planning.'

Tom bent over the form and read it out to Jackie. 'The insurance covers you for the building, fire, loss of profit in the event of the building burning down, theft, burglary, employers liability and public liability. It's a Combined Business Policy. I know your relevant details,' he went on briskly, 'and I'll complete the form for you. I just have a few questions I need to check with you. Do you have a working burglar alarm installed?'

Jackie dragged her attention away from admiring his curly brown hair and how his eyebrows ran almost in a straight line above his eyes. 'What? Oh, yes.'

'Any asbestos in the building?'

'Never seen any.'

'That's a no then, is it?'

'Mm, it's a no.' He had such a cute nose and straight jaw. She imagined herself running her hands through his hair and down his jaw…

'And you have two waitresses, yourself and a cook on the staff. Is that right?'

'Yeah, at the moment, but I'm going to get a new chef when the work is done.'

'That's OK, it won't make a big difference to the overall policy.'

Tom looked up and smiled engagingly at Jackie. Once more her heart lurched and her body tingled all over. She wondered if he had a muscular chest rippling beneath his crisp white shirt.

Tom put his pen and papers away. 'There. Enough of business for one day. Let's not spoil a lovely lunch. What about a coffee and a liqueur?'

He gave her his full attention again and Jackie was swept away for the next hour in a haze of Cointreau and light flirtation.

At last it was time to go. Tom took his leave regretfully. 'I have a desk full of work waiting for me, Jackie.' He patted his briefcase. 'I must get the ball rolling on this proposal form for you as well.'

Jackie was disappointed and it must have shown on her face. Tom bent down and kissed her lingeringly on the lips. 'It's only *à bientôt* not *au revoir*. We must do this again, maybe dinner next time and afterwards… I'll give you a ring soon. Give my best wishes to John Stampwick, he'll do a fine job for you.'

When he was safely gone Jackie made a dash for the Ladies' Powder Room. Wine, coffee and liqueurs had all combined to make her visit an urgent one. She dashed into a cubicle and pulled up the woollen dress to do battle with the pants again. The maxim what goes up must come down did not apply to them. They seemed to have a defiant life of their own and would not budge. No wonder rich Edwardian ladies had maids to get them in and out of their corsets. Jackie could see the sense of them as she heaved and tugged.

After ten minutes, by dint of breathing in at the same time as tugging, she freed herself from the corsetry. With huge relief she used the facilities and stuffed the pants into her bag. She might walk out looking a lot plumper than she walked in, but too bad. She was past caring. There was no way she was going to fight with those things again today, and anyway, Tom Young had left so it didn't matter.

She had a sudden thought. If he took her out to dinner she wouldn't be able to wear the magic-pants, not if … well, if things hotted up a bit. He wouldn't want to come across those would he? She would just have to starve and keep up the zumba dancing in the meantime.

CHAPTER 28

Barney arrived home late on Friday evening. He put his bag down in the hallway and looked around in dismay. Melissa had been left alone for the weekend whilst he paid a long overdue visit to his sister in Northumberland and his flat had suffered the consequences. The chair in the hall was piled with her coats and jackets, telling the history of her weekend outings, and the bureau was stacked with newspapers, magazines and dirty cups. Barney guessed her room would be in a similar state. Did that girl never put anything away? What did she think a wardrobe was for?

It was the same story in the kitchen: piles of take-away cartons strewn everywhere and the sink filled with more dirty coffee cups and wine glasses.

He felt his anger rising. Melissa had invited herself to stay rent free, and she was the laziest, idlest girl it had ever been his misfortune to meet. He had been tip-toeing around her and keeping her sweet for long enough, hoping he would learn something useful about Tom Young and his Trades Council outfit, but so far Melissa had not brought home the bacon.

He strode into the lounge, knowing exactly where she would be. Sure enough, she was draped along the length of the sofa, a glass of wine in hand, watching '*Life Below Stairs*' on television. Wordlessly, Barney picked up the remote and switched the TV off. Melissa sat up, spilling her wine on the sofa. Barney winced.

'Barney,' Melissa cried, 'what are you doing? I was watching that. The master had followed the servant to her attic room and was trying to have his wicked way with her.'

Melissa tried to snatch the remote from him but Barney stepped out of her reach.

'Melissa,' he started severely, 'I leave you alone in my flat for two and a half days, only two and a half days mark you, and look what I come back to. A bloody shambles,' he said.

Melissa pouted and lay back on the sofa. 'Oh don't start, Barney, I'm exhausted. You've no idea of the day I've had at the office. I don't know why you ever got me a job in that horrid place, it's a slave camp.'

Barney snorted with derision and threw himself into a chair. Melissa's idea of a hard day would be filing her nails and fetching a cup of coffee, from what he'd heard of her so-called work so far.

'Oh you can laugh,' she continued indignantly. 'Melissa this, Melissa that, phones going, faxes coming in and emails. Then everyone wants coffee, biscuits and sandwiches, typing. *Typing*, Barney! Since when did a receptionist do typing? I ask you. I'm supposed to be there to meet and greet, be a facilitator, not do their typing, that's minion's work. I tell you, Tom Young needs ten Melissas, not one. He's too demanding and if he goes on like this I won't stay. No, I won't, I don't care what you say, Barney.'

Barney listened to this tirade, alarmed at the hurt petulance in her tones. Oh God, he really didn't need this tonight, he was tired, but – he wanted to keep Melissa working for Tom Young a bit longer. Not that she'd done any work up to now that he could see, so what was she on about?

He gave her his full attention and asked gently, 'What's really been going on today, Melissa? You've enjoyed going to The Trades Council until now, so what's happened?'

Melissa was mollified by Barney's gentler tones. She sat

up and set her wine glass carefully on the table. 'It's just as I said, Barney. I've had to mind that awful office on my own all day whilst a certain other person, who shall remain nameless gets to swan off for a long, expensive lunch with a certain attractive café owner. I've been run ragged and couldn't even get out for a sandwich, let alone dine on minted lamb shanks like a certain nameless person did. He came back to the office looking like the cat that'd got the cream, with lipstick on his cheeks,' Melissa ended mutinously.

Ah! Barney was beginning to understand. Mentally translating Melissa's tirade it went something like: Melissa got left behind in the office whilst Tom Young took a lady out to lunch. He came back very happy after a long lunch with evidence of lipstick kisses on his cheek. Result: Melissa (a) hungry; (b) furiously jealous; and (c) exhausted from having to actually do a day's work.

Imagining the scenario, part of Barney wanted to laugh but at the same time he didn't want to alienate the girl. He composed his features in what he hoped would be a sympathetic look and patted her hand. 'Poor Melissa, let me pour you some more wine. I don't suppose you've had any supper yet, have you?'

'No,' she said dolefully.

'How about a nice omelette?' he suggested. 'I can whip us one up in no time and we can talk about things.'

Melissa brightened up. Food being brought to her always made her world a better place. 'Don't you want to know who the café owner was he had lunch with?' she asked, suddenly looking mischievous.

Barney was half-way out of the lounge. He stopped and turned, looking questioningly at Melissa.

'Only Jackie Dalrymple-Jones,' she said, a world of disdain in her voice. 'Fancy taking her to The Pear Tree. I would have thought the pizza shop down Old Gate would have done her fine.'

Barney clenched his fists and breathed deeply. Keep your face straight, Barney boy, he told himself, don't let her get to you. The Pear Tree; very nice. 'They obviously enjoyed themselves,' he managed to say evenly.

'Huh,' Melissa said spitefully. 'Tom Young certainly did. Do you know what, Barney?' Melissa picked up her wine glass again and took a thoughtful sip. 'I like Tom. I mean, who wouldn't, he's so handsome and all that, but I'm beginning to think he's a bit greedy.'

At last. Barney could hardly breathe. He'd waited so long for any nugget of information about Tom Young. Maybe it was coming his way now.

'How's that?' he managed to ask casually.

Melissa held her glass out to be refilled and Barney obliged, sitting down opposite her again, trying to look relaxed.

'Well,' Melissa snuggled down into the sofa, enjoying the attention. 'I know I shouldn't, but I couldn't help myself. I was so annoyed at being left behind when he swanned off, and I had to work *so* hard; so when he came back and asked to be put through to the London office brokers, I accidentally flicked the switch on that horrid complicated switchboard and listened in.'

Barney grinned knowingly.

'Accidentally, Barney, honestly.' Melissa was at her most wide-eyed, so he knew she was lying. 'Anyway, you'll never guess what he told this broker man in London, never in a million years.'

'No, probably not,' said Barney. He was very anxious to know and longed to shout, 'Oh just get on and *tell me* Melissa,' but willed himself to stay calm.

'He told them he'd just completed a new combined business policy for Jackie and was going to double the premium, just because he can! He knows she trusts him and doesn't know any different, and what's more, probably won't look anywhere else for insurance, so he's decided to get as much out of her as possible and that way the Company profits increase and so does his bonus.'

'As you say, Melissa,' Barney said evenly, 'maybe he's getting a bit greedy.'

After Barney had cleared up the kitchen, he began preparations for their supper, knocking seven bells out of the eggs he was beating up in the bowl. Tom Young was a crook, he was sure of it. Barney knew he had shady deals going on and Jackie was the first victim he could definitely point the finger to.

Unfortunately, he couldn't tell her yet; the trail would immediately lead back to Melissa and he needed to learn a lot more. But he hated to think of Jackie being ripped off in this way, even if it was her own stupid, pig-headed fault. Much as he disliked the idea, he must concentrate on Melissa for now. He laughed sourly. Who'd have thought it, dim Melissa being a key player in all this?

CHAPTER 29

Penny turned slowly round, looking at herself in the full-length mirror. Well, she might be fifty-two but she could give any woman of forty a run for her money, she thought. Even though she'd had three boys she'd kept her figure. The black ski pants and skimpy T-shirt suited her, outlining her curves. Penny brushed her black hair. How lucky she had been to discover Monsieur Antoine's salon last year; he'd taken years off her with his skilled tinting and cutting. She shook her head to and fro and watched with satisfaction as her hair swayed with her movements and fell back into shape. Yes, she would look good tonight however hard Enrique worked them.

She heard George coming up the stairs and blushing guiltily she gathered up the pile of discarded outfits from the bed and hastily thrust them in her wardrobe.

'Are you ready yet, Penny?' he called out. 'You've been up there for ages. How long does it take to find a T-shirt and shorts for a dance class? I have got other things to do with my Wednesday evenings besides hang about for you.'

He came into the room grumbling quietly. 'Bloody hell,' he said when he saw Penny. 'What's all the make-up and glitz for? I thought you were going zumba dancing, getting hot and sweaty with the girls. You look like you're ready to dance with Anton du Beke off "Strictly".'

Penny thought of Enrique, his glistening brown body and rippling muscles. Her mouth watered. She turned away from George and grabbed her coat. 'Don't be daft, George. I'm going out with Kate and Jackie, but that doesn't mean I don't want to look my best. I am a woman after all.'

'And what's that supposed to mean?' George demanded.

'Anything you like,' Penny replied and swept past him. 'Come on, I don't want to be late for my class.'

George backed the car down the drive and turned on to the main road. 'It's all very well for you, Penny,' he said as they joined the evening traffic heading on to the Harrogate Road. 'You only need a light tea before your class, but I've been working hard all day and I should be able to sit down to a good meal at night and take my time over it, not to a Mrs. Ebworthy's all-in-one TV dinner shoved at me as I walk in the door.'

'Oh listen to yourself, George.' What was wrong with him these days? Nothing she ever did was right, or enough, or at the right time… Surely he didn't begrudge her the zumba classes? He could come along and join in if he wanted to. It was a mixed class after all. No, on second thoughts she didn't want that, she enjoyed her time with Enrique too much. George's presence would put a stop to that.

'Are you saying I shouldn't go out? Just stay home and wait hand and foot on you all the time, because if you are, George Montague, you've got another thing coming.'

'No, I never said that,' George answered testily. 'I'm just saying I don't know why you have to go rushing off to this zumba class thing before I've hardly got in the door.'

'There, you see, there you go again. You're saying exactly what I said you were saying. You just want me to be a doormat at home.'

It was like a game of tennis, the same argument batted back and forth between them, all the way to the hall. George drove the car angrily into the car park, his wheels spinning, spraying up the gravel as he spun around and screeched to a halt.

Enrique was crossing the car park just ahead of them. He turned at the sound of the screeching tyres. He spotted Penny and smiled, turning back to meet her. As he came towards the car, Penny hurriedly gathered her shoes and bag and jumped out.

'See you later, George, 9:30, don't be late,' she called out and went to meet Enrique without a backward glance.

George watched them walk into the hall together, before driving off; a thoughtful expression on his face.

Jackie and Kate were there already, limbering up in the main hall as Enrique escorted Penny through the doorway.

'Like Lancelot and Guinevere,' Jackie joked, 'only Guinevere never wore ski pants and Nike trainers.'

Penny spotted them and came over to join them.

'Wow, Penny, you're looking very glam,' said Kate. 'I bet George thinks we're on a girls' night out, with you dressed to kill.'

'What, these old things!' Penny indicated her T-shirt and ski pants and tossed her head. 'And don't even mention George. He's just a self-centred cross-patch. All he could think about was his dinner.'

'I suppose at the end of a hard day's work...' Jackie began doubtfully.

'Nothing of the sort,' snorted Penny, 'he's just selfish. Thinks I should stay at home and slave over a home-cooked dinner for him.' She tossed her head again, hoping Enrique would appreciate the way her hair swung out and settled back into its bob again. 'It's time he learned I can have a life of my own.'

She began the bending and stretching exercises Enrique had taught them in the beginner's class. Kate and Jackie glanced at each other enquiringly.

'All is far from well in the Montague camp, by the sound of it,' Kate whispered.

'Ever since George discovered frocks,' agreed Jackie.

'We'd be the same.'

The class took its usual course, starting slowly to get everyone warmed up and moving to the South American rhythms and then getting faster and more furious in sound and pace as the night wore on.

From time to time people took time out and sat on the benches that lined the sides of the hall, to catch their breath and massage aching muscles.

Super-fit Enrique went relentlessly on, dancing all around the room, correcting a step here, a movement there, smiling and encouraging everyone. He came to Penny and danced behind her, holding her close to him and swaying with her to the music. Penny leaned back against him, eyes closed, a dreamy expression on her face.

Kate and Jackie were sitting it out on the benches, exhausted and sweaty after a particularly fast salsa. Kate nudged Jackie. 'That's not George she's dancing with, is it?'

'No,' agreed Jackie. 'I think our sexy Spaniard is getting to her. We'll have to watch out. In some ways Penny is such an innocent, I wouldn't like to see her get herself into something she never meant to happen.'

'Exactly,' agreed Kate, 'even though exotic Enrique does.'

The class continued for another half hour and Jackie and Kate re-doubled their efforts to vigorously dance off a few more pounds. Enrique moved away from Penny and led them again from the front, shouting and exhorting them on to even greater efforts until, as the music finally slowed, they all fell gratefully on to the benches in exhausted heaps.

Jackie stayed on her feet. 'If I sit down now, Kate, I'll never get up again. I'll get my towel from my locker and dry off and go and bring the car round.'

Kate nodded, too breathless to speak. After a few moments she managed to heave herself up off the bench. She saw Penny doing some last cool-down stretches and went over to her. 'Are you ready for the off?' she asked.

Penny stretched up her arms and swayed to and fro. 'There. Yes, I think so, Kate. I'll go and get my stuff. George might be waiting and we can't have that, can we?'

Kate rolled her eyes and didn't reply. Best not get embroiled in that one tonight.

With a lingering glance at Enrique, Penny went off with Kate to collect her things. Together they made their way back to the main front door. Jackie was already there and ready to go. There was no sign of George.

'We'll hang on a bit,' said Kate.

Penny shooed her off. 'No, it's fine, Kate. I'm a big girl you know. No-one's going to kidnap me before George arrives. Off you go and I'll see you tomorrow.'

Kate still didn't look happy at this. Penny gave her a playful push.

'Go on, I insist. George will be here any minute.'

Reluctantly, Kate went down the steps and into Jackie's car. Jackie was of the same mind. 'Shall we wait for George to turn up?' she said.

'Apparently not. Penny reckons she's all growed up and doesn't need a minder.'

In dribs and drabs the rest of the group came out of the hall, some walking away arm in arm up the road, others to their cars and driving away.

Penny waited by the door for George, her heart beating fast. She was aware that Enrique was still inside. He had not taken his usual leave of her, gently kissing her hands; so romantic, she thought dreamily.

Suddenly she was grabbed from behind and pulled inside the near darkness of the hallway.

'Pennee, my little Pennee, you are still here, alone.' Enrique slid his hands around her waist and spun her round to face him.

'George,' she stuttered, 'George is late.'

'Excellent,' breathed Enrique, 'the late George, the later

the better.'

Penny felt his hot breath on her cheeks and then he was kissing her, holding her in a tight embrace, pushing her back against the door. Penny felt excited and dizzy all at the same time. Enrique's lips were soft and firm. His tongue pushed at her mouth, seeking her out. Penny wasn't ready for this. She pulled away breathlessly. 'Enrique… I…'

'Pennee, beautiful Pennee, you tantalise me all night with your, oh so kissable, lips and sexy little body swaying in front of me. How can I resist you?' He made to grab her again.

Luckily, or unluckily, George screeched into the car park, spraying gravel in all directions. Penny twisted away from Enrique's grasp and dashed out of the door. 'My husband, George … that's him now. See you next week Enrique,' she called behind her, wiping Enrique's kisses from her mouth as she ran to get into the car.

As they moved off, Enrique stood in the doorway waving and smiling. George glanced at him and frowned. 'Who's that then?' he asked.

'That's Enrique, our teacher,' said Penny, fumbling for her towel and dabbing at her face.

'Enrique eh,' George said meditatively. 'Spanish charmer. You keep away from him, Penny.'

Penny laughed guiltily. 'Why should I do that, George? In any case, he's our teacher, we see him every week.'

'Hmph.' George packed a world of meaning into the expressive snort as he drove on through the dark streets.

No-one but George had kissed Penny in that way for thirty years and, now Penny came to think of it, George hadn't kissed her like that for, well, how long? Penny racked her brains, but it was so long ago she couldn't remember. Not that she could mention it; they weren't on kissing terms at the moment.

She turned to say something to him and stopped; her mouth sagging open in amazement. She leaned close towards him and inspected his face closely. Even by the street light that filtered into the car, she could see George looked decidedly odd. His face was bright red, pillar-box red.

'George!' she exclaimed. 'What have you been doing?'

'Doing?' he echoed. 'Running to and fro all night after you, that's what I've been doing. A man can't call his soul his own.'

'George' Penny said sternly. 'Out with it. What have you really been up to? Your face is brick red all over.'

'Well, if you must know, it's my five o'clock shadow. I hate it. It's always there, dark and bristly like an old shoe-brush stuck on my face. So I decided t have a go at getting rid of it and I bought one of those waxing kits at the chemist. You melt the wax and slap it on and when it cools you rip it off and it's supposed to take all your bristles with it and they don't grow back for weeks. Trouble is, when I ripped the strips off, half my face came with it.'

'Oh terrific, George,' Penny said. 'So now, not only do I have a cross-dressing husband who doesn't know who he is, but he looks like a day-glo lobster into the bargain.'

'Well speaking of red,' George said angrily, 'I'm not the only tomato face in this car. You're very red and flushed. What have you been up to?'

'Zumba dancing, George, you know very well.'

'That's what you *say*, he snarled.

'Yes I do say,' Penny defended herself. 'What else should I say? It's the truth.' She fell silent, guiltily aware that it wasn't the whole truth, the memory of Enrique's kisses too fresh to be pushed away.

'Zumba dancing never gave you that flush, I'll be bound. I'm still your husband, Penny. That Enrique had better keep away from you or he'll be sorry.'

Husband in a frock, waxing his chest and now his face. Whatever next? Penny wondered. She wanted a real man in her life and if George wasn't going to be a man, well ... we'll just have to see, she decided.

CHAPTER 30

Jackie turned over the 'Open' sign and heaved a sigh of relief. 'Thank God, 5:30 p.m.' she said, 'I thought it would never come. I'm not complaining, that's the best Thursday we've ever had, but enough's enough.' She looked across to Penny and Kate, wearily wiping down the tables. 'Let's take a break and have a cup of tea before we clean up. After all, we haven't had chance to catch up for over a week.'

Penny and Kate flopped down into the empty chairs. Jackie brought the tea and a plate of cakes across to the table.

'Eat up, they won't keep. Stan will be bringing fresh tomorrow. He's keen to see a certain fair-haired young lady?' She glanced across the table at Kate.

Kate smiled weakly. 'Probably. He's still very keen, but I'm not sure that I am.'

Instantly Penny and Jackie were alert.

'Is the romance not proceeding too smoothly?' asked Jackie.

Kate sipped her tea thoughtfully. 'I don't know what to make of him. It's like being with a double act, only he's playing both the parts.'

Penny and Jackie were hooked now. They both leaned forward, cakes suspended half-way to their mouths. 'Go on,' they said in unison.

'We went to the fair on the Green a week last Saturday,' Kate began. 'It was great, we had a lovely time. We went on all the rides and then on to the side-stalls. Stan won a huge teddy at the shooting gallery and gave it to me. He was such fun and so attentive, on the ball with everything and then suddenly it all fell to bits and it was like I was out with a different man.'

'Sounds fun to me,' said Jackie, 'two for the price of one.'

'Well it wasn't,' said Kate crossly. 'I have a well-known fear of heights, do I not?'

'Yes,' Penny and Jackie chorused again.

'So what does he insist I go on and won't take no for an answer?'

'Not the…?'

'He couldn't possibly…'

'All the way up there?'

'They say you can see all of York spread out like a carpet.'

'You can, and I did. Not only that,' Kate nodded solemnly at the gawping girls, 'first he called me "chicken" if I didn't go on it and then when I did, we got stuck. Not at the bottom where I might have stepped daintily off, or a little bit higher where I could have climbed down a ladder. No, *we* got stuck right at the very top for an hour and all he could do was babble on about his bearded Aunt Madeleine. She doesn't like heights but he took her on it too. Weird or what? And then to cap it all when we did finally get off, he couldn't remember where he'd left the car in the field where we parked up. We went round and round, clutching this bloody big teddy bear, for an hour or more. And then we had a cloudburst and it pelted it down for about 10 minutes, by which time we were soaked and the field was puddled. We ended up slipping and sliding about in the mud and still couldn't find the wretched car. In the end he put me in a taxi home. I seem to remember being here before with Stan.' Kate ended her story, took a cake and sat back.

'So date number three might not happen any time soon,' said Jackie.

'But it wasn't all bad,' said Penny. 'He behaved like a gentleman and he hasn't been down any dark lay-bys with you, as we thought he might, so why don't you give him another chance? Third time lucky. He might get his act together this time.'

Kate smiled wryly. Saturday night, home alone with a cheese toastie and the *X Factor*, instead of Stan and a meal in a cosy restaurant.

'As I said, part of the evening was lovely.' Kate stopped, remembering Stan's soft kiss at the fairground. 'Maybe if he asks me again…' She smiled and bit into a crumbly meringue. 'Seeing as how we're having post-mortems,' she said wiping the cream from her chin and looking at Jackie, 'what about you and that Trades Council fella, hot-to-trot Tom Young? Didn't you have a lunch date with him last Friday?'

Jackie blushed and looked coy.

'Oh yes,' said Penny. 'Mr Drop-dead gorgeous. Did you wear your magic pants like we said?'

'I did, but I'd sooner have a boa constrictor round me any day than those things. You can hardly walk or breathe in them and eating is definitely out. We went to The Pear Tree and you know what the food is like there.'

Kate and Penny nodded enviously.

'I could only manage a sliver of fish,' Jackie went on mournfully, 'and he ordered St. Emilion Grand Cru. Absolutely divine, but I didn't dare drink too much of it in case I needed the loo and that would have been impossible. But having said all that, it was worth it. I looked amazing even if I do say it myself. Svelte, that's the word.'

'So what did you get up to on this lunch of yours?' asked Penny.

'Well, Tom is an absolute sweetie. There were all the café insurances to sort out and bless him, he did all the forms himself. I mean, he could just have thrown them my way and let me get on with it, but all I had to do was answer a few daft questions and get back to enjoying lunch and drooling over him. He's so efficient. I've even received the policy documents already. He is absolutely gorgeous and talk about charm, he has it in spades. And the softest skin imaginable.'

'And how would you know that?' Penny demanded.

'Well, we had a little, shall we say, encounter. He's going to ring me. I can't wait,' she finished excitedly. 'What a kisser!'

Penny put her tea cup down and brushed the cake crumbs from her apron. 'Speaking of kissers,' she said. 'I had an interesting encounter after the class last week.'

Now it was Jackie and Kate's turn to stare.

'George remembered he's a man and got the hots for you again, did he?' Kate grinned at her.

'No, not George,' Penny said scornfully. 'He's still playing at being Georgina; only it might not be playing, who knows?' She leaned forward in her chair, looking down at her apron as she pleated it. 'I was waiting for George the other night, after the zumba class, do you remember?'

'Course we do, we wanted to wait with you, but you were having none of it. Told us to shove off,' Kate said.

'No I didn't,' protested Penny. 'Just didn't want you hanging about. Anyway, you'll never guess who followed me out?' Penny looked at them, wide-eyed and smirking a little.

'Well if this was the clincher question in *Who Wants To Be A Millionaire*, they can write me the cheque now,' said Jackie.

'It wasn't Enrique by any chance?' asked Kate drily.

'It was. How did you know?' asked Penny in surprise.

'Ooh, just a well-educated guess,' said Jackie.

'He kissed me,' said Penny dreamily, 'right there in the hallway. It was dark and I was in his arms.' She sighed ecstatically. 'It was so romantic.'

'Romantic, my ar…' Kate was exasperated.

'Exactly,' jumped in Jackie. 'You're playing with fire,

Penny, surely you can see that. Enrique's a player. He loves to play the older women in the class if they're daft enough to fall for it. And have you forgotten the teensy detail of your marriage to George?'

Penny tossed her head, as defiant as any of her teenage boys had been. 'Oh George. What about George? Half the time he doesn't even notice I'm there and if he does, he's asking my advice about his clothes. I want a man, Jackie, not an undecided.'

'Give him time, Penny,' Kate counselled. 'It might be just a passing phase, a mid-life crisis. Don't throw away thirty years of marriage for a poncey Spanish dancer.'

Penny continued to look mutinous. 'Well he's a fantastic kisser and that's a start. And what's more,' she ended, 'I hope he does it again'.

'Men,' said Kate. 'They're the cause of all the world's troubles.'

'Unless their Tom Young,' said Jackie dreamily.

'Or Enrique Gonzales,' said Penny enthusiastically.

'Or Stan Peterson and his Bertie bear,' said Kate wearily and got up to finish her work.

* * * * * *

That evening George opened the back door and went into the kitchen, slinging his bag on to the table. Overhead the persistent thump-thump of a bass drum reverberated through the house. He went through to the hall and listened. Latin American music was playing loudly upstairs. He went to investigate.

In the bedroom, dressed in a strappy T-shirt and tight leggings with a bandana tied round her head, Penny danced energetically, throwing out her arms and legs and wiggling her hips sexily in time to the music.

Unseen, George watched Penny as Penny watched herself

in their full-length mirror. She half-closed her eyes, pouted her lips and kissed someone beyond the mirror, all the while dancing sinuously to the salsa beat.

Feeling too much the voyeur, George crept back down the stairs and coughed loudly. He made his way back up, treading heavily and whistling loudly.

The music stopped abruptly. When he entered the bedroom Penny was perched on the bed wiping her face with the bandana.

'I liked the music, love,' George said cheerily. 'South American, isn't it? Puts you in the mood for dancing.' He sashayed about the room, miming a lively waltz. He pulled Penny off the bed and into a close embrace as he tried to waltz with her. 'This is no good,' he said, 'we haven't got the space to do it properly. I know - how do you fancy a night out tonight? Dinner at St. Olaves and dancing afterwards?'

'Is this guilt money? Have you been at the horses again?' she asked suspiciously. 'You know what you said after last time.'

'No I have not,' said George testily. 'Must there be a reason for a man to ask his wife out to dinner. Let's just be spontaneous and do it.'

This was so unlike George. Penny stared at him. He must be feeling guilty about something.

'There's plenty of time for a shower and we'll have a great night out.'

'You are going as George?' Penny asked anxiously, 'not Georgina?'

'George it is tonight,' said George. 'I know too many people around here; don't want to shock the natives.'

An hour later they were seated in the restaurant of St. Olaves and looking at the menu. Penny hardly recognised George in his charcoal-grey lounge suit. She had seen him in so many exotic silk and satin ladies' outfits that the sudden transformation into sober-suited man with neatly brushed hair came as quite a shock.

Penny wore an electric blue short sleeved dress, low-cut to expose her milky white cleavage. George eyed the dress enviously. Hell of a colour that blue. It would suit him. He wondered where she had got it from, but thought he'd better not ask and spoil the moment.

Penny was concentrating on the extensive menu, her brow furrowed as she tried to make sense of the gobbledegook. 'What's a slender cutlet of finely chopped pork in a natural skin accompanied by a fine rice of root vegetables and clouds of soft potatoes with a side serving of jus?'

'Bangers, mash, carrot and turnip in gravy,' said George shortly.

'Is that all? I can make that at home. Well what about Neptune's gifts from the sea surrounded by golden pomme de terre?'

'Scampi and chips.'

'Alright, try this. A buttery cloud of fluffy pomme de terres atop a sonnet of finely chopped beef, accompanying a medley of locally sourced root vegetables in a jus?'

'Shepherd's Pie.'

'Very good, George. You missed your way. You should have gone into advertising.'

'I'll say this for them, someone's got imagination. They make a lot of a little.'

After they had translated all the menu it came down to a choice between a trio of lamb chops or steak and ale pie, accompanied by another ' cloud of riced pomme de terre and onion jus.'

Waiting for their wine and 'fruits de mer' starters George and Penny looked about them. St. Olaves was a popular dinner and dancing venue and the tables were all occupied. George whistled tunelessly as he watched the couple at the next table deciphering the menu.

'George, don't do that,' said Penny, irritated by the noise.

'Do what?' he asked.

'That whistling thing. It's really annoying.'

George raised his eyebrows and was silent.

They sat quietly as waiters scurried to and fro carrying food and wine about the room. George began singing snatches of song under his breath. 'Don't put your daughters on the stage Mrs Worthington,' followed by 'It's a long way to Tipperary,' and then 'Summertime and the living is easy…'

Penny could stand no more. 'For God's sake, George, don't do that.'

'Now what? I'm not doing anything.'

'That awful, aimless singing. You know I hate it.'

'I'm not doing it.

'Yes, you are, you don't even know you are, so stop it.'

'How can I stop it if I don't know I'm doing it?'

'Just don't.'

Another long silence fell between them. George drummed his fingers on the table, then caught Penny's eye and stopped.

'They're a long time with our starters,' he said.

'They're busy, you can see that.'

Silence again. Penny decided to make an effort. 'Well, this is nice,' she began brightly. 'We don't often get time away together. We must have lots to talk about, catch up on.'

'Yeah,' said George.

'Well..?' Penny said encouragingly, 'what shall we talk about?'

An expression of panic flitted across George's face. 'I don't know. What do people talk about who've been married for thirty years?'

Penny thought about her job and the changes at the café, the zumba classes, her new sleek haircut and slimmed down figure. Well, if George wasn't interested…

The fruits de mer and lamb chops passed quietly, pleasantries being exchanged between them about the food and wine and little else. George attempted to make conversation, but Penny had withdrawn and was unresponsive. Vaguely he felt that somewhere along the line he had missed the boat with her, but didn't quite know how or what to do about it.

They decided against pudding in favour of coffee and liqueurs in the more intimate lounge area that encircled the dance floor. A four-piece band was tuning up on the small stage. Three men dressed in brightly patterned shirts and white trousers struck up a lively Latin American tune on their guitars, and were soon joined by the girl singing a song in close harmony with them.

Penny clapped her hands in delight. 'Latin American – salsa, tango. I can't wait.'

'I thought we were in for a bit of ballroom tonight. When I booked it on the phone, that's what the fella told me,' George growled quietly into his Cointreau.

'He must have got his weeks mixed up. Well we're here now, let's enjoy it. In fact,' Penny was suddenly cheerful, 'seeing as how it's a Latin American night, I'm going to be really adventurous and try a Tequila Sunrise. I've often wondered what one would be like. Now's the time to find out.'

George got up, pleased to get away from the racket on the stage. Well at least Penny was happy. He would have liked a nice bit of ballroom.

The evening was in full swing and the bar was three-deep in waiting customers. George queued patiently listening to the sound of Spanish guitars, hand clapping and foot stamping as Os Musicos got into their stride. Someone tapped him on the shoulder and George turned around. For a moment he saw a stranger and then recognition dawned.

'Therese?' he said uncertainly.

'Ssh, it's Terry here, mate. Good to see you, George. It is George, isn't it?'

'Yeah, I'm only Georgina to myself and when I come to the club, of course.'

'What are you doing here?'

'I brought my wife for dinner and dancing, but it's some Latin American group, all salsa and samba I expect. And you?'

'I just popped in for a drink. Manager's a friend of mine.'

'Come and have a drink with us,' suggested George. 'You've got to see the dress my wife's wearing. What a blue. It's amazing. I'd love something in that colour.'

'How are you going to explain me to your wife?' Terry asked.

'Well, I suppose she's got to know sometime and she knows everything else, so why not now?'

They collected their drinks and headed off to the lounge. The dance floor was already crowded and Penny was watching, smiling and tapping her feet. George introduced Terry to Penny. She looked puzzled at this new acquaintance until George explained how he had met Terry on a visit to a gay club. He could see Penny was shocked. Maybe this wasn't the best time after all.

'George, is this why we've come out tonight, so you can soften me up to tell me… Is this your…?' All the colour had drained from Penny's face.

Oh blimey, if there's a wrong end of the stick to get hold of, Penny will get it, thought George in exasperation.

'No, no, nothing like that, Penny love. I'm not gay, he's not gay.' He looked at Terry. 'You're not are you, lad?'

'No, I'm like you, George, I just like dressing up. I'm still a man underneath, but lovely dresses and fancy make-up, they just turn me on. Harmless enough. George is the same. We could be a lot worse, think of that, Penny. If we were drunks, gamblers or serial adulterers, now that would be something to worry about, but a few frocks, that's nothing.'

George could see Penny trying to frame words. Her

mouth opened and closed like a fish gasping for air, but none would come. He put the Tequila Sunrise in front of her. 'There you are, love, work your way through that. It will all seem a lot clearer then.'

Penny picked up the glass and drank it down in one. She caught her breath and coughed as she put the glass down and the colour returned to her cheeks. 'It's crystal clear to me now, George. You like being Georgina and he likes, what is it Terry, who are you?'

'Therese,' said Terry. 'I like to think of her as my alter-ego. George is the same,' he said helpfully.

'Alter-ego,' Penny mouthed experimentally.

George patted her hand. 'You just sit back and enjoy the music, love' he said. 'We don't want to spoil your evening.'

Was it spoiled? Penny wasn't sure. This was just another piece of information. George at a gay club and he'd never said a word... He says he's not gay, but then why...? She was lost in these new thoughts as snatches of George and Terry's conversation floated around her.

'See what I mean about that dress?'

'Electric blue, George, that's what you have to ask for. Try that shop in Kirkgate. She has stuff like that in all sizes.'

'Have you tried that new eye liner...?'

'No, don't go there. Wigerama on the internet, they're the best. See that one I had on last week? That's one of theirs.'

'My Bosom Friend? Yeah, I'll email you their web address. Fantastic. They made Therese what she is today.'

Suddenly a voice broke into Penny's jumbled thoughts. 'Pennee, beautiful Pennee, what are you doing here? You come for the music. No?'

Enrique, dressed to kill in tight white jeans and frilled satin shirt, was standing in front of their table.

'Enrique,' Penny squealed, 'what a surprise!'

'We both surprised then,' he said, smiling down at her, his lovely white teeth gleaming in his tanned face.

'Yes. My husband,' she indicated George, 'had a mad moment and brought me tonight. This is his friend, Terry,' she said with heavy emphasis.

Both men nodded hello. 'Are you with anyone or have you got time to sit a minute?'

'Os Musico are my friends. I sometimes come and sing with them.' Enrique sat down beside Penny. George and Terry quietly returned to their conversation.

Enrique eyed Penny hungrily. 'I loved you in your T-shirt and leggings,' he whispered slowly, 'but in that dress you look sensational. I cannot just sit here with you, Pennee. I want to hold you in my arms again. Will you dance with me?'

Penny glanced across at George and Terry. They were deep in quiet conversation. And not talking about the price of fish either, she thought resentfully.

'Yes,' she answered Enrique. 'I would love to dance.'

The band moved into a slow number and the girl crooned softly into the microphone 'I'll hold you in my dreams until I die…'

Enrique held Penny close. 'We do slow zumba eh? You know the steps, let us be as one and float away in our dreams together.'

Penny closed her eyes and gave herself up to the music. They drifted around the dance floor together, their bodies in tune with each other. For Penny it was perfect.

The song ended and the audience clapped enthusiastically. Penny raised her head from Enrique's shoulder, blinking as her daydreams ended.

'George is looking at us,' Enrique said, smiling down at her. 'I think he would like you back with him.'

Penny looked round. 'Oh, his friend has gone now, so maybe he's finally missed me.'

Enrique kissed her hand and escorted her back to the table and departed. George scowled after him. 'You want to keep your distance from him, Penny; he's all Spanish snake hips and charm. He's got you in his sights.'

Penny giggled. 'Ooh, I hope so, George, that's what makes zumba so exciting.'

CHAPTER 31

Penny brought Barney his tea and perched on the seat opposite. The Friday rush had subsided. 'Well if George is allowed a mid-life crisis I don't see why I shouldn't have one too,' said Penny.

Barney took a bite of his buttered tea-cake and considered this. 'I thought all women did anyway, it just has another name. Menopausal, isn't it?'

Penny looked indignant. 'Barney, it's no such thing, I'm too young for that yet.'

The door opened and Melissa drifted in. She looked about her with undisguised distaste. Spotting Barney, she walked over to his table, her eyes watching her feet as if she might at any moment step into something unsavoury.

'Hello, Barney,' she said. 'I'd just like a little word if you've got a moment.' She glanced at Penny and said sweetly, 'Just between us, I think.'

Penny moved off huffily and went to serve a new customer.

Barney tried not to show his surprise at Melissa's visit. He wondered what had gone wrong. He indicated the seat opposite and reluctantly Melissa perched on the edge of it.

She looked around the café, a frown creasing her beautiful porcelain-white forehead. 'I don't understand you, Barney,' she said in her high whiney voice. 'All the wonderful cafés there are in York and you choose to come to this, well … I don't know what to call it really! This run-down greasy-spoon place. Why, what is the attraction? It can't be the staff, they're all middle-aged and frumpy and the food … you can smell the fry-ups down the street.'

Melissa hadn't troubled to keep her voice down. Out of the corner of his eye Barney could see Penny nearly scrubbing the rose pattern off a tea-pot, and at her place behind the coffee counter, Jackie fiercely wringing out a dishcloth. The inside of his shirt collar suddenly felt too tight. He loosened the top button.

'Shut up, Melissa, and keep your voice down,' he snapped at her. Really this girl was the limit. He said in a louder voice, 'The food here is excellent and reasonably priced and the staff are extremely friendly.' He caught Jackie's eye. 'Most of them, most of the time. Anyway, what are you doing here? I take it you haven't come for your lunch?'

'Well no, not here at any rate.' Melissa watched as Barney drained the last of his tea from the heavy pot mug and shuddered theatrically. 'Thing is, Barney, I'm ravenously hungry, but I've left my purse at the flat so I haven't got any money to buy my lunch.'

'Can't Tom Young sub you?' Barney asked. Melissa had no more left her purse at home than he would leave his desk unlocked for her to nosey into. She was skint.

'Tom's boss has taken him out to lunch so I have to mind the office.' Melissa looked cross.

Barney grinned, 'And a wonderful job you are doing of it, my dear. Only,' he leaned closer in to her and whispered, 'I don't know if you've spotted it, but this is not the offices of the Trades Council.'

Melissa had been listening seriously until she realised Barney was joking at her expense. This annoyed her all the more. She stamped her foot in fury. 'I know it's not their offices, Barney, and if you don't want me to lose my job then give me some money so I can buy a decent lunch somewhere else.'

Melissa's outburst caused a sudden lull in the café

conversations. Everyone turned to look at them. Red faced and angry Barney reached into his wallet and extracted a twenty pound note. 'Just leave, Melissa, please,' he said quietly. 'Go and get your lunch where you like, just don't come here again.'

Melissa snatched the note triumphantly and managed at the same time to plant a kiss squarely on his lips. 'Darling Barney, anything you say,' and laughing, she was gone, banging the door behind her.

Barney sneaked a glance at Jackie, serving a spotty youth with a take-out coffee and chocolate cake. 'Different people like different lunches,' he ventured with a weak smile.

Jackie scythed a large slice of chocolate cake. Barney winced. Was it his or Melissa's head she had just chopped off? Jackie passed the cake to the youth.

'I hope you like it,' she said with emphasis, shooting a dagger's look at Barney. 'We like to keep up our reputation for quality.'

The spotty youth looked bemused. 'Your chocolate cake's the best in York, missus,' he said, 'Folk would come miles for it.'

Jackie smiled at him radiantly. 'Well, thank you,' she said and passed him the coffee, 'And just for that, have it on the house. It's nice to know some people appreciate us.'

When the youth had departed, Barney went to pay his bill. Jackie slapped his change down on the counter. 'And in future, keep that girlfriend of yours out of my café. I can do without her remarks ruining trade.'

'She's not my girlfriend,' Barney protested.

'Oh she kisses every man like that, does she? Tart,' Jackie said sourly. She turned away, not wanting to look into Barney's handsome face.

'She's just staying with me until she gets back on her feet. She has her own room.' Barney felt the whole Melissa thing was tying his life up in knots. How would Jackie ever believe anything he said again with Melissa kissing him like that? She just did it to make mischief, he was sure.

'I don't want to know your domestic arrangements, Barney, just keep that woman out of here.' Annoyed with herself for being so annoyed, Jackie took herself off to the office and slammed the door. Barney Anderson could have ten Melissa Gatenbys. What the hell did it matter to her?

Kate took Jackie's place behind the coffee counter. 'It's quite an achievement, Barney, when you think about it,' she said to Barney.

'What is?'

'I didn't think it was possible for you to be any more unpopular with Jackie than you already are, but I think you've just managed the impossible.'

'Make my day, Kate,' Barney said miserably and made his way out.

* * * * * *

As usual when Barney returned home that Friday evening, Melissa was stretched out on the sofa, drinking his wine and watching one of her interminable quiz shows.

Without turning around from the TV screen, Melissa waggled a hand over the sofa to indicate she had heard him come in.

Barney felt a surge of anger and disgust. She really was a useless creature and yet ... she was still at the Trades Council. He must tread carefully. 'Lasagne and salad OK tonight?' he called to her as he slung his jacket on to the hall chair.

'Marvellous,' Melissa cooed from the sofa. 'I'm starving.'

How Melissa stayed so reed thin was a mystery to Barney. She never took any exercise and yet ate like an athlete in training.

Later, when they were sitting down to supper, Barney

asked sardonically, 'You didn't die of starvation at lunchtime then?' as Melissa waded through a large helping of lasagne.

'Oh darling Barney,' Melissa said enthusiastically, 'you saved my life. However would I have got through the afternoon without you? I went to Betty's and had a lovely lunch with nice china and proper tea and everything.'

Betty's! Only the best for our Melissa, skint or not, thought Barney. Whilst I got soup and a tea-cake and a flea in my ear from Jackie.

Melissa broke into his thoughts. 'Lucky old Tom got some exciting news today, Barney.'

'Oh yeah.' Barney forked up some salad, hoping to hear a Trades Council titbit.

'You know I said his boss came today and took him out to lunch?'

'Mm mm.'

'You'll never guess what he told him,' she trilled.

Barney cocked his head in thought. 'Don't tell me, he's moving him to a prime posting in New York or Washington, or … or…' Barney mused aloud. 'I know. His wife's just had triplets and wants to go home to mum so Tom can have his job and move down to London. How's that?'

Melissa looked at him wonderingly. 'Why would he say all that when none of it's true? It was nothing like that.'

Realising Melissa would never see the joke Barney became serious. 'So what did his boss tell him?'

'Only that he's in line for a £50,000 bonus, Barney. Imagine that!' Melissa clasped her hands together as if in prayer and looked thrilled.

'Did Tom tell you this?' Barney asked.

'No. I just happened to hear them talking as I was passing the door,' Melissa said innocently.

As in, your ear glued to the door the whole time, thought Barney. 'So,' he said, 'what's this bonus for? It's a lot of money.'

'Apparently his insurance claims record has gone down and down each year and so if he can manage no claims against the company this year, that's his reward.'

'You mean, if he doesn't pay out on anything?' Barney looked hard at Melissa. 'Surely that's impossible.'

'Not according to Tom's boss. He said…' Melissa thought carefully for a moment. 'He said, "He must have a way with him", whatever that means.'

Barney frowned. Not wanting to reveal the depth of his interest to Melissa, Barney kept his voice light. 'Hang in there, Melissa,' he said, 'you might net yourself a rich husband yet.'

'Fifty thousand on top of his huge salary,' she said happily, 'and he's so cute, too. What's not to like.' She forked up a large helping of lasagne and stuffed it into her mouth, her eyes sparkling at Barney across the table.

And who's just signed up all the café insurances with him? Barney thought. I only hope nothing goes wrong with the renovations over the next month or two. Tom Young must have 'ways' I don't know anything about yet. But I need to find out.

CHAPTER 32

'We're not keeping that old thing, Walter.' Jackie took the cast iron frying pan out of the box.

'That's the best pan in the place, Jackie, you can't throw it out.'

'Watch me. It's a health hazard.' Jackie put the pan into the rubbish sack.

Walter took it out and wiped it lovingly with a cloth. 'Look at the sheen on that, Jackie. Years of fry-ups have gone into making this what it is today.'

'Yeah, a café owner's nightmare and possibly a "close-u-down order" from Environmental Health.'

'Environmental Health,' Walter scoffed. 'What do they know? All their stainless steel fittings and separating everything from everything. There's nowt wrong with this pan, it makes the best bacon and eggs in York.'

'Well it's not making any more, Walter,' Jackie said firmly. She went to take it from him but Walter backed away, holding on tight to the pan.

'I can't ditch this. We've worked together for forty years. I'll take it home.'

'Please yourself.' Jackie shrugged and carried on sorting through the utensils.

'Anyway, I don't need you in here interfering,' Walter grumbled at her. 'You must have better things to do. I can pack all this up myself.'

'Exactly, Walter and that's just what we're *not* going to

do.'

'Eh?'

'New kitchen, and new stuff to go with it. It's all on order, so a lot of this stuff can go to the charity shops or in the bin.'

'But there's nowt wrong with all this,' Walter protested.

Jackie raised her eyes heavenwards. 'Chipped mixing bowls, ancient wooden chopping board - outlawed years ago I might remind you; serving spoons with the paint flaking off the handles, probably into the soup. That's enough for me, Walter, they're going.'

'Marilyn never minded,' Walter growled.

'My mother was a tight-fisted old bat,' Jackie reminded him. 'She would have split a pea in two if she could, let alone lash out on new chopping boards and pans.'

'You shouldn't speak ill of the dead,' Walter said. 'She wouldn't have approved of all this new stuff.'

Jackie turned to face Walter squarely. 'Marilyn had her time here, Walter. Now it's my turn to make it into what I want. It's my future, probably for the next thirty years. It's not change for change's sake. We have to move with the times and I see things differently from Marilyn.' She turned back to her packing.

'She wasn't all bad you know,' Walter said gruffly, gathering up his favourite knives and boards. 'In her own way she loved you and wanted the best for you, she just had a funny way of showing it, that's all.'

'Yeah, I expect she did.' Jackie sighed. 'And you were friends all your lives, weren't you?'

'Aye we were, and I wouldn't have missed it.' He looked sad for a moment and then straightened up and said more briskly, 'I expect you're right, it's time to move on, but,' he picked up the box with all his bits in, 'I'm not parting with these. Memories of a lifetime here. I'll take them home. And I tell you one thing, I bet your new-fangled plastic boards and spatulas don't last half as long as my old wooden spoons.

Craftsmanship in them, not like today.'

'Pass the bearskins and we'll get back into the cave, Walter, then if we wait long enough, someone might invent the wheel.'

'Bah,' said Walter.

The late May sunshine streamed through the front windows and although it was Saturday the café was unnaturally quiet. Penny and Kate packed up the crockery and bottled drinks from the chilled cabinets. Penny filled a box with still and fizzy fruit drinks. She held up a bottle of dark red juice to Kate. 'Strawberry flavour, it says. You know what that means, don't you? Probably never seen a strawberry in its life. Just like that Mr Doggo dog food I buy. Chicken flavour it says. I don't know why they bother saying anything.'

Kate closed her eyes and took a deep breath. Ever since George had started cross-dressing, Penny's thoughts were jumbled up as if her brain had been in the washing machine. 'OK, what do you mean?'

'Have you ever tried to verify it as a fact?'

'I don't buy dog food, I haven't got a dog,' said Kate.

'Oh Kate, don't be so, so... If you did buy dog food you wouldn't go trying it, would you, to see if it really was chicken flavoured? So why do they bother?'

Kate realised she had made a mistake to give Penny her head on this one.

'I mean, the dog doesn't care does it? Chicken, beef, lamb, it doesn't need a name to it. It just wants a bit of meat.'

Kate gave up. They were a long way from strawberry cordial. 'So how are things between you and George?' she asked.

Penny closed the lid on the box of bottles and taped it up. 'A bit strained at the moment. He actually took me out for a meal the other night. I thought he was trying to re-kindle a bit of romance between us. How wrong can you be? He saw a chap at the bar he'd met at a gay club somewhere and that was it. They spent the rest of the evening talking frocks and make-up. Couldn't compete with that could I? But it turned out alright for me in a way. I had a lovely smoochy dance with Enrique.'

Kate nearly dropped the pile of cups she was packing. 'Right under George's nose?'

'Uh huh,' said Penny. 'Enrique had come to see his friends, so we had a dance together. It was lovely. George was quite cross, but serve him right, he should have danced with me himself.'

Kate wondered how tactful she should be in pursuing this line of questioning. But then, she was dying to know. 'So, if George has been to a gay club, has he decided he's…?'

'Gay?' Ever since she had found out George had visited a club Penny had pushed this thought away from her. Now here was Kate making her look at it. What if George did think he was gay? Tears stood in Penny's eyes and she felt very confused. Enrique with his Spanish charm was all very well and the flirtation did her the world of good, but put that beside thirty years of marriage between her and George and the three sons they had. Was George about to walk away from all that?

Seeing Penny's tears Kate kicked herself for being so tactless. 'Hey, come on, Penny. I'm sorry I asked. Let's talk about something else.'

Just then the kitchen door opened and Jackie came through dragging two large black rubbish sacks behind her.

'And you're not taking anything else,' Walter shouted at her as the door closed.

Jackie looked flushed and angry. 'Bloody Walter, bloody Marilyn. Between them they could have given e-coli, botulism and enteric fever to the whole of York.' She thrust her hands deep into the black sack and pulled out a rusty saucepan without a handle. 'Look at this! What the hell did he want to keep that for?' she demanded.

Penny gazed at it affectionately. 'He used it as a steamer for years, keeping food warm without drying it up in the oven.'

Jackie groaned. 'Oh, you're as bad. Well, it's all going.' She got up and dragged the bags outside to her car.

Penny and Kate returned to their work. The chiller cabinets were empty and wiped down. Penny fetched more boxes to put the rest of the crockery and cutlery in.

'It must be hard for Walter packing everything up after all this time,' said Kate.

'Yes, he's been in that kitchen for forty years, arguing with Marilyn just like he does with Jackie. He used to be so untidy but Marilyn knocked that out of him and I mean knocked it out of him. If he hadn't been such a gentleman, they'd have had many a fist fight.'

'And now everything's going to change,' said Kate.

'It's already changing for Walter, isn't it?' said Penny. 'Since he met Ellie Ward he's a different man – happy, cheerful, laughing, except when he locks horns with Jackie, of course.'

'It's lovely. Fancy finding romance at their age,' said Kate.

'They're only in their sixties, Kate. Plenty of life ahead of them yet.'

'Yeah, so romantic,' Kate said wistfully.

Penny looked at her sharply. 'Seeing as how we're discussing romance, what about you and Stan? Are you going to give him another chance?'

Kate hesitated. 'I don't know.' She looked confused as she tried to express her feelings about Stan. 'I really like him, Penny. All that bravado front he puts on when he comes in here, that's all that it is; just a front. When we've been out together he's been so funny and thoughtful and then suddenly it all falls apart and this completely different, disorganised, accident-prone bloke emerges. So, yeah, I don't know.' She smiled at Penny and picked up a full box of crockery and stacked it with the rest.

'Sounds to me like he deserves another chance,' said Penny, 'and then if it's a complete disaster third time round then fair enough But you never know, it might be third time lucky.' Penny smiled at Kate. 'Just be ready for anything and then you might enjoy it all the more.'

Kate was trying to work this one out when Penny said, 'Text him.'

'What?'

'Go on, you've got your phone, haven't you. Text Stan and suggest an outing, make a day of it. We're on holiday now the café's closed. It's a good chance to really get to know him.'

Chance her arm a third time? Well, why not? Going on past experience with Stan, anything could happen. Kate found herself almost looking forward to another chaotic and confusing date with Stan. Before she could change her mind, she picked up her phone and typed out the message – 'Kate's house 9am Saturday, bring boots and good jacket for walk over moors in day and cosy Scarbro' pub supper at night.' She looked down at the message and hesitated. Penny, peering over her shoulder, pressed the SEND button and the message went.

'Penny!'

'Oh go on, life's too short not to have an adventure. If he or Barney were ten years older I might have scooped either of them up myself.'

'Well keep your mitts off Stan for now. But Barney, he seems to still have Melissa around his neck,' said Kate.

Penny fetched another box and they started wrapping glasses in old newspaper. 'Melissa is nothing short of a menace,' said Penny. 'She's just using Barney and he can't seem to see it.' She paused, holding a glass up for inspection and discarding it. 'Chipped,' she said. And then, 'It's such a pity he and Jackie don't get on. They're just the right age for each other; both intelligent and sparky and he's such a softy. He would really take care of Jackie.' Penny sighed regretfully. 'Such a shame they dislike each other so.'

Kate stared at her. Couldn't Penny see what was going on right under her nose? Couldn't she feel the electric charge in the air when those two came anywhere near each other, the testosterone and pheromones dancing in the air between them? Kate decided to keep quiet. Perhaps it was as well if Penny didn't see it. Kate picked up the full box of glasses and stacked it with the others by the door. 'OK, just the last shelf of glasses now and that will be the lot.'

In the kitchen, Jackie's voice rose an octave. 'No way, Walter, absolutely not. I asked you to hire a proper van to transport the tables and chairs and left over stuff to Ivy's Tea Rooms, not borrow some clapped-out, dodgy rust-bucket from one of Barney Anderson's mates.'

'Oh, give over, Jackie, it's a perfectly good van. He's moved stuff for me before, sheep and ducks and the like. He's a good lad and he only wants his petrol money.'

'Oh, lovely! The café furniture arrives at Ivy's covered in sheep poo and God alone knows what else. No, Walter, get a proper van.'

'Can't,' said Walter crossly. 'Too late now. Barney's organised it and as it's a Saturday all the van hire places will be fully booked. The van will be clean as a whistle, I promise you. Just leave it to me and stop worrying for once.'

'Stop worrying! I'll be white haired and in a straitjacket if I work with you much longer. And now you've involved us with one of Barney Anderson's shady mates.'

'Barney hasn't got any shady mates.' Oh God, why were women so bloody exasperating. 'He can't afford to have any shady mates, not with his…' Walter broke off, aware of his promise to Barney not to reveal his profession.

'His track record,' Jackie finished for him scornfully.

'Yeah, that's about right for Dosser Boy.'

Walter gritted his teeth. 'It's a legal van with a legal owner. He will be here at 10:00 a.m. tomorrow and the van will be clean. Mr Stampwick and Co will have a clear field on Monday morning, if you get out of my way now and let me finish off here.' Walter glared at Jackie.

She walked to the door. 'How I would like to put my hands around your throat, Walter, and squeeze tight.'

Walter grinned at this, pleased to have got his own way for once. 'The feeling's mutual, Jackie, believe me.'

* * * * * *

Barney pulled up outside the Café Paradise promptly at 10:00 a.m. on Saturday morning. He tooted the horn and jumped out, going to the back of the van to move the blankets and rope ready for the furniture removals.

Walter was out of the door in a flash. 'What's happened to John?' he asked sharply.

'Got man flu,' said Barney folding the last of the blankets. 'I can drive the van on my insurance, so here I am at your service. Can't let a lady down in her hour of need, can we?'

'She's going to love this,' groaned Walter with his head in his hands. 'It was bad enough you had a finger in the pie in the first place, but now you'll be driving the thing.' He raised his head. 'She'll kill me, you know that, Barney. You are looking at a dead man.'

'Nonsense,' Barney said bracingly. 'Here we are, a man and a van. Let's be nice to each other and get the job done.'

He only hoped Jackie would see things that way too. When his friend John had phoned him that morning and croaked his excuses, Barney's heart had sunk. He knew he was the last person Jackie would want as removal man. But he quickly recovered himself. Maybe Jackie would see him in a different light today. They could have a nice run out to

Ivy's Tea Rooms on the outskirts of the city; maybe even stay there for lunch. Barney smiled. He would have Jackie to himself for at least two hours. Even she couldn't be snappy for all that time. He looked forward to watching her across the lunch table, dipping crusty bread into soup and popping it into her beautiful mouth…

'Barney!' Jackie exclaimed. 'You said it was a bloke called John.'

'John's got flu, so Barney's stepped in. Be grateful woman, he's trying to help.'

'If you'd done what I asked in the first place, I wouldn't need any help.'

'Too late for that now, lass. Everything has to go today, so just for once, try to be nice.'

Nice! She was always nice, wasn't she? It was only folk like Walter and Barney that drove her up the wall and now here she was, landed with both of them.

Before she could say any more, Barney appeared in the café, disarming her with his bright smile. 'Good morning, Jackie, here I am, your knight in shining armour ready to sweep you off your feet, or in twenty-first century parlance, a man with a white van come to take you to Ivy's.' Barney heard Walter's choked laughter behind him and ignored it. Nothing was going to stop him enjoying today.

'It's good of you to give up your time this morning,' Jackie began.

'I've plenty of it,' Barney said blandly. After all he was supposed to be unemployed.

'I suppose so.' Jackie was gruff. 'Well, shall we get loaded up and get on our way?'

Walter and Barney carried out the old tables and chairs and stacked them in the van. Barney carefully wrapped the blankets around them and secured them with the ropes. Jackie ferried out the boxes of glasses and crockery, filling the van right to the doors. They were ready to leave.

Suddenly Jackie felt unnerved at the prospect of spending time alone with Barney. She turned to Walter. 'Walter, I expect you and Barney have a lot to catch up on Do you want to go with Barney and show him where Ivy's Tea Room is? Lunch on me for a change.'

'Can't, lass,' said Walter, 'kind of you to offer but I'm out with Ellie this afternoon. My lady friend,' he explained to Barney.

Barney raised his eyebrows and smiled at Walter. 'Well good for you, Walter. She's a lucky lady. You go and enjoy yourself. I'm sure Jackie and I will get along just fine. She might call a truce for a day and enjoy a pleasant ride out and even have lunch on me at Ivy's.' He looked at Jackie. Just for once, say yes, he pleaded with her silently.

As if she had heard him she said, 'Yes, a truce it is. We don't see eye to eye most of the time, but I am grateful for your help this morning and lunch at Ivy's would be nice.' Even as she said the words she felt astonished at herself. Get a grip, Jackie, she told herself. Barney might be charming but don't get carried away.

Barney helped her up into the van and went round to climb into the driver's side.

'Good luck, lad,' Walter said. 'You're going to need it, spending a few hours with that one.'

Barney grinned. 'If she starts any nonsense I'll turf her out and she can walk home. That would teach her.'

Walter waved them off shaking his head. He was looking forward to a peaceful afternoon with Ellie and didn't envy Barney one bit.

* * * * * *

Stan and Kate had set off in the cool mist of the late May morning and had already walked for some miles high up on the North Yorkshire moors. Now, in the late morning, the sun had burnt the mist off and was streaming down on them.

Stan pulled his sunglasses from his pocket. 'Apollo is shining on us today, Kate. We must have earned his favour.'

Kate glanced up at him. 'Are you interested in the Roman gods?'

'Er, yeah,' Stan said guardedly. 'I find the customs and beliefs of other ages fascinating, especially the Romans as we know so much about them.'

'Yes, we're lucky in this country to have such a rich and varied history and much of it so well documented. I love reading about the Romans too.'

Stan grinned down at her. Things were looking good. Here he was on this beautiful day with the girl of his dreams, walking on the best moors in the world and now, to really put the icing on the cake, she loved history too. He bent down and kissed her gently on the lips. 'And you are wonderful,' he said softly. Taking her hand they set off on the moorland path that wound its way down to the river.

'Not only wonderful and beautiful, but clever too. I'm really glad you thought of a picnic. I'm starving already.' He hitched up the rucksack on his shoulders.

'As it was my idea to drag you around the moors I thought I'd better bring some food so we didn't die of starvation before tonight. That's if nothing crops up in the meantime to stop us finally getting to a pub meal.'

'Wretch!' exclaimed Stan and made to grab her, but Kate was like quicksilver and twisted away from him, running sure-footedly along the path down to the river. Stan gave chase but was hampered by the loaded rucksack. He didn't catch up with Kate until they landed breathlessly at the banks of the River Derwent. He shrugged off the rucksack and flung himself down next to Kate.

'Poor old man,' Kate teased, 'can't hack the pace any more.'

'And you are downright cruel,' he panted. 'You load me up like an old donkey, taunt me with past failures and then take off like a gazelle and expect me to catch you.' He sat up and took off his jacket, looking around him. 'This is a beautiful spot, Kate,' he said. 'How did you find it?'

'I used to come here with Mum and Dad and my brother when I was a kid. It was always a special place. It means a lot to me.' She looked at him shyly. 'I wanted to you to see it too.'

Stan was silent for a moment, touched beyond words. He drew Kate to him and they leaned back together against the soft grass of the river bank, watching the wide cool waters flow past.

Kate's picnic lunch was a success. The crusty salad baguettes, fruit and hot coffee filled them up. For Stan it was a real treat to have food prepared for him. He had spent so many weeks preparing meals for his over-fussy mother, in between walking her highly-strung poodle, that he'd forgotten how nice it was to have fresh food put before him.

He put his arm around Kate and lay back contentedly. Life didn't get much better. As long as those clouds kept scudding by, all would be well.

* * * * * *

At Ivy's Tea Rooms Barney and Jackie off-loaded the van and stacked all the old café furniture and boxes in an outhouse at the rear of the building. Ivy herself bustled out and thanked Jackie profusely. 'You're a chip off the old block,' she told Jackie. 'Marilyn would have helped me just the same. They'll give our Maureen a good start out at Haxby.' She beamed at Jackie. 'It's tough for youngsters to get a start these days. Thanks for giving her this chance.'

The idea of Marilyn *giving* anything away made Jackie smile and she hoped from the bottom of her heart that she was *not* a chip off the old block.

They went into the tea rooms for lunch and Ivy insisted they have whatever they liked. Barney was keen to pay, but Ivy would have none of it. 'You put your money away, lad, and find a table for you and your lass here. Mary will be over to take your order soon.'

Barney grinned at Jackie. 'Come on, my lass. Do as the lady says, let's find a table. I'm starving.'

Scowling, Jackie sat down at a table and stared at the menu. How dare he call her 'my lass.' She was no such thing and never would be.

Barney's smiling face appeared around the menu. 'Come on, Jackie, it was only a joke. A truce today, remember?'

Oh, those blue eyes in that handsome face. Why did he arouse such conflicting emotions in her all the time? One minute she wanted to kill him for winding her up and the next she had to control the urge to take that face in her hands and kiss it. She managed to mumble the words 'a truce' and hid behind the menu again.

They ordered lunch, soup and crusty bread. Barney was delighted. He couldn't actually feed her the bread as he'd imagined so many times, but at least he could watch and pretend. Maybe she would have a pudding – the soft chocolate torte and cream…

Jackie watched the pleased, faraway look on Barney's face and wondered if he was thinking of Melissa. She couldn't bear to sit through lunch looking at that idiotic grin on his face. They would have to talk about something. 'So what does your friend John, do with his van?'

Jackie broke in on Barney's thoughts and with an effort he dragged his mind back to mundane matters. 'John? Oh, he buys and sells stuff and shifts stuff about for people, that sort of thing.'

'Bit of a wheeler and dealer. Do you help him with shifting stuff, a bit like Del Boy?'

'Is that what you think I do with my time?' Barney was amused.

'Well I don't know.' Jackie looked doubtful. 'You can't spend all your time collecting your unemployment benefit and it wouldn't stretch to all the food you put away at the café, so I suppose you must help your friend out ... but you don't look like a Del Boy,' she finished uncertainly.

'I suppose I should be thankful for that,' he retorted.

Just at that moment, the waitress arrived with their lunch. Lovely lady though she was, Barney wished her to hell and beyond. Jackie might have gone on to ask him what he really did with his time, but the moment was lost and she was rabbiting on about Tom Young now and how helpful he had been sorting out her insurances and helping her find a good builder for the café renovations.

Barney listened with one ear. He didn't want to share this time with Jackie spouting on about Tom Young. He wouldn't touch the man with a barge pole but he knew he would never wean Jackie away from him.

He watched her dipping the bread into the soup and popping it into her mouth, her words going over his head. It was so much as he had imagined, he wanted to punch the air shouting, yesss, how sexy is that? Jackie, detecting his disinterest, tailed off her talk about the café alterations. Obviously she was boring him. Not everyone was going to be as enthusiastic as she was about Café Paradise. 'Sorry, I know I'm going on a bit.'

'What? No.' Barney started coming out of his fantasy. 'No, really, I can't wait to see it all. Just hope Stampwick & Co do a good job. And don't forget,' Barney leaned forward, a serious expression on his face, 'any time you need help, anything at all, Jackie, I'm always around. Please remember that. If it's OK by you, I'll keep popping into the café and see how everything is going. You never know when a man with a white van might be needed. Who knows, we might even make this a permanent truce.' Now he was really pushing it.

Damn and blast you, Walter Breckenridge, Jackie thought. See where your penny pinching has got me. Barney thinking he can drop in and out of my life as he chooses. Why doesn't he get a proper job? I'd have some respect for him then and things could be very different. But whatever ideas he's got, he can certainly shelve them. I don't need a handsome dosser in my life, or his feckless girlfriend.

Barney waved a hand in front of her face. 'Hello, anyone home?'

'I heard you, Barney,' Jackie said. 'I can't stop you calling at the café but there won't be anything to see for two or three weeks yet.' Feeling backed into a corner, Jackie knew she sounded ungracious but couldn't help it. 'You'll have to find somewhere else for your bacon and egg sarnies now. Try Mrs Grant's café down Ash Road just near Friargate. Café Paradise will have a very different menu when we re-open.'

'She's all cheap margarine and stale bread,' Barney said mournfully as they stood up to leave. 'Soggy chips and stewed tea, not to mention more fat than bacon in the sarnie.'

'Good white van man fare then,' Jackie said and handed him the keys he'd left behind on the table.

* * * * * *

Kate shifted her position in the crook of Stan's arm. 'My parents are away in America at the moment,' she said. 'Dad's on a lecture tour of American universities, giving them a broad sweep of English history; bronze-age barrows to medieval peasants and all things in between.'

'What an interesting man. That must be where you get your love of history from,' Stan said.

'Yeah, I suppose so. What about you? Where does your

interest come from?'

'Not from my parents, that's for sure,' laughed Stan. 'They are fanatical gardeners and serve on the boards of all sorts of charitable trusts for botanical gardens and the open gardens schemes. The talk is always of trees and planting. Unfortunately, since my mother broke her leg I am the gardener and the pampered- poodle walker.' Stan was wondering whether to tell Kate about the Roman Re-enactment Society, when heavy drops of rain began to spatter the remains of their picnic. He glanced up. A dark cloud overhead looked as if it was going to burst right over them and there were more gathering behind it. He sat up and pulled Kate with him. 'Looks like our time's up.'

They packed up the picnic into the rucksack and headed off along the path towards the car. Kate started to run as the rain increased in intensity.

'Be careful, Kate,' Stan shouted, chasing after her. 'Mind out for tree roots.'

His warning was too late. Kate tripped and fell, landing awkwardly across the path amongst the heathers.

Stan flung the rucksack down and knelt beside her. She was nursing her left ankle and wincing with pain. He looked at her anxiously. 'Is it broken?'

'I don't think so,' said Kate. 'I think it's just a bad sprain, but I don't think I can walk on it.'

The rain beat down, rapidly soaking them through. Stan grinned. 'Well this is nice: torrential rain, injured lady sitting in a bed of spiky heather and quite some distance to get to the car. Sounds like our kind of date. Nothing for it. Now, don't move.' He shrugged the rucksack on to his back and went to pick Kate up.

'You can't carry me all the way to the car,' Kate protested.

Stan smiled down at her, 'And what do you suggest I do? Leave you here in the pouring rain and go home.' He picked her up and kissed her tenderly. 'Just for the record, the rain is not my fault and I don't think it's my fault that you fell. This day is not a disaster; it is just a little setback. We're getting used to the unexpected. A sprained ankle? Huh, that's nothing. Hang on tight now.'

Two hours later they emerged from Scarborough A & E with Kate's ankle securely strapped up.

'You don't have a dog do you, Kate?' Stan asked as they headed for the car.

'No.' Kate was puzzled. What tangent was Stan going off at now?

'Thank God for that, walking my mother's poodle is quite enough. I thought I might be walking two now.'

Now they were clear of A & E and Kate was alright, Stan's mood was rocketing.

'Seeing as we've survived a third outing, you're still talking to me, and I haven't, as yet, done anything disastrous how about that country pub, log fire and fine wine you promised me?'

'The Nags Head just outside Scarborough, table for two booked for 7:30 p.m. Take me away from all this,' said Kate. 'I'm starving.'

* * * * * *

Stan paused beneath a magnificent magnolia tree in his mother's garden waiting for Tammie, the poodle, to oblige on his last walk of the night. Tammie looked up at him briefly with brown beady eyes and walked on, sniffing the ground about him. Usually, after half an hour of this battle of wits, Stan would give in and head off back to the house, Tammie tearing away in front of him eager to be back in his rightful place by the fireside.

But tonight Stan was serene. Tammie could snuffle about all night over the entire garden until he found the exact square inch he needed for his night-time toilet and Stan wouldn't even notice. Stan was deeply in love. Her sea-green eyes and smiling mouth had captivated him from the start and finally, finally they had managed an almost trouble-free date.

Whilst Tammie slowly trotted about the garden, Stan leaned back against the magnolia tree and dreamed of Kate, seeing her again across the table from him at The Nags Head, seeing her smile and laugh and talk and clink his glass in a toast to them both and finally remembering again the magical kiss goodnight, her soft skin and subtle perfume…

Tammie barked sharply breaking Stan's reverie. The little dog was trotting back to the house. Sighing happily, Stan straightened up and headed back to the house, hoping that for once Tammie had done the decent thing.

* * * * * *

Kate sat in the window-seat of her flat looking out into the dark May night. She watched the silver stars as they twinkled high above. Dave and her life in Cyprus seemed a world away now. She might have had two disastrous dates with Stan but it had been third time lucky today. Penny had been right to make her go for it.

She'd had a wonderful day with Stan. Even spraining her ankle hadn't been all bad. He'd carried her back to the car as if she were a featherweight and never once complained.

Dinner had been fun. He'd been so entertaining, recalling tales of his escapades on Walter's smallholding, chasing sheep, getting kicked by cows, chased and bitten by over-protective ganders. But he didn't talk about himself when Kate tried to draw him out. Like that time at Walter's when he didn't want to talk about the amateur dramatics…

Kate shivered in the cold night air. Perhaps Stan would open up a bit when they got to know each other better. In the meantime, if he kept kissing her like that, she wouldn't be responsible for her actions.

* * * * * *

Melissa was out on Saturday evening when Barney got back from his trip to Ivy's Tearoom. He slumped in front of the TV, watching an old episode of *Foyle's War*. A land girl was driving a tractor across a farmyard, whilst another drove a herd of cows into a byre for milking. Strong, independent women, Barney thought. He was surrounded by them - and in general admired them - except for Melissa who was a complete hanger-on, pain in the ass. It would be nice for once, just for once, if a certain woman would like to lean on him a little: let him slay a dragon for her; joust for her favour; anything.

He laughed wryly at himself and drained the last of the whisky in his glass. How caveman he was really. Yes, he loved women to get out there and do everything they wanted to do but, Barney had the insight to acknowledge his own personal dilemma. Underneath all that, he just wanted to love and protect her and keep her safe from everything in this rough old world.

He poured himself another large whisky. Why did I have to fall in love with such a prickly, independent woman? he wondered. Well get over it, Barney boy, she is not interested in you at all. How clear does she have to make it? He drank his whisky reflectively. She's only interested in that café of hers, so put her out of your mind.

Jackie's face swam before him, her blue eyes and soft lips taunting him. He swallowed the last of the whisky and hurled the glass across the room with all his might. It hit the wall and shattered into tiny pieces over the fireplace.

* * * * * *

Jackie poured the olive oil onto her salad and gently turned the leaves to coat them. Samson suddenly appeared through the cat flap and mee-owed loudly for his supper. Jackie reached for the packet of Kattibix. 'You've had your moment in the sunshine, old lad,' she told him. 'It's these, or go and catch your own supper. I've a new shop to pay for, so best salmon is strictly off limits now.' She shook the Kattibix into Samson's dish and got on with her own supper. Samson sat watching her intently.

She put her supper on a tray and carried it through to the lounge. Switching on the TV, she channel-hopped and found *Foyle's War* on ITV3. What higher delights were there for a cosy Saturday night in by the fire with a chicken salad and Samson for company?

Momentary pangs of envy passed over Jackie, as she thought of the friends she knew would be out to dinner and dancing tonight. Quickly dismissing these thoughts, she forked up her salad and tried to get interested in the programme. She admired the way the women dealt with all the heavy farm work and herded the cows as good as any man.

Finishing her supper she pushed the tray aside. Immediately, Samson jumped on to her lap and looked up at her. He mee-owed experimentally, checking if it was OK to be there. Jackie stared down at him in amazement. 'Are we entering sedate middle-age together, Samson?' she asked him. 'Saturday nights in by the fire with the cat and a glass of wine: is this it then?'

Barney's face came into her mind, his cheeky grin and beautiful speaking voice teasing her earlier on that day. 'We'll have to do this again, Jackie. I still haven't bought you lunch. You owe me a date.'

Jackie took a large gulp of her wine. Drat you to hell and back, Barney Anderson. Why do you have to torment me with your handsome face and sarky tongue? Why can't you get a job and make something of yourself? Why doesn't Walter or Stan help you out? They're your friends. If you got a life … had a life … maybe … oh why do you have to be in my life at all?

Unable to bear her train of thought any longer Jackie leapt up, sending Samson skidding on to the floor. He hissed angrily and turned to her with claws outstretched. 'Oh no, you don't,' Jackie said and shooed him out to the kitchen and through the cat flap, to take his chances in the late May night.

CHAPTER 33

It was Monday morning rush hour. Jackie slowed down and indicated left. It was a very tight turn into the parking area at the rear of the café, but today she didn't care how many cars backed up behind her or tooted impatiently. She would take her time and get it right in one. Stampwick and Sons, the builders, were coming and Café Paradise would soon be transformed.

In her mind's eye Jackie could see the new stainless steel kitchen in place and the smart wooden tables and chairs in the café, set out against the new cream-painted walls and linen curtains. It would look fresh and airy with just the occasional accent of colour in cushions or ornamental jugs perhaps.

Occupied with these images, Jackie steered the Fiat Panda into the café back yard only to come smack up against a huge black skip dumped in the middle of the yard. She braked sharply but too late; the Panda bumper buckled against the heavy steel of the skip and the tinkling of glass could be heard as the front headlights smashed.

'What the bloody hell…?' Shaken, Jackie got out of the car to survey the damage. As she was doing so, Mr Stampwick's van turned into the yard. He had to stop in the gateway as there was no room left in the yard. He climbed out of his van and looked at Jackie's car crunched up against the skip.

'Didn't manage to miss it then?' he commented.

'Didn't manage…' Jackie was incredulous. 'Who put this whacking great monstrosity here?' she demanded.

'Phelps Skip Hire. It says it on the side there.' Mr Stampwick folded his arms and surveyed the damage to Jackie's car. 'Bit of a mess like,' he said. 'You should ha' braked a bit sooner.'

'Brake! I know what I'd like to break.' Jackie tried to collect her wits and get a grip on the situation. 'Why is this skip thing stuck in the middle of my yard, so no-one can get in or out?'

'Well how else are we going to dispose of the old kitchen cupboards and fittings? They won't all fit in the back of my van so it has to be a skip. I ordered it for today, special like, and here it is.' Mr Stampwick regarded the skip proudly as if he had conjured it up himself.

'You might have told me to expect it,' Jackie said.

'And you shouldn't have been driving without due care and attention, young lady,' he said ponderously. He turned towards his van, where two youths were solemnly regarding the scene. 'I always told my lads there, Dennis and Brian. I said "You must always drive with proper care and attention to the road and everything around you, that way you won't go far wrong".' He let his gaze rest upon his boys for a moment. 'And so far that policy has paid off. Due care and attention, Miss Dalrymple-Jones, never forget it and you won't end up in a mess like this again.'

Jackie couldn't believe she was being lectured by her own builder for a situation he had created without even telling her.

'You'll have to shift it anyhow,' he went on. 'I need to get my van in here and get the tools unloaded. Can't do it on that busy road.'

'Of course Mr Stampwick.' Jackie snarled, 'We can't leave your precious van out on that busy road, can we? I'll just move my mangled car out of your way and then we can all get on.'

She jumped back into the Panda and started the engine. Very gently, she reversed away from the skip. She had left a tiny dent in it, nothing in comparison with the buckled bumper and smashed lights on her own car.

Mr Stampwick cautiously reversed his truck back out on to the main road and stayed there whilst Jackie manoeuvred out of the narrow gateway. The traffic was backed up way into the distance as Mr Stampwick majestically straddled the whole road, indifferent to the honking horns and shouts from impatient drivers.

Jackie got away and drove around the block. There was nothing for it, she would have to leave the car at the front of the café for a few minutes whilst she let Old Man Stampwick in and then take it to the garage

Ignoring the double yellow lines, Jackie pulled up outside Café Paradise and leapt out, leaving the engine running. She opened the door and quickly jabbed the code into the alarm to silence it. There was nothing worth pinching in the café now, but the insurance company demanded the alarm be set every night.

She hurried through and opened the back door. Mr Stampwick was waiting outside along with his two sons.

'Now, Miss Dalrymple-Jones, seeing as how we're all sorted out, I'll begin Monday properly by introducing you to my two sons here. Stampwick and Sons it says on the van now,' he said proudly, 'and these are the very same.'

He nudged forward a tall, skinny youth, who looked very like Stampwick himself. 'This is Dennis.' And bringing forth the other youth, a gangly, spotty boy, 'This is Brian.'

The boys shuffled their feet and mumbled a hello.

Mr Stampwick stepped inside and looked about the bare kitchen. 'Aye, it is as it is, Miss Dalrymple-Jones,' he said portentously. 'I remember it well.' He surveyed the scene. His sons, still waiting outside, rolled their eyes.

'Can we come in, Dad?' asked Dennis. 'It's a bit nippy standing out here.'

'Nippy?' John Stampwick said in surprise. 'You don't know what nippy is. When you've worked a few winters in ten degrees below, up to your waist in freezing water trying to find a cracked pipe, then you can say it's nippy.'

He made no move to let them in, just stood and looked about him ruminatively.

Conscious of her car engine still running and unsure as to the state of her petrol tank, Jackie beckoned the boys in. 'I'll leave you to start work,' she said with emphasis. 'I'm on a double yellow line with a bashed-in car, so if you don't mind I'll cut along. Don't want a parking ticket to add to my troubles, now do I?'

Mr Stampwick stared at her, coming out of his reverie. 'It's double yellow lines out the front, Miss Dalrymple-Jones. It's against the law to park on those and if a policeman comes along and sees the state of your car... Really, I don't know why you're wasting time here.'

Wasting time! There was only one time-waster in this kitchen and Jackie knew it wasn't her. Stampwick had a knack of putting her on the back foot every time. She would have to watch him.

When she got back to her car there was a ticket on it. The traffic warden was just walking away. Jackie snatched the ticket off the screen and raced after him.

'You've given me a ticket! You can't do that,' she panted. 'That's my café, I was only inside for a minute.'

'Yes I can, and oh no, you were not, madam. You're on double yellow lines *and* obstructing the pavement,' he told her sternly.

'But there was a skip parked in my space around the back and where else can I stop to open up my café?'

'Not my problem, madam. I just do my job. Pay the fine and don't park there again. If you're still there when I come

313

round again, that will be another sixty pounds.' The warden turned away and added as an afterthought, 'Half price if you pay within fourteen days,' and continued on down the street.

Jackie stared after him. The mean, miserable, little git; she hoped all traffic wardens rotted in hell. She looked down at the ticket in her hand. Sixty pounds! Well, happy Monday to you too, Warden 4051.

She stomped back to her car and drove off. Twenty minutes later, after queuing in the rush hour traffic, Jackie reached her local garage. She left the car in a bay outside and went in search of a mechanic. Andy had his head deep inside the bonnet of a Ford Focus and was banging at a recalcitrant nut with a monkey wrench. Jackie told him about the damage to her car.

'A skip,' he exclaimed. 'Well that wasn't going anywhere, was it? It's big enough, you can't miss one of those. Huh, and you didn't.' Andy laughed at his own joke. 'Didn't miss it, like. Couldn't you find your brake?'

Jackie regarded him silently. Did all men make such pathetic jokes? 'Just lend me a car, Andy, so I can get back to the café. I've got the builders in and I need to be there.'

Fifteen minutes later Jackie made it back to the café in the borrowed garage car. She was relieved to hear the banging and clattering of men at work. She walked through and listened at the kitchen door. She could hear a satisfying ripping sound. Cautiously she opened the door and looked in. Stampwick and Sons had not wasted any time. The kitchen cupboards were dismantled and young Brian was dragging them out of the door to the skip.

Mr Stampwick was taking the handwash sink off the wall. Seeing Jackie he stopped and asked, 'Did you get your car to the garage alright?'

'I did,' Jackie said, 'and a sixty pound fine from a miserable traffic warden, just to put the cherry on top of my cake.'

'I told you, you were breaking the law,' Mr Stampwick said with some satisfaction.

He put his huge hands around the small handbasin and gently prised it away from the wall. As he straightened up, holding it against his large frame, it looked like a doll's toy. He passed it to young Dennis who staggered away with it to the skip.

'Wants to eat his porridge in a morning,' Mr Stampwick observed, watching his son weaving his way outside. 'Lives on French fries, Snickers and coke. No wonder he's got no muscles.' Mr Stampwick clenched his fists and showed off his own biceps. 'Proper food and hard work builds these,' he told his sons. 'You'll only ever have muscles the size of peas on all that rubbish you eat.'

The boys had obviously heard it all before. 'Whatever,' Dennis mumbled under his breath.

Realising she wasn't going to get any sympathy for her car repair bill or parking fine, Jackie left the Stampwicks to get on and retired to her office to tackle a pile of much neglected paper work. She worked on, enduring the mix of hammering and loud pop music until she couldn't stand any more of it.

A change of scene was called for. She decided to treat herself to lunch away from the café. Tom Young came into her mind. Should she? Would she dare? Why not? They were overdue for a second date. Before she could dither and talk herself out of the idea, Jackie dialled Tom's number.

'York Trades Council, who's calling,' Melissa trilled.

When Jackie gave her name there was a pause at the other end. 'Oh, that dreadful … whoops, I'll put you through.'

Jackie need not have worried. When she shyly put her invitation to Tom he readily agreed to lunch. 'Great idea,' he enthused. 'I could do to get out of the office, but only for a short while I'm afraid. I've a lot of work on. The demand for good trades people has shot up with the arrival of the fine spring weather. How about spicy meatballs at Mario's, the new place near Fenwicks? See you there in half an hour?'

Jackie agreed and happily put the phone down. Even Melissa's rudeness couldn't dampen her spirits. Lunch with sexy Tom. With all the zumba dancing and salads at home, Jackie had lost a lot of weight and felt she looked good enough now to do without the magic pants.

Jackie hurried off to make her lunch date with Tom Young. She smiled to herself as she walked quickly along Blossom Street. As she neared the Citizens Advice Bureau, a young man rushed out of the door and cannoned into her, nearly knocking her off her feet. He dropped the briefcase he was carrying and reached out to catch her.

'I'm so sorry,' he said.

Jackie looked up. Barney Anderson held her in his arms and looked down at her, his face full of concern. Jackie caught her breath. Was she just waking up from a lovely dream? Barney wore a suit and tie. And was that really his briefcase there on the pavement? 'Barney?' she queried.

He smiled ruefully. 'Fraid so. I'm sorry, I shouldn't have been in such a hurry. Didn't look where I was going.'

Jackie looked up at the building, 'Citizens Advice Bureau. You must be in need of sound advice to go there. Is that why you're all dressed up?'

'Well actually…' Barney began, still holding her in his arms.

Jackie freed herself from Barney's hold, conscious of a fluttering in her stomach.

'Why don't I buy you lunch and I'll tell you all about it?' Barney suggested.

'Oh.' For an instant Jackie regretted making the lunch date with Tom Young. Then she remembered this was Dosser Boy and one day in a suit didn't make a professional of him. 'Can't,' she replied. 'I'm having lunch with Tom Young in five minutes. See you.' She hurried on, leaving

Barney standing on the pavement watching her go away from him.

'Jackie Dalrymple-Jones, I don't know whether to kiss you or smack you,' he said aloud.

A woman passing by said, 'Can't smack 'em these days, love, you'll get arrested.'

'She'll drive me to it one of these days,' he replied.

'Love,' said the woman, 'it twists your heart and turns your life upside down and inside out. But there, would you be without her?'

Barney wondered, at this rate, would he ever get the chance to be *with* her? He picked up his briefcase from the pavement and set off disconsolately down the street.

* * * * * *

Looking at Tom Young across the table from her at Mario's, Jackie acknowledged he was as charming as ever. He made flattering remarks about her appearance and asked intelligent questions about the on-going café renovations; not only asked but listened intently to her replies. In spite of this Jackie was conscious of a vague disappointment nagging away at the edges of her mind. She'd got her wish and somehow it didn't live up to expectations, like when she was a child and had excitedly waited for Santa and he'd left her a duff Christmas present after all those weeks of trying to be good and deserving of it.

Tom was telling her an amusing tale about a couple who were alleging their garden wall had just 'fallen down'. What they didn't know was that Tom knew their neighbours and had heard the tale of how Mr W had backed his Volvo estate into it at speed and knocked it for six. Jackie listened with half an ear, wondering why she didn't find him attractive any more. He was still charming and sexy but ...not Barney. When he'd held her in his arms outside the C.A.B., he smelled so fresh and clean, she wanted him to pull her to him and kiss her and keep on kissing her…

Jackie came to with a start and shivered. Tom looked at her with concern. 'Are you alright, Jackie? Not sickening for this flu that's going around, I hope.'

Jackie stared down at her plate of spaghetti and found it unappealing. 'I hope not, Tom. I must admit, I don't feel quite myself.'

They did not linger long over lunch. Tom had to get back to the office, something about a visit from his boss. He kissed Jackie goodbye and said they must meet again soon, have dinner one night. Jackie was relieved to leave it at that. She didn't know if she wanted another date with Tom. She didn't know what she wanted.

Walking back to Café Paradise, she thought about Marilyn. Perhaps she was more like her mother than she realised. Marilyn had always been a restless creature, wanting this, wanting that and then changing her mind again when she'd got it. Perhaps she was getting like her. Oh what was the matter with her?

She let herself back into the café and found Mr Stampwick sitting alone, eating his lunch from a battered tin box. 'Have the boys had their lunch?' she asked.

'I've sent 'em home,' Mr Stampwick said, replacing the lid on his lunch box.

'Home? Whatever for?' Jackie looked around the café. A few random sections of the cheap wooden boarding had been removed from the walls.

'You'd best sit down, lass, it's not good news.' Mr Stampwick brought a chair over for Jackie to sit on. He scratched his grizzled grey head, looking very unhappy.

Not good news, no boys, sent them home! Jackie didn't know what to think. Had Dennis or Brian crushed a hand with that huge lump hammer? Drilled through a leg with the electric screwdriver? She batted away images of the boys dripping with blood in the kitchen, lawyers-4-U, massive compensation claims, ruin…

'As you know, Miss Dalrymple-Jones, I always tell it like it is, no wrapping it up, just spit it out. It is as it is, that's always been my policy as you know,' he began.

Oh God, here we go, Jackie thought, we'll be all round the houses for the next half hour before he ever gets to the point. 'Cut straight to the chase, Mr Stampwick,' she ordered. 'No pussyfooting about, just spit it out. Where are your boys?' Jackie stared straight at him, looking deeply into his eyes. Mr Stampwick could not look away.

'At home with their mother by now, having egg and chips and a pot of tea, I expect.'

Relieved to hear nothing worse, Jackie was at a loss. 'I take it the boys are alright then?' she said. 'So what's the problem? You said it was bad news.'

'Aye, the worst really. Leastways I think so. It couldn't be much worse for you, lass.'

By now, real fear was talking hold of Jackie. 'What?' she shouted at Mr Stampwick.

'Asbestos,' he said unhappily. 'It's everywhere in this place; round the pipes, in the walls, in the roof. We can't touch it, lass. Some of it looks very old and unstable. You'd have to get a company licensed to remove and dispose of it in to sort all this lot out.'

'Asbestos,' Jackie whispered. 'Isn't it a fire retardant material?'

'Aye,' agreed Mr Stampwick, 'that's what it was originally put in for, in the days before people realised how dangerous it is. Get a bit of that into your lungs and it can kill you. The minute I saw it, I sent the boys away and put a mask on to take a better look. It's in a dangerous state, miss, and can't be left there. I can't do it. I'm just a jobbing builder. As I said, you'll need a licensed, specialist firm to remove it all and they can take it to a special disposal site.'

'So we can't carry on with the renovations?' Jackie's voice seemed to be coming from a long way off.

'No, sorry, but that's the law. Luckily I have other work I can go to. I can start again here when all the asbestos has been removed.' He got up and patted her shoulders awkwardly. 'I'm sorry to add to your troubles,' he continued 'but I'll have to send you a bill for all the materials I've ordered for here and for the skip and the time me and the boys have spent on the project already. And then there's the money I have to pay to Mr Young for getting me the work in the first place. But that's just between him and me, so keep that under your hat. You try ringing round a few firms, get some quotes for the work. Soonest started, soonest done, that's what I say.'

Mr Stampwick was full of sayings. Jackie wondered if he had one for every occasion. Quotes for the work – how much extra was she going to have to pay on top of the renovations? She'd only allowed a small amount for unforeseen emergencies. 'Have you any idea how much the work will cost? she asked.

'Don't be asking me questions like that, Miss Dalrymple-Jones,' said Mr Stampwick, gathering up his lunch and coat. 'I wouldn't like to put a figure on it. I never like to speculate on things like that.'

Jackie remembered Mr Stampwick coming to look at the café for the first time. She'd had to back him into a corner and threaten him with Walter's longest ladle before he would hazard a guess at a price. 'Live dangerously just for once, Mr Stampwick,' she suggested 'Give me the old ball-park figure.'

Mr Stampwick was at the café door ready to make his escape. He stroked his chin reflectively, looking about him. 'Twenty, maybe twenty-five.'

Jackie blinked. 'You don't mean pounds do you? she said slowly.

'Thousand. Twenty-five thousand mebbe.' He opened the café door and got safely on the other side of it. He looked back at Jackie through the open door. 'I'm sorry, Miss, sorry you didn't know it was there. By law, you should have done. There were new regulations from the Health & Safety Executive in 2006, but there, it is as it is. Marilyn didn't take too much notice of things like that. Look on the bright side, once it's done it's done, and you won't have to worry about it no more.'

Of course, Jackie marvelled, just put my hands on the twenty-five or maybe thirty thousand pounds I have in my little old piggy bank and problem solved.

Mr Stampwick cut across her thoughts. 'Mr Young at the Trades Council, he'll help you, lass. You'll have insurance against this kind of thing, just a question of putting a claim in.'

After he had gone Jackie sat in the empty café and stared about her. Mr Stampwick had made a thorough investigation in his hunt for asbestos. He had removed pieces of the old wooden boarding in several places around the walls, taken down ceiling tiles and even had the vinyl flooring up to look at it. He had propped everything back in place to cover up the asbestos, but even so, the whole place looked a wreck.

Thank God for Tom Young and the Trades Council. At least she had the place well insured and could get the work done through the insurance company. No doubt her premiums would go up dramatically next year, but she would face that one when it came along.

She got up from the chair and went towards her office. Mr Stampwick was right for once. Soonest started, soonest done.

There was a long silence at the other end of the phone when she told Tom Young. 'Tom, are you there?' she asked.

'Asbestos,' repeated Tom. 'Are you sure?'

'Sure as Mr Stampwick is and he was very sure. He

recognised it straight away and checked out the whole of the café. It seems it's everywhere and in everything; in the roof, behind the wall panelling, lagging the pipes, in the flooring, you name it.' Jackie tried to keep her voice light, keep herself positive. 'I know it's going to delay the renovations, but it's not the end of the world. At least it can be removed and disposed of.'

'At a great deal of expense,' said Tom.

'Which is why I'm phoning you, Tom.' Jackie was almost buoyant. They were already on their way to sorting things out. 'All that café insurance is going to come in useful for once. I would like to get a claim under way as soon as possible.' Once again there was silence at the other end.

'Tom?' Jackie looked at her handset. Sometimes reception could be poor in this cubby-hole of an office.

'I'm afraid you can't, Jackie,' Tom said gently.

'Can't what?' she asked.

'You can't make a claim. You said you didn't have asbestos in the building.'

'Well I didn't know, did I?' she said. 'Not at the time. How would I, if it's hidden away behind panelling and in the roof space and all the other places I can't see? I haven't got X-ray eyes, so of course I said no.'

'That's the point,' said Tom. 'You said no. You didn't say, not to your knowledge. If you'd have said that, your claim would now be valid.'

Jackie felt sick. 'Why didn't you tell me?' she demanded.

'You seemed so certain. I assumed Marilyn had had an inspection done, as per the 2006 Regulations relating to asbestos in buildings and none had been found. If you'd shown any hesitation, of course I would have advised you differently. I'm sorry, Jackie, I really am, but there is nothing I can do. In fact, because you didn't declare it and now it is found to be present, your whole policy with us will be void. I'm not sure my company would take the risk of insuring you in the future. I'm sorry, Jackie, but that's how it is.' Abruptly, he terminated their phone call.

Jackie sat at her desk and pondered on Tom Young. He'd been so cold, matter of fact. He hadn't even expressed any sympathy for her plight, just told her the cold hard facts. When she had been paying him a fortune in insurance premiums he had been all charm and good humour and now … now it was like talking to a cold stranger. The memory of Walter and Barney trying to talk her out of taking up with Tom Young and his crowd came back to her: Walter dead set against and Barney so serious, those blue eyes steady, his tone urgent in his sound advice.

What a fool she had been. She'd had the best advisors around her all the time and wouldn't listen, stubbornly going her own way. Walking blindly down the path to disaster; taken in by the fashionable, shiny set. Whatever had Marilyn seen in them? But of course, she'd been one of them, a wheeler dealer. Jackie laid her head on her arms and let the hot tears flow. Whatever was she going to do now?

CHAPTER 34

Walter was forking the old straw out of the lambing pens in his barn when he heard a car bumping up the track that led to his house. He left the fork on the barrow and went outside to see who his visitor was. There was still warmth in the May evening sunshine. Walter put his hand up to shade his eyes. He wasn't expecting Ellie until later in the day, Stan was still at work and few other people were brave enough to risk their cars up the rough track.

To his surprise, Jackie's borrowed car bounced up the track and slewed around the bend towards his door at some speed. Walter squeezed his eyes shut in case Jackie didn't hit the brakes on time and landed up against the old steel gates that opened on to his fields. Luckily, by a whisker, she did. In the accompanying silence, the smell of hot rubber filled the air.

Walter waited, but Jackie made no move to get out of the car. Now what's to do, he wondered. Jackie had only visited Walter's smallholding on a few occasions when she was small, a wide-eyed solemn little girl, hiding behind Marilyn's skirts, but as she grew more independent the visits ceased. Walter thought it must be twenty-five years or more since Jackie had been here at Claygate.

He watched her sitting hunched over the steering wheel staring out over the fields. She wouldn't be able to sit and watch his lambs gambolling about all afternoon. The little car was like a tin box on wheels and it would soon get boiling hot in there.

Walter walked over to the car and opened the door. 'Now, lass,' he said, 'it's a long time since you've been up here. I'm right pleased to see you. Is this a flying visit or are you going to get out of the car and come in and have a cup of tea?'

Jackie didn't answer, just carried on staring straight ahead. Walter remembered the day Marilyn died; how the shock of it had affected Jackie then, the same locked-in silence and white, tight expression on her face.

Walter kept his tone light to cover up his concern. 'Yes, Walter,' he said in a high woman's voice, 'tea would be lovely.' He helped Jackie out of the car as if she were an invalid and led her through his back door into the kitchen.

Standing inside the cool, dark room, Jackie seemed to come back to consciousness and looked around her. 'Claygate,' she said wonderingly. 'I haven't been here since I was a little girl. I remember it so well; it hardly seems to have changed at all.' She looked at Walter. 'You were always the one constant in my life, you know. Dad was always away on business or too busy to spend any time with me. Marilyn was at the café or the wholesalers or the Trades Council. But when I visited here or the café, you always stopped everything you were doing to spend time with me, gave me all your attention.'

Walter could hardly bear it. He turned away, not wanting Jackie to see the overwhelming love and pride that her words wrought in him. He sat her down at the table and went to make the tea. 'You don't take sugar do you? he said.

'There's asbestos in the café,' Jackie said.

Walter turned, tea-pot in hand, 'You what, lass?'

'The café's riddled with it, it's everywhere. Mr Stampwick found it this morning, after he'd taken the kitchen out. He and his lads went to start in the café proper and found some behind that old wooden boarding that covers the walls. So he looked further and he's found it everywhere: in the roof, round the pipes, in the flooring, just everywhere.' She turned anguished eyes up to Walter. 'He said it would cost about twenty-five thousand pounds to have it all removed and disposed of by a specialist firm, and the worst of it is the insurance won't cover it.' Tears rolled down Jackie's face as she tried to get the rest of the tale out.

Walter sat down and held Jackie in his arms as she poured out the story of the void insurance policy and Tom Young's uncaring attitude and coldness. As the tale unfolded, Jackie's sobs increased and her whole body shook in Walter's arms. He stroked her hair and soothed her. 'There, lass, don't cry like that. It will be all right,' he said over and over, 'it will be all right.' Strangely, it seemed the most natural thing in the world to be holding his child in his arms and comforting her, but it would need more than a sticking plaster to heal these wounds and make Jackie's world come right again.

When she had cried herself out, Walter led Jackie to the sofa beside the fire in the kitchen and sat her in it. He made the tea and handed her a mug. She took a sip and made a face. 'What's in this?' she asked.

'Drop of whisky,' said Walter. 'You've had a shock, lass. That'll warm you through and set you back on your feet.'

'It'll need more than that,' Jackie said dismally.

Walter brought his tea over and sat beside her. 'I'm right glad you came here, lass. That's the best thing you could have done. We'll sort something out tomorrow.'

'I've been trying all afternoon,' Jackie said quietly 'All the banks and building societies I know, but no-one wants to know. These are tough times we live in, Walter, and getting rid of asbestos isn't an investment.'

'We're not done yet, lass. Marilyn wasn't the only one with connections. I know a few folk that might stump up the money. I'll get on to it tomorrow. In the meantime, drink that tea.'

'I thought I was so clever, knew better than you and

Barney,' she said reflectively, watching the flames dance in the grate. 'What did you and Barney know about the business world? Neither of you had any experience, let alone any contacts with the Trades Council, so how could you possibly know anything? How wrong could I be? It's *me* that didn't know anything and now I'm in a monumental mess. No money for the asbestos removal and no café to operate in either. From worse to worse. I'll have to sell up and go back to the supermarket.'

'We all learn the hard way love,' Walter said gently 'but we'll come out of this upsides yet, you wait and see. Now,' he got up and rubbed his hands together, 'we're going to have a bite o' supper. I've a nice rabbit stew in the oven with some jacket potatoes. It will go down a treat.'

Jackie almost choked on her tea. 'Rabbit! As in fluffy bunny running about your fields?'

'No, an old buck past its prime. I did him a favour before the fox used him as a plaything. It's kinder that way, and gently stewed you'll think it's best chicken.'

Jackie looked unconvinced. Walter took no notice. He busied himself setting the table and serving out the meal. When he set it in front of Jackie she was impressed. 'I thought you could only do fry-ups,' she said.

'I do,' he said, splitting his potato and melting a large knob of butter over it. 'I just supplied the rabbit, Ellie did the rest. She's a first-class cook. Eat up, lass, you wouldn't get better at The Ritz.'

The stew was tasty and Jackie managed the lot. She didn't see a way out of her troubles, but somehow the world didn't seem such a black place as it had that afternoon. It was dark outside now and reluctantly Jackie went to gather up her bag and keys. 'I suppose I had better be getting off home, Walter,' she said tiredly. 'That was an amazing supper and I'm truly grateful to you, but if I don't make a move soon I might fall asleep in the car on the way home.'

'You're not going anywhere tonight, lass,' Walter said firmly. 'I'm not letting you go home to an empty house and be on your own to cry some more. No, that's not going to happen. You stay here the night and I'll look after you. I've got a good spare bed and I can find you some pyjamas. You can have a nice hot bath and a hot toddy, and with a bit of luck you'll sleep like a baby.'

Jackie managed a smile, 'That sounds like a good plan to me.'

Walter was relieved she hadn't put up more of a fight. He could hardly believe he had managed to get his own way so easily; she must be really done in not to argue with him for once. 'Right, I'll go and find some pyjamas,' he said, grinning back at Jackie.

He went off upstairs and returned a little while later with a pair of old blue and white striped flannelette pyjamas. Jackie was staring pensively into the fire but looked up at Walter's approach. Her eyes widened as he gave her the pyjamas. 'They might be a bit on the big side, but they'll keep you warm,' he said.

Jackie handled them wonderingly. 'Flannelette! I thought it had gone out in my great-grandmother's time. Fancy you still having some.'

'Steady on, lass,' Walter protested, 'I'm not that old. Lots of folk still wear flannelette, they just don't admit to it.'

'Do you have a matching nightcap and bedsocks?' she asked.

Ah, that was better. He could stand any amount of banter from her, a bit of temper, impatience; she could throw things at him, anything but that bleak despair she'd arrived with. 'Don't be cheeky, there's nowt wrong with flannelette. Go and get a bath while the water's hot, you'll be glad of those pyjamas then. There's only a coal fire in your room. I never got around to putting central heating in. You might find it a bit parky.'

'Do I get a hot brick in my bed as well? Will I need a candle to see by?'

Walter smiled back at her. She could tease all she liked; it would keep her spirits up.

Whilst Jackie was upstairs Walter made some telephone calls, first to Penny and then to Kate. He had formulated some plans for the next day but he needed to carry them out on his own, without Jackie in tow. He explained the situation to the girls and asked them to keep her busy tomorrow. 'Shopping and lunch and more shopping,' he suggested. 'Have a day out in York or to one of them Malls I've heard about, Leeds maybe.'

He kept his own plans to himself. Penny and Kate had to trust him on that one. 'Mr Mysterious,' said Penny.

'Very enigmatic,' said Kate.

But they agreed to his plan and would collect Jackie at 9:30 in the morning. Walter hoped, after all the arranging, that he would be able to sell the idea to Jackie.

Next he phoned Ellie. He wanted to see her tomorrow. Her future was bound up with his and she needed to know what he intended to do and why. He had a lot of explaining to do and he only hoped she would understand and agree. As he arranged to meet with Ellie, part of Walter marvelled that in the short time since Marilyn's death he had gone from no-one in his life to now having two women he cared about and felt responsible for.

Jackie arrived back in the warm kitchen sporting Walter's striped pyjamas and an old woollen dressing gown. She had lost a lot of weight since Marilyn's death, and with her slim figure and fair hair fluffed out after her bath, she looked young and beautiful and very like *him*. Walter caught his breath and steadied himself at the kitchen table. When her face had been fuller, she hadn't resembled anyone in particular, but now that her features were so clearly defined it was quite obvious to Walter who her father was. Would it be so obvious to others? Would Jackie notice? Now was not the time for such announcements, but he needed to talk to Ellie and very soon.

Jackie sat down by the fire and he made them both a hot toddy. Jackie relaxed against the cushions and sipped the hot whisky, listening as Walter outlined the plans with Penny and Kate for the next day.

'I want to be with you, Walter. You said you had some ideas and contacts that might be able to help. I need to be on the spot, not miles away spending money I haven't got on clothes I can't afford.'

'Leave me to look after my plans,' he said firmly. 'I could be all day scouting round and I don't want an inquisition from you at every turn. It would drive me bloody bonkers.'

'Oh, it's only my future we're talking here, Walter, that's all. If we can't raise any money, I might land up in a debtors' prison. Who'll come and visit me then?'

Off on one at the drop of a hat, Walter thought. Just like her mother. She didn't get that dramatic streak from him. 'Just leave me be to sort it out. If I don't have twenty-five grand for you by tomorrow night, I'll eat your hat and coat and that horrible cat and all. But I don't need you there breathing down my neck whilst I get it. So just go off with Penny and Kate and do what you're told for once in your life.'

They glared at each other for a few moments. Walter didn't let himself look away. This was one battle of wits he had to win. In the end Jackie sighed and sat back again against the cushions. 'Alright, seems like I've no choice.'

Mightily relieved Walter saluted her with his glass. 'Here's to Café Paradise for many years to come.' He took a long draught and relaxed for the first time that evening.

By the time she had finished the hot whisky, Jackie was yawning and her eyelids were drooping. After the stress of the day, the welcome and kindness she received at Claygate

Farm had overwhelmed her. Sitting next to Walter on the old kitchen sofa, she wanted to thank him for being such a good friend. She tried to formulate the words in her head, but everything was turning fuzzy and distant. Perhaps she would tell him tomorrow … when she could get the words … in the right.…

Walter finished his whisky and set his glass down on the table. He stood up and stretched. It had been a long day. He turned to tell her he would not be long for his bed. She was fast asleep, looking small and slight wrapped up in his dressing gown.

Walter shook his head. She couldn't sleep there. The fire would go out and she would get very cold. There was nothing for it. He picked her up and carried her upstairs and laid her gently in her bed. She didn't stir as he pulled the cover up around her.

Standing back he admired his handiwork. Jackie looked snug and warm for the night. What a day it had been. His own child seeking him out for comfort and advice and now for the first time in his life he had put her to bed. Walter shook his head. How much stranger could life get?

CHAPTER 35

It was late the next morning when the three women, laden with shopping bags, staggered out of a large department store in the centre of Harrogate and paused on the pavement to catch their breath.

'I'm starving hungry,' said Jackie 'Why don't we have lunch here? You've talked me into buying clothes I can't afford, so why don't we top it off with a very expensive lunch and I'll just go bankrupt in style?'

'Nonsense,' said Kate bracingly 'You needed new clothes. Your old ones are hanging off you since you lost so much weight. You can't go around looking like a bag lady.'

'Thanks,' said Jackie.

'The pleasure's all mine,' replied Kate. She looked past the Cenotaph dominating the square and across the road to Betty's Tearooms at the top of Parliament Street. 'We're lunching at Betty's today and before you have a heart attack, lunch is our treat. We have every confidence in Walter pulling out all the stops and coming up with the money and we're going to celebrate the new Café Paradise. The table's booked and the wine will be nicely chilled by now, so come on.' She took Jackie's arm and propelled her down the street.

Penny tottered on behind them, laden with bags. 'Don't worry about me, you two,' she called. 'I'll carry *all* the bags like the old pack-horse that I am and catch up with you in half an hour or so, if I haven't been knocked down by a car as I stagger across the road.'

Kate and Jackie turned back and took a bag each. 'Honestly, Penny, you always exaggerate,' said Kate. 'There's no weight in these at all, you'd have made it in twenty minutes and still had time for a glass of wine!'

Ten minutes later they were seated at their window table in Betty's, looking out on to the bustling crowds walking by in the spring sunshine.

'This is the life,' said Kate looking around her appreciatively. 'I could get used to this; being waited on by minions bringing me first-class food and wine.'

Penny sipped her wine and nodded agreement. 'This wine is lovely, chilled to perfection and look at this menu. It's going to be hard to choose, everything looks so good.'

Jackie looked at them both in amazement. 'Listen to the pair of you. We might all be soon out of a job and not a penny to bless ourselves with. We've just spent a king's ransom on clothes and now we're dining in the best café in Harrogate as if we haven't a care in the world.' Jackie shook her head. 'I told Walter last night I'll end up in a debtors' prison and it's looking more likely by the hour.'

Kate poured Jackie some wine. 'Enjoy this lovely wine and choose your lunch. Walter will come up trumps, you'll see.'

Jackie wanted to believe it, but how could a greasy-spoon cook from a back of beyond smallholding find twenty-five grand overnight? Jackie knew it was a lost cause but, in spite of that, the blow of losing the café would be softened by her finding how true her friends had been to her. Here they were doing their very best to cheer her up and give her a treat and Walter was working so hard in the background on her behalf. Jackie realised with a jolt how hard Walter had quietly worked for them for years and how little they had appreciated him.

'Betty's Yorkshire Rarebit sounds the business for me today,' Kate broke in on her thoughts. 'What are you going to have, Jackie?'

Jackie shook herself and gave her attention to Betty's menu. After a few moments she said, 'I like the sound of the smoked salmon omelette. Made with free range eggs, Scottish smoked salmon and served with mixed salad leaves.' She turned to Penny sitting next to her. 'Have you decided, Penny?'

'I think I'm going to have the warm seasonal quiche served with...' Penny broke off her attention caught by something at the window. 'Look at that,' she squeaked.

Kate and Jackie turned to look out of the window. Standing there, checking the day's menu posted outside, were George and a friend, both dressed to kill in new spring outfits and high heels.

'I'll kill him,' Penny whispered in anguished tones. 'He promised not to embarrass me any more, not to come out in public, and look at him.'

As if he heard her, George looked up and met Penny's horrified gaze. Momentarily he froze and then, digging his friend in the ribs, lumbered off down the street. Penny sprang up from the table. 'I'll have the quiche and fresh fruit cheesecake to follow, but first I have a little business to attend to.'

With her head held high she marched purposefully out of the café. Once outside she broke into a run and shouted at them down the street, 'George! George! Stop,' and waved her arm madly.

People were turning to look at her. Penny ignored them. 'Hang on, George, we need to talk.'

George stopped and signalled to his friend to walk on.

'Pipe down, Penny,' George said looking about him, 'you're attracting attention.'

Penny gawped at him. '*I'm* attracting attention. I like that. And I suppose you're not.'

'No, not at all. I'm just quietly walking down the street

minding my own business, blending in, and then you come along, running amok and shouting the odds. Thanks to you, the whole of Harrogate knows my name now.'

'George Montague, there's no way on this planet you're ever going to blend in dressed like that and if you think you do then you're fooling yourself. That's by the by anyway. You're supposed to be at work, at least that's what you told me this morning.'

'And you told me you were going into York with the girls,' George came back at her.

'We changed our minds, that's what we do according to you, isn't it? So we changed our minds and came to Harrogate instead to give Jackie a proper day out with a lovely lunch to take her mind off things. I've done what I said I was doing. Whereas you…' Penny looked up at George angrily. 'You promised me faithfully you wouldn't embarrass me again.'

'The job was cancelled for today and Frederika was free and suggested this trip at the last minute. You'd already gone, supposedly to York for the day and I was going to be on my own, so I thought why not? Bit of shopping, bit of lunch and home before you. No harm done.'

'No harm done!' Penny was incredulous. 'You could meet any one of our neighbours walking down this street, George, and you dressed up like a, like a … pantomime dame. It's disgusting and I've had enough. If you don't want to be a real man, a proper husband then just don't speak to me ever again, because I won't be speaking to you.'

With that Penny turned on her heels and marched away from him, head held high and tears streaming down her face. George stared after her open-mouthed. His friend, Frederika, approached him. 'She didn't take that too well did she?' he commented.

'Could be very quiet in our house tonight,' said George. 'She says she's not speaking to me and I haven't to speak to her.'

'I'd give it half an hour.' said Frederika, 'Never known a woman last out longer than that.'

'Ah,' said George, still staring up the street 'Let's hope you're right.'

Penny visited the Ladies to mop up her tears and tidy her make-up before re-joining Kate and Jackie at the table. She managed to look quite cheerful, not wanting to spoil their lunch.

'So now you see what I mean,' she said to Kate. 'You thought I was exaggerating, but now you've seen the real thing what do you think?'

'Well,' Kate began slowly, 'he looked very impressive. I loved the dress.'

'And the shoes and bag were divine,' added Jackie.

'I know. It was just the bad wig, make-up and five o'clock shadow that let him down.' Penny sighed. 'It's OK, girls, you don't have to be nice about it. He looks awful and will never pass for a woman, however much he tries. And I've had enough. I've told him if he doesn't want to be a real man I'll never speak to him again, and that's only the start. I don't want to be married to a half-man, half-woman, so he'd better look out. I want a real man,' she ended defiantly.

Kate and Jackie stared at her and then looked at each other. Kate's expression reflected Jackie's own thoughts. They would need to keep a close eye on Penny for a while. They both knew a very real man who would love to take advantage of a very vulnerable Penny.

What a day it was turning out to be and it wasn't over yet. Jackie only hoped that Walter would have some good news for her but somehow she doubted it. She smiled at Penny. 'Let's enjoy today, Penny,' she said gently. 'Everything could change tomorrow, maybe for the better.' She poured her some wine and raised her glass in a toast. 'To us,' she said, 'and a brighter future.'

They decided on coffee to round off the lunch. Whilst they waited for the waitress to bring it, Kate produced a cutting from the *York Gazette*. 'There's never going to be a good time to talk about this, so it might as well be now or never,' she said.

Jackie turned to look at Kate in surprise. Now what was coming? Not another catastrophe, please. One a day was enough.

'Walter started me off on it,' Kate continued, 'ages ago. He said I should be doing something else, not waste my history degree. I knew he was right, but I really enjoy my job at Café Paradise and I wasn't really looking for anything else.'

'There's a *but* coming, I can hear it,' Jackie said drily.

Kate showed her the newspaper advertisement. 'The York History Society is looking for a full-time advisor, with special reference to the Roman period and the re-enactment society. I could do that. I specialised in Roman history in Britain for my degree.'

Penny looked awed. 'Does that mean I'll know a real advisor then? I've never met one of those before. Fancy.'

'I haven't got the job yet,' Kate said. 'I would need to see what it involved first. I might not be suitable and even if I was there's plenty of time. The appointment doesn't start until September, so I'll still be around to help get the café up and running again.'

'They'd be stupid not to take you,' Jackie said. 'You'd do a brilliant job, you work hard and get on with everyone and I'm sure you know your stuff. What more do they want?'

Kate smiled at her. 'That's some testimonial. Can I have that in writing, I might need it.'

'Not likely, why would I myself to lose one of my best waitresses? I'll say you're sloppy and idle and they shouldn't touch you with a barge pole.'

Kate laughed. 'Thanks, friend.'

Penny looked at Jackie, puzzled. 'But you just said she was brilliant and then said she's sloppy … I don't get it. I thought you liked Kate.'

The waitress brought the cafétiere and set it on the table. Kate was nearest and poured the coffee out into pretty china cups. 'She does, Penny, we're friends.'

'But you're so rude to each… Oh, I get it, it's a joke.' Penny took her coffee from Kate and smiled.

* * * * * *

With Jackie out of the way Walter rode over to see Ellie. He parked his bike outside her back door. He was tired after the ride from his holding at Claygate to her cottage in the pretty village of Dunnington on the outskirts of York. 'You'll have to be thinking about a sturdy car, lad,' he told himself. 'Times change and you'll have to change with them.'

Ellie welcomed him with her bright smile and warm embrace. Soon he was sitting in her kitchen with a cup of tea and fresh buttered scone. Walter felt anew a sense of peace and contentment that had been missing from his life in all the long years he had wasted in yearning after Marilyn.

'You were very mysterious on the phone last night, Walter,' Ellie said, pouring a cup of tea for herself and coming to sit opposite him at the table.

'I had Jackie there,' Walter replied. 'She was upstairs getting a bath but I didn't know just when she might come down and I didn't want her to know anything about today.'

'This is getting better,' Ellie smiled at him. 'So come on, what's the story? You said you needed to see me urgently. What's it all about?'

Now the time had come, Walter didn't know where to begin with his story. What would Ellie think of him not acknowledging his child all these years? Would she think he had been weak and uncaring in just going along with

Marilyn's tale? Spit it out, lad, he told himself, it's the only way.

'I grew up in a poor part of York. Jackie's mother was my playmate. We were inseparable and we got into all sorts of mischief together over the years. As we grew older we had one very clear idea in our heads and that was we didn't want to live the kind of hand-to-mouth existence our parents had lived for the rest of our lives. We wanted out of that ghetto. I wanted my own place, the smallholding I've got now out at Claygate. I worked at anything and everything and saved every penny to put the deposit down on it and as far as I knew Marilyn was coming with me. It was going to be our new life together.' Walter paused and took a sip of his tea.

'So what happened?' Ellie asked.

'Out of the blue she told me she didn't want to be buried out in the country, it wasn't for her. And then she disappeared, just like that. I was broken-hearted at the time. I'd got the holding for us both, to make us secure in the future and then she was gone.'

'But she came back,' Ellie said.

'Yeah. Three years later, with a husband and child. She'd married a civil engineer, Barry Dalrymple-Jones. His offices were in York centre and he was doing alright for himself. He bought her Café Paradise and we met up again.'

Walter paused and emptied his cup. Ellie refilled it slowly, sensing he needed a few moments to collect himself.

'Thing is, Ellie,' he went on 'Marilyn and I, we were lovers before she took off and when she came back with Jackie in tow I did the sums and I knew she was mine. Marilyn denied it always, said she was Barry's, and by the skin of his teeth she could have been, but I knew. So I worked at the café all those years, stupidly still carrying a torch for Marilyn and keeping an eye on her and Jackie, watching her grow up, playing with her when she came in the café. Sometimes she even came out to the holding. She was my little girl. If I'd have left the café I might never have seen her again

Walter looked Ellie square in the face. 'I'm not ashamed of it, Ellie. Marilyn treated me badly and Jackie and I fight like cat and dog sometimes, but she's my lass through and through. I'd do the same again.'

Ellie took his hands in hers, 'Of course you would, Walter, and I wouldn't want it any other way. Does Jackie now know that she's your daughter?'

Walter looked into Ellie's concerned face. He'd got over the first bit; now for the next and possibly worst bit. He pushed his chair back and prowled about her small kitchen.

'Thing is, Ellie, Jackie's had the builders in Café Paradise renovating it and they'd hardly got started when they found asbestos everywhere. It's all over the building, even up in the roof. It's got to be removed by a specialist firm and disposed of safely. The builder reckons it's going to cost about twenty-five thousand pounds.'

Ellie put her cup of tea slowly down in the saucer. 'That's an awful lot of money, Walter,' she said quietly.

'Money she hasn't got,' he said grimly. He sat down again opposite Ellie. 'Thing is, Ellie, I have. I've been saving all these years. It would have gone to Jackie eventually anyway.' He stopped and took a deep breath. 'I love you, Ellie, have done almost since the minute I clapped eyes on you, and I want to marry you. But if I give this money to Jackie, we'll have nowt, we'll have to support ourselves from the holding and it's a hard life.'

In the silence that followed Ellie looked steadily into Walter's eyes. She took his hands again and a smile spread slowly across her face. 'You daft man, as if I cared for how much money you've got. I didn't take long to fall for you, Walter Breckenridge, and I'm glad you'll have nowt. We don't need it. Give it to the lass who does.'

'Does that mean you'll marry me, Ellie?' Walter asked.

'Yes,' she said softly and leaned across the table and kissed

Walter gently on the lips.

* * * * * *

Two hours later an elated Walter parked his bike outside the Citizens Advice Bureau in Micklegate in the centre of York and went inside to find Barney Anderson.

Luckily, Barney had no appointments and was busy catching up on paperwork when Walter arrived.

'What brings you into the city, Walter?' Barney greeted him. 'I thought with the café closed you would be enjoying some time away with Ellie.'

'No rest for the wicked, Barney lad,' Walter grinned at him 'I've finished lambing, I've silage to make and the vegetable garden to look after. There'll be plenty of hungry rabbits and their babies wanting their share if I'm not there to keep an eye on things.'

Barney ushered Walter to a comfortable chair and sat down opposite him. 'So, to what do I owe the pleasure?'

To his surprise Walter blushed pink and stammered out. 'Well, for starters I've just got myself engaged. Ellie has … you know … she said yes.'

'Well, you old dog!' Barney clapped Walter on the back and shook his hand heartily. 'Well done, Walter, so she's going to make an honest man of you?'

'Looks like it,' Walter grinned shyly back at Barney. 'But that's not really why I'm here. I need your help.'

Barney rolled his eyes in mock horror. 'Now what have you been up to? Isn't beguiling the loveliest woman in Dunnington enough for you?'

'Aye, she's enough for me, but now I have Jackie to consider. And she's got a big problem you don't know about yet.'

Barney was instantly sober and gave Walter all his attention. 'Jackie? What is it?'

'That Stampwick fella, her builder, has found asbestos all over the café, Barney, that's what.'

'Well can't he just box it in, that's allowed isn't it?'

'Aye, but it's everywhere they want to be working, putting in new pipes and cables for the kitchen and café. They can't work in amongst it. So it has to come out. And according to Stampwick we're talking twenty-five thousand for the job, removal and safe disposal by a specialist firm. He won't touch it.'

Barney whistled soundlessly. 'Yeah, it would be all of that money, I'm sure. I've had asbestos cases before and they're not cheap.'

'Thing is, Barney lad, she hasn't got the money to pay for it.'

'Insurance,' Barney came back at him promptly

'Nothing doing. Tom Young won't pay out. Says because she put a definite "no" to asbestos on the proposal form, that's it, the whole thing is null and void.'

'The crafty…' Words failed Barney. He got up from his chair and paced about his office in agitation. After a minute of pacing he said, 'And you mean to tell me he would let her go under? He's not getting away with this, Walter, not if I have anything to do with it.'

Walter had never seen Barney so angry. He was usually so calm, but now he was almost beside himself. Walter didn't fancy being in Tom Young's shoes when Barney got hold of him.

'When you've finished wearing the carpet out,' Walter said mildly, 'I have a suggestion to make.'

Barney paused in his pacing and looked across at Walter. 'Sorry, Walter, I'm just so furious with that man. What's your suggestion?'

'I have some money put by. I've discussed it with Ellie and I want Jackie to have it to get rid of the asbestos. That way she can get on with the café renovations as she wanted to.'

'Twenty-five thousand?' asked Barney. 'That must be years of careful saving, Walter. Are you and Ellie sure about this?'

'Course we are,' said Walter indignantly, 'Ellie's pure gold and do you think we'd stand by and see my girl go under when we can help her?'

Barney held his hands up. 'Sorry, that was stupid of me. Of course you'll help her. But why do you need me?'

'Because I don't want her to know it's come from me.'

'Why not? You're her oldest friend and sparring partner. Who better to help her out?'

'I know Jackie, she wouldn't take it from me. She'd think she was robbing poor old Walter of his life's savings. She doesn't know she's my daughter and I don't want her to, just yet. She's only recently lost her mother and now this café problem. I don't want to wade in with another major shock for her. No, the money has to get to her some other way and that's where you come in.'

Barney looked puzzled. 'I do? How?'

'You give her a cheque, make up a tale. I don't know where you can say you got the money from, some investor who wants to remain anonymous. Just make sure she gets it.'

Barney stared at Walter for a long moment and then burst out laughing. 'You can't seriously think Jackie would take a cheque from me, no matter who I said it was from? I'm Dosser Boy remember. She hasn't even let me buy her lunch, let alone give her a cheque out of the blue for twenty-five grand.'

But Walter wasn't taking no for an answer. 'I'll bring you the cheque in a couple of day's time and you get yourself round to the café. She'll be there and you can be the cavalry coming to the rescue.'

Barney looked unconvinced. 'General Custer's last stand, more likely,' he said glumly.

* * * * * *

The next day Barney was fully booked with appointments at work and couldn't get away until lunchtime. The minute he was free, he headed off to Friargate to see Jackie at the Café Paradise.

He knocked on the door, but as no-one answered, he tried it and found it was open. He walked in, calling out as he went, 'Jackie, hello, Jackie, are you there?' He walked through the café and poked his head around the kitchen door. Jackie was sitting still and silent in its ruins.

Barney stood in the doorway. 'Jackie?' he said quietly.

She looked up, startled, as he spoke her name. 'Barney? Where did you spring from?'

The café door was open, so I came on through, looking for you.'

'And now you've found me.' Jackie's voice was flat and expressionless. 'I can't offer you any coffee, I'm afraid.' She gestured to the empty kitchen. 'As you see, we're a bit short on equipment just now.'

Barney hunkered down by her chair. 'I've heard what happened from Walter. I'm so sorry, Jackie. You obviously had no idea about the asbestos in the building.'

'None at all; Marilyn never mentioned it. I just steamed ahead with the renovations, never gave such a thing a thought.'

'Surely it was on your insurance proposal form?'

Jackie laughed bitterly. 'Tom Young saw to all that. He rattled off a few questions over lunch and then said he'd see to all the forms himself. I said a "no" to asbestos and he didn't take it any further.'

'Of course he didn't, the scoundrel,' said Barney angrily. 'I bet he knew all these old buildings were bound to have asbestos in them and he very cleverly manipulated you to say no. That way he wouldn't have to pay up and lose his bonus.'

'Well he's not paying up and now I'm left with an empty café and no prospect of ever being able to get it up and running. Walter tried to help and get me a loan but hasn't been able to.' She looked up at him. 'If it's any satisfaction to you, I wish I'd listened to you and Walter in the first place and never gone near Tom Young and his awful Trades Council. But it's too late for that now.'

Barney couldn't bear the despair in her voice. He took hold of her hands and pulled her to her feet. 'Come on, I owe you lunch and I'm not taking no for an answer today. In the words of the immortal Baldrick, I have a cunning plan.'

Jackie offered no resistance and they were soon seated in an old church on Spurriergate with homemade soup and baguettes.

Looking at Jackie across the table, Barney could see how wan and white she had become. She looked so miserable. He wanted to take her in his arms and soothe all her troubles away, but he knew that would not be the answer just now. It was nothing short of a miracle he had persuaded her out to lunch today. She must be nearly beaten to come out with him.

He made her eat the soup and baguette and kept up a flow of small talk about his friend John and his latest escapades in his van. Jackie listened politely and toyed with her food. Eventually Barney said, 'And so he stripped naked and fell off the top of the cliff.'

'That was nice for him,' Jackie said absently.

Barney leaned across the table and took the knife and fork from Jackie's hands. She looked up at him. 'Sorry, Barney, what did you say?'

'Well I'd just said, "John stripped naked and fell off the top of a cliff".'

'Why did he do that?' she asked.

'He didn't. I just wondered if it might get your attention,'

Barney smiled gently at her. 'Well, now that I have, I think I might have some good news for you.'

Jackie tried to smile back at him. 'I could do with some, Dosser Boy, or I might soon be signing on at the dole alongside you.'

'And since when did you know that I sign on?' Barney demanded.

'I don't know,' Jackie replied 'just for ever I suppose.'

We'll leave that to one side for now, Miss Dalrymple-Jones,' Barney said grimly. 'That's an issue for another day. In the meantime, I think I can lay my hands on twenty-five thousand pounds for you.'

Jackie said nothing, but looked at him steadily. 'Now why didn't I think of that? Of course, Barney's bound to have the readies in his back pocket. He knows everyone, he's got connections.'

Barney grimaced. Even at her lowest ebb, she could still be sarcastic and rude and oh so, so wrong. 'As a matter of fact I have got connections,' he said. 'I know someone who sees Café Paradise as a good investment and would be quite happy to lend you the money.'

'With your circle of friends, I bet it's someone who wants to launder his drug money into a respectable business. Well I don't want anything to do with that, thank you very much.

'Oh God, Jackie, give it a rest,' Barney said impatiently. 'You've just said you wish you'd taken more notice of me and Walter, so take some notice now. I'm trying to save your business, not get you into bed with a money launderer.'

'Sorry,' Jackie said gruffly. 'Only how do I know what you've got up your sleeve? You seem to know some odd people.'

'Believe me, none odder than you,' Barney glowered at her. Would she ever cease to exasperate and annoy him with her blind assumptions about him and his friends?

'My investor friend is a legitimate businessman and, as I

said, knows a good investment when he sees one. He wishes to remain anonymous, as is his usual practice, and he is happy to provide the funds for the asbestos removal. The funds would be available to you in a couple of days time and in the meantime you could go ahead and line up a company to be getting on with it.'

Jackie stared at him searchingly for some long moments. 'I only have your word for this,' she said at last.

'Yes, you have to trust me on this one.' Barney stared steadily back at her.

'Yes, I do.' She paused. 'OK, I don't know why, but I trust you. If York's fairy godmother wants to lend me twenty-five grand, I would be happy to accept.'

Barney let a long slow breath out and had to stop himself from cheering. At long last this cussed woman was seeing a bit of sense. The cavalry had triumphed after all. Now he had gained her trust, he hoped they would be able to move forward, when he would get the opportunity to tell her what he really did for a living. Show her he was not the dosser boy of her imaginings, or white van-man's assistant. All he had to do now was go after Tom Young. The day of reckoning with him could not be far away.

Inside Café Paradise Jackie stared at her copy of the *Yellow Pages,* open at asbestos removal companies. Why was Barney being so kind to her? OK, he had all the time in the world at his disposal, but he was going to a lot of trouble on her behalf. It wasn't as if he liked her much. A mixture of emotions swirled around her brain. Amazement, relief, gratitude and embarrassment and regret for all the times she had sniped at him, swiftly followed by a deep longing and loneliness she could hardly bear. If beautiful Melissa wasn't on the scene…

* * * * * *

After delivering Jackie back to Café Paradise, Barney made his way back to the Citizens Advice Bureau and telephoned Melissa at the Trades Council. Keeping his voice neutral he enquired whether she would be home for dinner that evening.

'Ooh, are you going to cook something special for me, Barney darling?'

And they say the way to a man's heart… Barney thought bitterly. Melissa could always be relied upon to enthuse when food was being discussed and even more if someone else was cooking it. Well if that's what it takes to get Melissa in the right mood to spill the beans, so be it. Barney was certain Melissa knew a lot more than she was telling him up to now. He had kept her in style for weeks, now it was payback time.

'I'll cook whatever you would like,' he said, keeping his voice light.

'Ooh, Barney,' Melissa cooed in delight, 'could we have a nice thick sirloin steak and all the trimmings and … and…'

He could almost hear her thinking down the telephone line.

'And hot chocolate fudge cake and really thick cream to go with it,' she ended.

'Red wine for Madam and perhaps a teensy weensy nibble at the cheese board to finish,' he said, trying hard to keep the sarcasm out of his voice.

'Sounds divine, Barney darling. Maybe the St. Auger with some water biscuits and a nice Californian red to go with it. Ooh,' her excited voice squeaked down the phone, 'I can't wait for tonight. Is this a special occasion?'

'I think it might be,' Barney answered drily. 'As the advert says, "it's good to talk".'

CHAPTER 36

Barney left the office early and went shopping for Melissa's feast. He wished with all his heart that he was doing this for Jackie. He dawdled in the wine merchants, picturing Jackie waiting for him, him arriving home laden with the bags and then unpacking them with her and cooking supper together. Eating chocolate pudding by candlelight, drinking warm red wine and then, and then…

'Can I help you, sir?'

Barney jumped as the wine merchant's question broke into his daydreams. 'Er, sorry, I was looking for a beautiful blonde. I mean a good Californian red.'

By the time Melissa came home, Barney's preparations were complete. He had laid the table in the small dining room and put out flowers and candles. The wine was corked and nicely at room temperature and the food was all ready. Melissa drifted in, throwing her coat and bag over the hall chair as usual, and came into the kitchen to greet him.

'Barney darling, how exciting! How wonderful. What are we celebrating? Have you had a pay rise from that horrid old CAB?'

Barney smiled. Trust Melissa to always link events to money. 'No, I just thought, you know, perhaps you deserve a treat once in a while.'

Melissa giggled and kissed the back of his neck. 'Ooh, I love treats, Barney. Did you get that nice wine I like?'

'It's on the dining room table,' said Barney, scrubbing the

349

back of his neck as Melissa went in search of a drink.

Dinner was a big success. Barney cooked the steak rare, just as Melissa like it. Barney smiled to himself as Melissa chewed with relish, forking up the bloody meat in the same way as her ancestors must have done centuries ago. He pictured her sitting inside a cave wearing skins, holding a lump of meat and gnawing at it.

The chocolate pudding and cream slipped down easily and Barney tried to make sure that Melissa had enough wine to make her mellow, but not too much so she would fall off her chair immediately after dinner. Part of him disliked this method of enquiry but after all, she had free-loaded on him for months and, he only wanted information.

As Melissa attacked the cheeseboard with gusto, Barney felt the time was right to start his enquiries. 'Walter Breckenridge tells me Café Paradise has a lot of asbestos in the building,' he said conversationally.

Melissa spread the St. Auger cheese lavishly on a biscuit. 'Yes, well, it was bound to have it.'

Barney took a sip of wine. 'How's that then?' he asked.

'Well, all the other buildings on that street had it removed years ago. That's what Tom says.' Melissa popped the biscuit into her mouth and closed her eyes in blissful concentration.

'Oh, so he knew it was a possibility then?' Barney was careful to keep his voice neutral, already wanting to get Tom Young by the throat and knock his teeth down it.

Melissa swallowed and opened her eyes. She reached for her wine. 'Oh yes, more likely a racing certainty. Thing was though, Café Paradise was a good yield. Yield? Is that the right word? Anyway, Tom said it was a good yield, as his company had insurance on it for everything, the building, the business, Marilyn, the staff, public liability, oh, just everything. So he was raking it in from Marilyn every year and of course she never made any alterations, so wouldn't find any asbestos.'

'Whereas, Jackie…' Barney prompted.

'Yes, that was a bit of a bummer,' agreed Melissa. 'But Tom was clever. He took her out to lunch, filled her up with wine and asked her the question then. Was there any asbestos in the building and she said "no".' Melissa held her hands up as if in surrender. 'Fair and square,' she said, 'and that's what Tom put down on the form; quite legit.'

Barney was boiling with anger inside but somehow managed to maintain a rictus smile on his face.

'Oh yes, quite legit,' he agreed. 'But was he so hard up for business that he had to rely on Jackie's premium or was he just greedy?'

Melissa looked at him reproachfully. 'That's not very nice, Barney. I didn't think you could be so unkind.'

Hastily Barney backtracked; he needed to keep Melissa sweet. 'Sorry,' he apologised, 'that wasn't very nice. Tom doesn't deserve that.' He deserves stringing up and I'd like to be the one to do it, he added grimly to himself.

'Tom's not greedy, but if he'd suddenly turned away Jackie's business and then she found out about the asbestos, she would know he knew about it always and had still taken Marilyn's money. That wouldn't have been good for his reputation.'

Barney spluttered on his wine. Tom Young had the dodgiest reputation in York. Hadn't Melissa twigged on to that yet? He swallowed hard. 'No, I'm sure he is very conscious of his reputation.'

'He is,' said Melissa guilelessly. 'Mind you, I shouldn't be saying this, but he is really a very naughty boy, Barney. He doesn't know I know, but I do.'

Barney's interest quickened. Obviously there was more and he'd better be quick to hear it before Melissa downed any more of that wine. 'So what does he know, that you know that he doesn't know you know?'

This was much too complicated for Melissa, especially

after a bottle of red wine. 'Eh?'

'Tell me what you know about Tom Young?' Barney said slowly and gently.

Melissa giggled. 'Well, he doesn't know, but I found out that I could listen in to the conversations in his office, through a switch on the telephone switchboard. I did it by accident one day and he was having a boring conversation with some bod in London about a shipment of steel. I soon switched that off, but from time to time I would listen in just to see if there as anything interesting going on.'

'And was there?' Barney asked.

'Do you remember that day when I came to Café Paradise to borrow some money for lunch?'

Barney nodded.

'Horrid old Tom was taken out to lunch by his boss up from London and they left me all alone to mind the office on a mouldy old sandwich whilst they went to The Pear Tree.'

'Poor Melissa,' Barney attempted sympathy.

'Yes and I was cross with them. So I treated myself to lunch in Betty's; boo sucks to them. When they came back, full of good food and wine, they wanted coffee as well. Tom wanted proper coffee, all that cafétière lark and the best china cups. Imagine, Barney, *me* messing about with all that stuff. Yuk, all those ghastly foul-smelling grounds to spoon out and a fancy tray to arrange.'

'Clever girl. So they got their coffee,' Barney prompted.

'Yes and he sent me out and told me to shut the door behind me. Well that got my curiosity going, I can tell you. What was going to be so hush-hush that I couldn't hear it? So I flicked that switch on the switchboard and listened in.'

Melissa's eyes grew enormous in her head as she thought of the import of what she was going to say. 'That man, Tom's boss, he told Tom he would be in line for a fifty thousand pound bonus at the end of their financial year which isn't far away.'

Barney remembered Melissa telling him about this, but she had never mentioned it since. 'That's an awful lot of money, Melissa. He must be a very good agent,' Barney said mildly.

'Brilliant,' Melissa agreed. 'All he has to do is not pay out on any more claims for the rest of this year and the money's his. Top agent of the year. How good is that? So of course, there's no way he's going to pay Jackie out. He'd made sure she said a big 'no' to the asbestos in the first place and here's the double whammy. Because she said no and now she's found it that makes the whole policy void anyway, because the company take the view that she must have known about the asbestos and was covering the fact up. So Tom still has a clean sheet and will soon be fifty thousand pounds to the good, plus all the illegal rake-offs he gets from the Trades Council, when he recommends people like that old fart, Stampwick, for Jackie's café. What's not to like? He's a genius!' Melissa ended triumphantly.

Barney removed himself from the table before the urge to slap that stupid, spiteful face got the better of him. To think that Melissa knew all this time and was as cheerful as Tom Young to let Jackie go to the wall. Well, that was so not going to happen. But he had to be careful. Melissa might have had a lot to drink but she still might remember in the morning that she had told him all her secrets. He must move the conversation on and bury Tom Young's dirty deeds beneath a layer of small talk.

He opened another bottle of wine and picked up their glasses. 'Let's go and have another glass by the fire Melissa,' he suggested.

Glancing regretfully at the remnants of the St. Auger on the cheeseboard, Melissa staggered to her feet. 'Don't think I can manage any more,' she said.

'You can always finish it tomorrow,' Barney soothed and led her to the sofa in the sitting room. He sat down next to her and poured her some wine. 'Perhaps I'll get a pay rise from the Citizens Advice,' he said, echoing her earlier conversation.

Melissa tweaked his hair playfully. 'Yes, and then you'll get mega-rich and I might marry you, and not old Tom Young. It's hard, you see,' she hiccuped. 'Decisions, decisions, Barney. Isn't life just full of them?'

'Mm,' Barney agreed cautiously. Marriage with Melissa had never been mentioned before.

'You see, I like Tom and all that, he's lovely and he's handsome, but maybe just too old for me. But he's got shedloads of money, Barney, and that's not to be sneezed at. On the other hand, you haven't got shedloads of money, but you've got enough to look after me with and give me everything I want. Well almost.' There was a moment's silence whilst Melissa considered this prospect. 'Yes, I think so and you're ever so handsome, ever so ... such a fit body. I'd love to get all your kit off and sleep with you.' A mischievous smile flitted across her face. 'I know, that's what tonight's all about, isn't it. You want to seduce me, don't you? Have your wicked way.' Melissa giggled helplessly at this idea and took a long slurp of her wine. 'I'm ready when you are, Barney boy, bring it on,' she slurred and fell on top of him.

Barney was horrified. This was the last thing he wanted or envisaged happening. They had lived like brother and sister for months and here she was trying to rip his tie off and clawing at his shirt. 'Hey, Melissa,' he joked, 'you don't have to tear my clothes off.'

Gently he pulled her off and rolled her back on to the sofa. He put his arm round her and soothed her like a child. 'Let's just take this slowly eh? No need to hurry, no need to hurry.' He stoked her hair and kept on repeating, 'No need to hurry.' Melissa's eyes glazed over and after a few half-hearted attempts at his shirt, passed out. Barney waited until he was sure she was deeply asleep and then picked her up and popped her into her bed. She was young enough to sleep it off without too much of a thick head in the morning.

Barney sat deep in thought before the fire. Although he had been a solicitor for some years now, he could still be shocked by the cold-hearted duplicity of some people. He was deeply angry at the anguish Tom Young was putting Jackie through whilst seeming to have been her friend.

But now Barney knew all there was to know, everything was out in the open. He thought he saw a way of getting Jackie's insurance claim honoured and also, as Melissa put it, the 'double whammy' of depriving him of his fifty thousand pound bonus. He just had to keep his nerve.

CHAPTER 37

K ate was in buoyant mood as she drove to Southmere House early on the following Saturday morning. They were now into June and she hoped the beautiful spring weather would hold up for the Historical Society's re-enactment day today. She had decided to observe their activities at close quarters before putting in her application for the post she'd seen on their website, that they were re-enacting the battle of the Medway in AD43 as well as re-creating a slice of Roman life.

She was looking forward to the day and was only sorry that Stan could not have come with her. When she had suggested they have another outing on Saturday, Stan had turned all tongue-tied and confused on her again and made his excuses. Surely his wretched mother and her leg must be better by now. Was he always going to be at her beck and call, and tied to walking that wretched poodle of hers?

Kate sighed to herself. It always seemed to be the same. Just as she thought she was getting to know Stan and become at ease with him, he seemed to mysteriously slip away from her and become more distant. She wished she could work out what was going on. He had always seemed so open and unfailingly cheerful at Café Paradise, always ready with a laugh and a joke. But when she was alone with him, it was as if he was holding something back, something important. If only she could find out what it was.

So here she was, on her own again. Kate followed the

directions to the car parks and was waved into a space by a steward in a fluorescent jacket. Gathering up her coat and handbag she got out and locked up her car. 'You're here now, Kate,' she told herself, 'so enjoy it and learn all you can. Who knows, next season you could be part of it all.'

Following the gravelled path that led visitors down to the Roman camp that represented early York, with all its varied trades and hierarchies of people, Kate made her way on to the field to begin her investigations into the work of the Historical Society.

She met with a very busy scene. Roman soldiers and English peasants strolled about carrying their armour and weapons on to what must be the battlefield. Some way behind them, stretching away into the adjacent field, a large marquee had been erected with a number of tents behind it.

Curious to see what was going on, Kate picked her way around the soldiers and made her way across the field towards the large marquee. As she drew near, she realised it was being used to re-create a Roman villa of the day. She stood and watched as large chunks of painted scenery and mosaic flooring were carried in.

'Mind out, Charlie,' a voice shouted from inside the marquee 'You've got that wall in the wrong place. At this rate, Lucius Marcius will have his bedroom in his hallway. Let me get the other panel from the van and you'll see the right order then.'

Kate froze. She knew that voice. Before she could move away, Stan came rushing out of the marquee and cannoned into her, almost knocking her off her feet. His arms shot out and grasped her in a tight hold to break her fall.

'Sorry, love, I didn't see you there,' he said, setting Kate back on her feet. 'In too much of a rush as usual. Always am on re-enactment days.' Then he looked down at Kate and saw who he was holding in his arms. 'Kate!' he exclaimed, nearly dropping her again. 'What are you doing here?'

'Having a day out. What are you doing here? I thought you were going to your mother's. You weren't able to come out for the day, you said.'

'I never said I was going to my mother,' Stan protested. 'I just said I couldn't come out. I was coming here,' he ended lamely. He turned away, staring all about him, looking flushed and embarrassed.

'What's the matter, Stan, don't you want to be seen with me?' Kate was really puzzled. 'You know I love history. Surely you know I would have enjoyed this event today and yet you chose not to ask me.

There was a short silence. Kate turned and made to walk away. 'Well I'll let you get on, you're obviously busy. Sorry I interrupted things.'

Still Stan said nothing. Kate was a few paces back along the path, when Stan raced after her, calling her name. 'Kate, don't go. Wait, let me explain.' He caught her up and straddled the path in front of her, stopping her from going any further. He took her hands and said earnestly. 'There's nothing in the world I would have liked better than to have had you with me today, Kate, involved in all this. But I thought you might think it was stupid, spending my days playing at being Roman and organising pretend soldiers and battles. I wanted to tell you but Walter said not to, said you might be put off me.'

Kate looked into Stan's honest blue eyes and knew he was telling the truth. Suddenly a lot of things made sense. She started to giggle. 'Horse glue! And you said it was your friends who were involved in amateur dramatics. It was this, wasn't it?'

Stan grinned, relieved at her reaction. 'Yes it was, but I didn't want to tell you in case it put you off.'

'So when were you going to tell me your dark, dark secret?' she asked.

Stan scratched his head. 'I don't know.' He drew her

towards a garden bench above the path and they sat down. Stan turned towards Kate and held her hands tightly.

'From the first moment I saw you at the Café Paradise, Kate, I knew you were the girl for me. I fell head over heels in love with you and you've turned my life upside down ever since. But history and battle re-enactment isn't everyone's cup of tea and it's been a huge part of my life for years now. Supposing you hated the whole idea? Walter thought I should present a broader picture, talk about current affairs, theatre and music, that kind of thing and not bore the pants off you with history.' He knew he was gabbling but couldn't seem to stop.

Kate kissed him, slowly and lingeringly. When they came up for air Stan said, 'Does that mean you don't mind?'

'Mind! I'm delighted.' She stopped, struck by a new concern. 'You're not the only one with a confession to make,' she said.

'Don't tell me; you've got ten children tucked away, an ageing mother who will have to come and live with us and a Rottweiler with bad breath.'

Kate took a deep breath. 'Worse than that; I've got a History degree, specialising in the Roman period and I saw the job for historical advisor in the paper and so came today to see what went on.'

Stan stared at her, speechless. 'You never said...'

'Well, you never said...'

'That's amazing. You're amazing. Will you marry me, Kate?'

'Can I still apply for the Advisor's post?'

'Yes. Well, will you?'

'Yes,' Kate answered.

'Yesss,' yelled Stan and swept Kate up in his arms and danced about the lawns with her. Finally he put her down and taking her in his arms, kissed her.

The crowd gathered at the entrance to the marquee,

cheered and applauded loudly. Kate blushed and Stan waved them away. 'Get on with the villa, I'll be with you shortly.'

'Will you now,' said Kate 'we'll see about that, Mr Stan Peterson. Come here.'

* * * * * *

Jackie poured out a second cup of coffee from her flask. 'Cheers, girls, and thank you for coming to help out on a Sunday. That's the last of the debris cleared out and that skip can be taken away ready for Newnham's Asbestos Clearance to start work tomorrow.'

'Fancy Tom Young turning out to be such a rat,' said Kate.

'All that wining and dining and special magic pants and all. Wasted on him,' said Penny.

'Yeah, when I think of the agony I went through with those pants,' said Jackie. 'I could hardly breathe, let alone walk in them. All that food at The Pear Tree Restaurant and I ended up with a smidgeon of boring old fish. I should have had the most expensive dish on the menu and a hundred pound bottle of wine. That way at least I would have spent some of the huge fees he charges for insurance.'

'Ah, but the golden boy is riding to the rescue,' said Penny dreamily. 'I can see him now kitted out in shining armour, mounted on a beautiful white horse, sweeping you up in his arms and riding off into the sunset with you.'

'Or arriving on foot as usual in his scruffy denims and his old rucksack and maybe a cheque for twenty-five thousand,' said Jackie practically. 'He's supposed to be coming this lunchtime. I just hope it's all as legit as he makes it out to be, but at the moment beggars can't be choosers.'

'Well if I were twenty years younger I'd certainly choose him,' said Penny. 'He's just such a lovely man.'

'So how's it going with George?' asked Kate.

A mulish look flitted across Penny's face. 'It isn't going at all. In fact, I haven't spoken to him since our day out in Harrogate. I told him he would have to decide whether he is going to be George or Georgina. I want my husband back and if I can't have him, then I don't want him at all. There are other fish in the sea.'

'Fish, like Enrique?' ventured Jackie.

Penny blushed, 'Maybe.'

'Penny, he's just out for a good time. Would you throw away thirty years of marriage for that?'

'It's alright for you to say that, Jackie, you've got gorgeous Barney drooling after you, said Penny crossly. 'What have I got? A husband so absorbed in his cross-dressing antics that he's more interested in the latest style of wig or high-heeled shoes and spends hours discussing hair removal and bosoms with his mate, Frederika. Wouldn't you be more interested in snake-hips in that situation? At least Enrique remembers what men and women are all about, which is more than George does.'

Jackie hardly heard Penny's diatribe against George. Barney drooling after her? For a moment Jackie's heart surged and then cold reality set in. Penny as usual had got hold of the wrong end of the stick. Barney was friendly and helpful and very kind and she knew she was eternally in his debt. Look how he had helped her out over the Nina Mountford-Blayne affair. But no, Penny was misguided as usual. Barney had never shown the slightest interest in her. And even if he ever did, which of course, he wouldn't, there was always horrible Melissa in the background.

Her thoughts were interrupted by Penny's exclamation, 'Well you're a dark horse, Kate. Why didn't you say so first thing.'

'We were busy, I thought it would keep for later and now is the later.'

Penny turned to Jackie. 'It didn't take them long did it?' she said.

'Take who, what?' Jackie asked, her own confused feelings about Barney tumbling around in her head.

'Planet earth to Jackie,' said Penny. 'Kate and Stan, they're engaged!'

Jackie stared at Kate in amazement. 'Well, no wonder you look so glowing today. And I thought it was yesterday's sunshine that had done it.' She hugged Kate tightly. 'Congratulations, Kate. We'll have to hear all about it, every gory detail mind, spare us nothing.' Jackie was honestly delighted for Kate but looking into her radiant face she also felt a pang of envy. Finding love with the right man lit Kate up from within and she had a new sense of confidence and tranquillity.

They had just finished packing up their picnic lunch when Barney knocked at the café door. Kate and Penny glanced knowingly at each other whilst Jackie went to let Barney in.

'He does drool after her,' said Penny. 'I've seen him watching her in the café; he can't take his eyes off her. He'd have asked her out long ago, but she bites his head off every time she sees him.'

'Well she's not biting it off today,' said Kate. 'Look at them.'

Jackie and Barney were standing just inside the café door smiling at each other.

'You can hardly get a piece of paper between them,' commented Kate.

'Mm, why would you?' said Penny licking her lips, 'Barney the body. Well if you don't want him, Jackie…'

'I see you've got your helpers,' Barney smiled down at Jackie. Her face was streaked with dirt and greasy dust smeared her jeans. To Barney she looked beautiful and he wanted to kiss her gently on her full red lips … well, maybe not kiss her *so* gently.

Jackie glanced behind her and saw Penny and Kate watching them. 'They've been marvellous. I'm very lucky, they've helped me clear out, ready for Newnhams's starting tomorrow.' Jackie looked embarrassed. 'Actually, I went to the Chamber of Commerce for a recommendation. I know it's a bit like shutting the stable door and I should have taken your…'

Barney placed his finger over her lips 'Hey, that's all in the past. My mother has a saying "never go over old ground". Let's go with that and look to the future.'

'Your mother sounds nice,' Jackie said.

Barney grinned. 'She's the tops, you'd love her. Maybe you'll meet her one day. You'd get on really well.'

Jackie looked nonplussed. How would that ever happen unless he brought her to the new café?

'Yeah, she's into hippie beads, caftans, smokes pot and burns joss sticks.' Barney grinned at the alarm on Jackie's face. 'It's OK, she doesn't really. She's a pillar of the community; a Justice of the Peace and a fiendish bridge player. And if it's any comfort to you, she wishes I'd get a proper job too.'

Jackie smiled ruefully. 'Well I have to agree with her on that one. I know it's none of my business but you seem to be intelligent and well-educated and yet don't seem to be going anywhere.'

Barney looked at her steadily. 'Don't I? I know exactly where I want to go. I just haven't found the way to get there yet, but I will.'

Jackie didn't understand what he was talking about, but her heart beat faster and she flushed a rosy pink under his steady gaze.

Barney pulled his rucksack off his back and reached inside for the cheque. 'Speaking of getting there, you'd better have this then Café Paradise can be up and running again.'

Jackie took the cheque and looked at it. She gasped. 'It's

got your name on it.'

'Oh, if only,' Barney said. 'If I had the dosh it would have been yours yesterday, but unfortunately I don't. As I said the investor wishes to remain anonymous, so I had to pay it into my account first and then draw a cheque for you.'

In spite of a glint of a tear in her eye Jackie still managed a shaky riposte 'Of course, the dole can be paid in by standing order these day can't it?'

'I believe it can be,' Barney agreed mildly.

'I'm sorry Barney that was uncalled for,' Jackie was ashamed of the jibe. 'Thank you for rescuing me. First, Nina Mountford-Blayne and now, this. I suppose I'll be in your debt for the rest of my life.'

'I hope so.' Barney longed to say more, but with Kate and Penny as his audience, it would have to keep for another day.

'Invite me to the opening of the café and we'll call it quits,' he said and shouldered his rucksack again. 'A good red wine and a wedge of brie on crusty bread and I'm yours.'

If only, Jackie thought shutting the café door behind him.

'We'd best get a truckle in then,' said Penny after Barney's departure.

'And a case of Château Neuf du Pape,' added Kate.

'Hey, I saw him first,' protested Penny.

Jackie waved the cheque at them. 'Stop fighting children, we've got work to do.'

CHAPTER 38

Samson bounded through the cat flap carrying a mouse. The tail of the poor creature hung limply out of his mouth. He trotted into the sitting room where Jackie was lying on the sofa and dropped it at her feet. He stepped back a few inches for her to admire his gift.

Jackie was staring at the ceiling deep in thought and at first did not notice. He meowed loudly to attract her attention but got no response. Losing patience and feeling unappreciated Samson readied himself for further action. He launched himself on to Jackie's chest and meowed loudly into her face, patting her cheek with his paw.

'Ow, bloody cat.' Jackie sat up with a start and pushed Samson of her chest. Swinging her legs off the sofa she saw the dead mouse on the floor with Samson sitting proudly beside it.

'What the..? Yuk. Samson, I thought we had a deal these days. I feed you three meals a day and in return you keep all wildlife the other side of the door. We agreed, no presents. So why the mouse?'

She glared at Samson and he stared inscrutably back at her. The more he saw of humans the less he understood them. He'd brought her the finest mouse Mayfield Grove could offer and here she was shovelling it up and putting it out of the door. There was no pleasing some people. She could stuff her Kattibix. Next time he caught a salmon in the Ouse, he'd keep it for himself. Samson curled up on the chair furthest away from the fire, turning his back on Jackie as she sat down on the sofa again.

'Bloody cat,' Jackie said out loud, 'why can't you bring me something useful like a bit of salmon? Since when did you see mouse on the menu here?'

Samson curled himself into a tight ball and stuffed his head under his tail. He wasn't going to listen to any more of her diatribe. He sighed for the good old days when Marilyn was alive and fed him tinned salmon and fresh chicken, gave him the best seat by the fire or a warm lap to sleep on. Now he was lucky to get this old chair in the same room as the fire. Maybe it was time to think about a change of residence. After all, Clara, his friend from up the road, had done alright for herself moving into Number Twenty. He wondered if they would like another cat.

Oblivious to Samson's hurt feelings, Jackie lay back on the sofa again and resumed staring at the ceiling. She was supposed to be drafting an advertisement for a new chef, but had only got as far as 'New city café seeks innovative chef.'

New city café owner seeks six foot four, blonde, blue-eyed dosser boy, she thought dreamily. Duties include kissing café owner passionately, leading to … ooh, don't go there, Jackie, she told herself. She couldn't help it. Leading to her slowly unbuttoning his shirt and sliding her hands inside to caress his firm, muscular body. And how do you know it's firm and muscular? she asked herself.

I just do, came the reply. And then?

Jackie sprang up from the sofa, unable to bear her own thoughts. Yes, he had been very kind to her, he was always sweet and thoughtful, helpful; look at how he came to her rescue with his friend's van. But he was still going nowhere, unambitious, content with his dole handouts. Did she want to get involved with someone like that? And even if she did want to, he wouldn't look at a plain Jane like her when he had Melissa in tow. So why was she thinking about him anyway?

Feeling miserable Jackie hurled her writing pad across the room. It hit the wall, waking Samson from his nap. Thinking the book was aimed at him, he leapt down from the chair and fled. Jackie heard the cat flap bang and shouted after him, 'And don't bring any more wildlife back, Samson, or you'll be on the café menu next week.'

* * * * * *

Three weeks later Jackie came into the newly-fitted kitchen where Walter was unwrapping the new saucepans to put away into the cupboards. 'God give me strength,' she said.

'Now what, lass?' Walter looked up from his work. What was it going to be this time? Jackie and John Stampwick the builder didn't really hit it off and Walter could see why. Stampwick was a bit of an old woman and those lanky sons of his were in need of a good boot up the backside in Walter's opinion.

'He's only gone and put the coffee counter at the wrong end of the café. Where does he keep his brains?'

'Sits on 'em, I expect,' Walter said sagely.

'He must do, he's put it far too near the entrance. It would clog up the doorway and everyone would have to filter around it, stupid man.'

'Didn't he read the plan?'

'Yes, and then completely ignored it. Thinks his way is the best. Best! How can it be best to have the customers nearly falling over you as they come in the door?'

'I take it you've put him right?' If Walter knew one thing he knew Jackie wouldn't hang about in getting the details right about the re-styled café. Secretly he was delighted to see it all taking shape and with it Jackie's growing confidence.

'You bet I have.' She grinned. 'I tell it like it is,' she said, in John Stampwick's voice. '"It is as it is," he said. I told him it bloody well isn't and get the counter shifted *now*, or he'd have you to deal with and I knew he wouldn't like that. So he's in the process of relocating it even as we speak.'

'I'll take that as a compliment, lass, although I'm not sure.' Walter carried on unwrapping the saucepans. Since the night when she had come to him at the farm, a new closeness had grown between them. They still had their spats and that would never change, but Walter was content in the knowledge that she confided in him and even occasionally asked for his advice.

He had been surprised at Jackie's reaction when he announced his intention to retire from the café once it was up and running again. Her dismay was obvious.

'You can't leave me now, Walter. I need you.'

No, you don't. You'll have young Alastair you've taken on. He seems a fine young chef. He can do all your taramasalata and bunga bunga and he knows his antipasti from a Cornish pasty which is more than I do.'

'That's not the point.'

Now she had Walter mystified. She couldn't wait to engage a new chef before and never wanted to see a bacon buttie within a mile of the new Café Paradise, so now what? 'Well, what *is* the bloody point?' he demanded.

To Walter's amazement Jackie looked as if she were about to cry. 'Well … it's just that…, you know.'

'No, I don't bloody know.' Oh God, women! Why do they cry over nothing and never get to the point?

'You've always been here,' Jackie wailed, 'since I was a baby really. You've always been at Café Paradise and it won't be the same if you go. What am I going to do without you?'

For once in his life Walter was speechless. His girl couldn't do without him? He felt torn. He was looking forward to retirement with Ellie. They were making plans for Claygate. He thought Jackie would be happy going forward without him. Now what was he to do?

Jackie began stowing the saucepans away in the cupboard. Walter watched her trying to control her tears. Was this the moment? Had the time come to tell her the truth as Ellie said he must do?

'Supposing something happened to you and Jackie found your letter after your death, how do you think she would feel? Ellie had asked. All the unanswered questions, the 'why's'. Why didn't you tell her; or give her the opportunity to get to know her real father properly? No, Walter, you can't leave things like this. You must tell her and explain things properly.'

Suddenly Jackie turned to him. 'Isn't that typical of you, Walter. You're under my feet morning, noon and night for years, awkward, cantankerous and full of advice I don't want, always arguing with me and then the minute I ask for a little help and support at the re-opening, you're going to be off, like a bat out of hell.'

'We're too alike, that's why we always argue,' Walter said. 'You're a chip off the old block.'

'No, I'm not,' Jackie said angrily 'I'm not a bit like Marilyn or my dad. I never was. We never connected somehow.'

Walter looked steadily at Jackie and tried to breathe evenly. 'You're just like me, Jackie, a real chip off the old block.'

Jackie stared back at him. The new kitchen clock seemed to tick loudly above them. Slowly and very carefully, Jackie put down the saucepan she was holding. Her violet eyes couldn't get much wider. 'Are you saying…'

Walter took the saucepan from Jackie and sat her down on the kitchen chair. He reached into the inside pocket of his jacket and drew out a long white envelope and handed it to her. 'I think the time's come for you to read this.'

'I don't want to read anything, I want you to explain what you just said.'

'I hope God's ready for you when you die, lass,' Walter

said, exasperated. 'You'll be arguing the toss with him and Saint Peter at the pearly gates. I just hope your mother isn't in on the conversation as well, or God could have a nervous breakdown. Heaven isn't ready for the two of you.'

'The way my mother went on I'm not sure she's God's right hand help just now, more likely old Nick's.' Jackie turned the white envelope over in her hands. 'Much as I would like a philosophical discussion on the afterlife, Walter, right now I want to know what this is all about.'

'Just read the letter,' Walter said through gritted teeth. 'Just for once, do as I ask and don't argue.' He saw she was about to challenge him again so he walked away. 'I'm going to see what old man Stampwick's up to. I can read the plans, even if he can't.'

Walter walked out to the café and sat shakily down on the nearest chair. Now the time had come, he felt quite scared inside. He hoped Ellie was right. He could lose Jackie altogether once she knew the truth. After all, Walter acknowledged to himself, who would want him as their father? A smallholder and greasy spoon chef; not much to boast about.

In the kitchen, Jackie slowly opened the envelope and took out Walter's letter. She began to read.

Dear Jackie,

When I set out to write this letter to you I had it in mind to leave it with my Will so you could read it after my death. But since we have been getting on a bit better lately Ellie has made me see that I should explain things to you now before I die, as you might well feel very resentful towards me and to Marilyn if you didn't know before and had chance to get to know more about your real family before it was lost forever. Yes, I can already hear you thinking, cut to the chase, Walter. Well here goes.

As you know, Marilyn and I grew up together. What you

don't know, lass, is that we were always very close and as is the way of things, one thing led to another and we … well, you can imagine the rest. I worked and saved hard and bought Claygate for us both; we were going to live there happily ever after. But it didn't work out like that. One day Marilyn took off and I didn't see her for three years. She left a note just to say she didn't want this life, she wanted something different and this was goodbye. I won't dwell on how I felt, lass. I hope you can imagine.

I didn't understand it at the time, but when she came back three years later married to Barry and with a toddler in tow and he set her up with Café Paradise, I kind of understood. Marilyn was a city lass, no matter how much security I could have provided for her. After our hand-to-mouth upbringing, she wanted it all – a sense of financial security, control of her life, a life lived in the city and a well-heeled husband, even if she had to fool him into believing the child was his.

I can't wrap this up, Jackie love, Barry was never your father in a million years. I know this will come as a shock to you, but the truth has to be told. How do I know? Well, you look just you're your great-grandmother, my grandmother, Rebecca Matthews. You are the image of her. I can show you a photograph and then you'll see. Also the timing, lass, you could only be mine. She was already pregnant with you when she married Barry and I think he wanted to believe you were his, but maybe at the bottom of it he didn't really.

I always knew you were mine, but Marilyn always denied it and I can see why. I still loved her and I wanted to be near her and also to watch you grow up, so I stuck it out at the café all these years. I can't say it's been easy, but by heck, lass, it's been worth it. I know we argue a lot and you think I can be a complete pain in the arse sometimes, but under all that, lass I'm as proud as punch of you. You've had the guts to take on that café and give it a right good shake up. I know you'll make a success of it and I only hope you'll let Ellie and I stay in your *life and be part of it.*

Don't think badly of your mother. You have no idea of the awful life we had as youngsters. She did what was right for you and her at the time and I respected her reasons for doing it all those years ago. There's only me left now to set the record straight. I always loved her and always will, but the time's come for my life to move on, too. I only hope you and Ellie will be sharing it with me always.

This comes to you with a father's love and pride in his beautiful and lovely daughter.

Walter.

Jackie sat for a long time with the letter in her hands, her thoughts in a whirl. Images of her mother and Walter when they were younger danced before her eyes. No wonder she had gone to Walter in her time of trouble and need. Maybe blood was thicker than water. Is that why she had gone to him? Instinctively? Running beneath this was the picture of Barry Dalrymple-Jones. Somewhere deep inside, Jackie felt a huge sense of relief. He was not her father.

Only this morning, a short half hour ago, she had said she had never felt any connection to him. He had been a good father and provided for her, taken her out and about, but there was never that spark between them, that father daughter love. Now that she knew he was not her father, Jackie allowed herself to probe her feelings about him. Huge relief flooded over her. If she was really honest with herself, she hadn't liked him at all.

But Walter as her father? Grumpy, curmudgeonly, awkward, opinionated Walter? Yes and kind, honest and always looking out for her best interests Walter, Jackie thought. He had stopped everything to play with her as a child, let her run loose on his smallholding, showed her all his animals and spent time with her. Jackie drew in a sharp breath and sat up. How many times in those years had she wished Walter *was* her father! Had she ever said that to Marilyn? No, she wouldn't have dared.

There was a knock at the door and Walter's anxious face appeared. 'Are you plotting seven ways to kill me, Jackie? Because one of them is making me wait out there for half an hour. I'm ready to die of stress at any moment now.'

Jackie looked up at him, still holding his letter in her hand. Her expression was serious and gave nothing away. Walter's heart sank.

'I take it it's come as bad news, then,' he said, edging further into the kitchen.

'It has,' Jackie replied.

'Oh.' Walter's disappointment hit him like a hard fist in the pit of his stomach.

Jackie rose and came towards him. 'It's bad news that I never knew all this years ago.' Tears rolled down her cheeks as she put her arms around him and hugged him tightly. 'The man I wanted as my dad when I was a little girl.' Her words were lost as she sobbed into his chest.

Walter, never at his best with emotional women put his arms around her and awkwardly patted her hair. 'Come on now, lass, it's not a time for tears. I've lots to tell you yet, but it might have to wait a bit.'

'Why's that?' asked Jackie still buried in his now wet shirt.

'Old mother Stampwick's gone home in a huff 'cos I criticised his handiwork. You might have to pour oil on troubled waters to get him back.'

Jackie raised her head 'Oh no, that's all I need. What did you say to him?'

'Told him he was to building what I was to cordon bleu cooking and that was bloody useless.'

'Thanks, Walter, your first act as my father is to lose me my builder. What do you do for an encore?'

'Buy you a gallon of oil,' he chuckled.

CHAPTER 39

Early the following Wednesday evening Penny Montague carefully packed the last of the clothes she needed for her zumba class and the overnight stay at Lingley's Hotel in the centre of York and zipped up the bag. She checked her hair and make-up and nodded approval at herself. Monsieur Antoine had re-styled her hair in a sharp modern cut that suited her thinner face and figure; some of the benefits from the zumba classes. Satisfied with her appearance, she turned away from the mirror and made her way downstairs.

George was in the kitchen, dressed in his favourite green silk dress and reading the paper. Penny hunted for her car keys and, unable to find them, was forced to speak to George. 'Have you seen my car keys?'

'In the jug on the dresser, I expect, where you always leave them.' George eyed Penny's large bag curiously. 'Where are you going with that lot?' he asked.

Penny fished about in the jug and found her keys. 'Fancy, they were there all the time. where I'm going is for me to know. Zumba dancing, if you must know. I'll see you tomorrow.' She was out of the back door and into her car in a flash, deaf to George's startled questions.

He followed her out of the door, calling after her, 'Where are you going? Where are you staying tonight? Penny…?'

Penny ignored him and reversed out of the drive, screeching on the brakes to allow a car to pass by before roaring off into the June evening.

George went back into the house and slumped down at the kitchen table. What was going on with Penny these days? She hadn't spoken to him in the last two weeks unless it was strictly necessary, and then it was through tight lips. She wouldn't look at him. She came and went as she pleased, and now this. Out overnight. He wondered where she was going. And what's more, who was she going with? George knew Penny too well to imagine for one moment that she would be out on her own.

He sat up suddenly as the idea came to him. He stared wildly about the kitchen, appalled at his own thoughts. Surely not? It couldn't possibly have come to this, could it? She wouldn't do this to him, not his Penny; loyal, faithful Penny, good wife and mother to three sons. Another voice spoke in George's head. A newly-glamorous, honed and toned Penny, of independent means, who didn't need George any more, had maybe outgrown him; had maybe found someone else – that snaked-hipped Spaniard perhaps.

A horrible certainty descended on George. That night at the hotel after they had had dinner, you couldn't have got a piece of paper between Penny and that man when they were dancing, if you could call it dancing. It was more like the overture before the symphony proper begins, only they didn't have music on their minds. Penny was going to spend the night with him, George just knew it.

The dormant caveman in George awakened. She bloody well was *not* going to spend the night with him, not if he, George Montague, had anything to do with it. She was his wife and he loved her and he wasn't going to let any gyrating, smooth-talking Spaniard take her away from him. Unconsciously, George's huge hands formed themselves into tight fists. Young snake-hips would have to fight him first. He might be lithe and sinuous but George knew he was bigger and stronger and he had everything to fight for.

Tearing off his wig and kicking off his high heels, he

rushed upstairs and ripped off his voluminous dress. Casting it carelessly on to the bed George rummaged in his wardrobe for a dark shirt and trousers. A plan was forming in his mind. There were tall rhododendron bushes in the grounds of the meeting hall where the zumba classes were held. He could hide amongst them and watch for Penny coming out of her class and, more importantly, see who she came out with.

Twenty minutes later George parked his car in a lay-by a short distance from the Hall and walked quickly along the road, entering the grounds by a side gate away from the main road. He looked around carefully and, making sure he was not observed, concealed himself behind a bush close to the main entrance door. The muffled sounds of music from the zumba class wafted out on the May evening breeze. In a house overlooking the hall, a net curtain twitched.

Inside the hall, the zumba class was in full swing. Penny was enjoying herself. Now that she had attended the class for some weeks, she had learned all the routines and become a great deal fitter. She had much more energy, threw herself into the dances and revelled in her new found fitness.

Enrique was directly in front of her, moving his tanned, muscular body sinuously to the music, all the while calling out the movements. Penny enjoyed watching him and gave all her attention to imitating him. After half an hour of energetic dancing, Penny took a break, realising she would not have any energy left for the rest of the night to come if she continued to zumba at this pace.

She sat the next set out, resting on a bench at the side of the room, content to watch Enrique put everyone through their paces. He was tireless in his efforts to encourage everyone in the room to get the most out of the class. Penny wondered if he would still be able to perform later that night. She was looking forward to the two of them together at Lingley's Hotel later. They were so right together.

When the class had a short break, Enrique came over to her. 'Pennee, you are tired tonight of all nights?' he asked with concern, sitting down and putting his arm around her.

'No, I'm fine,' Penny answered. She smiled up at him. 'I'm saving myself for tonight. I want to be on top form and enjoy every moment.'

Enrique gave her a little squeeze. 'That's my Pennee. Tonight will be perfect you will see.'

Outside in the rhododendron bushes, George shivered as dusk overtook the bright May evening. He watched and waited as the cold penetrated his shoes. His feet grew numb and his legs ached with crouching down.

His long wait in the growing darkness came to an end as the music stopped. Soon after, the front door opened and a steady stream of dancers, young and old, made their way out of the hall, walking away down the drive or veering off to the car park in search of their cars.

George watched carefully, waiting for Penny to come out. It seemed that everyone else had departed except Penny and Enrique. He ventured out of his hiding place in the bushes, anger mounting in his breast. What was that Spaniard doing with his wife inside? George started towards the front door when a large hand clapped him on the shoulder, making him jump out of his skin.

'Good evening, sir.' A large uniformed policeman held George in a strong grip, whilst another shone a torch into his face. 'And what would you be doing skulking in the bushes at this time of night, if you don't mind my asking?'

George screwed his eyes up against the blinding light of the policeman's torch. 'I'm waiting for my wife. She's in there, zumba dancing, or perhaps doing a bit more, with the Spaniard that runs the class, Enrique something or other.'

'You usually wait for your wife in the bushes, do you, sir?' asked the policeman, keeping his vice-like grip on George.

'Of course I don't, officer,' said George irritably. 'Where

did you spring from anyway? Officialdom! There's spies everywhere these days. Can't a man wait for his wife without you poking your nose in?'

The policeman shining the torch shook his head sorrowfully. 'Now, sir, that's not the way to get out of your present trouble.'

'I'm not in any trouble,' George said angrily, trying to wriggle free from the policeman's iron grip.

'That's a matter of opinion, sir,' said his captor. 'A neighbour reported you lurking in these bushes for most of the evening and we come along and here you are. Still here. I'd call that a peeping Tom. Not looking good, is it, sir? If you were just waiting for your wife, you would have gone into the building long ago.'

'As you saw, officer, I was just on my way when you detained me.' George felt hugely frustrated at the delay in getting inside to see what Penny was up to right now. He struggled again to be free only to be seized by both policemen.

'Don't struggle any more, sir. You knew you'd been rumbled and were trying to get away,' suggested the policeman.

'I've told you, I was just going to go inside and look for my wife. Why don't we go in and you can see that she's still in there? She may be up to no good with that smooth talking Spaniard whilst we're wasting time out here.'

'Have a vivid imagination, do you, sir, or are you always this paranoid about your wife?'

'Please,' George begged through clenched teeth, 'can we just go inside and see?'

'What do you reckon, PC 591?' said the burly policeman.

'Check it out and then if there's no-one there, we arrest him and he can cool off in the cells for the night.'

They marched George up the steps and in through the front doorway of the hall. As they came into the dimly lit hallway, Penny and Enrique were making their way towards them. Penny stopped and cried out sharply, 'George, what are you doing here?'

George turned to the burly officer still holding on to him. 'You see, I'm telling the truth, that's my wife, Penny.'

'Is that right, madam?' asked the officer. 'Only we found this man lurking in the bushes outside. He's been there all evening, according to a nearby neighbour.'

Penny's eyes widened in amazement. 'Yes, officer, he is my husband, George Montague. Husband in name anyway. He spends half his time dressed as a woman, so he's as much a Georgina as a George.'

The policemen looked at George with renewed interest. 'Hiding in the bushes and dressing up as a woman, eh? We'll have to watch out for you.' Now that his identity had been established, the policeman relinquished his hold.

George took a few steps towards Penny. 'I was waiting for you to come out of that zumba class you allegedly go to,' he hissed angrily. 'I wanted to see where you were going after that. You sneaked out of our house with an overnight bag and won't say a word about where you're going. What am I supposed to think?'

Penny looked at him steadily. 'I'm not the least bit interested in what you think, George, but if you must know I'm going to Lingley's Hotel for the night.'

Just then Enrique came loping down the hallway towards them carrying a large bag. 'Are you ready, my beautiful Pennee? We have a long night ahead of us; we mustn't waste any more time here.'

George saw Enrique's bag. 'A long night ahead… With my wife? Oh no, you haven't, sunshine!' Before anyone could stop him, he charged up the hallway and caught Enrique a savage punch on the jaw, knocking him backwards and down on to the floor. Before Enrique could move away, George was astride him, gripping him by his shirt and shaking a dazed Enrique like a limp rag doll.

'Don't you *ever, ever* go near my wife again, you hear me?' Enrique groaned.

Penny screamed and the policemen rushed forward and dragged George off.

'Now Mr Montague, we don't want to be doing you for GBH as well as prowling, do we? I can see there is due provocation, but the magistrate might not see it like that.'

Red-faced and panting, George struggled in the tight hold of the two policemen. 'You heard him; he's got a long night ahead, with my wife! I'm not going to stand for that. What kind of a man do you think I am?'

'Red-blooded and perfectly normal I would say, sir,' said the burly policeman tranquilly. 'So why you want to go wearing frocks beats me.'

'There'll be no more frocks in my house,' George said forcefully. 'I'm done with all that. I can see where it's got me, nearly losing my wife.' He turned to Penny and drew himself up to his full six foot four. 'No more frocks, Penny, I promise. Just come home and be my wife again, I beg you.'

Penny looked at Enrique still lying on the floor, nursing his bruised jaw. 'If you're going to be a proper husband, George, then maybe. But I don't want you going around bashing up every man who takes a sideways look at me.'

George, too, looked at Enrique. 'He wanted to do more than look! What about your arrangements for tonight? I bet love's young dream there had more than a mug of hot chocolate on his mind at Lingley's Hotel.'

Penny smiled and helped Enrique to his feet. 'Yes, of course he did.'

George gaped at her.

'It's Kate's engagement party and Enrique and I are the floor show. We've been working on a routine and were, *are* going to perform it tonight, that's if Enrique's jaw isn't broken, and then join in Kate and Stan's celebrations before going to sleep in *separate* rooms.'

'Well, why didn't you tell me all this in the first place?' asked George.

'You'd still have punched his lights out,' said Penny. She looked pensive and then said, 'One thing I have discovered in the last six months since you turned into Georgina, is that I can manage perfectly well on my own, George. I've been preparing for independence in case you stayed as Georgina. I can support myself, go where I like and do what I like. I don't need you.'

The angry red colour that had suffused George's face drained away at Penny's words. 'But you just said "maybe" to coming home.'

Penny let go of Enrique and walked towards George. 'Yes, I did and I meant it. I *don't need* you, George, but,' she added softly, 'I do want you still. I'm not going to throw away thirty years of good marriage if there's a chance of the old George coming back.'

The two policemen stood by, arms folded watching the proceedings with interest. PC 591 sighed. 'Time we got back to the Station, PC 636. Doesn't look like we'll be locking anyone up this evening, after all. Let's go and have a cup of tea and a canteen doughnut. We've just got time before the pubs start chucking out.'

Making sure George would do no further harm to Enrique and that Enrique did not want to press charges for assault, they made their way to the front door. 'Enjoy your party,' said PC 591 to Penny. 'And just remember who's your dancing partner and who's your life partner tonight. We don't want to be coming to the Lingley Hotel to arrest the lot of you.'

Penny, held tightly in George's arms, smiled and thanked them. She wasn't going to be changing her life partner any time soon.

Seeing there was never going to be any possibility now

of a gentle seduction of the lovely Penny, Enrique gave in gracefully. He held his hand out to George. 'We don't fight any more, George. She is yours, but you let me dance with her tonight, yes?'

'Of course.' In victory, George could be magnanimous. 'I'm sure I'll enjoy the show and I wouldn't want to spoil Kate and Stan's party. That's if I'm invited?' he looked enquiringly at Penny.

Penny took his hand. 'Come on, let's go and get your glad rags on.' She kissed Enrique gently on the cheek. 'Thank you, Enrique,' she said.

Enrique looked puzzled. 'What for, Pennee? I didn't do anything, only zumba.'

'You and the zumba made me feel young and desirable again, so thank you.'

PC 591 raised his eyebrows and made his way down the hall steps. 'Cor, let's go and get that doughnut and a cup of tea. All this talk of desire, I need to sit down.'

His colleague agreed. 'But I'm not so sure about that doughnut, you know; I like a thick vanilla slice with all the custard coming out of the sides.'

'Or better still a slab of bakewell tart with lashings of custard on top.' PC 591 was really getting into his stride.

Their voices could be heard drifting back to the hall as they made their way to their panda car parked outside the grounds, moving on from the delights of cream cakes to the merits of their favourite desserts. Profiteroles, treacle sponge and custard and hot chocolate pudding seemed to be the favourites.

Watching them depart, Penny shook her head. 'Men! It's either sex, food or football with all of you. Come on, George, let's go.'

CHAPTER 40

Whilst Jackie was busy with the renovations to Café Paradise, Barney Anderson was making discreet enquiries amongst members of Tom Young's Trades Council. What he learned confirmed Melissa's story. Everyone paid Tom a cash backhander for finding them work through the Council recommendations. There had been much talk of Tom's connections and influence with the business community throughout York and the surrounding areas. It wasn't exaggerating to say that Trades Council members were enslaved by Tom Young. He appeared to have the power to make or break them. The cash 'donations' ensured a regular flow of work for members, even though they bitterly resented this practice.

Barney happily logged all this information and then moved on to researching Tom's career with UK Holdings PLC. As he studied the claims made through Lloyds of London, he found they provided a record of the progress of Tom Young's career. In the early days, the claims made by Tom on behalf of UK Holdings PLC were many and various, but as the years rolled on, the claims became much less frequent and, in particular, there was nothing logged for the whole of the previous ten months.

More discreet enquiries amongst Barney's old London friends in the legal and insurance community revealed that Tom Young would indeed be in line for a fifty thousand pound bonus if he could keep claim free for another two months. There was nothing illegal in this type of reward, only Tom Young's method of obtaining it. He had completed the proposal forms for Jackie, knowing that asbestos was found in all the other buildings in that area. He had deliberately defrauded her and her mother before her.

Jackie's wasn't the only case of Tom Young's malpractices that Barney had come across in his research. He had compiled quite a file about Young. Barney felt confident that he had a good case and decided it was time to pay Tom Young a visit.

* * * * * *

Tom Young was in an ebullient mood. It was a beautiful June day and all was going well in his world. John Stampwick had just stumped up four hundred pounds; his little gift to Tom in gratitude for getting him the work at Café Paradise. He still had another six hundred to come from getting Peter Zhimkov the big contract at his engineering works and five hundred from another member for a painting contract on the city's outskirts. Tom rubbed his hands and sat back in his luxurious office chair, putting his feet up on his desk.

The intercom buzzed. 'Mr Barney Anderson is here to see you, Tom. shall I send him in?' Melissa announced sweetly.

Tom sat up. Barney Anderson? Wasn't he that Citizens Advice Bureau solicitor? What did he want? If he was looking for a donation to keep them afloat, well, he could whistle for it, Tom thought. Always banging on about people's rights and entitlements and what benefits they could claim off the state for. They were bleeding the country dry. Waste of space the lot of them. The place should be closed down and would be if he, Tom Young, had anything to do with it. York City shouldn't give them house room.

Barney entered Tom's office carrying a large briefcase. He sat down, uninvited, in the chair opposite Tom.

Tom leaned back in his chair. 'Mr Anderson. Citizens Advice Bureau, aren't you?' Barney heard the veiled sneer in Tom's tone. 'And what can I do for that esteemed organisation?'

'Give Jackie Dalrymple-Jones the twenty-five thousand pounds you owe her for starters,' Barney said bluntly. Tom Young sat very still in his padded leather chair for a few moments. He remained leaning back but gripped the arms a little tighter. 'For one thing, I don't owe Miss Dalrymple-Jones any such monies and, for another, it's none of your business. So, if that's all you have come about, I'll wish you good morning.'

Barney made no move to go. 'It is my business, Mr Young,' he said pleasantly. 'I am Miss Dalrymple-Jones' solicitor. We can either settle this little matter between ourselves this morning or we can settle it in open court. That's entirely up to you.'

Court! Tom never liked the mention of courts and solicitors. Litigation always cost money and lots of it. What did this Anderson chap know? Ten to one nothing at all, but he'd better humour him. 'As far as I'm aware, Mr Anderson, my dealings with Miss Dalrymple-Jones have always been legitimate and above board.'

'I don't think taking money for insurance policies in the full knowledge that they could never be honoured is legitimate, Mr Young,' said Barney. Now that they were finally into the meat of the discussion, Barney opened his briefcase and took out a fat folder. 'I see you earned vast sums from insuring Mrs Marilyn Dalrymple-Jones and all the business insurance of Café Paradise in the past and continued to insure the present owner Miss Jackie Dalrymple-Jones in the same way.' Barney leaned across the desk and looked Tom full in the face. 'It's unlawful Mr Young. I have witnesses who can testify to the fact that you had full knowledge of the presence of significant amounts of asbestos in all the buildings in the same area as the Café Paradise and were certainly of the opinion that the café would be riddled with it too. You could not suddenly drop Miss Dalrymple-Jones from your clientele or suspicions would have been aroused at the subsequent discovery of the asbestos, so you completed the proposal form yourself and engineered the situation where Miss Dalrymple-Jones would readily agree to the phrase "no asbestos present". Staff at The Pear Tree Restaurant are very observant, I believe.'

Barney watched with satisfaction as the usually suave and urbane Tom Young gaped at him like a landed fish. Before Tom could collect his wits, Barney drove the point home. 'The form is completed in your hand Mr Young. Miss Dalrymple-Jones, a grieving daughter and very new owner of the café never had sight of it, and after you had filled her up with red wine, she was in no position to make the fine distinction between the statement about "no asbestos" and "no knowledge of asbestos." I think you would discover that a judge will rule in favour of Café Paradise and order that UK Holdings PLC honours the claim under Miss Dalrymple-Jones policy on the basis that you knew full well that asbestos was present at the property and therefore the company cannot claim that the policy is void. The Police and Crown Prosecution Service may also decide that a criminal prosecution is in the public interest. You could be looking at five years for fraud.' Barney sat back and added for good measure, 'But there, maybe, I'm being too generous. It could be seven to ten years.'

'That's preposterous and you know it.' Tom Young sprang up from his chair and took a turn about his office. He looked out of his first floor window at the crowds of tourists and shoppers thronging the streets below while trying to see a way to deal with this troublemaker, Anderson. He turned back to face Barney. 'Witnesses. Witnesses. Who are these witnesses? No-one knows what I have knowledge of and how I run my business but me. You're just trying it on. I bet she sent you. She's desperate for money, isn't she? No-one will lend her the money for that café so she's sending in the heavy brigade to try and twist my arm. Well, it won't work, Mr Clever-Dick Anderson. You can go back to your girlfriend and tell her it's no go.'

Feeling pleased with his confident showing, Tom Young sat down again and put on a relaxed air as he faced Barney.

At that moment Melissa buzzed. 'Would you like some coffee bringing in, Mr Young?' she asked.

'Most certainly not, Melissa,' snapped Tom. 'Mr. Anderson is just leaving.' Tom snapped off the intercom and stood up.

Barney made no move to leave. 'Well, I don't believe I am,' he said mildly. 'You see, we haven't finished yet. We haven't covered the little matters of your fifty-thousand pounds bonus from your company or your large rake-offs from members of the Trades Council.' Barney rearranged the executive toys on Tom's desk, and placing a rather fine crystal paperweight firmly down on Tom's papers, he said. 'The little arrangement you've got going with your boss in London is definitely unlawful. Jackie's claim would have cooked your goose in that direction, and taking under-the-counter backhanders to favour certain members of a Trades Guild over others is also criminal – I wouldn't bet on getting out of jail in under fifteen years, if I were you, unless you got remission for good behaviour.'

Slowly, very slowly, Tom automatically repositioned the toys on his desk, his face grey and sombre. 'I can deny it all, of course. You have no proof.'

Barney patted the file of papers on his lap. 'Proof a-plenty Mr Young. I know every claim you've made and, more importantly, refused during your entire career. I've interviewed hundreds of witnesses and collected statements of your dealings with them and believe me, Mr Young, when I tell you, there is a whole army of very unhappy and dissatisfied clients out there, all waiting to see you get your come-uppance. And as for your creaming off the readies at the Trades Council, well I don't need to go into that, do I?'

Barney's heart was beating fast. Had he done enough to convince Tom Young? He had spelled it out loud and clear and now maybe this disgusting leech of a man would pay up and Barney could get on his way before he gave into the temptation to punch him hard on the nose.

'Write a cheque for twenty-five thousand pounds to Miss Dalrymple-Jones here and now or I will issue proceedings on her behalf claiming the twenty-five thousand pounds costs of the remedial work, plus costs, which I would estimate at another five thousand pounds at least. I say nothing as to whether the police may wish to investigate your Trades Council activities, or the defrauding of policy holders with a view to your personal gain.'

Years of risk assessment and possible outcomes to situations had honed Tom Young's instincts for survival. Wordlessly, he drew open his desk drawer and brought out a cheque book. Quickly he wrote the cheque and tore it out of the book. Handing it to Barney, he said in a low voice, 'I admit nothing. This is purely a gesture of goodwill towards the daughter of an old and valued client. Just remember that, Anderson. And now get the hell out of my office and out of my life. If I don't clap eyes on you ever again, it will be too soon.'

Barney replaced the folder in his briefcase and tucked the cheque in with it. He rose to go. 'I would like to say I'm sorry you won't get your fifty thousand bonus, only I'm not. You're too greedy, Mr Young, and it will be your undoing if you don't watch your step.' Barney patted his briefcase. 'Always remember, Mr Young, I know where the bodies are buried and I would suggest straight dealings be the order of the day at the Trades Council in future. Remember, I will be watching.'

Tom Young rose from his chair and turned away. 'Just get lost, Anderson, I've had enough of your avenging angel act for one day.'

Satisfied he had achieved all he could, Barney left a defeated Tom Young to gaze down once again on the crowds passing below his window, and wonder, as he would wonder a thousand times in years to come, how the hell did that lanky, blonde-haired shit ever find out so much about him.

Once safely outside the Trades Council offices, Barney wiped the sweat from his brow and set off down the street at a brisk pace. A huge smile spread over his face. He was looking forward to presenting the cheque to Jackie. Only how was he going to explain how he had managed to get Tom Young to meekly hand it over in the first place?

CHAPTER 41

That same morning Walter and Ellie parked their car at the back of the café and walked around to the front to open up in preparation for the grand re-opening of Café Paradise. Warm June sunshine bathed the street with the promise of a fine dry day to come.

Walter fished out a small laminated card from his pocket and consulted it. 96 70 14. He grinned at Ellie as he unlocked the door and confidently punched the numbers into the keypad on the wall. 'Thanks for doing that, Ellie love,' he said. 'I could have done with this card years ago. You've no idea how many times the police came zooming down here ready to arrest me, 'cos I got the numbers wrong and I couldn't stop the bloody thing from wailing. In the end they mostly stopped bothering, but the neighbours didn't. The things they used to throw out of their windows at me and the language! I learned a few new phrases, I can tell you, and acquired some interesting items too. The fella up there threw *both* boots at me one morning and that lass at the end chucked a plant pot at me, with the plant still in it. It could have knocked me out. Good job I ducked.'

Ellie laughed, 'Get inside, Walter, and let's get on. You're full of nonsense, worse than Stan. I need a head start this morning. I promised Jackie I'd make sure everything was spotless and ready to go before her new chef starts and we need to check every inch of the café to make sure it's just perfect for when she comes in. We must make this a wonderful day for her, Walter. She deserves it after all the worry and hard work she's put into this.'

Walter put his arms around Ellie and kissed her. 'You're the best lass in the world, Ellie,' he told her. 'Thanks to you, I've got a whole new life and a new daughter. Lots to look forward to.'

Ellie pushed him away fondly. 'Yes, a flock of Wensleydale sheep being delivered tomorrow and six nanny goats and kids, not to mention my rescue donkeys next week. It's just as well Jackie's got a new chef.'

Ellie made her way into the kitchen and unpacked her basket of cleaning materials. She gave Walter a duster. 'Leave me in peace for a while. Go and chase any dust away in the café.'

Walter wandered back out to the café and looked around. He smiled happily at the scene. It was clean and bright, with new wooden flooring and fashionable tables and chairs. The restrained cream decor was broken here and there with splashes of colour from bright pictures and strategically placed lamps. Walter shook his head, almost in disbelief. That his stubborn, pig-headed daughter had achieved all this! He remembered the many battles she had had, not only with John Stampwick, but with plumbers and electricians who were quick to say a thing could not be done. But when his strong-minded daughter held out and said it had to be done, then somehow, magically, a way was found and this was the result; a beautiful place. Walter knew it would be a fantastic business and felt very proud of Jackie.

Fleetingly, he thought of Marilyn. What would she make of all this? Walter smiled to himself. She'd be shaking her head at all the money Jackie had spent on the project. Walter could almost hear the caustic remarks Marilyn would have made about this make-over. He shook himself and began to waft his duster about as Ellie had instructed. 'Rest in peace, Marilyn,' he said aloud. 'Our Jackie will do a grand job, you'll see.'

Walter prowled the café, checking every corner until he was satisfied that even if the Lord Lieutenant of the county dropped in for the opening, he wouldn't find a speck of dust anywhere.

As he checked the front windows the front door pinged and Penny entered the café.

'Morning, Walter,' said Penny.

'Morning, Penny,' Walter greeted her pleasantly. My, my! Being reconciled with George had done wonders for Penny, he thought. She was positively blooming. But there, she was back with a proper Englishman again. What she ever saw in that Spanish fella, Walter could never imagine. All garlic breath and gyrations in a G-string from what he'd heard. Walter was glad George had stopped all that nonsense with the frocks. A woman like Penny needed a real man in her life.

Penny interrupted his musings. 'You've missed a bit, Walter,' she pointed to a large smear high up in the window. 'You'll need the stepladders for that.' She made her way into the new ladies' cloakroom and closed the door behind her.

Typical woman, Walter thought. He looked around the café. He'd spent the last hour titivating every corner of it and then a woman comes along and immediately finds the only spot he'd missed.

The door of the café opened again and the morning sunshine streamed in, illuminating Kate's red-gold coloured hair as she strolled towards Walter.

'Morning, Kate,' Walter smiled at her. Kate looked blooming, he thought. She was a lucky lass to have found Stan. He was a good, steady bloke. He'd never get any daft fancies for frocks.

'Morning, Walter and what a fantastic one it is, too. We're going to have a great opening day. Stan's coming in later to help out.' She glanced up at the window. 'By the way, you've missed a bit,' she said and carried on to the ladies' cloakroom.

Oh God, women! For the thousandth time, Walter seriously wondered why God ever invented them. Or why he invented them with such bloody eagle eyes. He shook his head as he went to fetch the step ladders. It was unfair, men just didn't possess the squeaky-clean gene or whatever it was that women had.

As he returned with the step ladders, Jackie was standing in the doorway, surveying the café.

'Morning, love,' he said, setting the ladders up.

'Morning … Dad,' she said shyly.

Walter grinned widely at her, a tinge of pink in his cheeks. 'My lass,' he said happily. 'You've done a great job here, Jackie, I'm right proud of you. Café Paradise is really going places.'

Jackie looked up at the window. 'Only one thing, Dad…'

Walter looked at her in disbelief. 'Not you and all. How do you do it?'

Jackie grinned 'That's easy, Dad. I'm a woman, I look for trouble.' She patted him on the back and went off to join Ellie in the kitchen.

Walter positioned the ladders and climbed up to clean the smeared window. 'They don't need to look for trouble,' he grumbled to himself. 'They're just walking trouble to us poor men. Why I ever tangle with them at all I don't know. I need my head looking at.'

* * * * * *

The morning sunshine continued into the afternoon. After Jackie's opening speech and cutting of the ribbon at the door, Café Paradise had been full all day. The customers overflowed to the tables under striped umbrellas on the pavement outside.

The chef's new menu was proving a roaring success and with the new drinks licence, beer and wine flowed. Jackie, feeling hot and tired, manned the coffee and cake take-out whilst Kate took a short break in the newly refurbished staff room. Jackie was grateful for a brief lull at the counter. It had been gratifying to see so many old and new customers coming to her counter throughout the morning, many of them congratulating her on her brief opening speech of welcome and approving the new-style Café Paradise.

Jackie had put a lot of thought into her speech. She was very conscious how far she had travelled since Marilyn's death and wanted to express her thanks to everyone who had helped her on the often difficult journey to the re-opening of the café. Judging by the flush of pleasure on her friends' faces when she sincerely thanked them for all their support, Jackie felt she had got it right. Best of all had been the look on Walter's face when she had spoken of her pride in *both* her parents. Their years of hard work had given her a wonderful inheritance in Café Paradise and she thanked them both, particularly her father, Walter, who had been her strength and guide throughout the renovations, even though *sometimes* she hadn't always seemed grateful! Walter had blown his nose loudly and scowled fiercely at her, but his eyes were bright with pride and tears.

The only thing that cast a shadow over the re-opening of the café was Barney Anderson's absence. Jackie felt hurt and puzzled. He had said he wanted to come to the opening and she had sent him an invitation via Walter, who knew where Barney's lodgings were.

The brief lull was over and a new wave of customers entered the café. Jackie shrugged. She must put Barney out of her head. One minute he was saving her from financial ruin and the next he couldn't even be bothered to turn up to see the results of his rescue plan. Obviously she was not that important an item in Mr Barney Anderson's life. Tucking her hurt and sadness away, Jackie turned to smile and greet her new customers.

Nina Mountford-Blayne, accompanied by one of her young assistants, stood looking about her. Even though the day was warm and sunny, Nina made no concessions to the weather. She was dressed in a vivid red blouse and long floral trousers, topped off with a very long fur coat. As usual, she looked like a very exotic bird of paradise amongst a room full of brown sparrows.

Nina looked about her. 'So bland, darling,' she said, 'so boring. I might have known this would be the result. My design was infinitely better, more vibrant and exciting; you should have gone for it, not this…' She swept her arms out wide to encompass the café. 'Not these insipid and boring cream colours. I could have…'

Nina's young assistant must have been a new recruit and unused to her outspoken ways. Blushing vivid red to match her blouse, he tugged at her coat sleeve. 'Nina, I thought we were just popping in here for a coffee, not coming to criticise…'

Nina looked astonished. 'I am not criticising, Jason. I am simply telling the truth as I see it and I am right as always. My concept and designs for this café *are* infinitely superior.'

'Out!'

'What?' Nina Mountford-Blayne looked startled as Jackie came out from behind the counter and took her firmly by the arm. She escorted her to the door with a polite smile.

'I love my café just as it is, Miss Mountford-Blayne, and I don't need you or your vastly over-priced ideas anywhere near me. So in future, if you're thinking of making Café Paradise your coffee or lunch stop, please don't.'

Not waiting for Nina's reaction, Jackie returned to her waiting customers at the coffee counter. As she dispensed coffee and cakes, she realised how much her confidence had increased in the months since Marilyn's death. At the turn of the year she wouldn't have said 'boo', but months of dealing with tradesmen and council officials had given her new poise and decisiveness.

Café Paradise continued to be busy all afternoon. Penny and Kate were rushed off their feet, ferrying food and drink to the tables inside and out. Ellie worked flat out clearing tables after departing customers, cleaning and re-setting them for the next. Walter assisted Alastair in the kitchen and loaded and re-loaded the dishwasher in between times.

Jackie was mentally drafting an advertisement for new staff when Melissa and Barney walked in. They stopped to have a word with Ellie before approaching the counter, which gave Jackie time to take a few deep breaths to calm her beating heart and assume a serene expression to greet them.

'Hello,' Barney said, smiling across the counter at her.

As usual, and in spite of all her good resolutions not to go weak-kneed at the sight of the blonde dosser boy, Jackie's heart thumped uncomfortably in her chest. 'Hello,' was all she could manage back.

'Nice day for it,' said Barney laconically.

'Lovely,' she replied.

'You've had a good day by the look of it,' he ventured.

'Mm.'

'How's your new chef settling in?'

'OK.'

'Do you think you could manage a sentence next?' Barney asked, twinkling at her.

'Um.' Jackie blushed at her own inanity. For God's sake, woman, say something, anything, she thought to herself 'I thought Melissa didn't like this place,' she said. How stupid was that? Jackie immediately regretted what she said. She really didn't want to talk about Melissa at all, but couldn't think of anything more appropriate just then.

'Monstrous though Melissa is, and believe me, Jackie, she

really is, we are greatly in her debt.' Barney looked serious as he said this.

Jackie frowned. Since when was she in horrible Melissa's debt? The only debt she owed was to Barney's anonymous investor. That reminded her. 'I'm not in Melissa's debt, but we need to talk about repayments to your friendly investor person. Now that I'm up and running again, we'll have to fix something up.'

Barney looked around the café. The afternoon shoppers and tourists were beginning to depart and there would be a lull before the early evening wine bar crowd began to drift in. Melissa was already ensconced at a table with a bottle of wine and two glasses, waving away the menu Penny was offering her. He needn't worry about her for a while.

'No time like the present, Jackie,' Barney said firmly. 'We need to fix things up alright. The investor will need his money back. Can we go into your office and talk for a few minutes?'

At his words, the colour drained from Jackie's face. What was he telling her? She had trusted him, had been certain he would not let her down and now he was telling her the investor wanted his money back! Moving unsteadily out from her counter, Jackie motioned to Kate to take over and led the way into her office.

Closing the door behind them Barney smiled down at Jackie as she almost fell into Marilyn's old chair.

As if in her worst nightmare, Jackie looked up at him and whispered, 'The investor needs his money back? But you said … I can't possibly … I've spent it all … the asbestos removal; the café…' She couldn't go on; it was all too awful to contemplate and here was Barney, whom she had come to regard as a friend, smiling at her. Had the world gone mad? 'I trusted you … completely.'

Barney's conscience pricked him. How could he torment his love like this? He reached into his suit pocket and drew out Tom Young's cheque. Handing it to Jackie, he said slowly, 'The investor will need his money back because Tom Young has seen reason and coughed up the money for your insurance claim. You don't need the investor now.'

Jackie took the cheque with shaking hands and looked at it wonderingly. 'Tom Young gave you this? But what about the asbestos?'

Barney chuckled. 'Well, that's where we have to thank Melissa. Her nosiness paid off for once and she found out that Tom Young knew all along that there would be asbestos in this building. That's called fraud in anyone's language. I just had to point that out to him, and one or two other little practices of his that I knew about, and he saw the error of his ways and paid up.'

Jackie's eyes narrowed. She was not deceived for one moment by Barney's bland expression. 'There's a lot more to this than you're telling me, Barney Anderson. First you give me a cheque from Mr Anonymous, then you want it back and then you give me a cheque from Tom Young, that a month ago wild horses wouldn't have dragged out of him.'

Barney shrugged. Yes, I suppose that's a fair summary, but this isn't the time or place to tell you the whole story. That will keep.' He pulled Jackie to her feet and held her to him, their faces nearly touching. 'The best thing, the most wonderful thing, is that you're free, Jackie. You don't owe anyone anything now.'

Barney's eyes held Jackie's gaze for a long moment and then slowly and very gently he put his arms around her and kissed her. For a moment Jackie was passive in his arms and then, in dazed delight, she responded, kissing him back.

A long time later they came up for air, but Barney would not let her go. 'If you only knew how many times I have wanted to do that, Miss Dalrymple-Jones,' he told her. 'You're in my dreams, my work...' He drew her in to him and kissed her again.

The office door opened and Melissa staggered in, holding the now empty bottle of wine. 'I think I've had a little of your share,' she stumbled over the words. Seeing them locked in embrace she paused. 'Ooh, ooh, what's going on here then? Have you dumped me? Are you going out with Jackie now?' Melissa hiccupped and sat down on Marilyn's chair. 'It doesn't matter anyway, I've just met the new chef, Alastair his name is.' Her eyes grew dreamy. 'He's gorgeous; even more gorgeous than you, Barney, and I never thought that would be possible, *and*,' Melissa tried to drink from her empty glass 'he's ambitious. He's going places. Today York, tomorrow London, the Queen,' she proclaimed, swinging her glass around dangerously. 'He'll be chef to the Queen, you wait and see and I'll be right there alongside him. She'll probably make me her lady-in-waiting.'

Reluctantly, Barney released Jackie and took the glass away from Melissa. 'Of course she will,' he soothed. 'Just let Alastair get the job first.'

'She'll make him her head chef and he won't have to wear those stupid chef clothes; he'll get to wear a suit to work, like you do.'

Jackie smiled and shyly touched Barney's jacket. 'Your court suit; did you put it on especially for the opening today?'

Barney looked puzzled. 'My court suit?'

'Your suit for going to court in. That's what you said it was, once before.'

A slow smile spread across Barney's face. He took Jackie's hand. 'Do you know why I go to court?' he asked.

Jackie eyed him dubiously. 'No, but it can't be anything serious, I realise that now. Overdue parking fines or something? Perhaps you should get a good solicitor.'

Melissa squealed with laughter and rocked dangerously on Marilyn's chair. 'That's good, get a good solicitor. He's already got one! He solicits!'

Jackie eyed Barney nervously. 'You solicit? Not a pimpy

thing, surely?'

Barney gave up and took Jackie in his arms. 'I am a solicitor, stupid.'

Jackie gazed at him in stupefaction. 'A solicitor? You're telling me you're a real solicitor? But you can't be, your old clothes, you always look like you've slept in them.'

'They're about the only things he has slept with,' Melissa chortled. 'I could never get him into bed and, God knows, I tried hard enough.' She hiccupped again. 'Hope you have more luck,' she said to Jackie. She got up and weaved her way unsteadily to the door. 'Alastair's taking me to that new nightclub later. Don't wait up for me, Barney. I'll probably go back to his place. Don't want you cramping our style, do we? 'Spect I'll move in with him this week. Ooh, he's such a tiger. I can't wait.' She blew them both a kiss from the doorway and was gone.

'I feel sorry for young Alastair already,' said Barney.

'No need,' said Jackie. 'He's young and brash. He'll have Melissa sorted out in no time.'

Barney looked down into Jackie's magnificent violet eyes. He smiled and stroked her soft fair hair. 'Speaking of sorting out, you and I have a lot of it to do, particularly of this kind,' and he kissed her again

* * * * * *

Much later that evening, when Café Paradise was closed for the night and everyone had gone home, Jackie and Barney walked hand in hand around the familiar streets of York.

In the warm dusk, their steps took them towards the ancient Minster, the spiritual heart of the city. The sound of the organ rang out as it accompanied the rehearsing choir. They sat on a bench in the floodlit square and listened as Bach's Mass in B Minor rolled around them. When the practice had finished they sat on, reluctant to end the magical mood of the evening.

Holding Jackie securely in his arms, Barney regaled Jackie with tales of Tom Young and his handing over of the cheque and Melissa's unwelcome stay at his flat.

'I thought you lived in a squat,' Jackie said, 'thought you were just an unemployed dosser.'

Barney roared with laughter. 'I know I can look a bit untidy round the edges sometimes, but a dosser! Thank you very much.' He went on more soberly. 'When I left university I went to work for a big law firm in London and I was doing very well with them. Quite the up and coming young lawyer, so I thought. Then one day I was summoned to the senior partner's office and dismissed because they suspected me of embezzling funds from a client's account. They couldn't prove anything but didn't want me in the firm any longer, so I was going to be out on my ear. End of my budding London career.'

'They accused you of stealing!' Jackie exclaimed.

'Yes, and it would have ended my career. Men in suits, Jackie, men in suits. Anyway, I wasn't going to let it rest there and I followed the paper trail. It led back to the Company Secretary. He had six children and a wife with expensive tastes to support. I was offered my job back but by then I'd decided London wasn't for me and I headed back home to York.'

'Is that how you come to be at the Citizens Advice Bureau?' asked Jackie.

'Yeah and I really enjoy it, working with people who really need help. I may set up my own practice soon. There's a lot of kids out there who would like to get into law, they could gain good experience working with me.'

Jackie had so much new information to take in, it was almost too much, but she still had one piece of the jigsaw left to put in place.

'And what about your Mr Anonymous investor? Are you

going to tell me about him?'

Barney kissed the top of her head and held her tightly. 'Use that very beautiful head of yours, my love. Who alone on this planet *might* be able to lay his hands on twenty-five thousand pounds in a hurry and then want to lend it to you with no demands, no strings and no security? And what's more, wasn't even going to ask for it back.'

This last bit of information made Jackie sit up sharply. 'Walter? My Dad?'

Barney nodded. As the evening light faded, they sat alone in the dimly lit square in front of the Minster and Barney told Jackie of Walter's gift to her, keeping it anonymous because he knew she would refuse it. 'It was everything he had, but he wasn't going to see you go under. Nor was Ellie. She was right behind him.'

For the first time since Marilyn's funeral, tears got the better of Jackie. In a few short months she had gone from having no-one in her life but her sharp-tongued mother, to having her own Dad, as awkward and cantankerous as she was herself; lovely calm and funny Ellie, who would gently sort them all out, and best of all – she looked wonderingly again at Barney - this amazing man who had just told her how much he loved her!

Barney tenderly dried her eyes and took her in his arms. 'And wants to marry you, with Walter's permission of course,'

EPILOGUE

It was a golden morning in late September. Already the leaves were turning brown and beginning to drift gently to the ground. At the Claygate holding, Ellie was busy upstairs helping Jackie into her wedding dress. The cream silk dress fitted tightly at her waist and then fell in gentle folds to her feet. Ellie busied herself with the tiny covered buttons that fastened the dress at the back.

Walter, resplendent in morning dress and tall black hat, left the women to their preparations and went outside to put the white satin ribbons on the car. Irritated by the hat, he took it off and placed it on the dry stone wall beside the car. The car was already spotless, but still Walter inspected it all over before he began tying the ribbon around the wing mirrors and fastening it to the bonnet.

He was intent upon his task and did not notice one of Ellie's goats watching the proceedings with great interest. Only when he had finished and stood back to admire his handiwork did he notice that his hat was not where he had left it. He looked over the wall and saw the remains of it hanging out of Bertha's mouth.

'Bloody goats!' he exclaimed. 'Now what am I going to do? She'll kill me. A posh wedding in the Minster and me with no hat! I'm a dead man, I know I am.'

He turned around to go in and break the news to the women but was stopped suddenly in his tracks. Jackie was coming out of the house, with Ellie holding her dress up off the ground. Walter caught his breath. She was beautiful and she was his little girl; for a little while longer anyway. That's if he lived to see her to the church!

Seeing the panic on Walter's face, Ellie sighed. She hadn't been married to him for long, but already she knew what a genius he had for losing things. 'What is it this time?' she asked

'It's not my fault, it was your bloody nanny goat.' Walter looked at her pleadingly.

'What was?' Ellie had an unfamiliar dangerous note in her voice.

'Ate my hat.' Walter nodded towards the dry stone wall. 'I put it there whilst I fixed the ribbons on the car and when I turned around, Bertha had it in her mouth. Not much left of it either. Now, what shall I do?'

There was a short silence. Walter waited for the sky to fall in on him. Instead, Jackie and Ellie looked at each other and started laughing.

'It's not funny,' said Walter alarmed. Hadn't they understood? He had no bloody hat now for the wedding.

Jackie stepped forward smiling and kissed him. For a moment Walter felt he must be in a parallel universe. Posh wedding and no hat to go with and she kisses me! What's going on? he thought.

'It's alright, Dad,' Jackie smiled at Ellie who popped back into the house and returned with a black hat under her arm.

'What the…?'

'We know you so well, Dad,' said Jackie. 'We knew there was every possibility that some piece of the suit or hat would come to grief before the wedding; rip or snap or get lost, maybe, so we hired two sets of everything. That way, we had hopes of getting you to the church fully dressed *and* with the hat!'

'You'd better go before anything else happens,' said Ellie fondly.

Walter looked at Jackie. 'My lass,' he said proudly, 'you'll be the most beautiful bride York Minster's ever seen. Are you ready?' he asked.

Now it was time to go, nerves were almost getting the better of Jackie. 'Yes, Dad, I'm ready. Just don't trip over my frock going down the aisle.'

'We have to get there first and if we don't get a move on, young Barney might have had second thoughts and married that pretty young bridesmaid.' He held out his arm and Jackie slipped her hand through it.

'No, he'll wait,' she said serenely. 'That pretty young bridesmaid's his sister!'

CPSIA information can be obtained at www.ICGtesting.com
Printed in the USA
BVOW04s1404100414

350306BV00013B/490/P

9 781908 098931